Extraordinary Praise for

MORE THAN YOU'LL EVER KNOW

"*More Than You'll Ever Know* encompasses more than 30 years and delves into a love affair that destroyed a woman's life and helped her to reclaim the sense of self she lost to the 'cruel banality of motherhood.'. . . Each woman's desire to be known and understood is undeniably powerful. And, really, isn't that one of fiction's most critical functions—not to make us agree, but to strengthen our empathy muscles? . . . Perhaps that's another tract of fertile ground for this novel's discussion. Where, exactly, is the line between the forgivable and the unforgivable?"　—*New York Times Book Review*

"*More Than You'll Ever Know* is an intertwining story about ambition, motherhood, and more."　—Today.com

"A fantastic debut. . . . This is a sweeping novel, unflinching and evocative in its engrossing study of love, motherhood, sex, Mexico, journalism, and more."　—*Washington Post*

"Enthralling and beautifully written."　—*Boston Globe*

"It's difficult to believe that this masterful novel is a first book. Katie Gutierrez handles its dangerous turns like a Formula One driver. That elegance, darkness, even fear are deftly intertwined in the story make it a wonderful read."

—Luis Alberto Urrea, Pulitzer Prize finalist
and bestselling author of *The House of Broken Angels*

"I was enthralled with *More Than You'll Ever Know* from the very first pages of Gutierrez's rich and assured writing. A gripping and thoughtful exploration of motherhood and marriage, the complexity of female desire, and the consequence of our obsession with true crime, it's one of the best suspenseful dramas I've read in years. An exceptional, stunning debut—I absolutely loved it."

—Ashley Audrain, *New York Times* bestselling author of *The Push*

"An unapologetic, unflinching examination of love, sacrifice, and desire."   —Grace D. Li, *Washington Post*,
"8 Thrillers and Mysteries to Read This Summer"

"*More Than You'll Ever Know* is both compelling and resonant—a novel which grips you like a thriller as you are reading it, with characters and themes which linger in the mind like the best literary fiction. This is an unforgettable story, told brilliantly—one of those novels where from the first page you know you are in the hands of a writer of verve, confidence, and conviction."

—Ellery Lloyd, *New York Times* bestselling author of *The Club*

"What happens when a mother wants more? A seductive, urgent tale about desire, family, the pursuit of truth, and the art of story-telling, *More Than You'll Ever Know* will astonish readers with its vastness, romance, tragedy, and abundant heart. I became obsessed with Katie Gutierrez's restless, secret-keeping heroines and didn't want this book to ever end."

—Jessamine Chan, *New York Times* bestselling author of
The School for Good Mothers

"A tale of two families, a double life, and an ultimate act of passion that will have you on the edge of your seat. There are thrillers that tease, but *More Than You'll Ever Know* will haunt your dreams."

—Adriana Trigiani, *New York Times* bestselling author of
The Good Left Undone

"With beautifully written prose and razor-sharp insight, Katie Gutierrez draws us into *More Than You'll Ever Know*'s gripping and complex world. . . . Passionate, supremely intelligent, and thrilling."

—Jean Kwok, *New York Times* bestselling author of
Searching for Sylvie Lee

"A sprawling, stunning, twisting triumph. By turns heart-pounding and heart-wrenching, this is a story of marriage and murder, of the secrets we endure and the lies we tell ourselves to keep them. So achingly clever and stylish, *More Than You'll Ever Know* is a special novel from a very special writer."

—Chris Whitaker, *New York Times* bestselling author of
We Begin at the End

"With thrilling, atmospheric prose set against an intricate plot, Katie Gutierrez's debut *More Than You'll Ever Know* is a suspenseful mystery, a family drama, and an astute examination of motherhood, love, and secrets. I read this morally complex novel ravenously, desperate to discover the fates of the two women at its center. You won't be able to put this book down."

—Lara Prescott, *New York Times* bestselling author of
The Secrets We Kept

"A stunning portrait of female reckoning—Katie Gutierrez creates layered and vivid characters, forced to confront the complexities of their own desires. An immaculate novel that explores marriage and choice, partnership and autonomy, *More Than You'll Ever Know* is a wonder to behold."

—Danya Kukafka, bestselling author of *Notes on an Execution*

"As addictive as a real-life whodunit, with thoughtful attention to the ethical implications of the true crime genre, *More Than You'll Ever Know* explores how we entangle ourselves one choice at a time, and

what it costs to unravel the damage. Crystalline and multifaceted, this is a page-turner brimming with empathy."
—Julia Fine, author of *The Upstairs House* and *What Should Be Wild*

"Enthralling, breathtaking, and propulsive, *More Than You'll Ever Know* is the kind of book that only comes around once every decade. With hypnotic, shimmering prose set against a masterful plot, Katie Gutierrez has crafted an explosive modern classic—a groundbreaking, razor-sharp exploration of what it means to be a woman in all its complexity."
—May Cobb, author of *The Hunting Wives*

"This dual-POV slow burn thriller is a must-read for true crime lovers." —BuzzFeed

"An enthralling story that not only explores the human fascination with true crime but also deftly plumbs the depths of marriage and motherhood. Mystery fans beguiled by Donna Tartt's *The Goldfinch* and women's fiction readers who adored Taylor Jenkins Reid's *The Seven Husbands of Evelyn Hugo* will equally fall under the spell of this totally transporting tale."
—*Library Journal* (starred review)

"Satisfying . . . [Gutierrez] provides us with two fully rounded, vulnerable, and fascinating characters in Cassie and Lore. . . . Gutierrez imagines true crime's often one-dimensional female characters with sophistication and grace." —*Kirkus* (starred review)

"Katie Gutierrez's debut novel burrows straight to the heart of our cultural true crime fixation through an intense emotional dance between two seemingly different women. . . . *More Than You'll Ever Know* has all the ingredients necessary for a good thriller. But beyond the novel's well-executed, suspenseful structure, Gutierrez also clearly understands her characters, where they've come from and what they want and need. . . . Gutierrez has crafted detailed, vulnerable portraits of women searching for clues to their own survival. In the process, she unearths some truly compelling insights about our cultural obsession with true crime." —*BookPage*

"A masterful work of suspense." —PopSugar

"In her first book, Gutierrez has written a compelling, character-driven crime story that holds the reader's interest to its very end, which, yes, is slightly ambiguous, but then, as Lore believes, 'truth is a malleable thing.'" —*Booklist*

"Gutierrez's debut taps into society's preoccupation with true crime. . . . *More Than You'll Ever Know* is atmospheric and tantalizing, made even more impactful by rich character development." —Scribd

"Where are our true crime junkies at? Katie Gutierrez spins a mystery centered around motherhood, sex, journalism, money, and of course, true crime. . . . This gripping family drama will suck you right in." —Scary Mommy

"A gripping family drama, this book will make you question the role of marriage, family, and love." —Zibby Owens, GMA.com

"Exquisitely written, seductive." —*Milwaukee Journal Sentinel*

More Than You'll Ever Know

A Novel

KATIE GUTIERREZ

wm

WILLIAM MORROW

An Imprint of HarperCollins*Publishers*

MORE THAN YOU'LL EVER KNOW. Copyright © 2022 by Katie Gutierrez. All rights reserved. Printed in the United States of America. No part of this book may be used or reproduced in any manner whatsoever without written permission except in the case of brief quotations embodied in critical articles and reviews. For information, address HarperCollins Publishers, 195 Broadway, New York, NY 10007.

HarperCollins books may be purchased for educational, business, or sales promotional use. For information, please email the Special Markets Department at SPsales@harpercollins.com.

A hardcover edition of this book was published in 2022 by William Morrow, an imprint of HarperCollins Publishers.

FIRST WILLIAM MORROW PAPERBACK EDITION PUBLISHED 2023.

Library of Congress Cataloging-in-Publication Data has been applied for.

ISBN 978-0-06-311846-1

23 24 25 26 27 LBC 5 4 3 2 1

For my family. Los quiero mucho, mucho, mucho.

Part 1

CASSIE, 2017

By the time I read about Lore Rivera, my mother had been dead for a dozen years. Dead, but not gone. She was like my shadow, angling dark and long in the right light, inescapable and untouchable.

Everyone had loved my mother. She was a third-grade teacher who'd once told our class that history was written by those who had power and wanted to keep it. "So, when you read your textbooks, ask yourself who is telling the story—and what they have to gain by your believing it." My classmates had looked at me then, awed by my mother's educational subterfuge, and I'd smiled, proud she was mine, that I had come from her.

Every Friday night, she and I curled up together on the nubby tweed couch to watch *Dateline*. Sometimes our fingers brushed as we worked the matted tassels of our favorite blue blanket, and we giggled softly, as if catching each other in the act of something private. Then we'd wait for Stone Phillips, with his strong jaw and serious eyes, to reveal the endless ways one human being can harm another.

This was the midnineties in Enid, Oklahoma, still some time before my ninth birthday. My life was still ordinary. I hadn't yet learned that ordinary could be precious. So I got my thrills from watching the *Dateline* camera pan over photos of smiling blond women riding bikes and cutting wedding cakes, oblivious to their own tragic ends. I couldn't help but see myself in them, or see myself the way the camera might see me, a dead girl still living. I breathed in my mother's scent of snuck cigarettes and chalk dust as she pulled me against her side, and maybe that was the pleasure that started it all—from that nubby tweed couch, I explored an otherworld of danger without ever leaving the safety of my mother's warmth, thrilled in the closeness of the wolf's breath against a home made of brick.

Except it turns out brick walls don't matter when the wolf lives inside.

Later, once I stopped watching *Dateline* with my mother, once I stopped doing anything at all with her, I checked true crime books out of the Enid Public Library three or four at a time, slipping them into my backpack like contraband. I devoured *In Cold Blood* and *Helter Skelter* the way I imagined boys my age looked at porn, all that furtive grasping under covers. I was grasping for something, too. Some kind of dark knowledge, understanding. I slid my hands over their plastic covers, greased with fingerprints like mine. I read the other names on the borrowing cards—Jennifer, Nicole, Emily—and wondered if they, too, read about serial killers beneath the golden dome of their covers, grateful for something more frightening than their father's voice bleeding through the walls.

In high school, my clandestine obsession with true crime crystallized into clear goals: First, and most important, leave Enid, Oklahoma. Go to college. Become a journalist. Write the kind of books I had consumed, and that had consumed me, for so many years. Books that looked at the ugliest parts of humanity and asked: How did it come to this?

The year Lore Rivera entered my life, I'd finally landed pieces in *Vice* and *Texas Monthly*, but my biggest coup as an aspiring true crime writer was a part-time blogging gig for H2O, a television network whose market research had made it pivot from low-budget romance movies to true crime. Women, it seemed, had tired of watching pretty white couples fall in love among ice-skating rinks and hay bales. Instead, they wanted to know how many times you'd have to stab someone with that ice-skating blade in order to kill them, and whether bodies in those small farming towns ever stayed buried. And their appetite was voracious—not only did they want the "full-time crime" the network provided; they wanted a blog that would round up "the most interesting murders on the internet." No humdrum shooting would do. They wanted novelty. That's where I came in.

For fifteen hours a week and thirteen dollars an hour, I scoured the Web for killings that would make a jaded audience stop and click. I read national and local newspapers, scrolled through true crime message boards and subreddits, burrowed my way through 4chan threads like a spelunker of human grime. I created a set of Google alerts—terms like "murder," "dismemberment," "kidnapping," and "contract kill"—and every morning my inbox replenished like an hourglass overturned.

The best-performing murders were outlandishly gruesome with an element of either brilliance or ineptitude (the latter being far more typical). They also tended to have one thing in common: women ended up dead. Though only a quarter of all murder victims are women, when women *are* murdered, it's almost always by a man, and when men kill women instead of other men, well, that's when shit gets *creative*. Hacksaws and living burials and mysterious disappearances from tiny Cessnas. On a blog like ours, that's what sold.

That Friday morning, my top post was about a Florida man who'd bashed in his ex's head with a power tool after *she'd* caught *him* with another man. Then he'd partially dissolved her limbs in acid before chopping the rest into small enough pieces to fit into a five-gallon fishing bucket, which he'd taken to a swamp to feed to the alligators—except the gators were more enticed by the man's living limbs. He'd been forced to call 911, too badly mauled to dispose of the bucket's grisly contents before emergency responders arrived. Most of the comments were some gleeful form of *Karma's a bitch!*

I often wondered about my audience, most of them women, at least according to the market research. How did they interpret their pleasure at scrolling through the posts I curated? Did the human brush fires reduce their own miseries to matchstick flickers? Did the violence provide them with a language for their private suffering?

I wanted to think there was some of that, because more and more I felt like a forager of other people's tragedies, grinning as I presented them like trophies to an invisible bloodthirsty crowd. The woman in that fishing bucket—she'd been someone once. Maybe her baby teeth were still tucked away in a drawer somewhere, the way my mother had saved mine in that old felt jewelry pouch I'd found after she died.

It was hard to be proud of this kind of work.

I had one eye on the clock, counting down to when I needed to start packing for Fourth of July weekend with my fiancé's family, when my email refreshed with a Google alert: "Her Secret Lives: How One Woman's Double Marriage Led to the Murder of an Innocent Man."

I was so accustomed to dead women that, for a moment, I thought I'd misread the headline. Then came the prick of curiosity, instant and sharp.

The story was from the *Laredo Morning Times*, a local newspaper for a city a few hours south of Austin, where I lived. I clicked on the link. My screen filled with the bold headline and two black-and-white family photos, divided by a dramatic stylized tear. In the first photo, captioned 1978, a man named Fabian Rivera and his wife, Dolores, held a pair of oversize scissors at some kind of ribbon-cutting event. Her curly black hair was feathered over each ear, earrings dangling to her jaw. She was laughing, her cheeks round, chin slightly tilted, as though she'd been about to look up at Fabian. She wore a harsh shoulder-padded skirt suit, and Fabian stared at the camera with a small twist of a smile at the corners of his lips and eyes. Beside them, two dark-haired boys, twins—captioned as Gabriel and Mateo Rivera—grinned, as if they were doing bunny ears behind their parents' backs.

The other photo was taken in 1984. It was a studio portrait with a cheesy Christmas backdrop: glittering fist-size snowflakes suspended above the branches of a heavily ornamented pine. This time the same woman—Dolores—leaned into a different man, captioned as Andres Russo. He smiled broadly, his right arm around her shoulder. Dolores's palm rested on the shoulder of a laughing teenage girl, who wore slouch socks and Dr. Martens with her plaid skirt. Beside her, a boy of eleven or twelve was wide-eyed behind dark-framed glasses.

Nothing in either photo suggested a crack in the couple's intimacy—but then, my own parents had chopped onions and bell peppers side by side for fajita night right up until the very end. They'd held hands in the car, singing to the Eagles. On every anniversary, they retold the story of how they met: two nineteen-year-olds craving Baskin-Robbins on a rainy winter night. Fate.

The way things *seemed* meant nothing.

I took a sip of cold coffee and began to read.

Penelope Russo was 15 when she met Dolores Rivera, the woman who would become her stepmother—and change her life forever. It was December 1983, and they spent that first meeting decorating the Christmas tree in Penelope's father Andres's Mexico City apartment. The tree was small and artificial, because Penelope's brother, Carlos, then 12, was allergic to the real ones. The whole endeavor took 20 minutes, and then they went to Churrería El Moro for hot chocolate and churros.

Even from the start, Penelope could understand her father's infatuation with the new woman. Dolores was 33 years old, a successful international banker from Laredo who still had her job in the midst of the devastating peso devaluation. She was smart and magnetic, Penelope remembers, with sparkling brown eyes and a contagious laugh.

The memory, it is clear, comes at a painful price: to recall Dolores is to recall the pain of being deceived, the shock of trusting someone—*loving* someone—whose every word turned out to be a lie.

Already, my curiosity was mutating, growing limbs, sprouting new and reaching fingers. I imagined a part of my mother, left in me, quivering like a magnet sensing its opposite.

I had to know more.

The *Laredo Morning Times* didn't have much of a presence on Twitter, but on Facebook, local readers tagged each other eagerly, whittling the degrees of separation between themselves and Dolores: someone's aunt used to work with her; someone's dad had asked her to go around in high school; wasn't she the lady on that bank billboard on San Ber a few years back, the one close to the bridge? *Pobrecitos los esposos, imagine!* and *Qué agüite, did they take away her kids?* and *No fkn way, that's my neighbor! Always outside watering her jungle.* About half the comments were in English, the other half in Spanglish or full Spanish, so that I had to open Google Translate to understand them.

Occasionally, obvious outsiders chimed in: a man with an American flag as a profile photo wondering whether Dolores was still fuckable, or a ruddy-cheeked white dude in a fisherman's hat writing, *Fucking Mexicans.* Not one but two incels emerged from their semen-scented basements to say this was why women should be kept as sex slaves—it was the only way innocent men could protect themselves. To these comments, the women responded with variations on *Go fuck yourself, pendejo, no one else will.*

I wouldn't exactly call it nuanced commentary.

When the front door creaked open, I was still sitting on the gray love seat that doubled as my office. "Shit," I hissed, looking at the time. It was after four. My fiancé's family farm was three and a half hours from Austin with no traffic—as if there was ever no traffic—and they were expecting us for dinner at eight. I hadn't even started to pack.

"Hey, pretty lady," Duke called, his initial grin fading when he took in my open laptop, my socked feet.

"Before you ask," I said, meeting him at the door, "I'm not *quite* ready yet." Duke was broad and sturdy, his skin silty with sweat, and he smelled like pit fire and honey when I kissed him.

Duke hated to be late. That was the thing about growing up on a dairy farm: if you don't milk a cow or goat when you're supposed to, she'll wail and stomp in agony that *you* caused. So Duke had grown up doing what he was supposed to do when he was supposed to do it. I'd loved that at the beginning of our relationship, how he called and texted and came by exactly when he promised. But it didn't leave a lot of room for error.

"Work," I added, noticing the glimmer of irritation on his face.

"Oh." Duke's expression relaxed as he opened the fridge, making sure nothing would go bad while we were away. "The Antone's retrospective? I'm excited about that one."

Duke was highly supportive of my noncrime freelance work. To him my obsession was macabre, the way I could binge hour after hour of crime shows, from prestige documentaries to *Forensic Files*, depending on my mood; the stack of books on my nightstand with dark covers and long, bold lettering. The podcasts I listened to during my walks—once wandering eight miles around the lake because I had to hear just *one* more episode of *Serial*—and the message boards I returned to when I couldn't sleep, my late-night tumble of rabbit holes. The folder on my desktop labeled "Interesting Crimes," where I dropped articles and screenshots and early research. All of this in addition to working on the blog for fifteen hours a week.

But then, look where Duke came from. Parents who still held hands forty years later, who called on Sundays and sent dry-iced care packages of crème fraîche, goat milk yogurt, honey, and jams. Siblings constantly blowing up the group chat with photos and memes and personal news. Childhood memories of brushing horses' flanks until they shone like water, and *literally* coming home when the dinner bell rang. Even after meeting his family, I'd sifted through his stories for hidden resentments, secret trauma, and found nothing. He was boyishly open, untainted. I loved this about him. But it meant he believed people were inherently good and didn't like looking at evidence to the contrary. I never wanted to be surprised again, so I looked and looked until even my dreams were bloody.

"I filed the Antone's piece last week," I said. "No, I found this story about a woman—a *mother*—who was secretly married to two men at the same time back in the eighties. One of the husbands ended up murdering the other."

Duke gave a half laugh, throwing out some ham on the verge of going slimy. "Sometimes I wonder what it would be like to get normal work updates from you."

"Imagine how much effort it took to pull that off," I continued, powering off my laptop. "And *why*, you know? What makes a woman, a *mom*, do something like that? Not that mothers always put their children first"—I should know—"or even that they should, but this is something else."

"Yeah, it's definitely weird. But, Cass—" Duke jangled his keys, a nervous tic he never noticed.

I glanced up, on alert. "Yeah?"

He crossed the room to where I crouched, pulling my charger from the wall. "We've hardly seen each other lately. Can we take a break from work this weekend? Maybe leave the laptop behind and make it, like, a murder-free zone?"

I laughed, though my grip tightened on my charger. It was easy for him to suggest leaving work behind—it wasn't like he could smoke the brisket for his food truck at the farm. And if Sal called with a problem over the weekend, he'd obviously answer. The food truck was his business. Crime was mine. Sort of.

But he was right. For weeks we'd only been catching each other in moments: a twenty-minute dinner break at the food park; the occasional mindless movie on Netflix; half-asleep sex that almost felt like a dream in the morning.

"Okay." I exhaled as I set the charger down, already feeling strangely limbless. "Sure. Family time. No murder. Promise."

I-35 was, as expected, a parking lot. Duke bit back any accusations and asked me to text the group chat that they could start eating without us. In return, I resisted the near-constant urge to research Dolores Rivera on my phone. By the time the sky screamed with sunset, we were relaxed and holding hands, dreaming up honeymoon destinations—the food in Laos was supposed to be incredible, Duke said; I told him about an article I'd read about hiking glaciers in Iceland—drunk on possibility while ignoring every practicality, beginning with the fact that we had no money and hadn't planned a damn thing for the wedding itself.

It was nearly nine when we reached the farm, 150 acres bordered by a four-rail white wooden fence, with a stone sign reading *Murphy Family Farm, Est. 1985*. Duke's F-150 jolted and clanged on the rough gravel road as we passed the goat pen with its three-walled tin structure, where the goats slept on shelves at various heights like kids at summer camp. We passed the coop with three hundred laying hens and the cow pasture and stables and corral before finally approaching the shiny red milking barn and white metal store stocked with fresh milk and eggs, in-season vegetables, and the lavender soap and candles Duke's mom, Caroline, made by hand. Just beyond was the farmhouse. Wraparound porch lit up bright, double swing and rocking chairs waiting for desultory after-dinner drinks. The wine went down easy here. And peacefully, too. I still wasn't used to that.

Inside, we took off our shoes at the door, lining them up underneath the scratched and scarred entryway bench. The wide wooden planks were smooth underfoot, softened in places by faded rugs in shades of saffron and ocher. We followed the sound of laughter and conversation to the dining room, where everyone was sitting at the long farmhouse table that Duke's grandfather had made by hand right before shipping off to World War II. The table was set with burlap place mats and hammered copper salt and pepper shakers, and there were several open bottles of wine, evidence of fresh bread and butter, but no dinner. They'd waited for us. Of course they had.

"Here you are!" said Caroline. The low light from the wooden chandelier caught the three silver earrings curling up each ear as she stood. She wore her blond hair short and spiky, and when she hugged me, I melted into her strong, solid body. She squeezed Duke, then turned to his father. "Alf, come help in the kitchen, will you?"

Alf was slighter than Caroline, softer spoken, with a silver handlebar mustache and a Cowboys cap he hung off a brass hook on the wall. "With pleasure," he drawled.

"We told you guys not to wait!" Duke said.

His younger sister Allie rolled her eyes with a smile. "Like that was going to happen."

Allie was twenty-five, petite, with neat, clean features—bright blue eyes above youthful freckled cheeks. Stephie was in her sophomore year at Northwestern and apparently in the middle of urging Kyle, the youngest, to apply for the following year so they could be in school together again.

Five minutes later, we were squeezed between Allie and Duke's older brother, Dylan, cutting into herb-rubbed chicken that was somehow still tender and warm. Dylan bragged about Allie's latest barrel racing stats. She accepted the praise matter-of-factly, adding, "They never saw us coming." The conversation meandered comfortably. *How's the food truck, Duke—Hey, Cassie, did he ever tell you about the time—Can someone pass the potatoes—Mom, do we have any coffee milk this time—Did y'all remember to restock the shelves—When's Millie due to calve?*

Being here was like getting into bed at the end of a long day—warm, safe, comfortable. But I couldn't help wondering how many

Facebook comments had been added to the Dolores Rivera story since we'd left Austin. How many article shares? There was no way I was the only reporter who'd looked at the italicized line below the article—*Dolores Rivera declined to be interviewed*—and seen something else: an opportunity.

I'd felt it right away. An intimate story from the perspective of a rare female bigamist, whose crime *led* to murder? That was special. That could be big. *Harper's* big. *New Yorker* big. *In Cold Blood* had started as a *New Yorker* series. One long-form true crime piece to launch my career. I was so fucking sick of the blog, of being broke, consulting my overdue-invoices spreadsheet every Friday afternoon, sending my "just following up" emails, hoping to strike the right tone of polite assertiveness that wouldn't get me blackballed from the publication. If I didn't get paid at least five hundred dollars by the time rent was due on Thursday, I'd have to tell Duke—again. He'd say we'd figure it out—again. Suggest—again—we open a joint account. Wouldn't it be easier to pay all our bills from the same place? Less stressful? It probably was, for some people. And I wished I were one of them, I did, but the thought of combining our finances made me feel like burying myself alive.

"Cass?" Duke reached for my hand, teasing my marquise sapphire with his thumb. The ring had belonged to Duke's grandmother, and I always felt in it the weight of a family's history, its memories and unions. It made me feel like I belonged somewhere. "What do you think?" he asked, smiling.

"Sorry," I said, sheepish. Everyone was looking at me. "What do I think about what?"

Duke's jaw tightened. "Mom was just suggesting—"

"Offering!" Caroline waved her hands. "You can absolutely say no."

"Offering," Duke said, softening, "that we have the wedding here on the farm."

It had been seven months since Duke proposed. The cold Ferris wheel seat at the Trail of Lights had trembled beneath us, hovering over trees illuminated in bright primary colors, and the city itself had sparkled against the dark sky. My chest ached with an old, tender memory. I'd cried as I said yes.

But the average cost of a wedding in this country was thirty-five *thousand* dollars. Who had that kind of money lying around or was willing to go into that much debt for one day? Even the dresses on sale at David's Bridal, which I'd taken a tepid look at online, cost seven hundred bucks. And as soon as we decided on a location, they'd want a deposit, which we didn't have. So, we'd been stuck.

Now here was Caroline, offering the perfect solution, which I couldn't believe we hadn't already considered. I could see it now, the neat rows of white chairs arranged before a trellised gazebo Alf would make by hand. Caroline would bake a tiered naked cake, its buttery sides dusted with powdered sugar. Duke and I would walk to the altar together, and I'd officially become a part of a family where everyone had grown up sleeping with their doors wide open, no shouting to stifle, nothing to fear.

"Yes," I blurted. "Of course. I mean, right?" I said to Duke. "That's perfect."

Duke grinned. In the chandelier's low light, his eyes were the color of maple syrup spread thin. "It is perfect."

Caroline clapped, and Dylan went into the kitchen for the bottle of champagne Alf thought he remembered seeing in the back of the fridge.

My phone vibrated in my pocket. I froze midlaugh as Andrew's face filled the screen. An old photo, his skin red-gold in the sunset at Great Salt Plains Lake. Though his legs were out of frame, I knew his jeans were rolled to the knees, his calves immersed in the clear shallow water. My heart seized at the happy way he was looking at the camera. At me.

I was suddenly aware of my own heartbeat, its guilty thuds, as I declined the call. Andrew. He'd come into my life right as my mother left it. He'd saved me that summer. From my grief, from myself. But I never knew what might be on the other end of his calls, which meant I could never answer in front of Duke. There was too much he didn't know.

Too much to risk by telling him.

It was almost midnight when we crawled into Duke's old pine bed, my back to his chest, his hand on my hip. Sleep on the farm was usually like a hole I stumbled into in the dark, one moment tethered to the ground, the next falling. Gone.

But not tonight. Tonight, my thoughts kept flitting between Andrew and Dolores Rivera. If something was wrong, Andrew would have called again, I reassured myself. He would have texted me. And why was it that some people, like Duke, could hear about a woman who'd lived a complete double life that led to a murder, and simply *move on*, while others, like me, worried the threads of that story like yarn between fingers, scraping the skin raw?

Duke kissed the spot below my jaw that made me shiver. "I'm so happy we're going to get married here," he whispered.

"Me too," I said, though my mind was still on Dolores, thinking about the buy-in you'd need for someone to believe you're essentially alone in the world. What had Andres Russo's family and friends thought of his wife, a woman with a foot in two countries? Who had gone to their wedding? Didn't anyone wonder why she had no family in attendance, no friends?

My stomach lurched as I realized my own side of the aisle would be nearly as empty—everything, everyone I was missing creating its own gravity, impossible to ignore. The truth is it doesn't take elaborate lies, only being with someone who doesn't push to know the things you don't want to reveal.

When Duke's arm loosened around me in sleep, I pulled my phone off the charger and texted Andrew: *Sorry I missed your call. Is everything okay?*

The ellipsis appeared. Disappeared. Appeared again, followed by: *Yeah.*

I stared at the word until my eyes burned. *Yeah.* Simple, curt. He may as well have written *Fuck you.*

Okay, I responded. *I'll call you soon so we can catch up.* I hesitated, remembering the warmth of his skin on mine so long ago. *I miss you.*

This time, nothing appeared after the ellipsis. My heart was a comet trailing fire in my chest.

I put the phone away and closed my eyes, but I was viciously awake. Carefully, I edged out of bed, plunging my hand into my duffel bag and rummaging below jeans and tops and underwear until I felt the familiar comfort of cold steel. Then I pulled out the laptop I'd promised Duke I would leave behind.

I settled cross-legged onto the floor, my back against the bed. The computer chimed softly when I turned it on. Duke shifted as the room lightened with electronic blue. I held my breath, curved over the screen, dimming it with my body. After a moment, the covers stilled. His breathing deepened.

Exhaling, I pulled up the *Laredo Morning Times* piece again. Dolores Rivera and Andres Russo had been married for just under a year, together for nearly three, when Russo's body was found at the Hotel Botanica, a motor inn in Laredo, on August 2, 1986. It wasn't long before the police discovered that Russo, who lived in Mexico City, was in town to visit his wife, Dolores Rivera. (So why was he staying at a motel instead of with Dolores? Where did he think she lived?) He was believed to have been "shot the evening before, on a day temperatures soared to a record-breaking 117 degrees before a much-needed rain cooled things off."

The detectives at the time, Manuel Zamora and Ben Cortez, had questioned both Dolores and Fabian, but if she'd been a suspect initially (which of course she was), soon Fabian eclipsed her as a person of interest: a clerk had seen him leaving the motel around 10 P.M. on August 1, which turned out to fit squarely within the window of Russo's time of death.

Fabian was no criminal mastermind—he'd also left a partial print in Russo's room, and the slug lodged in Russo's body was later matched to ammunition found in Fabian and Dolores's home, ammunition used for the Ruger Mark II .22 caliber pistol Fabian claimed to have lost. The bullet had entered from the right side of Russo's chest, tearing through his eighth rib to lodge within the soft tissue of his lateral right back. It fractured the rib and punctured the lower right lung. Russo had drowned in thirteen and a half ounces of his own blood.

The reporter traded gleefully in these details, though I'd been writing my own grotesqueries long enough to know what they masked: a lack of any real insight into the crime. Not only the murder, but the crime that had led to the murder—Dolores's double marriage. Instead, there were quotes from Dolores's former stepdaughter, Penelope Russo, calling her a monster who'd used their family and thrown them away, like trash. As a treat, the reporter indulged in a little armchair pathologizing, questioning whether Dolores was a psychopath or merely a narcissist, and maybe that shouldn't have pissed me off, but it did—he was one step away from calling her crazy, that one word with the power to dismiss every aspect of women's emotional and intellectual lives, our motivations and desires. Which, especially in their absence, were the most interesting parts of this story.

The first search results for Dolores Rivera's name paired with Laredo were the article and its various comment threads. The paper's online archives only went as far back as 2005, with similar results for all other major Texas cities. Whatever had been written about her at the time of the murder was relegated to a reference library somewhere.

After the *Laredo Morning Times* piece, there was a retirement announcement from five years ago—astonishingly, from the same bank where Dolores had worked in the eighties. It featured what I assumed was a semi-updated headshot: Dolores with a thick, straight collar-length bob, her hair mostly still dark, wearing red lipstick and a matching silk shirt. Her brown eyes were warm, competent, and amused. She was still an attractive woman. Had she been in other serious relationships since the murder? Who would be able to trust her after what she'd done?

After the retirement announcement and an outdated LinkedIn page, the results lost accuracy, linking to Spanish GoFundMes and college volleyball game write-ups. I searched for her on social media with no results. Then I reopened the *Laredo Morning Times* article. There were Dolores and Fabian, with their hands on the oversize scissors.

And their sons.

Mateo and Gabriel Rivera must be in their midforties now. I started with Mateo: easy. He owned a veterinary clinic in San Antonio and reminded me of the serious runners at the lake, tall and greyhound-lean, with silvering dark hair. Mateo didn't have any personal social media, but the clinic maintained an enthusiastic Instagram account. In photos with animals, Mateo was almost always smiling: caught midlaugh between three lion-headed pit bulls at an outdoor adoption event, or beaming as he held a drooping pug puppy with an IV taped to its arm: *Clyde is off oxygen!* But with other people Mateo seemed serious, almost awkward—too much space between him and the person beside him in a group shot, a hand hovering instead of resting on a shoulder.

Gabriel, on the other hand, was a seasoned and prolific Facebook poster. He was a bull-necked high school basketball coach, with a black goatee and a gold class ring on one hand, a wedding band on the other. In clips of his games, he flung out his arms, eyes cast to the rafters, when players missed a free throw. With the volume off, the gesture looked almost rapturous. I could imagine his voice in the locker room afterward, though, bouncing off the dull, slatted metal doors: *Is this what we practice for? To lose the points that are* handed *to us?* Something about him—the predatory way he paced by the bench, the expansiveness of his gestures—made him seem like a yeller.

Then again, there were the photos of him with his sons. I stared at one in particular for a long time. Joseph and Michael were three and five. Gabriel was kneeling in patchy grass, his arms around them, the sons each wearing a neon green Velcro mitt. Over the skinny shoulder of the older one, Gabriel's eyes were closed. His smile was painfully tender. His wife, Brenda, had posted the photo tagging Gabriel, with the caption *Mi corazón*. For some reason, I took a screenshot.

Gabriel and Brenda, a "leadership consultant," whatever that meant, still lived in Laredo. They liked fried sushi rolls stuffed with cream cheese and jalapeños and had once won a radio contest to eat barbecue with the Eli Young Band at Rudy's and recently finished construction on a fortresslike stucco house in a subdivision called Alexander Estates. According to Google Maps, the neighborhood was right beside the high school where Gabriel coached. In a video Gabriel posted, he zoomed in on the edge of the cement driveway, which bore four handprints in a row, from large to tiny.

I scrolled through hundreds of photos on Facebook and Instagram, watching Gabriel's and Brenda's lives flow backward until they diverged and their future together was only one possibility out of millions. What a foolhardy thing, splaying yourself out like this for anyone to see, evidence of that very human desire to be known. Well, here I was, coming to know them like a tracker comes to know an animal through its scuffs in the dirt, its scent on the wind.

Startled, I realized Duke was no longer snoring. The room was silent. For a moment I swore I could feel his gaze raking over my back as I did exactly what I'd promised not to do on this trip. I turned around slowly, preparing for the shake of his head, the disappointed slant of his mouth. But he was asleep. Or at least pretending to be.

I scrolled forward again through Gabriel's photos, quick, deliberate. And there she was—Dolores Rivera. Rarely in the foreground and yet seemingly always *there*, part of the scaffolding of Gabriel's and Brenda's lives. She was proud in a gold gown in the first pew of a church for their wedding. Her hands covered in mushy orange baby food as she fed Joseph at a high chair two years ago. Standing at a basketball game, palms cupped into a megaphone around her mouth.

Picking up strewn wrapping paper at a kid's birthday party. That photo, in particular, made my breath catch. It reminded me of a day I tried not to think about, one that had defined my entire existence.

The point was this: despite the wreckage her choices left behind, Dolores hadn't lost her sons. Somehow, it seemed they'd been able to forgive her. How had they done that? How had she earned it?

I'd never been able to forgive my own mother. What would she think of a woman like Dolores, someone who'd wanted more than the life she had, or a different life, and spun one into existence?

Again, I looked at the brief, italicized sentence right below the article: *Dolores Rivera declined to be interviewed.*

Well, now that the story was out, maybe she would be ready to tell her side.

LORE, 1983

Outside the Aeropuerto Internacional, Lore Rivera shrugs out of her dark blazer and slips the pack of Marlboros—a dollar a pack, nearly twice what they cost three years ago, when things were good—from the zippered compartment of her tote. In Mexico, she smokes. Fabian would be shocked if he knew, and pissed at the unnecessary extravagance. This is part of the pleasure.

Mexico City is all pleasure to her. The wild swerving rush of taxis, the buses on their labyrinthine, timetabled missions, the orange canopy of smog suspended between the city and the clouds. She adores the three-minute walk through gasoline-soaked air to the Terminal Aérea, where she will take the metro to the Pantitlán station before changing lines, then walking the last ten minutes through the Centro Histórico to her hotel—a forty-five-minute trip, all forward thrust, shoulder to shoulder with more people than she'd see in a week in Laredo, whose entire population could be contained in just one of the shantytowns outside DF, thousands of shacks pimpling the hillsides, staggered against one another like drunks at the end of the night.

Her first few trips here, she was glad to be traveling with Oscar, another international banking officer. She'd never been anywhere bigger than San Antonio, never been swept along a human wave into a city that instantly inhaled her into its hot mouth of teeth and tongue. She'd never had to navigate a subway system or memorize maps in advance lest she mark herself a tourist. She was glad, then, to have Oscar to follow, to study. Now her aloneness in a city this size is intoxicating. Nobody knows her. She could be anyone. She could *become* anyone.

As Lore boards the metro, exhaling her own contribution to the smog, she is also exhaling the burdens of home: specifically, the sourness of Fabian's panic and his growing resentment that she will not panic with him.

Last night, she turned toward him in their dark bedroom. The cuates were asleep, finally, after Gabriel had thrown a fit because he was sick of fideo, couldn't they order a pizza, and a bedtime that extended past ten because Mateo, always anxious at the start of the school year, kept coming back out to double—no, triple—check that he'd put his homework in his backpack.

Lore had indulged in two fingers of Bucanas before bed, and she was loose-limbed and yearning as she slid against Fabian's back. She kissed his shoulder and closed her fingers around him, trying to ignore how his body tensed. She murmured, as if she could perform his desire for him.

"Lore." He peeled her hand away. "Stop."

"Why?" She kissed the nape of his neck, which needed a shave. Maybe she'd do it for him before she left tomorrow morning. "The cuates are asleep. And it's been so long—"

"I hate when you say that." Heat, the wrong kind, rose from his skin. "It's been a long day."

Lore sighed. "It's always a long day."

Fabian yanked the Tiffany lamp's brass cord. His black hair had already swirled into a pillow cowlick, the same one he'd been taming with Brylcreem since they were seventeen.

"How can you act like everything is normal?" His dark eyes were sunken, his beard unable to mask the downward pull of his lips as he sat against the oak headboard. "I'm going to have to lay off Juan tomorrow, and he's been with us almost since the beginning!"

"I know." The recession was all Fabian had talked about for months, the confluence of crises that had led to the peso's shocking devaluation from 23 to the dollar in 1980 to 150 to the dollar today—imagine, a peso worth less than a penny!—with predictions it would get ten, even twenty times worse before it got better. "You don't have a choice, though," Lore said, the way she always said at this point.

"I know that," Fabian snapped, then lowered his voice. "Did I tell you his mother's sick?"

Lore sighed. "Cancer, right?"

Fabian nodded.

"Everyone's getting cancer these days."

Fabian squeezed the back of his neck with one big hand, the hand that used to be rough as caliche from his ironwork. She used to love seeing him hunched over a furnace, dripping sweat as he curved what was once unbendable into elegant scrolls. Transforming it. Before the store opened five years ago, their small backyard was a jumbled, metallic playground, the cuates passing through gates leading nowhere, knocking on doors that leaned up against trees, as if they might open to another world.

Everyone needs doors, Fabian had said in the *Laredo Morning Times* article about the ribbon cutting. *Doors are a symbol of civilization. They separate the domestic from the wild. They protect what you love most.*

Fabian's passion, his poetry, had surprised her. She'd sparked with pride, framing the article and hanging it—naturally—in their entryway.

But Fabian had been wrong. When the homes stop being built, the doors stop being needed. The wild growing ever closer.

"Fabian," she tried, softer, turning him so she could dig her thumbs deep into flesh gone taut with stress. "Everything's going to be okay."

He pulled away, standing to loom over her. "That's easy for you to say. They need you."

"And that's a good thing, isn't it?" Lore said evenly. "For us, for our family?"

Fabian glared at her, his bowling ball shoulders hunched forward, and she caught an unwelcome glimpse of him in middle age—thick, an illusion of strength that would disappear when his clothes came off.

She knew what the real problem was: he was failing, for reasons outside his control, and she wasn't. Soon hers might be their only paycheck, and not a bad one at that. You could howl at the moon, but the moon wouldn't turn toward your pain. Your wife, though. Your wife the international banker, who cinched a gold belt around her waist and made the kitchen echo with the capable sound of her stilettos—your wife, whose job was, at least for now, secure—well, at her, you could howl. She would turn toward you, and you could turn her away, and in that moment, the power would be yours again.

"Chinga," he said, pulling a shirt from his drawer. "I won't be able to sleep now."

She heard his unspoken accusation: if only she hadn't touched him.

"I'm going to look over the books," he said. "Again."

He stalked from the room as if he'd slam the door if the boys weren't right down the hall. She sighed and looked at the clock: midnight. In only nine hours, she'd be driving to the airport in San Antonio. She'd open the windows and let the hot desert wind strip off the skin she was only too eager to leave behind.

Now, in the atrium of the Gran Hotel in the Centro Histórico, Lore gazes up at the golden dome of the stained-glass ceiling. From the center, three round peacock-blue skylights stare back like the eyes of God. The white marble floors are reflective as a lake, and the caged elevator carries people upward in a slow, dreamlike swoon. Joy slices like a knife between her ribs.

Along the border, things that are concrete, sharply defined, elsewhere are fluid. Banking is business, yes, but business is personal, always. You open accounts with relationships, not dollars, which is not something the big U.S. banks understand. Those national chains have no interest in operating in a small Texas-Mexico border town, and those who tried have not lasted. All they see in Laredo is a bunch of Mexican country bumpkins. They don't understand the power of the border, the flow of commerce like a river between countries. They don't understand the culture. How it's not enough to know your customers' names; you also need to know the state of their father's emphysema and that their daughter is salutatorian at Martin and that if you give them a camo baseball cap with the bank's embroidered logo, they will wear it so often their wife will forbid it in the bedroom. Now the big banks are floundering, with their risky investments and scattershot loans, while Lore's community bank is holding steady. They've had to be responsible with their funding, careful to whom they lend, but when customers struggle to make payments, the bank is able to work with them. And in better times, the customer remembers. This is how the table expands: to a game of Little League, the board of the Rotary Club, an extravagant wedding in Mexico City.

The wedding is tonight, the daughter of Fernando Santos, Mexican entrepreneur and owner of a slew of maquiladoras along the border, including two in Nuevo Laredo. Mr. Santos has been a customer of the bank for ten years, long enough to invite Lore and her colleague Oscar. But Oscar's first child will be born any day now, and even though Fabian scoffed at the invitation—how could he take time off right now?—Lore had accepted. It's good for business, she told him.

And she RSVP'd for one.

The whole hotel has been reserved for the wedding, and in the sun-shot atrium, employees scurry around a hundred round tables, calling out to each other as they arrange porcelain plates and gleaming silverware. Behind the bride and groom's table, florists make tender-fingered adjustments to an entire wall of roses and lilies. Lore watches from inside the caged elevator, touching one of the brass flowers. She wishes Fabian could see the intricate iron scrollwork.

In her room, Lore sets her bag down gently on the plush carpet. She sighs, running her hands over the king-size bed's ornate wooden headboard and the filmy white curtains; the dainty damask bench and dusky blue velvet chair. How strange to be somewhere so luxurious, so opulent, when Mexico is burning and Laredo along with it. They'd felt so lucky back in '80, '81, when they were mostly insulated from the national recession by the 1.5 billion retail dollars coming in from Mexico. But then the recession lessened demand for oil, oversaturating the market. Mexico's export revenue plummeted. Its foreign debt increased, coupled with an inability to pay it. In '82 the peso devalued, and then again, and again, and suddenly all that retail income Laredo saw from across stopped, like a faucet turned off. At the bank's last estimate, at least seven hundred businesses in Laredo have closed, leaving tens of thousands of people without a way to support their families.

At the window, Lore pulls back the thick curtains to see the Zócalo, the pulsing heart of the Centro Histórico. In the fifteenth century, the area was the center of the Aztec capital of Tenochtitlán. Now it's bordered by the Metropolitan Cathedral, built in sections over nearly two hundred and fifty years, and the National Palace and Federal District buildings, their stone facades soaked with sun and blood. Near the towering Mexican flag, tourists in jeans and T-shirts—they are the ones winning, the tourists—salsa dance before a street performer. She can nearly feel their laughter. Her chest seizes with the desire to join, join, join. To see Fabian's eyes glow rich as molasses in the sun, to feel his hand firm around her hip.

Fabian. She should call him. At the thought, the image of dancing-Fabian fades, replaced with the surly reality of her husband. She doesn't want to talk to him. Or—she doesn't want to talk to this version of him. If she could choose, she'd call upon the eighteen-year-old Fabian, who'd sat with her in a blind and said, "Close your eyes." She had expected him to kiss her. Instead, they had listened to the wind, to the birds, to, eventually, the soft scuffle of hooves, and when she opened her eyes there was a family of deer eating the corn they'd spilled from the back of his dad's truck. Two spotted fawns tugged at their mother's teats as she flicked them away impatiently, her jaws cracking the rock-hard kernels. Fabian smiled at Lore, shotgun by his side. "Don't," she said. And he laughed softly. "Of course not," he replied.

She looks at her watch: four o'clock. It will be cheaper to call him later tonight. Of course, there will be no "later tonight." The wedding will continue until morning, when everyone is too drunk to stand. In any case, she'll be home tomorrow.

She hangs her red gown in the closet and draws a bath. Light glints off the gold mirror. Drapery is tied back from the tub with gold rope, as if the tub is a stage, the actors moments from their entrance.

Waiters pass like ghosts between the tables, balancing silver trays of champagne and Don Julio on the tips of their fingers. A mariachi band in silver-buttoned pants and cropped jackets plays lively pre-dinner music. The ground nearly trembles with the room's heightened energy. There must be seven or eight hundred people here. Lore has always thought Laredo weddings are big, with all the various compromisos leading to hundreds of guests, some of whom the bride and groom hardly know, but in comparison they seem intimate and slipshod, like backyard carne asadas.

Lore is sitting with a group of Mr. Santos's more personal business associates: Jaime, his architect, and his wife, Mariela; Ramón, his CPA, and his wife—Lore had to ask twice to make sure she wasn't mistaken—Ramona; his cardiologist, Dr. Olivares, and his wife, Cynthia; and Andres, his daughter's professor and adviser at the Universidad Nacional Autónoma de México. Lore wishes there were more entrepreneurial types at her table, but there will be plenty of time to network in the guise of celebrating.

The other women lean toward each other as they sip their champagne, touch the elaborate floral centerpieces as they talk about the beauty of the ceremony, the jaw-dropping length of the bride's mantilla. What they're really talking about, Lore knows, is how much it all must have cost. She joins the conversation, though her ears are with the men, who are essentially having the same discussion.

"His businesses must be doing well," Dr. Olivares comments.

Ramón, the only one at the table who would know besides Lore, answers politely. "Fernando is very dedicated."

"I wonder where she bought her dress," Ramona says. "Here or in New York."

Cynthia scoffs. "DF has some of the best shopping in the world. Why would she go spend six times more in New York? Especially now?"

"Because it's *New York*," Ramona breathes.

"What do you think, Lore?" Andres asks, and for a moment she isn't sure which conversation she's supposed to be following. "You said you're in banking?"

"Yes," Lore says, finishing her first glass of champagne as another is seamlessly placed before her.

"How has the devaluation impacted the retail sector on the border?" Andres asks, and Lore is amused that he, too, had an ear in both conversations, bridging them with academic ease.

"Honestly," Lore says, "it's like a bomb has gone off." She thinks of the women squatting to comparison shop for generic canned goods and bagged cereal on the bottom shelves at H-E-B, and how many more men there are outside Dr. Ike's, waiting to jump on flatbeds that never come. She thinks of all the CERRADO signs and rolled-down security grilles downtown, as if everyone inside has simply vanished.

Andres angles himself toward her slightly. "Tell me more," he says.

Lore looks at him more closely. He's around forty, she guesses, with black hair swept back from his forehead and tucked behind his ears. His eyes are a clear, startling green, like a broken bottle catching sunlight. Proud nose, heavy eyebrows giving him a look of earnest concentration. His Spanish is clipped, some of his *s*'s missing—she can't quite place his accent, but he doesn't sound Mexican.

"Well," Lore says, "Laredo's main industry is retail. Now . . ." She trails off, thinking of Fabian, wondering how it went, firing Juan. The city smells like desperation. "Without that income from across, nearly a third of the city is out of work."

"A third." Andres shakes his head. "Unbelievable."

"And to think, we were at ten percent only two years ago," Lore says, remembering what she now knows was a boom time, Fabian asking his mom to babysit while he swept her off to the Cadillac Bar, or surprising her with a pair of gold-and-topaz earrings lumpy inside her pillowcase. They were planning to remodel their house. The peso devalued before they had a chance. At least they aren't one of the thousands who needed to abandon a construction project midbuild, the city scattered with the carcasses of dreams.

"What about the maquiladoras?" Andres asks. "Fernando owns several dozen, doesn't he?"

"Yes," Lore says, "though mostly in Juárez. But you're right: Mexican income, returned to the U.S. through purchases, plus U.S. manufacturing jobs to provide the materials for assembly—in normal times it's a win-win. But when you don't have buyers for the final products . . ." She opens her hands on the table, then realizes with a start that she's not wearing her wedding rings. She put all her jewelry in the safe before sliding into her bath. She touches her chest, where her gold locket usually rests, and encounters only skin.

"How old are you, Lore, if you don't mind my asking?" asks Dr. Olivares, peering at her through square-framed gold glasses.

His wife, Cynthia, swats him on the shoulder. "Ay, Héctor. You're the one showing your age."

The table laughs, Lore along with them. She's used to this—older men first assuming she's a secretary or maybe a new-accounts rep, then reappraising her suspiciously when she opens her mouth. She doubts Dr. Olivares would ask Oscar, if he were here, for his age, though he is actually two years younger than Lore. But this is the way things are in the business world—perhaps in any kind of world, and especially in Mexico. If she were to show offense, she would be committing that ultimate sin of femaleness: oversensitivity. She's learned better than that.

"I'm thirty-two," Lore says.

"And how long have you been with the bank?"

"Let's see," Lore says, though she doesn't need to think about it. "It's been eight years now."

Lore had started as a teller when she was twenty and believed she would return after her six-week maternity leave. How naive she had been then, how utterly unprepared for the brutality of motherhood. Cooped up in their tiny rental during the cuarentena, family streaming in and out without warning: Marta with tortilla soup, Mami with her brusque and capable hands, Fabian's mother dispensing useless advice, his father with cigars, not realizing or caring how little she could spare Fabian for forty backslapping minutes in the backyard because those two tiny newborns were too much for her to handle alone.

Six weeks after the cuates were born, they were still under six pounds each, with red-soled feet the size of fallen leaves and wild, heart-stopping cries like cats in heat. Her nipples were crusted with scabs, every letdown triggering a warm gush of blood between her legs. She was still healing from a third-degree tear, her body split from one intimate end to the other. The idea of returning to work was laughable and cruel, like a soldier rushing back to battle with skin flapping open, metal buried in his body, festering. And so, the weeks turned to months and the months to years. She finally returned when the boys were in preschool, starting again as a teller and rising through nearly every position until her most recent promotion to officer, three years ago.

Andres smiles at her, warm and knowing. "Did you always want to be a banker?"

"I wanted to be Robinson Crusoe," Lore says wryly, as waiters place salad plates before them. "Life on a desert island seemed like heaven to me as a kid."

"Even with the cannibals?"

Lore laughs. "They couldn't have been worse than my siblings. Besides, Crusoe was free to be who he was there. Not perfect. Not even always good. I longed for that kind of freedom."

"What's wrong with being good, though?" asks Mariela, the architect's wife. Her cheeks are flushed at the high points. "The world respects a good woman."

"Does it?" Lore spears an overripe tomato. Guts spill. "Or does it just appreciate a meek one?"

Mariela's cheeks flame brighter, but after that, dinner continues seamlessly: over buttery filet mignon, they discuss the architecture in DF and whether President Reagan will go on to a second term. Their wineglasses refill as if by magic, until Lore has no idea how many glasses she's consumed. Then come the after-dinner drinks: port, more sipping tequila, playful mango shots with sugar-spice rims. The mariachi band has been replaced with a popular Mexican band everyone knows—a surprise, judging by the bride's strangled shriek of joy. The table empties of everyone except Lore and Andres.

Lore knows she should drink water, but she and Andres are laughing, talking with exuberant ease, and it feels so good to not be worrying, for once. They talk about how, for him, this is the first month of the new year—he lives by the academic calendar, he says, and August has that fresh-start sparkle that others feel in January. So you're either five months early or seven months late, Lore jokes, and he says late. Argentineans, like Mexicans, are always late.

"So that's where you're from," Lore says. "Argentina. I've been trying to figure it out."

"Buenos Aires." A shadow crosses Andres's face.

It's Lore's job to be informed of international affairs, so she knows he's referring to the military junta and the Dirty War, the last seven years of state terrorism in which tens of thousands of political dissidents—many of them students, activists, journalists—have been killed or "disappeared."

"The election is coming up, isn't it?" she asks.

Andres nods. In his eyes, guarded, cynical hope. "October. Let's hope for the return of democracy."

"What was it like to grow up there?" Lore asks, and he tells her about his childhood, how he misses the graffiti and street art that make even the wealthiest neighborhoods feel like raw silk, on the edge of unraveling. Lore tells him about City Drug, the 1930s apothecary-turned-soda-fountain where she used to take the bus after school, ten cents for a bag of pistachios white with salt, making her mouth water to think about even now.

"So tell me, Ms. Crusoe," Andres says sometime later, with a lazy smile. "Couldn't your boyfriend make it tonight?"

"Boyfriend?" Lore laughs, glancing automatically at her ring finger—but of course, it's bare. Though, has she really not mentioned Fabian or the boys all night?

"I don't have a boyfriend," Lore says, and before she can finish, Andres is out of his seat, hand outstretched.

"I was hoping you'd say that," he says. "Dance with me?"

Lore will look back on this moment again and again over the years, naming every detail back to life: how Andres has loosened his bow tie, giving Lore the startling impulse to undo it completely; the long, elegant fingers on his waiting hand, which she will later discover smell like oranges from his morning café de olla; the irresistible chaos of the dance floor, pulsing now within her chest. A simple misunderstanding, an incomplete sentence, leading to a moment when everything that will happen has not yet happened, and so every possibility still exists: Lore could decline the dance. She could tell him she doesn't have a boyfriend—she has a *husband*. She could realize she hasn't had so much to drink in months and remember her beautiful king-size bed upstairs, a haven of uninterrupted rest. In this moment, Lore's life forks.

But she doesn't know that yet, and who ever does? Lore looks up into those shattered-bottle eyes that are suddenly electric, and though his stare flusters Lore, it electrifies *her*, too, because how long has it been since she's been looked at this way, with such fierceness of curiosity, as though she might be anybody? And it's only a dance, after all.

CASSIE, 2017

On Tuesday, the day after we returned from the farm, Duke and I had our usual coffee and toast together before he left to start the brisket. For the perfect caramelized bark, he'd season the meat with only salt and pepper, dusted from an old shaker two feet above the glistening prime beef. Then he'd begin the eight-hour smoking process, a whole workday before the food truck's window even slid open. Duke was as obsessive as I was about work, only his nourished people, while mine—well.

I spent the next three hours combing through my murder alerts and writing the day's blog posts. Man sets wife on fire after believing she'd been poisoning his pot roast. Kid fresh out of high school plots his octogenarian godmother's murder in hopes of inheriting her house. Man dismembers young girlfriend who wants no part of his group sex lifestyle. Below each post, a fuchsia link like a lipstick stain, tempting readers with *You May Also Like*. What a strange word to use in this context—*like*. I imagined readers flitting from post to post as if gorging on a box of chocolates, liking them right up until they felt sick.

I wanted out. Or no: I just wanted different. I might be a dirty little cog in the true crime industrial complex, but I still loved the genre. When it's done right, true crime tells us who we are, who we should fear, who we are always in danger of becoming. Under a careful investigative eye, someone opaque briefly becomes transparent. Even if what's revealed is ugly, it's true. And nothing is more beautiful than the truth.

After a sad bagged-salad lunch, I reread the Dolores Rivera story. Though the article was ostensibly written for the thirty-year anniversary of Fabian's sentencing (a lazy claim on relevance), there was so much about the murder the reporter didn't even address. How had Fabian found out about Dolores's double life, and how long had he known before killing Andres? How had he known where Andres was staying? Why take his rage out on the other man, instead of the woman who'd duped them both? I wondered why Andres's body wasn't found until the next morning—at a hotel, somebody should have heard the gunshot. And why had Fabian accepted such a harsh plea deal instead of taking his chances in court? This was the *definition* of a crime of passion. Any half-decent attorney should have been able to plead down the charges.

And finally, Dolores. Had she seen Andres that day? Had she known Fabian killed him before he was arrested? Was she haunted by her role in both men's downfall, or—a cynical thought—was any part of her relieved to be free of them?

I made a spreadsheet with every name referenced in the piece, along with any contact information I could find. The Laredo Police Department didn't have an online FOIA request form, so I left a voicemail with the records division. Then I started a rudimentary timeline: the year Dolores and Fabian married, the approximate year their sons were born, the date and place Dolores met Andres, the date they'd been married, and finally the murder and Fabian's arrest. There were only ten days between the last two.

I worked in a state of heightened focus, like the few times I'd taken Adderall in college to write four papers back-to-back. If I was right about the potential for a story from Dolores's perspective, I had to be fast.

Relationship fraud is typically a man's crime, with the FBI identifying most common targets as women over forty who are divorced, widowed, and/or disabled. Money is usually the end game. In 2016, more than fifteen thousand relationship scams were reported to the FBI's Internet Crime Complaint Center, with losses over two hundred million dollars. The real numbers were probably much higher.

The stories were easy to find. Whirlwind romances, women who couldn't believe their luck: He was a doctor, a soldier, an entrepreneur. He was handsome, charming. He took her out on his motorcycle, on his speedboat, in his convertible. He proposed after only a couple of months. Arms snaked around each other's waists at courthouses and chapels, eyes shining. But the travel. The money he needed to borrow until the real estate deal came through. The errant piece of mail with a different name. The disappearing act. Heartbroken and humiliated, the women were forced to move in with aging parents or continue working the jobs from which they'd been set to retire. What was taken from them would never be recovered.

I'd read, once, that hypnotism only works on the suggestible—those who are willing and ready to suspend disbelief, to focus at length and with wholehearted intensity on an alternate version of reality. Perhaps the men who preyed on these women were like any other criminals—hunters, adept at spotting those with the capacity to believe.

In the course of my double-life research, I came across only one other American woman known to have been secretly married to two men at once, and it had nothing to do with money.

The writer Anaïs Nin was forty-four, married to an investment banker named Hugo, when she met Rupert Pole in 1947. He was twenty-eight and film-star handsome, though his acting fell short of his looks. They met in a Manhattan elevator on their way to the same party, and when he got the impression Nin was divorced, she didn't correct him.

Eight years after they met, Nin finally agreed to marry Pole. She lived in six-week stretches, swinging from New York to California, where Pole was now a forest ranger. She maintained her double life for the next eleven years, the truth recorded only in her diaries and what she called "the lie box."

By 1966, Nin was achieving some fame, and both husbands were claiming royalties on their tax returns. Mostly, though, Nin sounded tired of the lies, so she chose to reveal the truth to the man she believed would stay: Pole. And he did. He even agreed to annul their marriage for the sake of her royalties. And years later, when cancer was ravaging Nin's body, he shuttled her to doctor appointments, administered her injections, and dialed Hugo's number to help her maintain the ruse of their marriage. When she died, Pole rented a small plane and released her ashes above a small cove near Santa Monica. Her diaries, all thirty-five thousand pages, were left to Pole, and he honored Nin's wishes by publishing less censored versions of them over the years. When Hugo died, Pole scattered his ashes, too, above the cove. Then Pole returned to the home he'd built for himself and the woman he'd loved, in spite of it all.

Nin was guilty of the same crimes as the men I'd read about—manipulation of trust, exploitation of love, theft of dignity—but told in her own words, her story took on a kind of mythology, even tragedy. Nin herself was like the lie box she kept, the dutiful sole record keeper of what must have been an extraordinarily lonely inner life, pressed like a dried flower between the two she'd lived. Ultimately, Nin had wanted to tell her story, even if it was after her death.

I hoped Dolores Rivera wouldn't want to wait that long.

Online White Pages spit out nine Dolores Riveras, each with a helpful list of family members. It was easy to find the Dolores related to Gabriel and Mateo Rivera, but I'd need a premium membership to unlock her phone number and address. Instead, I tried a property records search.

One result.

I plugged the address into Google Maps and switched to Street

View: the house was one story, clean white brick with a dark shingled roof and extravagant flowering hedges encircling the exterior. A silver Volvo was parked in the semicircular driveway; the license plate was blurred, with no discernible bumper stickers to indicate the driver's age or interests. Still, unless Dolores rented or owned a house under a different name, it seemed promising. Besides, hadn't there been some Facebook comment about her "always watering her jungle"? Maybe I was reaching, but those hedges might fit the bill.

I navigated up and down the street, splashed with shadows from mature trees, brick mailboxes, and the occasional garbage can that hadn't been brought inside yet, or perhaps these were the first to be taken out for the next day's pickup. I circled the house from all angles. It almost seemed possible to force open the front door with the heat of my gaze, the pressure of my finger.

I felt I was closing in.

It was hard to breathe through the early July humidity as I headed out to the food park. The cleaning crew was back at the cobalt midcentury modern duplex next door, an Airbnb property rented for $150 most nights and $500 during ACL or South By—stupid, unimaginable money. The duplex had gone up quickly last year after the original house, a falling-apart 1950s bungalow like ours, had been razed.

I'd fallen in love with Austin immediately after dragging my two suitcases to my fifth-floor dorm in the Castilian for my freshman year at UT. Through the small windows, the smells of weed and patchouli and Madam Mam's Thai floated from the Drag below. Austin could almost still be called weird back then. There had been Leslie, riding his bicycle downtown dressed only in a leopard thong and stiletto sandals. Racing turtles at Little Woodrow's or playing chickenshit bingo at the Little Longhorn Saloon, not because some Austin listicle told you to, but because you'd heard about it from a longtime local, already a dying breed.

The East Side, where Duke and I lived, used to be a mostly Black and Latino neighborhood, with families who'd been here for generations. Even thirteen years ago, though, you could see the cranes. The skeletons of high-rises and hotels, the way modest streets would eventually be thrust into shadow by behemoth mixed-use condo developments. Our neighbors now were architects and coders, bar owners and tech start-up CEOs, transplants from San Francisco, Portland, Seattle, New York. Duke and I were part of the gentrification, I knew—two white thirtysomethings paying ridiculous rent for a house some other white person, far richer than us, had bought from its original residents, likely pushed out by rising property taxes. But we'd been in Austin for nearly half our lives, and I liked to think we were among those clinging to something original, trying to keep it from being destroyed.

At the food park, diners were red-faced and cheerful as they drank Shiners or rosé from plastic cups, hairlines damp despite the whirring efforts of four black fans. There were only three trucks, including Duke's BBQ, a repurposed Airstream painted with abstract cows and pigs floating in a neon sky. I had sprayed and lacquered the picnic tables candy-apple red, imagining how they'd look in Duke's Instagram photos. I realized afterward that I'd inadvertently re-created the scene of our first date.

Duke had been in culinary school when a mutual friend had set us up five years ago. He offered to make me dinner at his apartment. Did I have any dietary restrictions? How did I feel about pork belly? But two-thirds of murdered women are killed by men they know—why make it easier? Instead, I suggested the South Austin Trailer Park and Eatery.

Over Torchy's Tacos at a long red picnic table, Duke told me he wanted to open a restaurant one day. "With a name like Duke, I was destined for barbecue," he joked. He told me that making brisket was both a science and an art. There was a language to it: the point and the flat, the grade and the wrap. A whole culture around how to trim the meat, whether to wrap it with foil or peach butcher paper, how to manage the stall, what to use as the base wood. "Making brisket is an act of love," he said. "When it's good, when it's real, there's nothing better." I couldn't believe there was a man alive who would say the word *love* on a first date, even if he was talking about meat.

I had fallen for Duke quickly. Or no—not fallen. Falling sounds too careless and violent, scraped knees and jarred bones. I came to love him quickly. He was easy to love, because he was easy to trust. He answered every question I asked him, from how many women he'd slept with to where he wanted to be in five years. If he liked something, he said it. If he didn't like something, he said that, too. If he had a secret self hidden within, it was so well concealed that even he didn't know about it.

I was behind a group of men in line, able to watch Duke for a few moments before he noticed me. He was attentive, with spring-coiled energy and a ready laugh, an ability to forge easy connections with people that I envied but also wasn't sure I wanted for myself. It was safer to keep a distance.

When the men cleared away with their beers and I stepped forward, Duke's grin softened, became more personal than all-purpose. He leaned through the window to kiss me. "You know you could just come around back. VIP access."

"I know." I waved at Sal, a fifty-something guitarist with an unironic black mustache, standing behind him. "But I like to get the whole Duke's experience."

Duke pulled two Shiners from the fridge, and we sat at one of the tables, where our carved initials were now lost among hundreds.

"Guess what?" I said.

Duke twisted the tops off our beers, passed mine across. He smiled. "What?"

"Remember that story I told you about—the woman with the double marriage?" One of my legs bounced beneath the table, fine powdery dirt sneaking into my sandal. "I've been doing some research. I left a message for police records but I'm too impatient, so I found one of the old detectives and—"

"Hang on." Duke frowned. "Is this for the blog? I thought you didn't have to do extra reporting."

I made a face, took a cold gulp of beer. "Not for the blog. I want to write a real story about this."

"But—" Duke slapped at a fat mosquito on his tawny forearm. "The guy's in prison, right?"

"Five more years."

"So then? It's over. Why are you reaching out to the detective?"

A curdle, deep in my belly. He didn't get it.

"Crime is rarely *over* for the people involved," I said. "The impact lingers. Anyway, the story's really not about the murder. I have to know about it, but I'm much more interested in *her*. Dolores."

"Why, though?" Duke glanced back at the Airstream, making sure Sal had the line covered. Sal gave him a thumbs-up.

Every crime story begins with the writer's obsession. And for the last twenty years, you could say my obsession had been double lives.

My parents had loved traditions. Every Christmas my father made us Swiss Miss hot chocolate, the kind that came in packets with mini marshmallows, before we drove around to admire all the houses draped in white lights like wedding gowns. Every summer we went digging at the Salt Plains National Wildlife Refuge, our rasping shovels searching for the selenite crystals with hourglass-shaped inclusions found nowhere else in the world except for this salt-encrusted land that was once covered by an inland sea. My parents, in those years, had seemed so predictable and familiar, as if nothing they could do would surprise me.

One time I walked into the kitchen and found them kissing. My mother's back arched against the counter, her legs slightly spread, one of my father's in between. He ran a hand up her white T-shirt, palming her breast while she crumpled a fistful of his blue shirt. Their mouths moved over each other, sensual and almost savage. I watched for a few moments, cheeks burning, before scurrying back to my room. I thought about that kiss often, after. How it looked like love, but also looked like pain.

My father had been scheduled to work on my ninth birthday. He was an aircraft mechanic at Vance Air Force Base. I used to stare at his hands, each groove stenciled black with oil. The night before my birthday, he squinted over the *Better Homes and Gardens* recipe for strawberry shortcake. "Does room-temperature butter mean butter *left out* until it reaches room temperature?" he asked. "Or *warmed up* until it reaches room temperature?" My mother laughed at his typical precision with language. "Maybe you can write a Letter to the Editor," she teased.

Had there been tension between them that night? A sharpness on his breath? That's the thing when you discover another side to a person you thought you knew. No memory is safe from cynical revisiting. You search for clues with the benefit of hindsight, desperate to believe your intuition hadn't failed you so catastrophically. But in my memory my mother nudged him with her hip when she needed to see the floury magazine page. My father's glasses steamed when he opened the oven. And my own soft, broken-in happiness: completely unremarkable.

The next day, after my friends' mothers had bundled them up in marshmallow parkas and hustled them out into the frosty December evening, I followed my own mother with a trash bag stretched open like a cat's cradle—the living room a graveyard of wilted streamers, frosting-smeared paper plates, and half-drunk Kool-Aid cups. Jim Croce, my mother's favorite, played on the radio: "Bad, bad, Leroy Brown, baddest man in the whole damn town." We sang *damn* more loudly with each chorus and I was wild with laughter, hardly believing my mother was letting me swear in front of her.

That was when my father walked through the front door, his hands dwarfing that morning's coffee thermos.

"John! You're home early!" My mother's palm flashed white as a star as she beckoned him to come join us.

Then a thud and something rolling at my feet—the golden urn that held my granddaddy, ashes spilling in sickening clumps, breaking into talcum-fine powder. What's left of a man.

For a moment, silence. Then my father, red-eyed and mouth slack and one of those baseball-mitt hands, a strike so fast it couldn't have been the first. The blow caught my mother in the chest with a dull, bony thwack, and she gasped, an absence of sound more than a sound itself, something that seemed to pull the air from my own lungs. My bladder pinched, warmth between my legs. The three of us staring at each other like strangers at a car wreck, shocked at the devastation. Then suddenly my father gagged and lurched down the hallway to the bathroom.

"Mommy." The word squeaked out, the first time I'd called her that in years.

She fell to her knees. Gently, she pried the trash bag from my fingers and let it drop. A cup rolled out, Kool-Aid leaking on the gray carpet. She pulled me against her, my ear to the waterfall rush of her heart. "It was an accident," she whispered. "Nothing happened. Okay?"

I nodded, desperate for her story to overtake mine.

"Cassie, you can't tell anyone about this." My mother's sharp cheekbones flushed as she gripped my shoulders. "No one. Do you understand?"

Of course I didn't understand. But I nodded again.

"Come on," she said, looking at the front of my purple Levi's. "I'll turn on the shower for you."

That was the beginning.

After that, I still earned good grades, laughed on the monkey bars, talked about boys and played the Ouija board at slumber parties. I blew out candles pretending every birthday didn't remind me of the one when I'd lost everything that mattered. But I also gave in to the obsession that started with *Dateline*. I read crime books and saw myself not only as the potential victim but as the killer's closest family, forever scarred for not recognizing the signs. I saw myself in the detectives, driven to understand those who shed their human skins to act on their darkest desires. I wanted to carve open the perpetrators' skulls, hold their brains in my hands and sift through the folds to find where the rot began, how it had spread.

But, of course, I also saw myself in *them*. In those people who split themselves in two.

Maybe I recognized a piece of myself in Dolores Rivera.

I couldn't say that to Duke, though. I'd told him only that my father and I didn't get along. That my mother had bound us together and after her death we'd drifted apart. It happens. Duke had looked sympathetic. He couldn't imagine a family like that, and he'd brought me into his own with no hesitation. Now it was too late. I couldn't tell him about the years of bruises and silence without also revealing that I was no better than my parents. Maybe worse.

"I don't know," I answered Duke. "I guess I'm interested in how women, in particular, can reconcile these seemingly incompatible parts of themselves and then . . . go on living their lives. She's an extreme example of that."

Duke nodded, though he appeared unsettled. "What makes you think she'll talk to you?"

I flinched.

"No," he said, reaching for my hand. "I just mean if she didn't want to talk to the first guy."

"Not that I'm a nobody who writes for a trashy crime blog?" I tried to joke, but my tone was sharp. "I don't know, Duke. I guess I'm hoping she'll see that I really *do* want to hear her side."

"Well," he said with a grin, "if anyone can convince her, it's you, Cass. When are you planning to get in touch with her?"

"That's the thing." I grinned back. "That detective? He tracked down Fabian's case file for me. I'm going to Laredo tomorrow."

LORE, 1983

Time passes in waves, one song flowing into the next before stopping so that bride and groom can cut the cake, plates delivered to tables as the music starts again. Andres leads effortlessly, Lore his graceful shadow, their bodies linked hand to hand, hip to hip. Lore's hair keeps slipping from its bobby pins, and she pulls out the rest, dropping them on the nearest table while Andres goes to the bar for fresh drinks.

While she waits, dabbing at her moist cheeks with the knuckles of her thumbs, she briefly imagines an alternate reality, one in which Fabian were here. Would they be dancing like this, sweating and breathless? Or would they still be sitting at their table, she hunched resentfully toward him as he talked of the recession, the store, the uncertainty that's tearing him apart before her eyes? The answers fill her with quiet, unassailable sadness.

When Andres returns, his starched shirt is wilting from the heat of his skin. He hands her the drink and says, with a mischievous smile, "I need to cool down. Do you feel like taking a walk?"

And because Lore's mind was so freshly on Fabian, on the grim, heavy state of their marriage, to which she will be returning tomorrow, she smiles back and says, "I'd love to."

Outside, the Zócalo is mostly quiet. The Mexican flag ripples in the breeze, and the Cathedral and Federal District buildings glow gold against the black sky, the edges of the clouds even now smeared orange with smog.

"Where are we going?" Lore asks, as Andres takes her hand to cross the street. The touch feels gallant, as though he wants to ensure she won't trip on her gown. But when they reach the other side, his fingers remain entwined with hers. Lore's stomach clenches, yet she doesn't pull away.

"When you need to take a breath, there's only one place to go." Andres reaches down to the peg of a motorcycle and hands her a helmet. "The lungs of the city."

Lore stares, helmet dangling from her hand.

"Haven't you ever seen a helmet before?" he teases.

"I thought we were going for a walk."

Andres laughs. "It would be a long walk to the Bosque de Chapultepec. Only a fifteen-minute ride, though. But only if you want?"

Lore stares at the bike—its slim black lines, the narrow seat rising up over the rear tire, too small, surely, for her to sit on, and what about her gown?

"Have you ever ridden before?" Andres asks.

Lore says the first thing that comes to mind: "My mother would kill me." Then she laughs, imagining Mami's face. Her mother—a stoic, commanding presence in the home, whom no one, even Lore's father, ever dares cross—is a woman of extreme phobias in the outside world. She hyperventilates in crowds; she has never boarded an airplane and would throw herself in front of a bus before climbing on a motorcycle.

"Don't be afraid," Andres says. "It's—"

"I'm not afraid," Lore interrupts, and she isn't, she is greedy for all the world she has not tasted. She lowers the helmet onto her head, fumbles with the strap below her chin before letting Andres fasten it for her.

"Go ahead." Andres holds the bike by the handlebars. "Slide to the back."

Lore hikes her red silk gown up to her thighs, swings a leg over. Her perch feels high and precarious, impossible to maintain.

Before Andres climbs on, he says, "When I turn, don't resist it—lean with me. If you get scared, tap me and I'll slow down. Okay?"

Lore nods, keenly aware she's on a kind of adventure. (Don't resist it.) Only once, briefly, before the bike growls to life, does she realize nobody knows where she is, she's riding off with a man whose last name she doesn't even know, though what good would a last name do if he meant to hurt her? Then Andres pulls away from the curb and Lore squeals, a small echoing cry inside her helmet. With one hand, Andres joins her hands at his sternum, holding them there for a moment before returning his hand to the handlebar.

Then they're off.

Lore falls in love with riding in seconds. It's the immediacy of it, nothing separating her skin from the city. The rushing pavement is a shocking reminder that life is fragile, separated from death by only a gossamer veil, and somehow this closeness to the beyond heightens every sense: the smells of gasoline and cigarette smoke punctuated by pockets of mysterious sweetness; the roar of the engine and wind in her ears; the taste of wine on her tongue, the feel of her body wrapped around Andres, her limbs performing silent measurements—his waist narrower than Fabian's, his legs longer. His eyes, when she catches his occasional glances in the side-view mirror, are more lined in the corners, his hair losing its black-tie restraint and flying back to whip her helmet. She's forgotten they have a destination. She could ride with him all night, learning a new language of pointing and squeezing and patting. People waste so much time talking when talk so often conceals more than it reveals.

Sharply, she thinks, You shouldn't be with him at all—what are you doing?

Before she can answer herself, they arrive.

The Bosque de Chapultepec, more than fifteen hundred acres of history and nature. Andres bypasses the first, oldest section, where, on Lore's last trip, she'd lingered in the Museo Nacional de Antropología, gazing at artifacts from the Aztec, Maya, Toltec, and Olmec, wondering at the hands that made them, the empires that fell. She'd meant to rent a pedal boat on the lake and eat lunch in the shadows of the castle at the peak of Chapultepec Hill, but before she knew it, it was time to head to the airport.

Andres passes the second section, where a roller coaster's sinuous curves rise above the treetops. Finally, he stops at the third, least developed area. Lore's ears ring in the sudden silence.

Andres climbs off first, holding the handlebars again as Lore stiffly swings her right leg back onto the ground. Her body is shaking. She hadn't realized how tightly she'd been holding him.

"So?" Andres grins as Lore unstraps her helmet. "What did you think of your first ride?"

Her cheeks are sore from smiling. "Not bad," she says, and they both laugh.

Tomorrow, the park will be bright with picnic blankets and soccer balls. Tonight, the quiet is dense. A canopy of feathery leaves blocks the sky, and the trail absorbs their footfalls. It's like they're in a tunnel, surrounded and concealed. She looks up, stumbles. She's never seen trees so tall. Andres catches her by the elbow.

"They make me dizzy too," he confesses, and she laughs, charmed. "You know some of these ahuehuetes are more than a thousand years old? The name means 'old man of the water.'"

Lore grazes her fingers along a rust-colored trunk so wide it would take twenty people to bracelet their arms around it. "Do you think they're disappointed there's no water in sight?"

"DF rests on the clay of the old Lake Texcoco," he says. "The clay is constantly collapsing because of the overextraction of groundwater. DF has sunk as much as nine meters since the start of the twentieth century. So I guess you could say we're never far from water."

Lore stops, looking at the path. How can something that seems so steady be so fragile, so impermanent?

They walk on, and in the silence, as her mind and body begin to come down from the wine, the dancing, the ride, Lore realizes how little she knows about him.

"So," she says. "You're a professor. What do you teach again?"

"Philosophy." Andres glances down at her. "Mostly second-level courses right now—Ethics, Logic and Reasoning, The Nature of Reality, stuff like that."

"The Nature of Reality?" Lore bumps him with her shoulder. "Come on. That's not a real class."

Andres laughs. "You'd fit right in."

Lore feels quaint. She's only ever known people with degrees in solid, practical subjects, if they have degrees at all. "What is philosophy . . . for?"

"For?"

"You know. People study business to work in business. Finance to work in finance."

"Ah." Andres kicks a branch out of their way. "Do people study philosophy to become philosophers?"

"Right. And what do philosophers . . . do?" Lore hates how her questions are emerging, ignorant and a bit judgmental. Once, she'd told her father she wanted to learn French, and he'd stared at her before erupting in big, laughing-at-her laughter. *In Laredo?* he'd scoffed. *You want to learn how to snowshoe, too?* She hadn't realized she had this part of him in her. "I'm sorry," she starts.

"Don't be. Philosophy can seem abstract, but it's actually about things that influence our everyday lives: reason, language, existence, values. Is there a best way to live? Is it better to be just or unjust, if you can get away with it? What does it mean," he adds, with a smile, "to be 'good'?"

Lore starts, remembering their conversation at the wedding table. Robinson Crusoe.

"Believe it or not," he says, "philosophy has given us Isaac

Newton's work, which is now classified as physics. It's given us disciplines like psychology, sociology, linguistics—even," he adds, "economics. And while many students of philosophy go on to academia, others practice law or journalism, or even, God help us, politics. To study philosophy is to learn how to be curious, to think critically, to ask questions, to reason. At least, that's what I hope to teach my students."

Lore can't help but think of Fabian, who would see philosophy as self-indulgent and unnecessary. They live in a world of *things*, after all. A world of iron and heat, solid and understandable. And yet, look at the recession: What is money if not an idea? An idea with the power to liberate or enslave.

Fabian. Right now, he's sleeping alone in the queen-size bed they bought so proudly as newlyweds, whose oak headboard Lore religiously cleans with lemon Pledge every Sunday, just like Mami taught her. Fabian, who trusts her without question, because she's never given him reason not to. Fabian, her first love, whom she'd always believed would be her only love.

And yet here she is, walking so close to Andres she can feel the heat of his body, and when he slides an arm around her shoulders, asking, "Cold?," she nods, her arm slipping around his waist as if disconnected from her mind.

Lore suddenly blurts, "I've never done this before."

"What?" Andres smiles. "Ridden off with a stranger to a secluded park in a foreign city in the middle of the night?"

She croaks a laugh. "Yes. That."

"Your mother wouldn't approve?" he teases.

Lore startles, then remembers saying Mami would kill her for getting on the bike. She can hear Mami's voice now, the clarity of her disappointment: *¿Lore, qué estás haciendo?* For a moment, she can't breathe.

Andres stops. "Hey," he says softly. "I'm sorry, is she—has she passed?"

Lore swallows, and there is no reason for what she says next except that a part of her must know. A part of her is already building the scaffolding.

"It's just hard for me to think about her sometimes," she says. "What about you? Did your parents approve of you being a philosopher?"

"My father was a surgeon. He expected me to be a different kind of doctor."

"You're a doctor." Lore tries to move past her implication that her mother is dead with a joke. "I feel bad, calling you by your first name all night."

"So you should," Andres says. "'Doctor' only from now on, please."

"Very well, Doctor," Lore quips, and then she has another moment of heart-stopping recrimination. What is she doing flirting, walking arm in arm with this man, this *stranger*, in the middle of the night? She pulls away slightly, letting the cool air fill the space between them. "And your mother?"

"She would have approved of anything I did, if only I'd done it in Buenos Aires."

"I guess all mothers want their children close." Lore thinks of Gabriel and Mateo, who feel very far away in this moment.

Lore asks him about Buenos Aires, and Andres tells her about growing up in La Recoleta, where the rich had fled to avoid yellow fever at the end of the nineteenth century. "You should see it one day," Andres says, and she is startled by his image of her, a woman who might go places she's never been. When he tells her about the cemetery, all she can picture is the cemetery on Saunders, which is a nice enough place to be dead but sounds nothing like what Andres describes: five thousand above-ground mausoleums, elaborate monuments made of marble imported from Paris and Milan, marble so shiny the living can see their reflections in statues of the dead. When he was a boy and wanted to escape his mother's suffocating love, he used to go there.

Lore tells him how, back when she'd wanted to be Robinson Crusoe, she'd felt a seed of wildness in her, something that didn't belong. Sometimes she walked out to the railroad tracks and waited in the middle for the shiver to start beneath her feet, for the glare of headlights to fill her vision. She waited for the horn to sound, an elephant's trumpet wail, for the shriek of metal on metal, and imagined her skeleton rattling beneath her skin, trapped and giddy as pebbles jumped at her ankles. Finally, at the last possible moment, she leaped aside, laughing as she picked stickers off her bare arms and legs. The high lasted for weeks afterward. While everyone else was numbly performing the rituals of their days, she was fully alive, because she'd chosen to be.

She tells Andres about Hurricane Alice, the 1954 storm meteorologists had predicted would cause "moderate" flooding, when in reality the Rio Grande swelled to a monstrous sixty-one feet, the second highest crest ever recorded. She was too young to remember it, but in an inexplicable postcard Mami had shown her, the muddy water was thick as cement, swallowing the new four-lane bridge so that only the red-roofed turret of a building stuck out like a hand waving for help. They'd had to destroy the remnants of the bridge with dynamite, Mami told her, in order to build a new one. For the next two years, people risked their lives crossing by canoe.

Lore used to ask Mami to tell her the story of the flood, as if it were a dark fairy tale. But she never told her mother about the dreams, each one the same, even now: Lore trapped in that cement-thick water, the pressure building until it eventually wrenches her apart and she becomes liquid, a part of the flood, engulfing roads and cars and homes, sending trees crashing onto roofs, collecting debris with a mighty, destructive force. It's this destructiveness Lore remembers when she wakes—the pleasure of it, the power. The closest she's come to feeling it in real life was when she gave birth to the cuates, roaring as her body ripped, swimming in unnameable fluid. And somehow women are expected to forget this afterward, how they are the closest thing to God, breaking themselves open to create new life. Motherhood is supposed to be quiet and pretty. But motherhood is not pretty. Motherhood has teeth.

Mateo and Gabriel. Their hot-dirt scent and thick dark hair and long-lashed eyes. She remembers holding their naked newborn bodies to her chest, stricken by how close this kind of love—wild, primal, consuming—felt to terror, like standing at the edge of an abyss, one foot dangling. Yet, somehow, Mateo and Gabriel are not enough for her. Being a mother is not enough for her, which is why she returned to work despite Fabian's earnest urgings to stay home. And maybe this was the first rift between them, the way he didn't understand what the job meant to her, and if he didn't understand that, how could she think he understood *her*?

She wonders sometimes if Fabian, too, has a secret side, a more alive side, but any attempt to peel him back these days ends with irritation. It's as though her desire to know him better—to know him differently—is another extravagance they can't afford.

She doesn't tell Andres, of course, about Fabian or the cuates, but what she reveals feels so raw, so true, that it eclipses the fundamental untruth of her omissions.

They share little things, too, each tiny artifact of memory standing in for something larger. She doesn't know how long he was married, or when he divorced, or why, but she knows he has two kids, and that his fifteen-year-old daughter recently joked about who would start dating first, she or him, and this joke tells her that his kids are comfortable with him, that he is a good father. She doesn't know where exactly in DF he lives, but she knows he collects sand from every beach he visits, lining the small jars along his bathroom windowsill—and this tells her he is a dreamer.

"Do you want children?" he asks her at one point.

Her opportunity, one of so many, flickers before her like a candle's flame; she blows it out. "I'm not sure," she says, and the answer feels honest because she changed the question in her mind to *Do you want* more *children?* In this way she lets herself think she's being as truthful as he seems to be.

"They're like bombs," Andres says, with an understanding laugh. "They blow up every familiar thing in your life. But then you look around and realize that somehow things are better this way—that only what matters remains."

Lore kicks off her strappy sandals, letting them dangle from a fingertip. The hem of her dress, which she bought at Sanborns for thirty dollars, back when people still shopped, will be ruined. She doesn't care. When she looks up at Andres, she recognizes the look in his eyes, a look she's seen only once before, at the Plaza Theatre in 1967, just as Benjamin arrives at the church, screaming Elaine's name, in *The Graduate*. Her first kiss with Fabian.

Her heart catches as Andres leans lower, and she can smell the wine on his breath as he murmurs, "Mexico City, the constantly sinking land. Even now, we're sinking. Do you feel it?" His hand moves to the nape of her neck.

"I feel it," she whispers.

His mouth is a velvet box, opening beneath hers. The seed of wildness, long neglected, breaks open and takes root, and she winds her fingers through his hair, presses her hips against his. He's hard against the thin fabric of her gown as he runs a heavy hand from her hip to her breasts. She stumbles a little as he guides her backward, until the rough bark of a tree chafes her bare shoulders. When he begins to raise her dress, it takes every weakened reserve of willpower to push him away, breathless.

"I'm sorry—" Lore gestures to the tree, the path, the sinking land that will take them with it. Shaking, she smooths her dress over her thighs. "I can't—"

"No, no." Andres steps back, shoving a hand through his hair. "I'm sorry, I don't usually—"

"I think we should get back to the hotel."

"Of course." His eyes, from what Lore can see in the darkness, are clouded with desire, and she feels a throb of lust, to be looked at that way. Andres holds out a hand, says, "I'll be a gentleman, I promise," and Lore gives a shuddering little sigh as she laces her fingers between his.

On the bike, Lore wraps every part of herself around Andres. She'll never see him again after tonight. Thank God. But for now, she wants him to feel her heartbeat against his back and know something real about her.

CASSIE, 2017

The drive from Austin to Laredo was about four hours down I-35, the same highway I followed from Enid when I was seventeen years old.

Enid was a place people stayed. You saw it every Sunday, three or four generations gathering for their usual diner lunch, a church on every corner to accommodate the weekend worshippers who, like my parents, went home to their secret lives. It would have been so easy to stay—in-state tuition at OU, move back home afterward to save money, that old trick of the "temporary." But my plans, my dreams, would have died there. I could feel it, the way paper curls away from a flame before its edges blacken with burn.

So, despite the one person holding me there—Andrew—I left.

I glanced at my phone as it jostled in the cupholder. I still needed to call him back after our brief text exchange at the farm. When was the last time we actually *talked*? Guilt sat like a boulder on my chest. It was hard to imagine, now, the intimacy that held us together the summer after my mother died—the way, with the weight of his body anchoring mine, I finally didn't feel alone. I'd whispered so many promises to him in the dark, imagining them landing on his skin like bubbles, diaphanous membranes bursting at the touch. But in the end, he had to stay, and I wouldn't give up my future, not even for him.

Later, I told myself. I'd call him later. When I could give him my full attention. Not when I was entering San Antonio, traffic bloating the highway, the air conditioner of my old Corolla weakening to streams of lukewarm air every time I slowed down.

This morning Duke had hugged me as if I were heading off to war. "Be careful," he said. "Laredo used to be on the news all the time. Kidnappings, murder, goddamn decapitations. Don't go anywhere near the border. Promise."

I bit back my irritation. It seemed like such an ignorant, white-person thing to say, to assume, that "bad hombres" were lying in wait at the river. Last night, I'd stayed up until 3 A.M. researching. Across the bridge, in Nuevo Laredo, the Zetas cartel had split into warring factions. Videos filmed there showed armored tanks speeding by parked cars, behind which civilians hid. Recently, the bodies of five women and four men had been dumped on the sidewalk outside a Nuevo Laredo home, along with a handwritten note: *This is not a joke, nephew.* In a YouTube video taken at an outlet mall on the U.S. side, the woman filming uttered a stream of Spanish as artillery fire rang out in the near distance, as if she were a soldier in the Middle East instead of a shopper looking for a good deal on a Coach purse. Still, despite Laredo's bad rap because of its proximity to Nuevo Laredo, the FBI ranked it as one of the safer cities in Texas.

"I'll be fine," I told Duke.

As I drove farther south, flat sepia ranchland replaced the green Hill Country. Signs for grass sales and exotic whitetail hunts, blown tires curled like black snakes on the highway, pastures freckled with cattle and the spiny, mysterious silhouettes of oil drilling equipment. On the median, trunkless mesquite trees surged from the earth like half-buried bodies, and cactus lined the railroad tracks where graffitied freight trains bore their heavy cargo north. A plastic bag caught on a fence post waved like a wedding veil in hot gusts from passing traffic.

An hour south of San Antonio, signs warned, PRISON AREA: DO NOT PICK UP HITCHHIKERS. I slowed to sixty as I passed the sprawling gray mass. The sun glared white-hot against hundreds of small square windows. There was something disturbing about how evenly spaced out they were, how utterly identical in shape and size. This was where Fabian Rivera was serving his thirty-five years.

If Dolores agreed to speak to me, I would need to request an interview with Fabian at some point. But one thing at a time.

After Cotulla, still an hour north of Laredo, only Spanish radio stations came in clearly. An AT&T billboard advertising international rates read: HAHAHAJAJAJA. Eighteen-wheelers now had Mexican license plates. Every few miles, I reflexively slowed before the white and green Border Patrol vehicles parked beneath the gap-toothed shade of mesquites.

The sun bounced off the long white flanks of semi-trucks as I eventually passed a customs station off the northbound lane of the highway. Two rows of cameras on either side of the southbound side flashed as I drove through. A few miles later, a billboard inexplicably featuring a blonde in a velvet colonial gown welcomed me to Laredo.

Nothing else indicated I'd reached a city. No spray of silver high-rises, like San Antonio or Austin, or quaint Main Street, like Enid. Laredo emerged first as a stream of billboards for a mall and fast-food restaurants before opening to gray industrial parks, a smattering of secondhand car lots, and trailers with bilingual advertisements for naturalization assistance. I was on mile marker nine before I saw a hospital and strip malls, H-E-B and Starbucks and Chick-fil-A.

This was where I exited to meet Detective Ben Cortez.

Outside, the air felt scalding. Heat bore down from above and radiated up from the black asphalt parking lot, pressing against me from all sides.

"Jesus," I muttered, already sweat-slick when I stepped inside the frigid Starbucks.

I spotted Cortez immediately. Sitting on a bench seat, back against the faux brick wall, he radiated retired cop: mid- to late sixties, thick cinder-block-gray hair, belly straining the buttons of a worn denim shirt, a casual slump to his shoulders though he scanned the room with bristling awareness. He clocked me as easily as I did him. It was my blond hair. I seemed to be the only white person in this space, possibly—I realized with discomfort—for the first time in my life.

"Detective Cortez?" I asked, approaching.

"That's me." Cortez stood, and a gold belt buckle the size of my hand caught the light. His handshake rubbed my knuckles together.

"I appreciate you making the time to see me." A folder peeked out from beneath his newspaper, a cardboard box on the bench seat beside him. It took every ounce of restraint not to reach for them. "Thanks again for helping me out."

"My pleasure." Cortez lowered back into his seat. "Like I said on the phone, I'm retired. Got all the time in the world now."

The light words were edged with something bitter. I'd found Cortez on Facebook, and he'd responded to my direct message in minutes. I pictured him sitting in a dark room at home, scrolling through his news feed, wondering where the day had gone, where his life had gone. When I'd asked on the phone whether the case file would still exist after thirty years, he'd chuckled. That had told me everything I needed to know: he would help me, as long as he could feel some of that old power while doing it. I had no problem giving him that.

"So," I said, after buying myself a coffee. "This was a quick close for you guys. Three weeks, right?"

"Well," he said, all gruff modesty as he pulled out the folder, "it fell like dominoes after we figured out it had nothing to do with drugs."

"Drugs?" I repeated, surprised. Maybe the border connection was more important than I'd thought. "Why did you think that?"

Cortez licked his finger and turned the pages. "Motel, no forced entry, single gunshot to the chest. Wallet's missing. First glance, seemed random. Cold."

"His wallet was missing?" I pulled out a notepad, checked to make sure the recording app on my phone was running. "So, it was staged to look like a robbery?"

Cortez scoffed. "More like the perp panicked and tried to throw us off track."

"Right . . ." I trailed off. "But panic would suggest lack of intent, wouldn't it?" Which one was it? Had Fabian gone to the room to kill Andres, or had he only wanted to talk, and things got out of hand?

"Well, now you're getting into lawyer stuff." Cortez smiled, still friendly, though with a new set to his jaw. He was here to relive the triumph of a quickly closed case, not to be interrogated for a nuance he clearly hadn't thought mattered at the time, let alone thirty years later. As long as he could still walk out of here with the case file, I needed him on my side.

"It must have been tricky to ID Russo," I said, leaning forward. "Without his wallet. How'd y'all do that?"

Cortez relaxed. Men who need control are so easy to manipulate. All you have to do is give them what they want, right up until the moment you take it from them. "Passport was in his bag," he said. "Plus, motel records. Got no answer on his home phone so we tracked down the ex-wife. She was the one who told us he was in town to see the new wife."

For a moment I let myself imagine that phone call. However Andres's ex may have felt about him at that point, he was still the father of her children. Maybe she could hear Penelope and Carlos in the next room. Maybe she'd waited a few minutes before telling them, if only to extend the percentage of their lives they thought their father was in.

Quietly, I said, "You must have looked at Dolores Rivera as a suspect."

Cortez laughed. "Damn straight. Then it turns out she's already married!"

Three teen girls squeezed into the table beside us, giggling. "Pero ¿lo *viste*?" one of them asked, and laughed that immortal teenage laugh. Cortez cut them a look, and the girls on the bench side slunk away like mercury toward the wall.

"How did you eliminate Dolores?" I asked.

When Cortez turned back to me, the girls laughed again, lower, conspiratorially this time. I resisted the urge to meet their eyes, to align myself with them in some way.

"She alibied out," Cortez said. "And wasn't like the guy was a genius. Used a gun registered in his name, left a partial print in the room, got ID'd on his way out. Plus, he and the vic were seen arguing outside the Rivera house the day of the murder. I mean, you do the math."

"Andres Russo went to their *house*?" I hated how much it thrilled me, imagining Andres's finger on the doorbell, the two men staring at each other. The disbelief that must have melted their bones. This story was too good.

Cortez nodded. "Neighbor witnessed their altercation."

"And Dolores?" I asked, pen poised. "Where was she at the time?"

Cortez flipped through the folder. "Around four thirty P.M. that Friday—doctor's appointment. She had alibis all throughout the evening, including TOD. Weird thing is—" Cortez took a gulp of coffee. "She actually alibied Fabian Rivera. Said the family was all together from about nine P.M. on. Held firm, too, till everything else fell to shit. Pardon my French."

"Wait. Why would she do that?" If Dolores had falsely alibied Fabian, she must have either believed he was innocent or known he was guilty. Already, it felt crucial to determine which one was correct. Because if Dolores had loved Andres, wouldn't she have wanted justice? And if she hadn't loved him—or if she'd loved Fabian *more*, enough to protect him with a false alibi, why had she compromised her entire life to marry Andres?

Cortez stared at the patio, where two crows fought over something stuck in one of the iron grooves of a table. "Who knows? Seems like lying's just what she did."

"Right . . ." It must have been so easy for them to leave it at that, once they had evidence against Fabian. It's easier for men to dismiss a woman than attempt to understand her—especially a woman like Dolores, who didn't just cast off societal expectations but burned them to the ground.

"Between us," Cortez said, turning back to me, "I would've rather put that woman away than the poor cabrón she was married to. Not his fault, you know? I mean, in the eyes of the law, yes, but . . ."

Heat crawled up my neck, slow but relentless, until I felt it staining my cheeks. Whatever Dolores represented to Cortez—as a cop, as a *man*—apparently it was worse than murder, and he had no problem saying that out loud.

"Well," I said, standing. "Thank you again for your time." I gestured for the case file. "May I?"

Cortez looked surprised. "Don't you want to hear more about the murder?"

I smiled tightly. "It's not really that kind of story."

Outside, I used the hem of my shirt to open my car door, scalded my hand on the metal seat belt buckle as I dropped my bag and the case file on the passenger seat. The AC, pathetically outmatched, blew hot air at the untouchable steering wheel. I searched the sky, longing for a good Oklahoma storm. The metallic, earthy smell of water in the atmosphere, charcoal clouds rolling in like a stampeding army. My mother could always predict storms. "Mares' tails stream with the wind," she'd say, pointing. "The storm is coming from the east." Or: "Look how the top is flattened like an anvil; the anvil is pointing in the direction the storm is moving." As a girl, I had been in awe of my mother's ability to decipher the sky. Later, I told her, "It's basic science." I didn't need to touch my mother to hurt her.

I plugged Dolores's address—or the address I hoped was hers—

into Google Maps. I wanted to drive by, see if I could get a better sense of whether or not she lived there. If so, I'd park somewhere, read the case file, then try to make contact. If not, plan B was to track down Gabriel Rivera's house. Thanks to his Facebook posts, I knew the name of his subdivision, what his home looked like, the four handprints in the cement driveway. I could find it, easy. But it's always better to reach a source directly.

According to my research, more than a third of Laredo residents lived below the poverty line, but the north side of town was all new construction, shells of whole neighborhoods rising from the ground as if 3-D printed. Gated entries, golf courses, sprawling hacienda-style homes with stone fountains and oversize clay pots spilling bougainvillea. I drove past a country club, every tennis court full despite the gruesome heat.

Dolores lived—maybe—on a cul-de-sac a few blocks away from the country club. The silver Volvo I'd seen in the satellite image was missing, so I parked near the mailbox. If the neighbors noticed me, they'd probably assume I was texting someone or checking directions. Women—well, white women—are so rarely seen as threatening.

I took photos one after another, zooming in on the whitewashed brick, the terra-cotta potted plants beside the cherrywood door, the chest-high bushes flush against the house's facade. Roses, I thought, though they looked . . . wilder. Almost unkempt, the blooms ballerina pink and mauve and fuchsia, threading through thick greenery. There was something insistent about them, something defiant.

"Can I help you?"

The voice came from the passenger window, facing the street. A baseball cap shaded the woman's flushed cheeks. She looked to be in her late sixties, wearing a sleeveless white linen top and athletic shorts, as if she'd changed from pants but left the shirt on, her plump shoulders dark and freckled. She was holding a leash, and a black Lab, shiny as an oil slick, panted at her knees.

I recognized her immediately. Shit.

"Can I help you?" Dolores Rivera asked again, her tone sharpening. She looked at my phone, still open to the camera.

I locked the screen. "I'm sorry, I was just admiring your roses. What kind are they?"

She softened, patting the dog's head. "L D Braithwaite, mostly. But also Mary Roses and Tess of the d'Urbervilles. The Marys hang on the longest come fall, though. Do you garden?"

"Oh, no," I said, forcing a casual laugh. "Whatever's the opposite of a green thumb, I have it."

Dolores smiled. "I wouldn't have known what a trowel was before I retired. Do you live around here?" She glanced around, frowning, as if she'd know if I did.

"No." My mind raced—I shouldn't have come yet. I shouldn't have been so impatient. I should have read the case file, decided on the best approach. What a stupid fucking mistake, the mistake of a trashy crime blogger, not a real journalist. But I couldn't back out now. I had to make this work. "You're Dolores, right?"

Her wrist flicked to hold the leash tighter. "Yes . . . And you are?"

"Cassie Bowman." I took a deep breath. "I was actually hoping to talk to you."

Dolores peered into my car: the laptop bag and cardboard box on the floor, the folder on the passenger seat clearly marked POLICE DEPARTMENT HOMICIDE CASE FILE.

Her entire body stiffened, as if her bones had been reinforced with steel.

"You're a journalist." She nearly spat the word, as if it were a slur. "Are you with him? The one who wrote that horrible article? ¿Que no tienen vergüenza—"

"No," I broke in. "I'm here because I don't think that piece was fair to you. I want to tell your side of the story."

Dolores's fingers closed around the leash, pulling slightly. She scoffed, her gaze hot and direct. "Please. You don't know me from Adam. Why would you care about 'fair'? Come on, Crusoe," she said to the dog, and began walking toward her door. "Pinche newspaper reporters," she muttered.

I scrambled out of the car. I couldn't turn around and go home, back to the blog, to feeding women's murder to an audience that consumed it like candy, quick hits of shock and disgust converting to an empty sugar rush of pleasure in the brain. I wanted more, and this could be the start, right here. I had to make her see it, make her want it as much as I did.

"I don't write for any paper," I called after her. "And I think your story is worth much more than two thousand words anyway."

Dolores stopped. Slowly, she turned around. "What do you mean?"

I approached her, breathless, until we were standing directly across from each other. She was shorter than I'd expected, at least four inches below my five-seven, with a soft, matronly body, a body for pulling grandchildren close. Her eyes were a burnished bronze, her face thoroughly lined, like paper that had been folded and refolded so the creases themselves were soft as suede. There were two age spots on one temple and constellations on her hands. She'd disappear in a crowd the way older women do, the adventures and passions of their youth tucked far from view of a society that's lost interest in them.

"A book," I blurted. "I think your story could be a book."

Dolores's eyes narrowed. "A book. And why would I want to do that after going through the humiliation of being written about multiple times now?"

"Because I wouldn't be writing it *about* you," I said. "I'd be writing it *with* you."

Dolores laughed, and for a moment I saw the phantom of a different Dolores, younger, whose warm, throaty amusement could make heads turn. "You'll excuse me if I don't see the difference. Thanks, but no thanks."

"Wait!" I gritted my teeth so hard pain shot to my head. "Just—listen. Please."

The dog, Crusoe, whined, and Dolores said, "He's thirsty."

We were standing directly in the sun, my clothes sticking to damp skin, arms reddening. There was a roar in my ears, a rough wind. I knew what I had to do, though I felt sick at my willingness to do it.

"My dad," I said, before I could think better of it. "He used to take me fishing every weekend. We caught channel catfish and saugeye and brought them home to my mom to cook for dinner. After our neighbor had a heart attack, my dad mowed his lawn for six months. He collected our other neighbors' newspapers during their annual cruise so it wasn't obvious they were away."

Dolores crossed her arms. "He sounds nice. Why are you telling me this?"

"Because he *was* nice." I swallowed my nausea. "He also beat the shit out of my mom."

Dolores searched my face, and I forced myself to let her see the pain and shame at the core of who I was. "I'm sorry, mija," she said quietly. "No child should have to see that."

"I've never told anyone before," I said. "Not even my fiancé."

She touched my shoulder, so quickly I could have convinced myself I imagined it, if not for the warm impressions her fingertips left behind. "So you're telling me . . . why?"

"Because I want you to know I understand what it means to lead a double life," I said, surprised by the tears choking my throat, by how tempted I was to tell her the rest. But I stopped myself in time. Remembered what I was doing here. "I get why you'd be wary. But this is a chance to set the record straight. To tell *your* story." I paused. "One secret-keeping woman to another."

A glint in Dolores's eye looked, for a moment, like excitement. As if she, too, could feel the possibilities. Then she looked over my shoulder and a veil slid over her face, subtle but impenetrable.

"Go home," she said, though her voice was kind. "And take care of yourself, mija."

LORE, 1983

Laredo always seems like it shrinks in Lore's absence, reduced to forty-mile speed limits and hand-lettered signs for window tinting and elote desgranado. As always, she adjusts. She can feel it already, the return of her Laredo self, scheduled and regimented. Places can do that to us, can't they? Trigger the brain into a kind of muscle memory, so that as Lore turns into Hillside she's wondering whether the cuates have eaten supper and if Gabriel has done his homework—not Mateo, he always does his right after school, even on Fridays, while Gabriel waits till the last minute—trying to remember when she last went to H-E-B and when the electric bill is due, an onslaught of domestic responsibility that casts last night's walk in Chapultepec Park in a surreal glow, the way dreams seem bizarre only after you've woken.

Outside her front door, Lore touches the decorative Florence grille Fabian made by hand. He'll never know, she thinks, and it feels like a promise—to herself, to Fabian, to God. He'll never know because she'll spare him the pain of knowing, but there is something sad, too, about this piece of her, this piece of their lives, to which he'll forever be blind.

"I'm home!" she calls, stepping inside.

She drops the keys to her little red Escort in the wooden bowl on the console table, catches sight of herself in the round, gold-framed mirror—hair pulled back into a low scrunchied ponytail, circles beneath her eyes from lack of sleep, a jittery liveliness to her face, a smile she keeps biting back.

Fabian calls, "In the kitchen!"

Lore takes another moment, flips through a teetering stack of bills, the mouths of the envelopes already jagged with opening. She can imagine Fabian's rough fingers slitting the paper, pulling out the bills and stuffing them back in, helpless with rage. Power, water, health insurance, house insurance, car insurance, money funneled to companies to protect them if the worst happens when the worst is already happening. She wonders when Rivera Iron Works will join the grim ranks of failed businesses, then scolds herself. She needs to believe in Fabian. She *does* believe in Fabian.

The cuates are yelling and laughing from their game room, where they're no doubt slumped on their plastic beanbag chairs playing *Star Wars* on the Atari. They emerge, arguing about something in the game, right as Lore is about to step through into the kitchen.

To the untrained eye, Gabriel and Mateo are identical down to the length of their dark lashes, the sharp Cupid's bow of their lips, the way they stand with feet planted wide apart, naturally unafraid of taking up space in the world. She remembers holding them both to her breasts, these babies whose movements inside her she'd memorized, and sobbing to Fabian, "I can't tell them apart! What kind of mother can't tell her own children apart?" Fabian had laughed, helping to support one of their heads, and said, "Chinga, neither can I." They searched for a birthmark or bump that would help differentiate the boys, eventually settling for painting Gabriel's big toenail purple before snipping off their hospital bracelets. As the days passed, though, Lore began to notice differences, starting with the way they nursed: Gabriel with an impatient, shallow latch that shredded her nipples and made him spit up, and Mateo with a kitten's lapping gentleness, never quite getting enough. Within weeks, Lore and Fabian no longer needed the toenail polish and wondered how they ever had. Now she feels a surge of relief at her sons' limited understanding of her: To them, she is only a mother. Not a woman, capable of desire and deception.

Mateo lifts his full eyebrows. "Dad's making you something special for supper."

"Ooh," Gabriel adds mockingly, as though Lore should be embarrassed.

Fabian is standing at the stove. Two rib eyes, freshly seasoned, glisten on the cutting board beside him. Steak is Fabian's specialty, always crisp and salty on the outside, pink as a rose on the inside. The round glass kitchen table is set with their wedding china—glazed porcelain with a garland of blue flowers, rimmed in gold. The wineglasses are crystal, the ones they usually pull out only at Thanksgiving and Christmas, and there's a bottle of red at the center of the table.

"Fabian!" Lore gives a startled laugh. "What's all this?"

"I know, it's a splurge, but . . ." Fabian gestures her closer as he settles steak to pan, and she hesitates. Then she goes to him, giving him a kiss while the boys *ewww* and *gross* and smoke hisses up toward the range hood.

"I'm sorry," Fabian says quietly. His warm brown eyes meet hers and hold.

"For what?"

"The other night. Before you left. You know."

"Oh." Lore ducks her head into his shoulder. "Don't worry about it."

"No, I was a *D-I-C-K*," he says, with a glance at the boys, who are standing by the refrigerator like puppies waiting for scraps. Lore doesn't remind him they're twelve, not three.

"Dad said—" Gabriel starts, delighted.

Lore cuts him off with a pointed stare. She squeezes Fabian's hand. "Seriously, don't worry about it."

Fabian smiles. "Okay, well, dinner will be ready in ten. Cuates have already eaten."

"You know what that means," Lore says to the boys. "Showers. Gabriel, you're first tonight."

"Mom," Gabriel whines. "We're in the middle of a game!"

"We were at the ranch all day," Fabian says. "You guys stink."

The cuates laugh. It's one of those incomprehensible boy things: they love to stink.

"The ranch sounds fun," Lore says, leaning against the counter as Fabian flips the steaks. "With tío Sergio?"

But the boys are already edging out of the room. One of their wordless communications, an attempt to sneak out before agreeing to take showers.

"Showers," Lore says again. "And wash your hair! Then you can play your game, but only for thirty more minutes. Have you all done your homework?"

"Yes, Mom." Gabriel rolls his eyes, and panic flashes across Mateo's face. Seeing his brother's expression, Gabriel says, "We both did. On Friday. Remember? Before we ordered pizza?"

"Oh, yeah," Mateo says, with a relieved grin.

Fabian looks at Lore, grinning. "Miss us?"

She laughs, a crack of guilt opening in her chest.

The small kitchen heats up quickly; even the wood cabinets, when Lore opens them for water glasses, feel warm as skin. Sweat prickles beneath her arms, and she can smell the dingy remnants of air travel—the recycled plane air, the stale reek of cigarette smoke. Every so often, she thinks she catches a whiff of Andres's cologne.

"Salad's in the fridge," Fabian says, turning off the stove, transferring the steaks onto a cutting board. She takes the salad and ranch dressing to the table while he wraps the meat in foil to seal in the juices before slicing.

At the table, Fabian pours the wine with a flourish, pausing for a moment over her glass. He grins. "How's the cruda?"

Lore laughs. "Ay, please, I was one of the first to leave the party." It was true, after all.

"Why?" Fabian holds up his wineglass, and she clinks it. "That doesn't sound like you."

Lore murmurs noncommittally, though a part of her glows at his knowledge of her, how she hates reaching the end of a good night. When they host family, she's always the one waving the bottle, asking, ¿Uno más?

"Just a lot on my mind," she says. Though Lore doesn't want to dampen Fabian's mood, it will be a no-fail subject changer: "How'd it go with Juan?"

Fabian cuts grimly into his steak. "He begged me for his job. Begged, Lore. He practically fell to his knees."

"Oh, no." The image is horrifying—proud Juan, who serves as an usher at St. Patrick's, where they go to Mass at noon every Sunday. Fabian and the cuates probably saw him at church today, passing around the basket for the offertory. "Fabian, what did you say?"

"What could I say?" He looks up at her, and for a moment Lore thinks he's actually expecting an answer, a solution that will let him call Juan in the morning and make things better, the way Fabian always tries to make things better. "I told him how sorry I was," Fabian says, "and that as soon as I can, if he still wants the job, I'll hire him back."

"Well, that's something." Lore sips her wine. "A lot of employers wouldn't say that."

Fabian grunts, forking steak into his mouth with sharp jabs. "Anyway," he mumbles, "how was the wedding?"

"Oh, my God, Fabian, you wouldn't believe it," and Lore describes every opulent detail she can remember, every fragment of conversation she thinks he'd find amusing. She feels like she's creating the night more than recalling it, emphasizing and erasing like an artist at her easel, until this alternate version feels more immediate than its fading counterpart, and so, too, does the man before her. How could she? How could she just . . . forget him? It's this pinche recession. It's making everyone crazy.

Once Lore has cleaned the kitchen and the cuates are in bed, Fabian opens a second bottle of wine and they take the glasses to their bedroom. Before she can take a sip, Fabian's lips are on hers.

"Hold on," she laughs, fumbling to set her glass on the nightstand. "Let me take a shower. All the travel—"

"I don't care." Fabian's hands are at the buttons of her shirt, nimble and sure. "You were right. It's been too long."

Interrupting the moment would ruin it, but letting Fabian continue to kiss her feels like daring him to discover the invisible hieroglyphics of another man's hands on her skin and lips, so she does the only thing she can—pulls him with her to the shower, where she grips the rippled ledge that holds their Suave shampoo as Fabian pushes inside her, water dripping from his head to her shoulders as he kisses her neck. She closes her eyes, remembering the Bosque de Chapultepec, her back against a tree, Andres yanking up her dress. She imagines the cool air, the dress ripping, her hands and arms scraped on ahuehuete bark, and one hand dips between her legs, one finger, a tiny motion, and then she is crying out, and Fabian thrusts twice more before groaning into her hair. When she turns around, she is almost surprised to find herself here, with Fabian, but she is glad, too.

The first alarm goes off at 5:50. Fabian rolls toward Lore today, instead of away, and she sighs and burrows against him. His chest hair makes her back itch, a familiar, younger feeling, reminding her of when they used to sleep skin to skin all night long. When the second alarm goes off ten minutes later, she groans and throws off the comforter.

Last night, after the shower, they'd turned on *Late Night with David Letterman*, dipping into the second bottle of wine as they laughed at interviews with John Candy, Teri Garr, and Dom DeLuise. It felt like a vacation, a reprieve. But she's paying for it now, head throbbing, and the usual resentment crawls up her throat as Fabian stays in bed while she goes to make breakfast. It was one thing when she stayed home with the cuates all day, but *still* she's the one in charge of sating everyone's morning appetite, rewarding them all for the hard work of sleeping, like no one else could pull a soggy box of waffles from the freezer and slide the icy disks into a toaster.

Lore trudges to the kitchen, turning on lights and brewing a pot of coffee, making noise the way she always does. She might never get to wake up with a leisurely shower, like Fabian, or breakfast hot and ready, like the cuates, but she'll be damned if she's going to tiptoe around like they're all a bunch of kings in the last few minutes of royal slumber.

The kitchen is U-shaped, with dark oak cabinets, Formica countertops, and green-and-cream striped wallpaper that reminds Lore of Christmas. When they'd moved in, she'd planned to replace the wallpaper with something more modern, a geometric design, maybe, in warm colors that would complement the Saltillo tile with which she'd replace the linoleum. Now they're stuck with everything they'd intended to fix.

They bought the house three years ago, at the height of the boom. The gray brick ranch in Hillside was such a step up after the two-bedroom condo they'd been renting while they saved for a down payment. She remembers how the cuates, then nine, had instinctively chosen "their" room, not realizing it was possible to have one each. The house was ten years old, practically new, but she and Fabian still made plans: updating the wallpaper, for one. And the master bathroom, where Lore dreamed of adding a Jacuzzi so she could light candles and sink into scented bubbles after the cuates were in bed. And the backyard, more than big enough for a pool! She and Fabian would invite the whole family over for carne asadas, fajitas sizzling over charcoal while the kids cannonballed into sun-toasted water. But the only thing they'd gotten to was building the carport out back so she and Fabian weren't constantly asking each other to move their car to unblock the other. A narrow driveway built for two vehicles bumper to bumper—whose good idea was that? Now at least they each have their space, Lore in the driveway and Fabian in the carport, complete with an automatic wrought iron gate he fabricated himself.

Lore sighs, glancing up at the skylight she'd once found romantic and now hates for the way it silhouettes the Rorschach blurs of bird shit. When the waffles are stacked, she strides to the cuates' room and opens their door. Gabriel lies spread-eagled on top of the covers, his skinny chest—he recently started sleeping shirtless, and she'd caught him flexing in the mirror—rising and falling. Mateo sleeps on his stomach, arms stiff and straight at his sides. Their hair is rumpled and wild, the sun striping their carpet and the piles of dirty clothes and Nerf guns. They're in seventh grade this year. Soon they'll be teenagers. How is that possible? Only yesterday they were at her breasts, slack-jawed and determined, connected, even when they pulled away, by delicate silver strings of saliva. Now they're all so . . . separate. She can feel the passing of time, its devouring mouth at her back, and has an overwhelming urge to draw their bodies close, as if that might keep them young like this forever.

"Morning, calabazas!" Lore turns on their light, and they groan.

"Mom!" Gabriel throws an arm over his eyes. "Do you always have to *do* that?"

Lore's sentimentality fades. "Breakfast. Apúrense, before it's cold."

This gets them, as always. Coltish limbs unfolding, exaggerated yawns, gusts of morning breath as they push past her through the doorway, no greeting or recognition.

While the cuates eat, she heats the curlers and blasts her copete under the blow-dryer. Fabian leaves right after seven, a cold waffle in hand and two vertical lines already carved between his brows. Then Lore hurries the cuates into the car, calling out a stream of reminders. The boys, even Mateo, are forever forgetting to ask her to sign their permission slips, and with the new school year just begun, there are more than usual.

"Mom, can you at least try not to be late today?" Gabriel meets her eyes in the rearview mirror as she inches forward in the drop-off line. "It's super hot outside, and it's boring."

"Only boring people get bored," Lore says by rote, one of Mami's old lines. She'd missed seeing her family for their regular Sunday lunch yesterday. Maybe if she has time this week, she'll pick up Whataburger and take it over to her parents' house for a visit.

Gabriel is right, though: not even 8 A.M. and the sun is already bleaching the sky white. The city is under water restrictions—no sprinklers, no mangueras—and everything that should be green is brown or yellow, dead. August is the worst month. Everyone short-tempered with heat, impatient for the modest turn toward fall. What will Christmas be like this year, with few places left to shop and fewer still who can afford to? When retail is the bulk of a city's economy, watching each store close is like watching the town itself begin to wheeze, its lungs weakening with astonishing speed.

When you need to take a breath, there's only one place to go—the lungs of the city.

The memory of Andres's words, his husky voice, nearly takes Lore's own breath away. She wonders where he is, what he's doing—whether he's remembering her, wishing he'd asked how to reach her. Why hadn't he?

The Zócalo had been humming to early-morning life, the streets already choked and belching, when they made it back to the Centro Histórico. For a heart-stopping moment, as Andres passed the hotel, a thrill had risen up in her: Where would they go? What would they do? But he only parked against the sidewalk half a block away.

They walked hand in hand to the entrance, and Lore saw that the wedding was still being dismantled.

"Well," he'd said. "Tonight has been one to remember, Dolores Rivera."

Her married name in his mouth caught her like a splinter: her seating card. But if the night had been so memorable, why hadn't he asked for her phone number? Maybe he, too, is less available than he seemed. The thought makes her unreasonably jealous, as if she has the right to expect anything of him.

In the back seat, Gabriel is pointing to someone out the window as he and Mateo talk in the strange, truncated twin language they developed years ago, as toddlers communicating in grunts and clicks and odd combinations of vowels and consonants. She'd panicked, thinking something was wrong with them, some kind of speech impediment or handicap. Then they'd laughed, decipherable to her again.

"Okay, off you go," she says, pulling up, finally, to the drop-off point. She's already exhausted. Unexpectedly, though, the boys each lean forward and kiss her cheek, and the sweetness of the gesture briefly revives her.

The bank is only five minutes away. For all Laredo has grown, it's still a small town, insignificant to the rest of the world. Here they are, resorting to asking the federal government for help—job training programs, grants for development, aid to education, anything—and what's happened? Nothing.

You're one of the lucky ones, she thinks. So stop complaining.

But isn't that even worse? Wearing blinders to the reality of a situation because it's not that bad for you, at least not yet?

Downtown is a tight grid of one-way streets, bordered by I-35 on the east, Park Street on the north, and the Rio Grande on the south and west. This is where Laredo started, its original footprint, and this is where its soul remains—in the San Agustín Cathedral, the Plaza Theatre, the courthouse, the faded facades of innumerable tienditas selling knockoff fashion and shoe shines, jewelry and perfume. In the eight years Lore has worked at the bank, she's never seen downtown like this: stores boarded and barred, the remaining owners standing behind counters, staring at empty streets. It's a gauntlet of guilt before Lore finally arrives at work.

But the guilt falls away as she enters the lobby. It's the smell: Windex and Pine-Sol mixed with cigarette smoke and coffee, and something else, something papery and mysterious—money. It's the smell of her own ambition, the home she's made for herself here.

In the break room, someone has brought three dozen foil-wrapped tacos, and despite herself—she could really stand to lose fifteen pounds—she takes one. She can tell by the heft that it's barbacoa, and her stomach growls as she pours coffee into a Styrofoam cup.

"Hey!" someone calls, and she turns around to see Oscar. "So? What'd I miss? How was the wedding?"

"Boring." Lore winks. "More important—does the world have another Martinez to contend with?"

Oscar is tall and lanky, with thick blond curls that make most people mistake him for a gringo. He can't stop grinning, already reaching for his wallet. "Mijo was born on Saturday morning. Eight pounds, three ounces, twenty inches, not counting his—" Oscar raises his brows suggestively.

"Ay, Oscar." Lore laughs, swatting his shoulder. What is it with men, starting the penis bragging from birth? "¡Felicidades! How's Natalie?"

"Good, good." He smiles, and Lore can see the wonder on his face, the way Fabian had looked at her once the cuates were in her arms, stunned by her power and sacrifice. She hopes Natalie enjoys it, because it doesn't last.

When Lore's extension rings that afternoon, she answers without looking up from the credit analysis she's reviewing.

"Yes, I'm looking for Ms. Crusoe," the caller says in accented English. Lore is about to say he has the wrong number when she recognizes the voice, the teasing nickname: Andres.

She slides out of her wheeled chair with a clatter, holding the phone while she circles her desk and kicks the office door shut.

"Andres! Hi. How did you get this number?"

"Just call me Sherlock Holmes," he says with a laugh. "I dialed information. I hope that's okay? After we said goodbye, I realized I hadn't—"

"Of course," Lore says, before biting her lip. No. This isn't okay! She's been trying all day not to think about him, scenes from the weekend replaying in some recess of her mind, a whole other world secretly unspooling.

"How are you?" she asks finally.

"I'm . . . missing you," Andres says, almost shyly. "That must sound ridiculous."

"No." Lore's cheeks go warm. "It doesn't."

"That's a relief. I've never been good at playing games."

Lore takes a pen between her fingers, tapping each end on the desk like a seesaw. "Did you ever try?"

"Of course," Andres says, and he tells her about his lab partner in college chemistry. He'd had a crush on her all semester, and finally, after a late study session, they kissed. "My friends were telling me to play it cool—'Tranquilo, tranquilo, girls don't like you breathing down their necks.' So a week went by, and I did nothing."

Lore groans.

"Exactly. She started getting more and more fría—not laughing at jokes, canceling study sessions—but somehow, I thought this was a good thing."

"That she was pissed off?"

"Of course," Andres says, deadpan. "Because it obviously meant she wanted me to ask her out."

"Did you?"

"Right before she convinced the professor to let her switch lab partners. She never spoke to me again."

Lore laughs, and Andres laughs with her. She is amazed all over again by the ease of their conversation, how unhesitating Andres is to share stories of his romantic past, however innocent this one was. She wonders what Fabian would have been like if she'd met him as an adult. Would he have told her about ex-girlfriends and old heartbreaks? Somehow, she doesn't think so. Fabian could always talk about the future for hours, obsessed with goals, progress, a destination. She had loved this about him at seventeen, when most boys couldn't see past Friday night. But as an adult? *What does it matter?*, she can imagine him saying.

"What about you?" Andres asks, a smile in his voice. "Do you play games?"

Lore doesn't know how to answer. She's playing games now, isn't she? Pretending to be someone Andres can call without guilt or reservation. But is this who she is? A pretender?

She and Fabian met on a double date. Her childhood friend Jenny had set it up; it was Jenny's second date with Fabian, and she asked him to bring a friend for Lore. Arturo, another Martin football player, had the shadow of a mustache on his otherwise baby face, and used his pizza crusts to beat a rhythm on the table at Wizard Wicks. Jenny kept sneaking bright-eyed glances at Lore, nudging her beneath the table with one of the patchwork boots she'd bought on their last trip to Payless. But it was Fabian who had Lore's attention. Broad-shouldered and quiet, with quick flashing brown eyes that made Lore wonder what he was thinking and—to her chagrin—how much he really liked Jenny.

The four of them went out two or three more times. It happened subtly, the way Fabian and Lore took opportunities to be alone together. "You get the tickets, I'll get the snacks," Lore might say to Arturo, and Fabian would press a five-dollar bill into Jenny's hand for the tickets and say, "Popcorn?" They would disagree on this later, but Lore remembers Fabian saying, in this same concession line at the Plaza, "I think I'm going to break up with Jenny." He was looking straight ahead, and for a moment, Lore thought she'd misheard him. Then he glanced down at her, a question in his eyes. She said, "Well, I'm going to break up with Arturo," though "break up" was too strong a phrase for what they were, still two strangers, really, thrown together like broken magnets, easily pulled apart.

And, yes—this does not make her teenage self a great friend. But she didn't pretend. When Fabian smiled at her, she smiled back. And when Jenny called her crying, after the breakup, Lore didn't deny it when she demanded, "He likes you, doesn't he? And you like him." Lore only said she was sorry, and when Jenny called her a puta and hung up, she quietly accepted that their friendship, which began in CCD classes before their First Holy Communion, was probably over. So she was selfish, perhaps. But she hadn't pretended to be otherwise, and there was integrity in that, wasn't there? So this, now—what she's doing, or not doing—isn't who she *is*.

"No," she says to Andres. "I don't play games."

They talk for almost twenty more minutes. The call must be costing Andres a fortune, though he shows no desire to hang up. They laugh at how they spoke Spanish at the wedding and now English because he is calling her in the U.S.; they recognize they are different in each language, more limited in expression in their second one, so Andres switches back to Spanish and Lore feels a shiver of recognition, as if a song has struck a memory, and when he asks her why she's quiet, she says she's thinking of the Bosque de Chapultepec. Andres sighs, and she swears she can feel his breath in her ear.

"I loved kissing you," he says, his voice lower, intimate.

A slow, delicious burn in Lore's chest. "Me too," she whispers. Her office, suddenly, feels charged with unfamiliarity. The wood-and-metal clock on the wall, the plastic mat beneath her chair, the dot matrix printer with its reams of continuous paper—all slightly foreign now, tilted, with the illicit thrill of this shared memory.

The question hangs, though: What now? What happens when two people, for one night, close a great distance, and want to do it again? What happens when one of them is already committed to another?

Lore glances at her watch, crashing back to reality. Time to pick up the cuates.

"Andres, I have to go. But . . . I'm glad you called."

"Can I call you again?" he asks hurriedly. "On Friday, maybe, if I can? I have office hours . . ."

What if she'd said no? What if she'd closed this door that is barely open? All three of them—Lore, Andres, and Fabian—might be happy, blind to the dark fates they'd eluded. All three of them might still be alive.

But there is no alternate future. There is only the one Lore creates with one word: "Yes."

CASSIE, 2017

I hadn't planned on staying at the motel where Andres Russo was murdered. I'd only wanted to see it. But even after failing miserably with Dolores, I couldn't make myself go home. I'd brought an overnight bag just in case, and at sixty-five dollars a night, Hotel Botanica was cheaper than most other options in town. If I was going to stay anywhere, I might as well stay here. After all, there was still a chance she'd change her mind—I'd left my contact information beneath a rock on her front porch.

Hotel Botanica was set apart from the string of Motel Sixes and La Quintas along I-35 by what seemed to be an appeal to families. Yellowed waist-high trellises separated the aluminum-sided room doors, all of which faced a central courtyard. In the small, leafy pool area, three children splashed around a broken waterfall feature, the red plastic rocks dry and cracked. A little girl performed clumsy, elaborate jumps into the pool, limbs starfished, a slap of water on her belly. "¡Mira, mami, mira!" she yelled, water streaming from her pink polka-dotted bikini as she stared toward the cabaña, where two couples drank beer from plastic cups and occasionally waved back toward the pool. Tejano music played. A sign on the bar advertised two-dollar tacos.

My sunburned arms stung as I followed the cement walkway toward my door. This goddamn heat. If anything, it was worse at five than it had been at noon. I understood now why the *Laredo Morning Times* article had specifically mentioned the 117-degree day. Lesser things drove people to acts of madness.

I dumped my bags and the cardboard box on the coverlet of the queen-size bed, which matched the rust-orange zigzag carpeting. The mattress was set on a faded, scratched wooden platform base. Two barstools were tucked beneath an empty shelf that did double duty as a breakfast table and desk. The only other piece of furniture was a long mahogany buffet table beneath the wall-mounted flat-screen, flanked by two large fake ferns.

When I'd first read the *Laredo Morning Times* article, I'd imagined the shot ringing out in a quiet hotel—adjoining walls, carpeted hallways—and wondered how no one had heard it, but here, on a night like this, it wouldn't get dark until after nine. Maybe the music had been blasting, all accordion and bass, the pool filled with people drinking and splashing. Maybe an eighteen-wheeler had bleated its horn at the same time. Maybe everyone had assumed someone else would call the police.

Meanwhile, Andres Russo had bled out in his room.

As much as I'd read and written about murder over the years, this was the closest I'd been to an exact spot where someone's life had been taken. A familiar, morbid draw overcame me, the kind of reverent zeal I'd felt reading about Ted Bundy's kills for the first time. Those sorority girls, asleep in their beds. The way you might close your eyes on an ordinary day and end up beaten to death, shards of skull and teeth flung like gruesome confetti around the same room where you'd once studied, giggled, tried on lipsticks and personalities, had sex, and dreamed of where your life might go. A chiaroscuro of the macabre and mundane, the nearness of the two transforming me into a rabid voyeur of that final experience.

I wondered in which room it had happened, how many people had brushed against Andres's ghost without feeling it. I closed my eyes, imagined him lying on the floor—blurred and featureless though still somehow distinct in my mind, that sweater from the photo in "Her Secret Lives" drenched in blood.

I shook myself, checked my phone: no calls or texts from Dolores.

Why the hell had I said I was writing a book? If Dolores had bothered looking me up, she must have laughed. As if landing a piece in *Harper's* or the *New Yorker*, the way I thought I'd been envisioning, wasn't hard enough? Yet, now that I'd given it voice, it felt obvious. *Of course* I wanted to write a book about her double marriage. I would write the hell out of this story, and it would practically sell itself. And after that, I'd have some *legitimacy*. A real career, not a part-time blogging gig I could lose at the whim of a giant media corporation deciding to "restructure." I'd have some money in the bank—maybe not a lot, but more than I had now, surely, enough to have *some* cushion in case of an emergency, not like today, when I'd had to put gas and motel on my credit card, which was already dangerously close to maxed out. All I needed was a chance.

I ate the refrigerator-hardened deli sandwich I'd bought at a gas station before tipping a heavy pour of six-dollar cabernet into a coffee cup. Then I opened the case file. Incident reports, evidence log, witness statements, search warrant, arrest warrant, crime scene photos—a treasure trove, irresistible.

According to Dolores's statement, she hadn't known ahead of time that Andres was coming into town. He'd first arrived at the bank where she worked around nine in the morning on Friday, August 1, but Dolores had been in a board meeting, which, according to the receptionist, couldn't be interrupted. The receptionist had told Andres to return after two that afternoon. When he'd come back around four, Dolores had been at a doctor's appointment, the first stop in a string of corroborated alibis. Andres had left a note for Dolores with her colleague, Oscar Martinez, who had given it to her when she returned to the bank close to five. The note itself had never been recovered. Dolores had thrown it away that afternoon, she said. Maintenance had emptied the trash cans on Saturday, and by Monday the garbage was collected. In her statement, Dolores said the note read, *I'm sorry I missed you.*

I frowned. *I'm sorry I missed you?* It wasn't like this was a friend who'd stopped by on a whim. This was her *husband.* Her husband, who apparently had no other way to find her than to visit her at work. Her husband, who'd apparently just found out from Oscar Martinez that Dolores was married to someone else. Could that really be all the note said—no details, no contact information? But if it had said something more, or different, why had she lied?

I flipped through to the next witness statement. Around 4:30 in the afternoon, Andres and Fabian were seen arguing outside the Rivera house.

[Witness name redacted], who lives at [witness address redacted], waved when a car pulled into Fabian and Dolores Rivera's driveway. He initially believed it was Mrs. Rivera, who always parked in the driveway, but an unfamiliar man, later identified as the victim, Andres Russo, emerged instead. [Witness name redacted] was unloading groceries when Mr. Russo knocked on the Riveras' door. [Witness name redacted] states that his attention was caught when he heard Mr. Russo say, "That, there, she's my wife!" pointing to something inside the house. Mr. Russo then showed something to Mr. Rivera; [witness name redacted] could not identify the item. [Witness name redacted] states that Mr. Rivera yelled, "Get the fuck off my property!" [Witness name redacted] states that before Mr. Russo reentered his car, he told Mr. Rivera he was staying at the Hotel Botanica, and that they "needed to talk."

Well, that explained how Fabian had known where Andres was staying. Except, how had he known the exact room number? The hotel clerk had spotted Fabian returning to his car but said they'd never spoken. And if Andres had known Dolores's address, why leave a note—or stay at a motel—at all when he could wait for her at her home? I opened the basic timeline of events on my laptop, adding to it as I went, and started a separate document of questions.

Between 5:00 and 5:30 that afternoon, Dolores's brother-in-law, Sergio, had picked up Fabian to go to the family ranch, where Fabian was alibied until he was dropped off at home around eight. Dolores, meanwhile, claimed to have gone straight home after work because she had plans with her kids. A cashier at Wendy's remembered her and the twins ordering Frosties around 6:30. Lore had then taken them to the movie theater at the mall. She still had their receipt and ticket stubs. The movie cashier commented on how nice it was, teenage boys not being embarrassed to see a movie with their mother, especially a blockbuster like *Aliens*.

After that, they went home. In her initial statement, Dolores had claimed Fabian was there when they arrived around 9:15 and remained there all night. She had called her sister close to 10:30, placing her at home until after 11. But Fabian was seen at the motel between 10:00 and 10:30. Andres's time of death, established by his body temperature, was estimated between 9:00 and midnight, making that ID damning.

I took a few sips of wine. Fabian must have confronted Dolores about Andres. If they'd fought and Fabian had left . . . Had Dolores had any idea where Fabian was going? Or what he was about to do?

I set my cup on the nightstand. My tailbone ached from sitting heavily on the bed for the better part of two hours. The room had felt cool earlier, when I'd come in from outside. Now a thin sheen of sweat had formed under my arms and between my breasts. No wonder—the thermostat was set at seventy-nine. I lowered it to seventy-five, where Duke and I kept ours. Then, after a moment, stabbed the down arrow several more times. I wasn't paying the electric bill.

After a quick shower, I spread the crime scene photos—about

three dozen, all taken vertically—across the bed. They formed a dark collage, a cross between precious artifacts to be handled with care and something lewd and forbidden I shouldn't be seeing—and shouldn't *want* to see. But I did. I always did.

Andres Russo lay with legs splayed on the cornflower-blue carpet, a strip of skin visible between his socks and jeans. A jagged, star-shaped hole in his gray T-shirt (of course it wasn't the Christmas photo sweater), photographed close-up with a scale beside it. His shirt darkened to eggplant around the wound, dry and stiff as a paper airplane. Left arm close to his body, his hand—his nail beds, his gold wedding band—stained with blood, as though he'd tried to stanch the inevitable gush. His other arm was flung out wide, palm up, fingers half-curled. His skin was oyster gray, his face caricatured in death: the prominent nose and heavy brows, lips twisted. I wished I could place my fingertips on his closed eyelids and lift them. I wanted to see what Dolores had seen the night they met. I wanted to see what Andres had seen the night he died.

For now, the photos were the closest I could get. In them, the room's venetian blinds were closed, a window air conditioner unit spotted with condensation. The white pillows on the queen-size bed were lightly rumpled on the left side, as if someone had briefly leaned against them. The black telephone, slightly askew on the wooden nightstand beside the metal hotel key. Gray canvas duffel bag, unzipped. Across from the bed, a long, low-slung TV armoire similar, but not identical, to the one in my room. Remote control in place beside the wood-paneled TV. One empty highball glass, two empty mini bottles of Scotch. A hand towel crumpled on the white counter beside the bathroom sink. The bar of soap stuck, gummy, to the drain. Toilet lid down.

Scattered around Andres were small yellow numbered placards beside items of interest. Some were incomprehensible to me, the blood, in particular, imbued with mysterious hieroglyphic meaning. Others—fingerprints—were obvious.

Every surface was covered in sooty black smudges. Fabian's fingerprints had not been found where they might be expected: the interior or exterior door handles, the bathroom sink or tub, or Andres's belongings. But because the door handles had been cleaned of prints altogether, the detectives had speculated early on that the perpetrator hadn't worn gloves but, rather, wiped where he might have touched, leaving more room for error. It was the placard marked nineteen that gave police the lead they needed: a partial fingerprint on the wooden platform base of the bed.

I brought that photo closer to my face. Why would his fingerprint be there? I lowered myself beside the bed. He'd need to be on his knees. Maybe he was checking whether Andres was breathing—though he'd be closer to Andres's ankles than his chest. Maybe he was waiting for Andres to die. Maybe he needed to brace himself against what he'd done: a low crouch, shallow breaths, ears ringing. Was it here, in this spot, that he'd decided to take Andres's wallet?

I glanced around the room. Most men kept their wallets in their back pocket, but if that was the case, Fabian would have needed to move Andres, and there would be some evidence of that. Maybe Andres had tossed the wallet beside the hotel key on the nightstand. Maybe Fabian had seen it in this low crouch, casting desperate glances around the room. But if he'd been hoping to obscure Andres's identity, he hadn't thought about the passport, which, according to the evidence log, had been tucked neatly into an interior pocket of Andres's duffel bag. Not to mention that in 1986, Hotel Botanica was almost new, a decent family motel with appropriate record keeping. But most people don't think clearly after committing a murder. Killing gets to people.

I pored through the photos again. That strip of skin between Andres's sock and the hem of his jeans, black hair sprouting from a bony shin. A piece of himself he hadn't meant to show.

A strange image rose: Dolores, naked, her shoulders gleaming silver beneath a blood-orange sun. The dark curls of her youth falling tangled to her waist. Teeth like a shark's, one ancient row tucked behind another. Her fingernails—long, sharp as arrowheads, and eerily pearlescent. The soles of her feet worn smooth and hard as diamonds.

Then I thought of the woman I'd met today, her linen shirt and running shorts, thighs dimpled in the unrelenting sun. The ways we can hide in plain sight.

I woke up at eight in the morning with a dull pulsing behind my eyebrows, a tremble in my fingers. I'd stayed up until four reviewing the case file. The empty bottle of wine on the motel nightstand caught the accusing morning light. I felt all six dollars of that hangover.

I grabbed for my phone, hoping for an early-morning message from Dolores. Nothing.

After checking out, for lack of anything better to do, I drove to Mall del Norte. This was where Lore and the twins had seen *Aliens* the night of the murder. Not surprisingly, that theater was long gone. There was a new one, with stadium seating and reclining leather chairs. The two kids working the box office hadn't even been alive back then.

I left and aimlessly ended up back on I-35 South, swerving off just before accidentally joining the line for Nuevo Laredo on the bridge. I turned down a narrow one-way street, trying to regain my bearings. This part of town was *old*. Not in a historic, Main Street way, but worn the way things get when they are abandoned to the elements. Spanish-signed storefronts and blistered red awnings, women browsing racks of pleather Betty Boop purses as children pointed to windows bright with cheap plastic toys. Men smoking, shoulders slumped, on the stoops of battered convenience stores. A Casa de Cambio (money exchange, according to Google Translate at a red light) on every corner.

Through the dilapidation, there was a sad echo of a kind of splendor. A plastic banner for an electronics store hung incongruously across a building with a sleek marble facade, as if it had once been a bank or high-end department store. Beside the tiny Border Beauty Supply was a tall brick building with mosaic-tiled bald eagles hovering, regal, over arched windows. The four-story courthouse with elegant white columns overlooked a plaza with globe streetlights, where brown-skinned men sat on benches beneath the shade of mature oaks. It felt like a different country, which of course it used to be.

I ended up at an outlet mall, a cheerful, garish monstrosity wildly out of place a block from the tiny Mexican storefronts I'd just passed. Instead of turning right into the parking lot, I turned left onto dirt. Mere feet in front of me was the Rio Grande, a wide swath of brown water separating one country from another. The two riverbanks looked identical—long, flaxen weeds and inhospitable snarls of mesquite. The vantage looked familiar, and I realized with surprise that the YouTube video of near-distant artillery fire must have been taken nearby. I couldn't imagine it now, not with this unbroken sky and motionless ribbon of water, murals for Coach and Banana Republic beckoning behind me.

I opened Andres's autopsy report, imagined a cold room, chrome shining. On the table, Andres reduced to the sum of his parts: he was six feet, two inches tall, weighed 195 pounds. No facial hair, teeth in good repair. No needle marks or tattoos. Bloody liquid found in nostrils. His heart weighed 400 grams. Its surface was smooth, glistening, and transparent.

The slug was seen through X-ray, then extracted and submitted as evidence. It was, as the *Laredo Morning Times* reporter had written, "later matched to ammunition found in Fabian and Dolores's home, ammunition used for the Ruger Mark II .22 caliber pistol Fabian claimed to have lost." It washed up on the bank of the Rio Grande days later.

I couldn't stop staring at the slug. Such a small thing. Innocuous and almost pretty, like a golden teardrop. A fraction of a second. The curl of one finger, and Andres's life was over. But what had brought him to that exact moment?

My phone rang—a Laredo area code. My heart jumped.

"Cassie Bowman speaking," I answered, too eagerly.

"I was reading that article again." Dolores Rivera gave a mirthless laugh. "No sé por qué—I have the damn thing memorized. Do you know what really bothers me?"

"No." I tried to keep my voice even, casual, as if we were picking up right where we'd left off.

"Penelope," Dolores said. "The things she said: 'She used us. Then threw us away, like trash.' What does she think I used them for?"

"I'm not sure," I said. "Did you ever reach out to them again? After . . . ?"

"Yes! I wrote them letters, for months. That pendejo got everything wrong. He thinks I'm a psychopath. That I didn't love anybody." Dolores's voice vibrated. "He can't even imagine the truth."

"And what's that, Dolores?" I held my breath. "What's the truth?"

For a beat, she didn't answer. Then: "I loved everybody. ¿Me oyes? I loved them all."

The hair on my arms floated up in the slant of sunlight through the window. She did want to be understood. And I wanted to understand her. I set the autopsy report on the passenger seat.

"Dolores," I said, "let me help you tell your story."

She exhaled, long and slow. "One condition."

In that moment, I would have given her anything. "What?"

"I don't want to talk about the day—" She faltered, the strength in her voice giving way to something softer, bruised. "The day Andres died. Everything else, fine. But not that day. I don't want to relive it. And it's not—that's not how I want either of them to be remembered."

I bit my lip, canines sharp. Her double marriage was the story I wanted to tell—but we couldn't just pretend the murder didn't happen. It was, after all, how everything ended. I glanced at the open autopsy report. Obviously, her memories of that final day were more valuable, but if it came down to it, I could get most of what I needed from the case file.

"Okay," I said. "Deal."

The space between us trembled.

Finally: "You know where I live."

Part II

LORE, 2017

Tenía mucha energía nerviosa as I waited for the gringa reporter to arrive. I scurried around wiping the granite countertops, hiding mail in the bulging junk drawer, and giving the floors a quick pasadita with the Swiffer to pick up any of Crusoe's stiff black fur, which he shook off every time he came inside.

Crusoe had been an impulse decision. I'd bought him on the side of McPherson near H-E-B three years ago. He was the wildest puppy in the litter, with a bounce like his legs were pogo sticks. I'd never wanted a dog, didn't even know why I'd pulled over, but after holding him to my chest, I couldn't imagine going home without him. "Tiene mucha energía," the woman selling him had warned. I'd smiled tightly and said, "Pues, qué bueno, yo también."

His tiny claws were sharp on my chest as I drove to Petco to buy dog bowls and chew toys, apologizing when he peed in three different aisles with his shaky little squat. At the register, I paused at a machine that would stamp a tag with your pet's name. I stared into his cocoa eyes and thought of the café de olla Andres used to make, and the name just came to me: he was Crusoe.

The thing about a spontaneous act is that the consequences are long-lasting. The puppy chews the furniture, destroys the bougainvillea, becomes a dog. The dance becomes an affair, which becomes a marriage, which becomes a murder.

Which becomes a pact.

I thought of the gringa reporter, the way she'd tried to win my trust by telling me about her family. She wasn't the first one to approach me after the *LMT* article. The first was another gringo, a fast talker with a New York accent. He was in his fifties, according to Wikipedia, and he'd written three true crime books, one of which was a bestseller. But when I told him I wasn't interested, he said, "I'd prefer your cooperation, but I don't need it." ¡Qué descarado! Imagine writing a book about someone who didn't want to be written about! Apparently, these crime writers did it all the time by using other sources, like the guy from *LMT.*

That one's call had been so out of the blue. It was like being hit on the back of the head, waking up to find your purse gone, your car stolen. Things taken from you purely because someone else wanted them.

Yesterday, through a gap in the curtains, I had watched Cassie Bowman leave a note on the front porch. She went back to her car and waited, like a hunter sitting in a blind, except I wasn't some dumb animal, and I wouldn't give her the satisfaction of taking the bait.

Ten minutes after she left, I scuttled outside and plucked up the note, a breathless feeling in my chest, stupid. It was only her name and number. *Please call me.* I tossed the piece of paper on top of the other mail on the island. Then, just in case, I stuck it to the fridge with a magnetic pig.

I reheated flautas for lunch, bone dry. It was too hot to garden, so I busied myself cleaning the hall bathroom, the one I thought of as belonging to my grandsons, with the fuzzy bathmat and Mickey Mouse potty, the faint scent of urine and Johnson & Johnson shampoo, the same kind I'd used on Gabriel and Mateo. How history repeats itself, si la dejas.

At six, I considered the half-empty bottle of Chardonnay in the fridge. What I really wanted though, for the first time in years, was Bucanas. I pulled a dusty bottle from the liquor cabinet, gave it a sniff. Age was supposed to be a good thing, right? I poured two fingers into a heavy crystal highball and went out to the back porch.

At dusk, the heat was finally contained, like fire in a lantern. The air smelled like jasmine and potting soil and the occasional pungent whiff of dog turd. I sat on one of the wicker chairs and tucked my feet beneath Crusoe, his belly bathwater-hot against my skin.

I took a sip of Bucanas, pictured it forging a path through me like the ants in that ant farm Mateo had begged me for when he was eight, rivulets through the sand. That ugly word from the *LMT* article—*psychopath*—hissed through my brain. Penelope, thinking I was a monster. I shouldn't have been surprised. She'd written a letter the first time Fabian was up for parole. Talking about the impact of Andres's death on her and Carlitos—the drugs and alcohol, Carlitos's own arrests for petty crimes. She argued that Fabian should remain in prison, but it was me she wanted to punish. And I deserved it.

The sky darkened and I finished my drink, slapping at zancudos. Somehow, without even realizing it, I had made up my mind.

I called Gabriel once I was in bed, hair soaking through the shoulders of my bata.

"Mom." His voice in my ear was irritated, as if I'd interrupted something important, which, fine, maybe I had—it was a Friday night. "What is it? Everything okay?"

"Sí, sí," I said. "Todo bien. ¿Y tú?"

"Fine." Then, "I'll be right there!" he called, no doubt to his wife, Brenda. "Sorry. We're about to eat."

I looked at the clock on my nightstand—nine thirty. "¿Tan tarde?"

"Joseph isn't sleeping again. We just got him down. Anyway, what's going on? Is that pinche writer from New York still bothering you?"

"No." I smiled, satisfied. "I'm going to talk to someone else."

"Wait," Gabriel said. "What? Mom, you should have talked to us first! ¿Qué piensas?"

"Oye," I said sharply. "Soy tu madre, no tu hija. You don't scold me, and I don't ask for permission. That's how it works."

"Obviously." Gabriel's voice was bitter. "Okay, explain, then."

"She wants to tell my side of the story." *One secret-keeping woman to another.* She had no idea.

"Ay, Mom, don't be naive! She's a reporter. She—"

"Just listen!" I snapped. "She's young. Not a lot of experience." I didn't tell him about that blog, all white and bright pink like it was regular celebrity chisme instead of people killing each other con machetes y quién sabe qué. I also didn't tell him about her story in *Texas Monthly* about the fiftieth anniversary of the UT sniper. It was good. It made me cry. "If I talk to her, that other writer has nothing. Who would publish his book, without my perspective, if someone else has it? He'd have no reason to keep snooping around."

Gabriel was quiet. Considering. "Okay. So it gets him off our backs and it might not even go anywhere if she doesn't know what she's doing."

For some reason this bothered me, how easy it was for him to dismiss Cassie Bowman, aunque this had been my reasoning, too.

"Well, I don't know about that," I said. "But at least I can try to control what she writes."

"Forget about controlling it, how about *stopping* it?" Gabriel's voice rose, and I imagined him pacing in front of that obscenely big TV that took up practically a whole living room wall. "Look—I'm *coming*!" he called again to Brenda. He was going to wake Joseph if he kept that up. He lowered his voice, presumably so Brenda wouldn't hear. "I just don't want everything with Dad and—"

"Ya sé, ya sé," I soothed, the way I did when the cuates were little and constantly scraping off their top layer of skin, blood blooming to the surface. *Ya sé, ya sé, I know it hurts,* I would say, before wiping their cuts with alcohol, knowing it was about to hurt even more before it felt better. "Don't worry, mijo—I know what I'm doing."

It crept back into me then, this long-slumbering part, sniffing itself awake. The part of myself I'd discovered with Andres and buried since his death. The part that only came alive—powerfully, desperately, impossibly alive—when I risked everything I loved.

So I'd called Cassie Bowman.

And now I waited.

CASSIE, 2017

I rang Dolores's doorbell, laptop bag cutting into my shoulder. Rose-bushes flanked the front door. Up close, the flowers looked wild and out of place in the tidy suburban neighborhood, a spiraling universe inside every bloom, the scalloped edge of each petal almost savage. Their fragrance hovered, thick, and I almost gagged. That smell—my mother's funeral.

I was about to ring the bell again when the door opened. Dolores stepped out wearing another sleeveless white linen blouse, this one with tiny pink and green flowers embroidered on the collar. Her jeans were faded almost white at the knees. Her once long, curly black hair was mostly silver, cut to the collar and blow-dried straight. She wore gold studs on slightly elongated earlobes. So *ordinary*, so unassuming. Aging can be a kind of disguise.

"Hi," I said, wishing I'd brought coffee or doughnuts instead of showing up empty-handed.

Dolores nodded. Though she had invited me here, she pulled off her gardening gloves slowly, deliberately, as if I had interrupted her without warning. "Pase," she said, holding the door open.

Inside, the house was air-conditioner crisp. Dolores led me into a formal living room right off the foyer. White walls, red Persian rug, stiff antique furniture. A sterile, unused room, at odds with her garden-casual appearance, the verve in her coppery eyes.

"So how does this work?" She perched, arms crossed, on the edge of a velvet Victorian settee. "Do I need to sign anything?"

I sat across from her in a floral chair with curved wooden arms. "Not yet," I said, as if I'd done this before. I pulled my phone and digital recorder from my laptop bag. "But I'd love a verbal commitment that you won't talk to any other reporters."

Dolores snorted. "Like if I want to talk to more than one of you."

"Fair enough. For the record—" I gestured toward the digital recorder. "This agreement for exclusive rights was made on July fifteenth, 2017, between myself, Cassie Bowman, and Dolores Rivera."

"Lore," she said. "That pinche article kept calling me Dolores. No one calls me Dolores. He couldn't even get that right."

"Lore," I said, the two syllables clumsy in my mouth. All that research and I had fumbled this most basic, crucial thing. "Sorry."

"Also—" Lore leaned forward, businesslike. "For the record. Nothing about that day." A minute shift in expression, an inward crumpling. "Everything else nomás."

"It's the everything else I'm interested in," I assured her, thinking again of the case file in my car, how I'd pored over the crime scene photos so long last night that I'd dreamed of Andres—his eyes sewn shut, me picking at the threads, picking, picking, my fingers coming away stained with blood.

This seemed to satisfy Lore. She leaned back against the green tufted velvet, glanced at my sapphire ring. "So, when's the big day?"

"Next May." I gave a self-deprecating laugh. "In theory."

"What does that mean?"

"We haven't actually planned much. Weddings are expensive."

A single spear of sunshine pierced through the taupe curtains beyond Lore's head, bisecting her thigh. She kept moving her hand through it, playing with the light. "They don't have to be," she said, almost teasingly.

"You're referring to yours?"

She raised her full brows. "That's why we're here, isn't it?"

"We'll get there," I said. "Let's start at the beginning. Were you born here? In Laredo, I mean," I added, flustered, in case she thought I was asking if she was born in Mexico, though why should that be offensive? Jesus. Off to a good start.

Lore's smile was amused, as if she could read my mind. "I was. Mami started having us young, at twenty-one. Five of us in seven years—imagine? By the time she got to me, there wasn't even time for the hospital. She just squatted in the bath and lifted me out of the water herself. Papi apparently fainted, right at the end. Men. All he had to do was watch, and he couldn't even do that." She laughed, though it sounded brittle, painful. I made a note to come back to her father. "After that, she supposedly looked Papi in the eye and said, 'Unless you push the next one out yourself, she's the last.'"

I smiled. "What did your dad say?"

"Pues, what could he say?" She laughed again. "Mami was the boss."

"Tell me more about your parents. What were they like?"

Lore ran one fingernail beneath another, wiped a smear of dirt on her jeans. "Papi was once-a-marine-always-a-marine. He woke up at dawn. Did his push-ups and pull-ups and then took Mami a cup of coffee in bed. Their room was right next to my sister's and mine. We used to hear them turning pages of the newspaper in the morning, talking and laughing quietly."

"So they were happily married?"

"If there's one thing I've learned," Lore said dryly, "you can never say for certain what goes on in someone else's marriage. But yes. I think so." She paused. "Mami once told me it's impossible to get everything from one person. That at best, we get eighty percent. The other twenty, ni modo, we have to find it somewhere else."

"Like where?"

Lore shrugged. "Papi loved talking politics, not feelings, so Mami had her comadres. She'd pull up a chair to the phone in the hall and giggle like a teenager."

"What did they talk about?"

"What do you talk about with your friends?" she snapped. I had the sense my questions were disappointing her. "Their husbands, their kids. The novelas they were watching, Sunday's sermon at Mass. Whatever."

"And that was enough?"

She rubbed at a smudge on the glass table with the hem of her shirt. She couldn't seem to stop moving. "The way they looked at each other. The way Mami looked at him. Yes. I'd say it was enough. What about you?"

"What about me?" I asked, startled.

"What do you think of the eighty-twenty rule? With your fiancé."

"I guess I've never thought about it like that." Not that I believed in soul mates, but I didn't love the idea of inevitable lack in a relationship, either. Had Andres fulfilled Lore's twenty percent? Even if he did, why go so far as to *marry* him?

"Let's start with the easy one," Lore insisted. "What's your eighty?"

"Okay." I hoped she wouldn't notice the heat rising to my cheeks as I considered. "Family."

The first time I'd met Duke's family, out at the farm, they'd asked me everything under the sun—except about my parents. Duke must have warned them in advance: mother dead, father out of the picture. I'd been grateful for his foresight, their consideration. I was happy to come to them as if I'd burst spontaneously into existence.

"Your dad," I said, before Lore could press me to think about the remaining twenty percent. "Is he still alive?"

Lore shook her head. "Heart attack. In eighty-six. One of those they call 'widow-makers.'"

"Eighty-six," I repeated. "The year—"

"Yes." Lore's gaze was clear and strong, almost defiant. "A few months after . . . everything."

The horror settled over me slowly, like drizzle darkening pavement. Lore had lost Andres, Fabian, and then her father. All practically at the same time.

"After Papi died, Mami never spoke to me again."

Our eyes met, and I wondered who looked more stricken.

"What about your father?" Lore asked.

My breath caught. "What about him?"

"Did he ever hit you?"

"No." The room felt smaller, hotter. No one had ever asked me that before. How could they? "But I knew to stay away when he was drinking."

"So it was your mother's fault?"

"Of course not!" What kind of feminist would I be if I blamed the victim? But my defensiveness gave me away. Because, yes, after a while, I had blamed her. For reaching for his glass—*John, it's getting late*—as if she didn't know what could happen. If she wasn't going to take me and leave, how much of our pain might have been avoided if she'd just let him do what he was going to do anyway?

"Did she ever leave him?" Lore asked.

"In a sense," I said. "She died when I was seventeen."

Lore blinked. After a moment, she said, "Mami passed last year. You think it'll be easier once they—and you—get to a certain age. But it just makes you feel like a little girl again, looking for her around every corner."

We were quiet. How unexpected to have found this commonality: We were both daughters, after all. Motherless.

"How did she die?" Lore asked.

There was a disarming bluntness to Lore's questions, a slicing away of the bullshit that usually fills a conversation. It was unsettling, though also, if I was being honest, exciting.

I swallowed. "Childbirth."

Lore looked surprised, no doubt doing the math. It had been an unplanned pregnancy, at forty. An even greater shock than my mother's age, and mine—almost seventeen—was the fact that my dad, who'd been sober for almost two years by then, had recently relapsed, again. I couldn't imagine how she'd let him touch her in that way. Was it before or after the time he'd elbowed her into the corner of a side table with such force a lump swelled like an orange on her thigh?

He went back to meetings, stopping drinking. And she got anemic, her lips white until she swiped them with tinted lip balm—Burt's Bees, the faint smell of peppermint. She leaned her whole body against his when he helped her off the couch, eyes closed against the onslaught of dizziness. He kissed the top of her head, held her for as long as she needed.

By the time she was eight months along, he had five months of sobriety. He cooked every meal, reminded her to take her iron supplements, walked her to and from the bathroom. Once, I went into their bedroom to ask if I could spend the night at a friend's house. The murmur of their voices over the shower, my father saying, "It's okay, Lisey, I've got you." I imagined my mother's veined belly distended and slick between them, my father running a washcloth along her back, and couldn't bear it. How could she trust those hands?

My father had called me again and again that night. He followed with texts: *Come home now. Not much time. Cassie, please. At hospital. It's happening. CASSIE COME NOW!* I pretended I hadn't seen them. It was probably a false alarm. And if it wasn't, I didn't need to hear my mother panting and moaning, the dutiful husband slipping ice chips between her chapped lips and reminding her to breathe the baby down, the way they'd been practicing. The whole thing violently and inviolably intimate.

When I finally arrived at the hospital, the room was dim. My father was slumped in a chair beside the bed, head in his hands on the thin hospital mattress. His shoulders shook, but he didn't make a sound. The new baby, born three weeks early, yowled like an injured cat from his clear plastic bassinet. Behind that there was only silence; it felt wrong, the sense that something essential had been shut down, like a house without electricity. The machines beside my mother were black, their cords disconnected.

I inched closer. "Mom?" I touched her forearm. Her skin was cool. Her eyelids thin as parchment paper, still as marble. "Mom?"

My father looked up, his gaze unfocused. "She's gone."

"What—"

"She hemorrhaged." He ran his hands over his face, pulling them away wet with tears. "Placental abruption, they called it."

"No." I shook her, and the hospital gown slipped off one pale shoulder. I readjusted it, shook her harder. Her head lolled to one side, horrifying. "Mom? Mommy?"

"Cassie, enough!" In one fast motion, my father reared up and reached across her body—that's what it was now, a body—to grab my wrist. I yanked it away, stumbled backward. A sob winding up my throat as my father collapsed back in the chair. "She thought it was back labor," he continued, faint, as if he hadn't just crushed the small tendons right at my pulse point.

They'd rushed to the hospital, he said—all those anxious texts, me ignoring them at a party I hated, pretending to drink Natty Light from a Solo cup, a sourness I could still taste. The pain had circled around to her abdomen. Then, without warning, before the fetal monitoring tubes had even been attached, a gush of blood. "It happened so fast," my father said. He'd looked around, wondering where the sound had come from—a bursting bag of IV fluid, maybe. The blood must have been everywhere. I stared at his boots, the toes now darkened to black.

A wail ripped out of me as I finally collapsed against my mother. My tears trailed her cheeks, pooled in her ears as I begged her to please, please come back. For so many years I'd hated her for staying—and now she was gone. Permanently, irrevocably gone.

The baby was crying, too, high and hysterical, struggling against his flannel hospital swaddle. His eyes, shiny with antibiotic ointment, still balled shut, as if he couldn't bear to look at the world he'd come into.

The baby. My new brother. Andrew.

We brought him home after a few days in the hospital. My mother had already filled dresser drawers with neatly folded onesies and zip-up playsuits, prewashed in Dreft baby detergent. The leg holes of those onesies gaped around his tiny thighs. His arms and back were covered in dark, downy hair, his skull as soft as bruised fruit. He was otherworldly, not quite human. A creature that didn't belong in the outside world.

It was my summer break, and I insisted on keeping Andrew's bassinet in my room. My father was too wrecked with grief to protest with any conviction. I fell asleep to Andrew's grunts and woke up every other hour to warm his formula at the kitchen sink. I used the horseshoe-shaped pillow someone had given my mom at her baby shower, leaning against the headboard of my bed as I eased the plastic nipple into Andrew's searching mouth. I was the one who ran a washcloth over his body before his umbilical stump blackened and fell, the one who cried as I removed the last remnants of sticky white vernix from his skin, feeling as though I were erasing my mother from his body. I watched YouTube videos until I figured out how to strap him to my chest with the long yellow piece of fabric my mother had bought. I took him to the library for story time, where he mostly slept, and for long walks around the neighborhood, naming the world for him. I was the one who saw his first smile, the first time he pushed up to his elbows, the first time he rolled over. All those tiny monumental achievements that only reminded me of his utter helplessness, his total vulnerability.

I considered taking Andrew with me when I left for UT in August. But I was only seventeen, and his sister, not his guardian. Even if I was granted custody, I'd need an apartment instead of staying in the dorm, and a real job, not work-study, to pay for rent and day care. It seemed impossible. I thought about staying. I really did.

Or maybe that was just something I needed to tell myself.

I'd sobbed as I held Andrew in the driveway. "I'll be back soon," I whispered in his seashell ear, kissing the silvery moon of his cheek. "I promise."

Andrew's whole head glimmered blond in the sun. His eyes were shifting from gray to green, like our mother's. They were wide and watchful as I passed him to our father, as if he knew.

My father stared down at him, almost dazed. He wore his wedding ring. His shoulders were pitched forward after years of working on airplanes. He did not look like a violent man.

But if he started drinking again—which was almost certain with the grief, the stress—how would he deal with Andrew's witching-hour screams? Would he even get up when Andrew needed to eat at night? Where would his anger land, without my mother or me there to catch it? All it would take was one hard shake, one drop to the floor. Every instinct to protect my baby brother screamed inside me.

I left anyway. I chose my future over Andrew's safety. And I had continued to do so every day since.

Lore listened with her whole body. A sheen of tears made her eyes burn copper. Was this how she had pulled it off? A sleight of hand, the magic of making you believe in the intimacy of your connection because you were the one made vulnerable? Now that I'd told the story, one I'd kept to myself for so many years, I felt raw, embarrassed, ashamed. I glanced at the recorder. I wouldn't transcribe this part. I wished it could be that easy to erase it from Lore's memory, to reclaim the power I'd given her. At the same time, I felt light and dizzy, as if I'd been untethered from something anchoring me in place for a long time.

"And how is your brother doing now?" Lore asked. No judgment. All warmth. "How old is he?"

I cleared my throat, trying to keep my voice from trembling. "Twelve. He always says things are fine."

But then there was his recent late-night call, at the farm. The one I had yet to return. And besides, since when had our family's silence meant anything other than secrets?

"Guilt is a terrible bedfellow," Lore said quietly. "I couldn't look at mine, either."

LORE, 1983

Andres calls Lore on Friday, and then the following Wednesday, then Friday again. Lore asks him to describe his office, so she can imagine him as they talk, and it becomes a kind of game—they describe everything to each other.

They describe their childhood bedrooms, Lore's with the two twin beds pressed against the walls, a wooden dresser between them, where her older sister, Marta, claimed the top two drawers and Lore the bottom, the closet where Lore tried on all of Marta's clothes while her sister was in class at Laredo Junior College. And Andres's bedroom, unshared because his parents had struggled to conceive him, and after he was born, his mom had four more miscarriages before they did whatever parents do to stop having babies. His mom always told him he was the light of her life, her miracle, and what teenage boy wants to know he matters that much to his mother? "Now that she's gone, I wish I'd treated her better," Andres says, his regret sharp through the line.

They describe their current homes, his a tenth-floor apartment in Tlatelolco, a massive housing complex about fifteen minutes away from the Centro Histórico. The name recalls some long-forgotten day of her adolescence, Mami and Papi sitting in front of their staticky TV, snapping, "Ya cállense, we're trying to hear," to the kids.

"The massacre," Andres says, "before the sixty-eight Olympics."

"*Yes*," Lore breathes. She remembers now—the horror of the Mexican army and police opening fire on thousands of unarmed protesters, *students*, claiming they'd been provoked, at which point Papi, who'd served in World War II, had shouted, "¡Pinches mentirosos!" and left the room. An estimated three hundred had died. "Were you there?"

"No," Andres says. "I've only been here four years, since the divorce."

His fifteen-year-old daughter and twelve-year-old son—the same age as Gabriel and Mateo, and she can't help wondering, briefly, dizzyingly, if they'd be friends—have their own rooms in his apartment, he tells her. They stay with Andres every other weekend, alternating holidays, and two weeks in the summer. Lore is surprised at how American their custody arrangement seems, and with the first tinge of bitterness, Andres says his ex-wife likes rules. Her name is Rosana, and she, too, teaches at the UNAM. They married young, at twenty-four, only a year after meeting and a year before their daughter, Penelope, would be born. Lore nearly blurts, *You think twenty-four is young? Try twenty.* She stops herself in time.

When Lore describes her home, she doesn't tell him about the JanSport backpacks dumped on the living room floor during the cuates' daily race to the television. She doesn't tell him about their bedroom—the crumpled grass-stained shorts, the forgotten glasses of Coke fermenting to sticky sweetness in the sun, the football-patterned wallpaper border right at the seam of the ceiling.

And, of course, in her telling, the T-shirts and plaid buttondowns and worn jeans on Fabian's side of the closet disappear. Their bed smells only like dryer sheets and her shampoo. No Gillette razor at the sink or dark hair flecking the drain. His creased leather cowboy boots by the front door, gone. No venison in the freezer, no blue-and-white Chevy truck in the driveway. The home she describes is sterile and lonely, with none of the comfortable mess of family life.

It's a sneaky, ugly feeling, this systematic erasing of her family. Like tempting fate, whispering to the universe that she wants them gone. Which isn't true at all.

For months after Lore gave birth, she spent her sleepless hours weeping silently as she stared at her newborn sons, asleep in their bassinets, imagining their possible deaths one by one. She killed them so many times in her mind, convinced she had to conjure every excruciating detail, endure every horror completely in imagination to protect them in reality.

One night, she fell asleep with Mateo breastfeeding beside her in bed. Gabriel's shriek awoke her, and she saw that Fabian, still snoring, had stretched a heavy arm across Mateo's face. Mateo's mottled red legs kicked. Lore gasped, shoved Fabian's arm away, and drew Mateo to her chest, too shocked to even cry. Later she stroked the soft spot on Gabriel's head, letting him pummel her breast with his jerky little fist, whispering, "You saved him." She didn't know how he knew to scream right then, but he knew. It wasn't a coincidence.

She forced herself to stop imagining their deaths after that, sure she had invoked this danger. She feels similarly now, erasing her family with Andres—the fear of invocation.

But the calls are short, and the rest of the time there's no escaping her family's *realness*. In fact, there's only room for thoughts of Andres in the edges of her days: idling behind other mothers (always mothers) in the school drop-off and pickup lines; during her evening shower, rushed because the cuates have used all the hot water; and her favorite, before dozing off to sleep, when time belongs to her alone.

And how quickly memory turns to fantasy. Sometimes she imagines them riding the caged elevator at the Gran Hotel. She curls her hands around the bars of the iron car, stares down at the dancing wedding guests as Andres lifts the red silk of her dress and slides his fingers inside her. She imagines the crowd below suddenly stopping, tilting their heads up, watching.

Everyone fantasizes, she tells herself. Men sneak their *Playboy*s and *Hustler*s, obsessing over women whose allure could never survive the relentless banality of marriage, motherhood. Imagine those parted lips pursed grimly at the sink, hands scrubbing burned milanesa off the pan; those endless legs unshaved for weeks; heaving breasts smashed tight in a sports bra during the rare, clumsy half hour of home aerobics, every movement a second behind the neon-leotarded women on the screen. It doesn't work. Fantasy never holds against the assault of reality. That's why it's so important. A safe outlet. An escape hatch to nowhere.

But women have no such magazines, nor do they have dedicated spaces to act out their desires, should it come to that. La "zona de tolerancia," a walled compound of brothels, strip clubs, and cantinas only three miles south of the border, is nicknamed Boy's Town for a reason. Women have only the potent force of their imagination. And that's all Andres is to Lore. Despite the phone calls, he is, essentially, a figment. The memory of kissing him as unreal as the idea of making love with him.

Fabian had three girlfriends before he met Lore and slept with one of them. Lore had only ever kissed one boy before him, in a truck that smelled like dirty socks and stale Whataburger fries.

In their bedroom later that night, she told her sister, Marta, about the boy's dry lips and darting tongue. Dismayed, she asked, "Is that what kissing is always like?"

Marta laughed. "Bad kissers are bad in all kinds of ways."

Lore wondered if bad kissers could be trained. She wondered if, perhaps, *she* was the bad kisser. The idea mortified her. So, at sixteen, Lore made up her mind: she would kiss as many boys as possible in order to identify the anatomy of a kiss. She knew, of course, what girls who kissed a lot of boys were called, but she couldn't concern herself with such things. This was in the name of science.

But before she could begin her research, she met Fabian on that fated double date with her friend Jenny. Fabian became Lore's second kiss, a tooth-to-tooth fumble during *The Graduate.* At first, disappointment washed over her. Then self-doubt—she was the common denominator. Then they laughed and Fabian leaned in again, and she could tell this was different. He kissed her slowly at first, then touched her tongue gently with his, as if asking permission. When she opened her lips, his kiss was languorous and smooth. Fabian always tilted his head to the left, so she learned to kiss with hers tilted to the left as well. This was the only kiss she knew, and it hadn't changed over the years, except to become less frequent, more intentional. Now, if Fabian's lips opened beneath hers, it was because he wanted sex, and if she reciprocated, inviting his tongue into her mouth, he assumed he would get it. Otherwise, he kissed her chastely, hellos and goodbyes and glancing affection no more intimate than the accidental graze of a stranger's elbow on the street.

We're too young for this, Lore finds herself thinking. But after sixteen years together—nearly half her life—what can she reasonably expect? She often wonders what other people's marriages are like behind closed doors. But marriage is a temple that protects its own secrets.

Still, despite her old, adolescent curiosity, she's never strayed. She's always considered herself lucky, meeting the love of her life before the world had a chance to harden them against each other. And it's not as if she's never had the opportunity. Lore is no Cindy Crawford, but she knows she could have had any number of men in DF hotel bars. She's never even considered it. She loves her husband. She loves her sons. She would never compromise her life with them.

And yet—here she is. With thoughts of Andres crowding the periphery of her mind as she makes pancakes and checks pre-algebra homework and folds load after load of laundry—válgame Dios, the pinche laundry, materializing like dark magic on the floor by the washer, as close as anyone can get to the chore itself—and takes the boys to basketball and track and makes small talk with stay-at-home moms, who still, though none of their kids are home during the day, judge her for working, even in this economy, and of course she has to actually work, and then it's dinner, something easy because Lore hates cooking, and cleaning the kitchen, because it's always been a point of pride with Fabian's mother that Fabian's father never had to lift a finger around the house and now this is Lore's burden to bear, and she has to listen, really listen, when Fabian tells her about the store's abysmal sales, and brainstorm ways to get customers through the doors, which Fabian will automatically reject because people aren't buying, and then finally, finally the cuates are showered and asleep and she's in bed, and now she's grateful Fabian is too distracted and upset for sex because it means she can close her eyes and conjure Andres, who is, of course, all too real.

Rivera Iron Works is a thousand-foot showroom attached to an aluminum-sided warehouse off McPherson Road, a street that barely existed when Lore and Fabian were growing up; go much farther north and the city is still all monte. Fabian was proud to open in this newer part of Laredo. It was symbolic, a way of telling the city that Rivera Iron Works would grow with it. He hand-forged the ironwork for the showroom's double doors, each scroll curling into a gold leaf—growth, Fabian had said, new life—protecting the frosted glass behind them.

At the ribbon cutting, Lore had stood at his right shoulder, the midday sun beating down as Fabian addressed the Chamber and their first customers. "Thank you," Fabian had said, "for inviting us into your homes." She'd looked up at him, touched by his earnestness, right as the *LMT* photographer took the picture. She likes that it's this moment they captured—his pride in the store, her pride in him.

On this Saturday morning in October, there are only four cars in the lot. Fabian has let two other employees go since laying off Juan in August. Now it's Fabian, one fabricator, one saleswoman, and the bookkeeper. A skeleton crew, he calls them, for ghost customers.

Inside, the showroom smells like metal and cinnamon potpourri. At the counter, Olga, the saleswoman, hurries to close the morning paper.

"Morning," she says to Lore, then grins at the cuates. "Let me guess. ¿Quieren paletas?" She's already pulling two chile-covered mango lollipops from her drawer, and Lore's mouth waters as the cuates thank Olga.

"Can we go to the warehouse now?" Gabriel asks Lore, ripping the plastic wrapping off his paleta. He steps on the edge of his skateboard, flipping it up toward his hand. The cuates love riding their skateboards down the ramps. When they were younger, Lore worried they'd get too close to the fabricators, drawn to the orange sparks flying off the metal, but they've learned to keep an awed distance—besides, the work is small these days.

"Go for it," Lore says. "But no skateboarding with sticks in your mouths. I'll call you when it's time to go."

This used to be their Saturday ritual, Lore and the cuates picking up Fabian for lunch at Shakey's Pizza, plates piled high with pepperoni pizza, fried chicken, spaghetti from the lunch buffet. The cuates would hover over arcade games. Lore and Fabian would relax with cold Coors while old Charlie Chaplin movies played on the back TV. They haven't done it in months, but the fridge is empty and Lore thought it'd be a nice surprise for Fabian.

Normally, there's music playing, Top 40 on repeat. Today there's nothing to disguise the lack of customers as Lore threads her way through the existing inventory of doors, handrails, fireplace screens, and home accessories to Fabian's office, where he squints at his IBM monitor. He prefers working on paper, but Lore insisted that computers are the way of the future.

"Hey, boss," she says lightly, dropping onto one of the folding chairs opposite Fabian's desk. She used to tell him his office needed a woman's touch: it was all cheap wood paneling and haphazardly stapled blue carpet. But even when times were good, he hadn't wanted to spend money on himself.

Fabian rubs his bloodshot eyes. "When will it end?"

Lore feels a flicker of alarm. "You're not . . . going to have to let anyone else go, are you?" she asks, low. Olga has four kids and a disabled husband.

"Not if I can avoid it. Especially this time of year."

Lore nods, exhales. "Hey, I was thinking—maybe it's time to hire an ad company. I know it's an expense, but we need visibility right now."

Fabian is gaping at Lore as if she's suggested a trip to Europe: I hear Paris is lovely this time of year! "Lore, what the hell is the point of 'visibility' when the people who are seeing you can't afford to buy anything?"

Lore bristles. "The point is, maybe you could reach the people who *can* afford to buy."

"And who are those people? Seriously, who are they? I want to know."

Lore grits her teeth. The idea she had of them earlier, laughing over a beer at one of the long communal tables at Shakey's, fizzles.

Fabian sighs. "Sorry. Look. I actually do have an idea. But you're not going to like it." He grabs a printout and begins tearing off the perforated edge, a clearly unnecessary task to avoid meeting her gaze.

"What is it?" Lore asks.

"Austin." He risks a glance at her, and she understands why he was hiding his eyes: for the first time in months, they're lit with possibility. "Things are still moving up there. Homes are being built. I could go, meet with builders, form some relationships. Maybe even open a new location."

Heat smolders in Lore's chest. "Let me get this straight. Hiring an ad person is ridiculous, but you want to open a *second location*? Four hours away?"

Fabian turns back to the paper in his hands, as if he's suddenly too busy for her. "I don't know yet. But if there's business up there, then that's where I should be."

"And me?" Lore gestures to the open office door. "And the cuates?"

"Like I said," Fabian says, "I didn't think you'd like it."

"Well, of course I don't like it!" Lore hisses. She closes the door, much more gently than she wants. Olga doesn't need to hear their business. "I work full-time. And I'm supposed to take care of the cuates on my own for—how long, exactly?"

Fabian doesn't flinch. "Months, at least. I'd come down whenever I could. You have our parents, not to mention your sister. You know she and Sergio love spending time with the cuates."

"That's not fair."

"What?"

Lore shakes her head, stung that after all this time, he still doesn't realize. "You think after trying for so long, Marta wants to help raise someone else's kids?"

"Ay!" Fabian shoves a pencil into a sharpener, the whine filling the room. "'Help raise,' that's a little dramatic, don't you think?"

"If you're gone for months? Not really! And where will you even stay?" She hates how already, she's using *will* and not *would*, taking his proposition from the conditional to the inevitable.

"You remember Joseph Guerra?" he asks. "From Martin? He has a guest room I can use."

"You've already talked to him," Lore says.

Fabian nods.

"Fabian," Lore starts, but she doesn't know how to finish. "What about the store?"

"Well . . ." Fabian meets her eyes, and she understands. In the early days, she came to the store every day after working the teller line. While the boys careened around playing hide-and-seek behind doors and gates, Fabian taught Lore how to take inventory, run payroll, process payments, and balance the general ledger. *If anything happens to me*, he said seriously, *I don't want anyone taking advantage of you.* He was always thinking ahead.

"I'm not asking for much," Fabian says. "Come in on Fridays, run payroll. Saturday mornings, go over the general ledger. Stop in every once in a while, so Olga and the guys know there's still someone in charge. That's it."

Heat spreads in Lore's chest like blood from a wound. "Oh, that's it! Sure, just take over everything involved in caring for this family!"

His eyes flash, but his voice is calm. "We're supposed to be partners. Remember?"

Lore glares at him. She used to take such pride in that word, in the image of them linked arm in arm, stronger together than apart. But Fabian gone for months—that doesn't feel like partnership. It feels like abandonment.

"Fabian, what about—" She's scrambling and she knows it. "Diversifying? What else could we sell here that people already need?"

"All anyone here needs is work," Fabian snaps. "We're a bunch of starving dogs circling each other, wondering who will take the first bite."

Lore wants to say now he's the one being dramatic. Then she thinks of the warehouses the bank has leased, one after the other filling up with vehicles and mobile homes, whole cities on wheels locked away. She knows he's right and that this whole "discussion" has been a farce. His mind was made up before she even walked into his office.

She picks up her purse from the chair. "When do you leave?"

He doesn't hesitate. "Tomorrow."

CASSIE, 2017

For every story told out loud, there is the story we only tell ourselves. And behind that—somewhere, often out of reach—is the truth. The trick is telling them apart. And with Lore, that was going to take time.

I had planned to drive home to Austin on Saturday, but I couldn't pass up the chance to spend at least half of Sunday with her, too. After leaving her house on Saturday night, I used my emergency credit card to check back in to the Hotel Botanica.

I stayed up until nearly 3 A.M. transcribing as much of our interview as possible. Afterward, when I still couldn't sleep, I pulled out Fabian's case file. I'd promised Lore I wouldn't ask about the murder. But after meeting her, it seemed even more tragic—and intriguing— that Andres had been killed as a result of her minute decisions, all her seemingly harmless justifications. Because people aren't just murdered in moments; they're murdered in all the moments leading up to that final act. That's what makes true crime so addictive. Godlike, you're allowed to see the intricate chain of events leading to the end of someone's life. You realize that everything you do, every decision you make, might bring you, too, closer to the abyss. Briefly, your own life feels precious.

As I paged through the file, three things still bothered me: the unknown reason for Andres's visit, the unrecovered note he left—supposedly without contact information—and Lore alibiing Fabian. I wondered again if she could have initially thought he was innocent. In their life together, had he ever given her reason to suspect he could be violent? So far, it didn't seem that way.

There was something else, too. Laredo was small. If Lore had left the bank downtown around 5:15, as she'd stated and security footage had confirmed, she would have been home no more than fifteen minutes later. Her next public sighting was at 6:30, buying Mateo and Gabriel Frosties at Wendy's. That, in itself, seemed strange to me—taking her kids out on a carefree outing after learning Andres was in town, knowing her double life could be on the verge of collapsing. Or maybe that's why she'd done it—to get them out of the house, in case Andres rang the bell. (She wouldn't know he'd already confronted Fabian.) The twins had been playing basketball at a nearby park with their friends Rudolfo Hinojosa and Eduardo Canales until six; it would have taken them maybe ten minutes to walk home afterward. That meant, technically, there was a gap in Lore's alibi between, say, 5:15 and 6:15.

If Andres *had* told Lore where he was staying, it would have taken her ten minutes to reach the motel, then another fifteen to get home, leaving her with a maximum of thirty-five minutes with Andres. Significant time, but time that didn't matter when applied to his murder, since she was on the phone with her sister during his time of death and Fabian had left damning evidence behind. But, assuming I wasn't way off base, why would she have lied about seeing him?

How had everything come to that terrible end?

Morning light was sneaking between the venetian blinds when Duke called on Sunday.

"Hmm?" I answered, face half buried in the pillow.

Duke laughed. "Good morning to you, too. Sorry, I know it's early. Just wanted to wish you luck today."

I smiled, turned onto my back. There was a water stain on the ceiling, a murky outline of a hole that had since been patched. "It's okay. My alarm would've gone off soon. I want to review my notes from yesterday."

There was a pause. I realized Duke had been hoping for something else.

"And it's good to hear your voice," I added. He'd been at the food truck when I called last night, and our conversation lasted less than a minute.

He laughed. "Yours too. So—what's she like?"

I thought about Lore's direct stares and intrusive questions, feeling unfaithful to Duke at the memory of all I'd revealed to her about my family, things I hadn't told him in our five years together. Lore was going to extract payment for her stories, and already I knew—I would never refuse.

"Charming," I said finally. "But not in a superficial way. More like because she doesn't seem to care whether you like her or not."

"Huh," Duke said. "Sounds like someone else I know."

"Me?" I laughed, though my initial pleasure quickly turned to sadness. "I'm not like that at all."

"Whatever you say," Duke said, a smile in his voice. "Hey, I've got to start the meat. Be safe, okay? And call me later."

I packed my laptop bag and checked my bank balance. Goddamn it. My credit card auto-payment had gone through, and I was about to dip into overdraft, which made my chest tighten no matter how many times it happened. Unexpectedly, I found a loose twenty in my bag, enough to pick up coffee and breakfast tacos from Stripes, which Lore had said were her favorite. I'd smiled politely. Gas station tacos? God help us. At least they were cheap.

But the barbacoa and chorizo con huevo were simple and flavorful, the tortillas thin with a delicate dusting of flour. We ate on the back patio, where Lore's gardening gloves rested on the table, dark and fragrant with soil, while her black Lab pretended not to be intensely interested in what we were eating.

Crusoe. She'd named her dog Crusoe, after Andres's nickname for her. So many years later, Lore still wanted the reminder of Andres. This told me she'd loved him.

"Lore, have you had other relationships since"—I chose my wording carefully—"Andres died?"

Lore offered Crusoe the last several bites of barbacoa, which he ate gently from her hand. "No."

"Not one?"

"Not one."

"What about sex?"

Lore gazed at the bougainvillea that poured over the back fence. Her profile was somber, her face shaded as though with a widow's veil. "Not that, either."

Thirty *years*, alone. "Why?"

"I was greedy. I had the love of two good men at once. And it destroyed them both."

Something nagged at me. Inside, Lore's house was orderly and minimal, with its white walls and placid gold-framed watercolors. But the front yard had those barely tamed English roses, and back here, glossy-leaved climbers covered the fence, palms sweeping like women's skirts in the breeze. Lipstick-pink bougainvillea and what Lore told me were oxblood lilies, Mexican mint marigolds, and petunias surrounded a small, fenced-in veggie garden. The house and the yards seemed to belong to two different people.

"So now you're, what? Punishing yourself?" I asked.

Lore folded her greasy foil into a neat triangle. "Not punishing. Evening the scales, maybe. How many men have you loved?"

And so the morning went, the two of us like the calmest, most precise butchers, applying our blades with just enough pressure to separate flesh from bone. After a while, I could predict when Lore would ask me a question—always right after she revealed something particularly private or painful about herself. After she told me about feeling like she was erasing—almost killing—her family in her phone calls with Andres, she asked how I would most like to die. I was surprised to have an answer ready: any way but how my mother went, here one moment and gone the next, her body scooped out and hollow.

"What about you?" I asked.

"Motorcycle crash," Lore said, no hesitation.

After a slapdash lunch of Oscar Meyer turkey sandwiches, Lore said, "Let's go for a drive. You should see the places you're going to write about."

Her voice was almost scolding, as if I should have suggested it myself, which I would have, if she'd given me the chance.

"And DF." She turned left on McPherson Road, then swore in Spanish as a car with Tamaulipas plates cut in front of us. "Do you plan to go there? What about learning Spanish?"

Lore's reference to Mexico City as "DF" still caught me off guard—I'd had to Google it yesterday. Now, I almost laughed. An international trip? A language course? I'd be lucky if my card wasn't declined at the gas pump on my way home. And why would I need to learn Spanish if I was going to write the book in English? But Lore was giving me dubious sidelong glances, as if suddenly questioning her decision to work with me.

"Yes," I said. "Definitely. Eventually."

"Are you going to write the book as me or as you?" she continued.

I frowned. "What do you mean?"

She gestured out the windshield. We were leaving behind the FINANCED BY and OPENING SOON signs, the digital billboards for plastic surgery—*Dream it, Achieve it!*—the strip malls that looked like movie sets, a diminutive French Quarter and Times Square, places trying to be other places. A few miles south, the homes were older, with burglar bars, well maintained, the dry grass trimmed, vehicles tucked into carports with tin roofs. A little farther and all the signage was in Spanish. Brick buildings cracked, fissures snaking through homes and businesses as if an earthquake had juddered the foundations. Only a few miles separated Lore's country-club-adjacent home from leaning chain-link fences, El Bufalo Pawn, back seats of cars propped on peeling front porches. The income disparity was staggering.

"This is my city," she said. "My *home*. When you write it, is it going to feel like my home, or like some place you came to see for a weekend?"

I was an outsider, Lore meant. Sometimes, though, it takes an outsider to see things clearly. To tell the truth.

"Honestly?" I said. "Probably both."

Lore grunted.

"Why did you stay here, after?" I asked. "Why didn't you start fresh somewhere else?"

"We were in the worst recession to hit Laredo in God knows how long," she said. "Our house would have sold for pennies on the dollar, if it sold at all. Besides, the cuates were starting their junior year. All their friends were here. How could I take away the one stable thing left in their lives?"

It was one of those strange contradictions that drew me to this story, to Lore: love and duty had kept her in Laredo, but they had not kept her from leading her double life. How did she decide between right and wrong? When to sacrifice and when to claim what she desired, no matter the cost?

Lore slowed as we drove through El Azteca, her childhood neighborhood. I looked out the window at Spanish colonials with yellowed stucco walls and missing clay shingles; tiny Pueblo-style homes the same color as their dirt front yards; two-story neoclassicals with white columns and rusting burglar bars, probably installed midway through the area's decline.

"The Spanish were the first to settle here," Lore said, gesturing. "Only a few families, sometime in the 1700s. It was a part of 'New Spain' at that point. Then Mexico won its independence from Spain, and Texas from Mexico, before it became annexed to the United

States. That's when the river became a border. It used to be just a river."

I nodded, though Lore's swift tour of history only made me aware of how much I needed to learn.

Eventually, Lore parked in front of a small, weathered white clapboard house on a narrow street cluttered with twenty-year-old cars. "The house was left to all of us when Mami died," she said. "My sister, Marta, and I alternate cleaning it once a week, and my brothers rotate yard duty. Eventually, if none of the grandchildren want to live here—which they won't—we'll make the repairs and sell it, but for now . . ." She shrugged. "We can't bear to see it go."

We climbed out of the car, and I followed Lore beyond the house to a weed-choked creek hardly more than a drainage ditch. When Lore was a kid, she said, there were a few spots where small waterfalls formed. She and her siblings used to play here for hours, returning home with their skin layered in salt and silt, clothes and shoes covered in burrs.

She nudged a stick away with the toe of her worn green Nike, then reconsidered and picked it up.

"We used sticks like this and pretended we were Colonel Santos Benavides, holding the Union Army at bay during the Battle of Laredo." She laughed. Then she caught my blank stare and rolled her eyes. "The Confederate States used to export cotton to Mexico through here. During the Civil War, the Union deployed two hundred men from Brownsville to destroy five thousand bales of cotton in the San Agustín Plaza. But Colonel Santos held them off with only forty-two men of his own."

"I didn't know about that," I said.

"Surprise, surprise." Lore's hair stuck to her temples and neck. A rivulet of sweat puddled in the fleshy hollow of her clavicle.

I remembered what my mother had once told our class: *History is written by those who have power and want to keep it. So when you read your textbooks, ask yourself who is telling the story—and what they have to gain by your believing it.*

"Lore," I said impulsively, "why did Andres come to Laredo that day?"

Lore's face closed. She tossed the stick in the creek, where it briefly submerged before bobbing up again, dark and slick as an eel. "¿Ya? You're already breaking your promise? Maybe Gabriel was right. Maybe I shouldn't be talking to you."

I resented the threat, implicit and effective. Lore seemed to think I would write only what she wanted me to write. But that hadn't exactly been my promise. I hadn't exactly promised her anything at all.

LORE, 1983

Fabian was right about one thing: Marta is a godsend.

Unlike Lore, Marta loves to cook, and she comes over every other afternoon to make huge batches of flautas, chiles rellenos, and encilantrada. Lore loiters until Marta waves her away with a plastic spatula. "Go!" she says. "Help the cuates with their homework, do whatever." After dinner, she cleans with the same organized fervor, leaving the kitchen smelling like Fabuloso, leftovers neatly packaged in the fridge.

Tonight, after the cuates are in bed, Lore pours herself and Marta a hearty glass of wine each, and they retreat to the velour sectional in the living room.

"I feel like I'm stealing you from Sergio," Lore says, curling her legs beneath her.

Marta rolls her warm brown eyes. "Ay, he heats up leftovers and watches football. He's in hog heaven."

Lore laughs.

At thirty-four, Marta is a part-time physician's assistant who has longed for children since her early twenties. She and Sergio started trying right before Lore found out she was pregnant, and the sisters were thrilled, imagining themselves draped in ugly muumuus, complaining about their swollen ankles together. They talked about how close their kids would be, more like siblings than cousins. They'd go to the same schools, vacation together in San Antonio and Port Aransas. At carne asadas, Sergio and Fabian would stand at the barbecue pit and joke, "Do they even need us?" God, they were so young. Lore twenty and Marta twenty-two, newlyweds both, never once considering that life might not go as they'd planned.

The day Lore received her blood test results, the four of them celebrated in Lore and Fabian's tiny kitchen. She and Marta primly sipped Sprite while the guys downed cold Micheladas. They were sure, so damn sure, that Marta's positive test was right around the corner.

But as Lore's belly ballooned, Marta's remained stubbornly flat. Then, during Lore's first ultrasound at thirteen weeks, Dr. Sosa had said, "Well, look at this—double trouble!" Two babies, the way it should have been, except Lore was hoarding them both. Though there was no way of knowing the months would stretch to years, Lore sobbed in Fabian's steaming-hot truck. "It's not fair—it's like I've taken her baby." Fabian laughed, kindly, rubbing her sweaty back as she dripped snot onto his shoulder. "It'll happen for them soon," he said. "Just you wait."

Marta was stoically supportive throughout Lore's pregnancy. When Lore was violently sick in the first trimester, Marta made gallons of her special tortilla soup, the only thing Lore could stomach. In the sixth month, Marta threw Lore's baby shower, fifty of their tías and primas eating shrimp cocktails at Pelican's Wharf, playing baby-themed Lotería and gasping in delight every time Lore laid a new onesie across the lavish, obscene globe of her belly.

After the boys were born, Lore stopped asking Marta for monthly updates. They only talked about it when Marta brought it up, in her matter-of-fact way. "Another year," she'd say to Lore on New Year's

Eve. "Thirty-four," she said on her most recent birthday, meeting Sergio's eyes over the chocolate frosting of her Holloway's cake. "Make a wish," he said back. She closed her eyes, and everyone looked away, embarrassed by the clarity of her longing. Afterward, Lore squeezed Marta's hand. "Plenty of time," she whispered, and Marta's eyes flashed with something complicated and painful before she smiled and squeezed Lore's hand in return.

Lore is careful, even in her most trying days with the cuates, never to complain to Marta. And when, four years ago, Fabian started talking about having more kids, Lore only shook her head. "The cuates are more than enough," she said, gesturing at the expansive mess of their living room. The truth was, she would have loved a daughter. But she couldn't present her sister with another grainy sonogram, watching the tiny muscles of Marta's jaw twitch with the effort to smile instead of cry.

Now the idea of more children is unthinkable. Lore lost herself in those early years with Gabriel and Mateo. If you'd asked her then what her favorite meal was, her favorite movie, her favorite hobby, she wouldn't have known. It was as if Lore—the person, the woman—had disappeared, consumed by Lore the mother. The idea of taking maternity leave again, molding her life around a baby's insatiable need while also making sure the cuates were fed and clean, their homework done, chauffeured on time to school and sports—and the house livable, groceries bought, bills paid, her marriage nurtured: quicksand. By the time she clawed her way out, she wouldn't recognize herself.

Motherhood is the thief you invite into your home.

"So how's it going in Austin?" Marta asks.

Lore shrugs, playing with her gold locket. A gift from Fabian on their tenth anniversary, a miniature gap-toothed picture of the boys on one side, a wedding photo on the other. "He's working on a bid right now for a big house on Lake Travis, you know, one of those casotas with thirteen balconies and a boat ramp." They laugh, because in fact, they don't know such houses. "So he's bidding everything: doors, stair railings, fences, driveway gates—even if we get a partial, it'll be the biggest sale we've seen in months."

"Ay, ojalá que sí." Marta makes a quick sign of the cross. "And the store?"

"Super triste." Lore surreptitiously glances at her watch as she swirls her wine. "It's like a funeral home in there. Or no—an ICU, where everyone's waiting to see who will die next."

"You're so morbid," Marta says, and they laugh. "You must miss him," Marta adds, and for a disorienting moment, Lore thinks she's talking about someone else.

"Of course," she says. Then, after a beat, "You'd miss Sergio, wouldn't you?"

Marta grins, swirls her wine with a lazy wrist. "Not for the first week. Maybe two."

There are so many other questions Lore wants to ask: Do Marta and Sergio talk, really talk? Are they still curious about each other? Is it possible to avoid that horizonless plateau in which you do and say the same things out of boredom or comfort or fear, and does Marta think you can love one man and still feel something for another?

Because Lore does love Fabian. Yet, in the month he's been gone, the landscape of her heart has changed. Even now she can feel it, her heart, broken up into many windows and doors, each one opening to a different room, a different world. Her heart is shape-shifting, with some of those doors and windows locking and shrinking, preventing entry into worlds gone spooky with reeds, glinting garbage can lids, ripped curtains, broken things; while others slide open bit by bit, allowing access to rooms that have long since grown stale but quickly begin to gleam; just a peek, her heart says, open that door wide enough to press your eye to the crack, to see what is there, or what could be there.

She glances at her watch again. Almost ten. Andres will be expecting her call.

Lore finishes her wine and gives an exaggerated yawn. Marta takes Lore's glass and rinses them both, as if this is her house.

"See you on Sunday?" Marta asks at the door, slipping her slouchy tan purse over her shoulder. "Don't forget the pan dulce for Mami's birthday."

Lore draws her sister close. "What would I do without you?"

The cuates are spending the night at a friend's house, and Lore prepares for her call with Andres like a date in reverse: she uses her Ponds cold cream to remove her makeup, pulls the scrunchie from her hair, rummages in her drawer for the kind of nightgown she used to wear for Fabian on special occasions. There aren't many of these, and they're slightly too small, the satin snagged in a few places by the rough interior of her wooden dresser.

She squints at the calling card in amber lamplight, finger trembling as she stabs the endless digits into the phone. She's told Andres she's having issues with the phone line, incoming calls not coming through. She has no idea if this is plausible, but he didn't question it. In the meantime, she's given him the phone number of the pay phone outside the bank in case he tries to reach her one night anyway. It's not a perfect solution, but it'll do until she thinks of something better.

"Hello?" Andres answers, the way he always does, in husky, slightly amused English.

Lore smiles. "Hello."

"I was beginning to think you'd forgotten." He makes it sound like a confession, and also teasing, sexy.

"Never." As always when she talks to him, Lore's senses stagger to life. She can feel the seductive curl of his voice, taste the licorice darkness.

"How was a part of your day?" he asks. It's another thing they do now, sharing one precise piece of their day, something surprising or moving or funny. She loves how it makes her look for those moments, preserving them so they take on a kind of magic.

"I spoke to a prospective customer," she says. "The owner of a big freight company. He's looking to open a jumbo CD, upward of a hundred thousand dollars."

"That sounds promising," Andres says, questioning. It's not the type of day-piece they usually share.

"It's good for something else, too."

"What's that?"

"Well, did I mention he's from DF?"

His breath hitches. "Does that mean . . . ?"

"I have a meeting with him next Friday."

Andres is quiet for a few moments. "How long are you staying?"

"The bank booked the tickets," Lore says, "so I leave Saturday." The regret in her voice is real, but she's also relieved. Until tonight, she wasn't even sure she was going to tell him. Talk is not touch, after all. If they were to see each other in person . . .

"That gives us Friday night," Andres says with a tinge of wickedness. "That's if—you're not having dinner with the client, are you?"

"I am, unfortunately."

"Of course. Then—a nightcap? Or . . . Maybe you'd like to see the view from my apartment?" He laughs. "That was terrible."

Lore laughs, too. "Let's not get ahead of ourselves," she teases, though of course they're already ahead of themselves, or perhaps twelve years behind. She squeezes her eyes shut at the thought of him ever learning about Fabian, how completely she's misled him.

No, not misled—deceived.

"Fair enough," Andres says, though the wickedness hasn't disappeared, and she feels a quick, painful-sweet pang of longing between her legs. "Tell me," he says, as if he can read her mind, "what are you wearing?"

And so she describes the satin nightgown, the lace that falls at the tops of her thighs, the deep V at her chest where she dips her finger, the swell of her breasts. She doesn't tell him about the snag, or the way the satin stretches tight over her belly, or how the lace has become descosido at the edges. She doesn't tell him that her panties are faded green cotton. When he asks, "Are you wet?" she swallows hard, slips a finger between her legs. She's never used her own hands as proxies for someone else's desire. She is surprised by how desirable she feels.

"Yes," she whispers.

"I want to taste you," he says, and Lore closes her eyes, giving in to the fantasy once more.

Despite the occasional loud calls to maintain El Azteca, to preserve it—as if a neighborhood can be pickled, held forever in a jar—Lore can feel its crumble. The neighborhood is Laredo's proud great-grandfather who insists on living alone, though his bones are already turning to ash.

Her parents refuse to leave. This is where they were born, three streets in either direction, and this is where they say they will die. Even though I-35 now cuts them off from downtown—and even though downtown itself is dying—Lore understands. Home is home.

"Are we almost there?" Gabriel asks from the back seat. "I'm hungry. Can I get a concha?"

"You can see we're almost there." Lore glances in the rearview mirror to make sure he hasn't touched the white Holloway's box. "And no. Not until after lunch."

"What are we eating?" Gabriel asks.

"What do we always eat at Belo and Bela's?" Lore asks, anticipating the platters of fajita, golden barbecued chicken, and chicharrones in all their crispy guilty pleasure.

"Well, then, we have a problem." Gabriel snickers. "Mateo's a vegetarian now."

Lore laughs, turning onto her parents' street. "Since when?"

Mateo grasps the passenger seat to pull himself forward, straining against his seat belt. "Mom, do you know how they kill cows?"

"Very humanely," Lore says, though she isn't sure of this at all. She'd prefer not to think about it.

"No!" Mateo says. "They're supposed to be dead before they're cut up, but sometimes they're not, and they get their tails and hooves chopped off and their bellies sliced open, and they're still alive! Did you know that, Mom?"

"I—" Lore is thrown by the bloody imagery. She parks on the street behind Marta and Sergio's truck and turns around to look at Mateo. "I'm sure that's not true. Where did you hear that?"

"It is true!" Mateo says, insulted. "They're scared and hurting, and did you know all of that goes into the meat? When we eat meat, we're *literally* eating their suffering." He shudders.

Gabriel has been uncharacteristically quiet. Now he says to Lore, "We couldn't sleep the other night, so we watched TV in the game room for a while. You were talking to Dad on the phone." With a smirk, he adds, "Mateo had nightmares."

"Did not!" Mateo says, jabbing his thumb into the seat belt buckle to release it. "Anyway," he says to Lore, "that's why. You shouldn't eat meat, either. No one should! Not until they treat the animals better."

It takes a moment to register: Fabian never calls after the boys' bedtime. She must have been talking to Andres. The cuates could have overheard her! What if they innocently mentioned the call to Fabian?

"Okay." Lore takes the key from the ignition, shaky. "You don't have to eat meat if you don't want to, Mateo."

"Is Belo going to make fun of me?" he mumbles.

"Probably." Lore's father will think this is evidence of a weaker generation of men.

"I won't eat it, either," Gabriel says to Mateo, and they grin at each other, the twin grin. In her womb, their limbs had been intertwined, indistinguishable, as they pushed her belly up in different places, her skin like sand dunes reshaping in the wind. Now here they are, still each other's fiercest protectors.

"Well, then, that makes three of us," Lore says as they head for the house.

Lore's childhood home is an unintentional shrine to the past: the kelly-green shag carpeting in the living room that covers a loose floorboard in the corner, the whole thing pulling up like a scab for the perfect diary hiding place; the black rotary phone on a lace-covered hall table, where she used to whisper to Fabian on the occasional daring late-night call; the tiny galley kitchen—woman-sized, she and Marta joke, no architect or builder ever considering the need to accommodate a man's height with a higher ceiling.

All the furniture is the same heavy wood polished to a lemon-scented shine. The white walls are almost spartan, save for the occasional crucifix or biblical painting, a blue-robed Madonna cradling her improbably blond infant, her eyes holding the knowledge of future sorrow. Lore's mother loves white walls. With five kids, she used to say they were the only peaceful thing in the house. Once, Lore's brother Pablo brought in used matches he'd collected from around the rusted barbecue pit outside and ran them all over his bedroom, creating wild charcoal loops and swirls. Lore remembers how he wailed when Papi—after the belt—handed him a brush and a can of white paint and said, "Fix it." Pablo had sobbed, "I already did!"

God knows how her parents had done it with the five of them. Papi had inherited his own father's store downtown, selling secondhand jewelry and home electronics. Mami had stayed home until Lore, the last one, was finally in school, and then she'd gone to work at the store. Their house was small, only three bedrooms, and if her parents struggled with money, which they must have, the five of them never knew. There was always enough food, and Mami worked miracles on the sewing machine, turning outgrown jeans into shorts, old sweaters into vests, dresses into skirts. On weekends, the kids took turns "helping at the store," which usually meant smudging the glass cases with their fingerprints, leaving early with a dime for pistachios at City Drug. They roamed the city like a pack of wild dogs, feral and fearless. Such innocent times. The world is different now. Though perhaps every generation feels this way; the children grow more insulated from one kind of danger while others grow out of the gloom.

"¡Hola, hola!" Lore calls, pushing open the front door with her hip as she balances the Holloway's box and her mother's wrapped birthday gift, a pair of plush house slippers from Dillard's. Her mother deserves a little luxury.

Lore's greeting is lost in the din. There are Marta and Sergio, Marta wearing jeans instead of scrubs, for once; and Lore's brothers, Pablo, Beto, and Jorge, and their wives: Lisa of the fairy-tale strawberry-blond hair; Melissa, all biting sarcasm and legendary tortillas; and Christie, who even now, all these years after joining their family, has not yet found her voice among them. Mami is bustling around the table, straightening the edges of place mats, and Papi is limping back and forth from the yard with platters of sausages and fajitas. The kids, all eleven of them, ranging in age from three to fifteen, weave in and out of rooms calling, "Did you find it? Where was it?" Gabriel and Mateo instantly disappear among them, with Lore shouting after them, "Did you say hi to Belo and Bela?" Then her attention turns to her brothers, sitting with beers cracked. "Ay, qué padre. None of you can go help Papi?"

Pablo, the youngest of the three and her closest sibling besides Marta, grins. "What, Fabian's gone so you have to nag us instead?"

Beto, the oldest, laughs, claps Pablo on the shoulder. Only Jorge groans and stands. "We've only been out there with him for an hour, but what the hell?"

"Oh." Lore grins, chastened, then ducks into the kitchen to leave the Holloway's box. From the fridge, she pulls out the jug of Carlo Rossi sweet red wine and fills a glass. She's told Mami time and time again that white is chilled, red is served at room temperature. Mami just flicks her hand and says if Lore doesn't like it, she doesn't have to drink it.

"Can I help with anything?" Lore asks Mami, giving her a kiss on the cheek.

"Looks like you've helped yourself already," Mami says, arching an eyebrow at Lore's wine.

"Which one do you want to be," Pablo calls to Lore, "the pot or the kettle?"

Lore laughs. "Oh," she says as Papi returns with what must be the last trays of meat, "before I forget." She glances toward the hallway, making sure the cuates are out of earshot. "Mateo is a vegetarian now," she says with a straight face.

"Veggie-qué?" Papi wipes his brow with a pot holder, ignoring Mami's glare.

"Vegetarian," Lore stage-whispers as the kids' voices grow closer—they can always sense when food is about to be served. "He saw something on the TV about how the animals are treated—don't ask—and he's giving up meat in protest. Gabriel, too, in solidarity. Me too," she adds with a wink, grabbing a sausage link.

"Lore, grace!" Mami scolds, and Lore drops the sausage onto her plate.

Papi shakes his head. "Cuando ustedes eran niños, you ate what we gave you or you didn't eat at all. Los estás chiflando, Dolores."

Lore fights the urge to snap at him. They're too alike, she and her father. They've butted heads her whole life. "They're allowed to have convictions, Papi. It's a good thing."

"Convictions!" he scoffs. "They'll forget about this in a week."

"We'll see." Screw it, now she really won't eat meat, at least today. If Gabriel can show his support, so can she.

"I think it's sweet," Christie says unexpectedly.

Jorge, who's brought in the smell of cigarette smoke, says, "Sure, say that when we're eating pinche *tofu*."

Christie flushes. "There are worse things."

"Tofu's pretty damn bad," Pablo chimes in. "Has anyone tried it?"

They all look at Lore, as if suddenly she's the authority on vegetarianism. "I don't even know what it looks like," she says, and they all laugh. "Is it white? It's white, right? And squishy?"

"¡Niños!" Papi bellows.

The kids rush in, a stampede of child-sweat and wild hair, a couple of the young ones still clutching handfuls of pecans from the trees out back. The mothers rise to cut strips of meat into bite sizes and ladle rice and beans into plastic bowls, while the older kids bury their torsos in the fridge looking for the coldest Cokes. Mateo and Gabriel appear at Lore's side, Mateo's eyes anxious as he glances at his grandfather. Lore gives her father a warning glare. Papi says, "Boys need iron. You think I got these by eating broccoli?" He flexes, showing off biceps still burly from daily push-ups and pull-ups, and for a second, Gabriel looks torn. But Mateo sets his jaw and says to Lore, "No meat."

"No meat it is," Lore says, and serves both boys extra rice and beans.

Lunch, as usual, passes quickly. They talk about who's taken the kids to see *A Christmas Story* and begin making plans for Thanksgiving, which will be here in less than three weeks. A tense hush falls over the table as they all consider Christmas, and then Papi, forever a marine, brings the subject back to the Beirut barracks bombings last month, nearly 250 marines and 58 French paratroopers killed by two simultaneous truck bombs.

"Cowards," Papi says, sinking his teeth into a pork rib. "These 'Islamic jihadists.' No match for us on the battlefield, so they hit us at rest."

"Never mind about that." Mami glances pointedly at Papi. "We have something we need to tell you all."

Silence descends.

"What is it?" Jorge asks gruffly. "Your health?"

"No, no." Mami waves the idea away like a bad smell. She glances again at Papi, who slices aggressively into his sausage. "Es la tienda."

Dread settles like a fist behind Lore's ribs.

"Mami, no," Marta gasps.

"What?" Pablo looks between them all, as if he's missing something. "Is the store in trouble? That much trouble, I mean?"

Papi's knife clatters to his plate, startling Lore. "Mijo, what did you think? All people want to do is sell their shit, not buy any. It is what it is."

"You're not closing?" Beto says. "The store's been around for seventy years!"

"Seventy-two, but who's counting?" Papi says bitterly.

"What about a loan?" Lore asks, though banks are under more pressure than ever to ensure their loans can be repaid, and clearly her parents are in no position to do so.

"Ay, Lore." Mami's bare face reddens with irritation. "Don't you think we tried that?"

"And?" Lore asks.

Papi lifts his chin. "The bank said no. So we found another solution. A . . . private lender."

Oh, God. While banks are heavily regulated, there are dozens of fast-cash places scattered around the city, sketchy lenders offering quick turnaround loans in exchange for collateral, with interest rates rivaling credit cards, fleecing struggling customers with up to 30 percent interest.

"You're not behind on payments, are you?" Lore asks evenly.

Her parents don't answer.

"How many months?"

Mami glances at Papi, bites her lip. "Three."

"Ay, Mami." Marta puts a hand over their mother's. "Why didn't you tell us? We could have helped you!" She turns to Lore. "What does this mean?"

"Did you put up collateral?" Lore asks. "The car? The house?" She knows her parents have nearly finished paying it off.

Papi sits up straighter. He and Mami look at each other, and Lore can imagine the sleepless nights, panic mounting. The store folding anyway. Why? Why didn't they come to her?

"The house," Papi says, and Lore can hear in the flint of his voice how hard this is, admitting his struggles, his mistakes, to his children.

"What's going to happen now?" Marta asks Lore, her voice rising. "They won't—I mean, they can't—foreclose, can they?"

They can and they will. Those private lenders are little more than loan sharks, and in times like these, they smell blood.

"It depends on the terms," Lore says. "Do you have the loan doc?"

By the time Marta brings out the red velvet cake she baked for Mami, they've formed a plan: all the siblings will pitch in to help repay the loan, which is no small sacrifice. Pablo is worried the restaurant he manages will go under soon, which would leave them with only Lisa's teaching income. Beto and Melissa are both real estate agents. Jorge is a school principal, but Christie isn't getting her yearly bonus at the law firm where she's a secretary. Marta only works part-time, and there are industry rumors that despite recent deregulation, a savings and loan crisis is on the horizon, which doesn't bode well for Sergio's job. Only her parents and Fabian work directly in retail, and yet the heavy hand of the peso devaluation has struck each of them. They are all wobbling.

Then there's the issue of her parents' retirement. How much have they saved? Next year Papi will be eligible for 75 percent of his social security benefits, though how much can that be? Mami won't be eligible for another four years. Papi is on 60 percent disability, but Lore doesn't know what he receives for his monthly VA check. Her parents are private people, and proud. It's always felt unseemly to pry into their finances. Now she has no choice.

As they're getting set to leave, Lore suddenly remembers her trip to DF on Friday. Her nail beds tingle with a nervous current of electricity.

"Oh, hey," she says to Marta as they collect purses and Ziploc bags filled with meat. "Would you be able to pick up the cuates from school on Friday and keep them overnight? Work trip. I'll be back Saturday evening."

Marta's face brightens. "Of course! If the weather's nice, we can take them to the ranch."

"They'd love that." Lore smiles gratefully. There is nothing better than someone you love loving your children, and Marta loves them generously and unconditionally. If anything ever happened to Lore and Fabian, she'd want the twins with Marta. The thought comes complete and unbidden, and Lore shakes it off with a chill.

CASSIE, 2017

It was almost six, and I had a four-hour drive back to Austin ahead of me. In Lore's driveway, we stood hugging-distance apart, arms at our sides. It was like coming out of a trance. So much between us, so much left to say. The scope of this project felt vast, unfathomable from end to end.

"So." Lore shielded her eyes from the sun, casting her face into shadow. "¿Ahora qué? What happens next?"

In an ideal world—that is, if I had money—I would rent a place in Laredo for a few weeks, spend several hours a day with Lore. Let the stories unfurl in a continuous dream. But there was no way to make that happen.

"Well, I can come down again in a few weeks," I said, though even that was probably a stretch unless I made it a day trip. "In the meantime, I'd love to continue our conversations over the phone."

Lore shrugged. "You just tell me when you'll be calling, and I'll answer."

"How's six o'clock in the evenings?"

"Fine."

Then, to my surprise, she stepped close and traced what felt like a *t*—the sign of the cross, I realized—on my forehead. I could smell her rose-scented body lotion, see every gray hair layered like tinsel above a bottom layer of black. She murmured something in Spanish, her breath soft on my face, followed by "May God bless you and keep you safe." Then, with a brisk squeeze of my shoulders, she walked away.

I was still standing there, unexpectedly moved, when Lore shut the front door.

The Austin skyline was sequined silver against the velvet night, welcoming me home.

Duke and I ate a late dinner of grilled cheese and brisket sandwiches, talked about Lore over nearly two bottles of wine. I'd barely touched alcohol in college. I couldn't separate it from the dread of seeing my father pour his first glass, the rage at what it had done to my family. I was afraid of whatever parts of him might lie dormant in me. But with Duke, I'd discovered the way wine softened my harsh edges, made the world feel more inhabitable. Sometimes I wondered if this was how it had started for my father. If everything that becomes too much starts out as just enough.

Like Dolores and Andres. Entire lives destroyed because of one dance.

After dinner, Duke pulled me into the bedroom, pushed me playfully onto the unmade bed. I laughed, reached for him, let him pin my wrists over my head. He kissed me, and my body responded, even though my mind was still on Lore.

Before I could change my mind, I mumbled against Duke's mouth, "Do you think it's weird that you've never met my family?"

His lips stilled, his weight heavy before he shifted to brace himself on his elbows. Outside, the neighbor's German shepherd emitted a throaty, staccato series of barks, and a car's headlights swept across our tangled miniblinds, illuminating the frown between his eyebrows.

"No," Duke said. "Well, I mean, maybe at first. For a long time, I thought it was just me. Like maybe you weren't sure about us." He shrugged, a motion I could feel more than see, the flicker of a faded hurt.

"Really? I didn't know that."

He rolled off, facing me in the darkness. "I didn't want to pressure you."

"And now?" I asked, fingers in his hair, tracing the landscape of his skull.

"Now what?"

"Is it weird?"

"Well, now it's normal," Duke said. "It's just you."

Duke's answer, though it was the one I'd thought I wanted, teased open a maw of sadness. Lore had described those Sunday lunches with her family in such detail, with such love. It made me ache for something I'd never really had. Or had briefly before losing it. At least I had those memories, though, of my mother and father and me, back when I'd thought we were happy. Not Andrew. He'd never been a part of that family. He only had my father, and I didn't truly know anything about their life together.

I'd spent that first Thanksgiving and Christmas after leaving Enid at my new roommate's house, blushing with pleasure when, on Christmas morning, there were gifts for me under the tree, too. I didn't see Andrew again until summer. I ran to him, arms outstretched. He wrapped himself around our father's leg and hid his face. Those three months we spent together scrubbed from his memory like the vernix I'd scrubbed from his skin. It felt like another death.

Later that summer, though, once Andrew had warmed to me again, I took over his evening bath routine. Every night, I examined his chubby pale arms, the soft pouch of his belly, the backs of his knees and nape of his neck. I looked for marks that couldn't be explained by stumbles I'd seen. I never found any. So, when August came, I left again. I still thought of his unmarked baby body when I needed to reassure myself that he was okay, as if that flimsy long-ago "proof" mattered even one day, one hour, one minute after I drove away.

"Hey." Duke cupped my cheek, discovering my tears with his thumbs at the same time I realized I was crying. "What's wrong?"

I wanted to laugh. I wouldn't even know where to begin—except I had begun, with Lore, and maybe that's why the past felt so close. It was easier with strangers. Easier to bend toward that sweet-tender lure of intimacy. There's nothing to lose by exposing yourself. With Duke, I had everything to lose.

"I . . . miss Andrew," I tried. "I'm such a terrible sister. He called me at the farm, and I still haven't called him back."

Duke stroked my hair, kissed the corner of my mouth. "It's hard to be close when there's such a big age difference, that's all."

"Yeah." I felt the churn of more tears coming, and I fought them back.

Duke's lips found mine in the darkness, and I let them part automatically, dulled by a disappointment I didn't fully understand.

Over the next six weeks, my conversations with Lore slipped into a comfortable, familiar rhythm. Sometimes we talked for hours. Occasionally I interrupted to clarify a timeline or ask how she felt about a particular moment—both at the time and in hindsight—or for physical detail. Her memory was uncanny, conjuring settings and conversations with such photographic detail that I wondered if she restored the fuzzy spots with imagined re-creations: maybe a little better than the originals, or a little worse, for effect.

Lore continued asking blunt, intrusive questions of her own: How often did Duke and I have sex (about three times a week, usually drowsy, after he returned home from the food truck and pressed against me in bed, a dreamlike quality to it that contrasted with my pleasant soreness in the morning, so real and concrete, a secret my body carried through the day); had I ever been unfaithful (no); when I'd last seen my father (two years ago, when I'd spent a secretive hour checking all his old hiding spots for booze, feeling twelve years old again). Our mutual interrogation was becoming its own kind of addiction, an experiment in how far we could push, how much honesty— or at least the perception of honesty—we could demand. How much we could give.

On a Wednesday in early September, I was halfway through a new blog post—a man who had killed a couple for unfriending his daughter on Facebook—when Mateo Rivera called me.

I had left a message for him at his veterinary clinic weeks earlier, around the same time I'd sent Gabriel a Facebook message. Lore was painting a vivid picture of her marriage to Fabian, one of love and also loneliness. But plenty of women were lonely in their marriages without having an affair or marrying someone else at the same time. I wondered, especially in the context of Fabian later killing Andres, whether she was leaving anything out. Other than Lore, who would know that better than Gabriel and Mateo? I wondered how they'd found out the truth about their mother, how they made sense of what their parents had done. How their parents' actions had altered the landscape of their lives, who they blamed, and to what extent. What did Gabriel tell his children about why their grandfather was in prison? How did this kind of legacy get folded into a family's identity?

But Mateo hadn't returned my call, and Gabriel had written in all caps, *NOT INTERESTED*, as if I were selling magazine subscriptions. When I tried again, he responded, *Read the room—fuck off!* The aggression was startling at first, and then I laughed. I had pegged him as a yeller.

Now Mateo wanted to talk. "How about Chuy's, near Schertz?" he asked. "Seven o'clock?"

"Sure," I said. "Sounds great."

I phoned it in for the remaining blog posts, typical it's-always-the-husband murders, so I could focus on my questions for Mateo. I was grabbing my laptop bag to head out the door when he called again: A couple's dog had just been hit by a car. They would need to say their goodbyes. Could I come to him instead?

The sixty-mile drive south took more than two hours through the slog of rush hour traffic. It was after seven when I reached Mateo's clinic, located in northeast San Antonio among older strip malls with Mexican restaurants and car service places. At the Catholic church next door, two towering conifers flanked a bronze fountain where water fell in glimmering sheets.

Inside, the clinic smelled like fur and shampoo and the stale-fries odor of pet food. The walls were eighties wood paneling, covered in bright canvas paintings of French bulldogs and Siamese cats. In an aquarium along the back wall, clown fish flitted in and out of half-open treasure chests. Invisible dogs barked, a disorienting, distant cacophony.

"We board pets here, too," explained the girl behind the semicircular front desk. Her blond hair, woven into a loose side braid, glowed beneath the fluorescent lights. She'd introduced herself as Maggie.

"How do you like working for Dr. Rivera?" I asked, taking a seat. "What's he like?"

"Oh, he's great!" Maggie blushed. I looked at her more closely. She clearly had a crush on Mateo. At *least* a crush, depending on whether Mateo was the type of man who could resist a woman twenty years his junior. In photos, he didn't wear a wedding ring. "He's so good with the animals," Maggie continued. "Even the real scaredy-cats that shiver and shed all over the place end up loving him. Honestly, that's become one of my mottos in life: If my dog doesn't like you, don't let the door hit you on the way out, you know?"

Before I could respond, a back door opened, and Mateo Rivera emerged. He was dressed in blue scrubs and held the door for a couple in their fifties. The man wore dusty jeans and steel-toed work boots, and the woman clutched her brown leather handbag to her chest. The man cradled a towel-wrapped form in his arms. One black paw hung out, and the woman tried to tuck it back in, crying.

Mateo touched the covered form. "He was lucky to have you two."

The husband nodded gruffly and shook Mateo's hand before pushing through the front doors. The woman wiped her nose, fumbling with her purse as she approached Maggie at the counter.

"No, no." Mateo touched her shoulder. "Váyase a casa."

A fresh film of tears glassed the woman's eyes. "¿Está seguro?"

Mateo nodded, his expression gentle. "Claro que sí."

"Gracias." The woman let the purse fall to her side. "Que Dios lo bendiga."

After she left, the room was quiet, heavy. I thought of my childhood dog, Wags. He'd slipped under a gardenia bush one day to die. We'd had a funeral for him in the backyard. I'd written a eulogy in my Tweety Bird journal. There were afternoons I fell asleep draped over his mound of dirt.

"You must be Cassie," Mateo said. He didn't move toward me.

I stood. "I'm sorry," I said. "That must have been difficult."

"It always is."

He led me to a small office stuffed with a desk, three chairs, and a mahogany bookshelf too large and baroque for the space. Among the glazed Mexican pottery, framed diplomas from Texas A&M University, and veterinary reference books was a framed black-and-white photo of a couple and five children. I recognized the clapboard siding behind them—Lore's parents' house.

"Your grandparents?" I asked Mateo, gesturing toward the photo. I wanted to pick it up, maybe take a picture with my phone.

Mateo slid behind his desk and nodded. "The bookshelf was theirs, too."

"It's beautiful," I said. "What were they like?"

When he didn't respond, I said, "You didn't charge that couple for euthanasia."

"No." Mateo adjusted a slanting wall calendar. September was a bullmastiff puppy, lolling sleepily on a sheepskin rug. "People walk in here with a loved one alive in their arms and they leave with a body to bury or cremate. The last thing they need is to pay for the favor."

"That's very decent of you. I'm sure it's appreciated."

"We make up the cost elsewhere." Mateo grinned. "Boarding is exorbitant."

I laughed, startled, and for a moment he looked pleased by my reaction, unexpectedly boyish. His smile faded when I pulled out my digital recorder. "Do you mind?" I asked.

"Actually." Mateo held up a hand, all business again. "I want to be straightforward. I think it's a mistake, my mother talking to you. I don't trust you or any other reporter to do right by our family."

"Well." I echoed his dry tone. "That was straightforward. You could have said that over the phone and saved me the trip."

"This is a family." Mateo leaned forward, an urgency to the curve of his body. "*My* family. How would you feel if strangers banged down your door, demanding to hear about the worst time in your life, then published it for the world to see?"

I thought of my mother's funeral, friends and neighbors descending with wet rabid eyes, an emotional feasting on my family's misfortune.

"I don't get the sense that it *was* the worst time in your mother's life," I said gently. "At least not before Andres died."

Mateo flinched at the mention of Andres's name. "Well, it was for us. Or does that not matter to you, the fact that my brother and I don't want this book written?"

"Dr. Rivera, I intend to treat your family's story with respect. I—"

"But that's just it." Mateo shook his head, as if genuinely baffled. "It's *our* story. What gives you the right to pick at it, scavenge it for your own gain?"

That word—*scavenge*. I saw myself as Mateo must see me—hunch-shouldered and long-beaked, scarlet neck like a question mark—and recoiled from the image. A moment later, I reconsidered. Maybe I was a vulture. After all, where most people see an end in death, crime writers see a beginning. I thought that was beautiful.

"I get that this is uncomfortable for you," I said. "But if your mother wants to talk to me, that's her right."

Mateo opened the shallow center drawer of his desk and pulled out a checkbook. "What will it take for you to reconsider?"

I laughed, sharp and incredulous. "Are you . . . trying to bribe me?"

Mateo's amber eyes held something of Lore in their unflustered directness. "You've never written a book before. You only have a few bylines aside from that"—his voice soured—"blog. This is a big swing for you."

Heat crawled up my neck, where I knew it would stain my skin like marks from invisible fingers. "Good thing I'm not afraid to hold a bat."

His mouth twitched, a surprised almost-smile. He rolled a pen between his palms—*click rasp, click rasp, click rasp*—and I couldn't help it: I wanted to know how much he was willing to pay.

"I don't mean to insult you," he said. "I remember what it was like to be starting out, barely scraping by, student loans up to here. I'm just saying, I'd like to help you."

Without breaking our stare, which made me prickly and hot, I turned on the recorder. "I don't need financial assistance from you, Dr. Rivera. Tell me, does your mother know you're making this 'offer'?"

The corners of his eyes pinched.

"I didn't think so," I said. "She's a grown woman. How would she feel to know her son doesn't think she's capable of making reasonable choices for herself?"

He drummed his fingers on the desk. There was a light square on his wrist where a fitness watch might usually sit. "I was hoping we could keep it between us."

"If I said yes, you mean." I laughed. "Trust me, your mother would know something was up if I suddenly decided to abandon this project. Which I'm not going to do. Not for any reason."

Mateo closed his eyes and pressed his knuckles between his eyebrows. "So that's a no, then."

"That's a no."

"It almost destroyed us, you know." Mateo's jaw was sharp, clenched. "It did destroy us. But we managed to move on with our lives. To come back together. And now here we are again, because you think it's a good story."

It sounded damning. But his objections ignored the fact that Lore *wanted* me to write this book. He and Gabriel were the ones trying to silence her. Who was more wrong here?

"My mother died before I got to ask her anything real about her choices in life," I said quietly. "You don't know how much I wish she'd left behind journals or letters, anything that would help me understand her better."

Mateo considered me, a lingering, open gaze. "I'm sorry to hear that."

I nodded. Then I asked, "Do you think you've forgiven her?"

I expected him to shut me down. Instead, he set his checkbook back in the drawer and closed it. "Most of the time."

"It must have been hard, though."

His gaze was distant and fractured, as if trying to look at too many things at once. "We moved in with my aunt and uncle after everything. Then we both left Laredo for college." He focused on me with that unnerving directness. "Sometimes you just have to leave."

My mouth went dry, and for a moment I wondered if, for some reason, Lore had told him about Andrew; if my secrets were actually safe with her. But no. Mateo simply understood. He, too, had been harmed by his parents' secret selves.

"But?" I held my breath, ready for him to remember who I was and why I was here. Though maybe he saw something of himself in me, as well.

He shrugged. "She's my mother."

The tangled glittering history in those words—the generosity of his heart—made the veins throb at my wrists.

"How about Gabriel?" I asked. "Was he able to maintain a relationship with your mom?"

"Not until the kids came." Mateo turned a frame on his desk to face me: Joseph and Michael, I knew from Gabriel's Facebook. Squinting up at the camera, noses white with sunscreen, swim trunks drooping with water and sand.

I smiled. "Adorable. And you? No kids?"

Mateo turned the frame back around and held it, staring at his nephews' windblown hair and sparkling baby teeth. "No."

"What about your father? What's your relationship like with him?"

He didn't look up from the photo. "He's in there, I'm out here. It's hard to find . . . points of connection."

"How do you feel about what he did?"

Mateo set the frame down, too hard; it fell over, and he righted it. "Can you even imagine what it was like, opening the door to someone who tells you everything you believe about someone you love is a lie?" Mateo's voice trembled; all ten fingers pressed into his desk. "He did what he felt he needed to do. Of course, I wish he hadn't. I wish none of it had happened, which is why," he said, standing, "I also wish this whole damn thing would go away. Please," he added, a final plea. "Think of my nephews."

"They'll find out one day anyway," I said. "At least this way, they'll hear it in your mother's words."

Face-to-face like this, Mateo reminded me again of a greyhound, the ropy muscle and sinew, bright soft eyes. He extended a hand toward the door. "Your words, you mean."

LORE, 2017

In September, I drove up to San Antonio to celebrate my birthday with the cuates. They didn't like me driving. Mateo would come to Laredo, he said. We could go to Palenque Grill or wherever I wanted. Pero por amor de Dios, I was turning sixty-seven not ninety. My blood sugar was "slightly elevated, something to watch." And my body was taking longer to warm up in the mornings, knees locking, ankles stiff. But even Rolexes need constant motion to keep telling time. I took Crusoe, con su "mucha energía," for a two-mile walk most evenings. I knew the slide of wet soil beneath my nails, the sun at my back, and it was then I felt young, Marta and I digging holes in the dry grass of our childhood backyard, excavating cold silvery worms from hiding.

Besides, the whole point was to get out of Laredo, out of the same old, same old, for a little while. Talking to Cassie was making me restless. It was making me want things.

I admit, though, the highways did make me nervous. How suddenly the two lanes of I-35 widened into three, then four, with exits flying at you one after the other. At the hospital mural of the child with angel wings, I made the sign of the cross and a wild last-minute swerve left onto 281. I was sweating but grinning. I was glad I'd told Gabriel I wanted to come early, instead of driving up with them tomorrow. I would die for my grandsons, pero road trips with them? No, thank you.

I passed the Pearl on my left, apartment buildings on my right. Now that I had left all the mugrero of downtown, there were gentle hills and thick green live oaks all around. As I drove to Mateo's town house near the Quarry, I felt my vision widening—exactly how I used to feel when the plane landed in DF. As if I'd had tunnel vision before and now I didn't. I could breathe deeper, too. It made me want to cry: this was all it took, a little drive to San Antonio.

In the five years since my retirement, my life had become so small. One of the cruelest parts of getting old is how unnecessary you become, like a helium balloon released by a child's hand, floating and forgotten, drifting toward the inevitable pop. Suddenly I was needed again—by Cassie and her ambition, and by my family. It was up to me to define our legacy.

Mateo made Parmesan risotto for dinner. It was only the two of us at the town house he'd bought after his divorce two years ago. I still wasn't sure what exactly had happened with him and Liane. I assumed it was all the stress and financial hardship of the IVF. Mateo never talked about it. He was like Fabian that way, holding his disappointments close.

He was forty-six now. He'd have to marry someone much younger if he wanted to have babies. And if he didn't, well. He'd be saved from certain heartbreaks, yes, but what about when he was old, and I was no longer around? Not that I'd needed to take care of him for a long time. I just hated to think of him todo solito here. Whenever I asked him if he'd met someone, if he was on all esos dating apps, he'd smile and say, "When there's someone worth meeting, you'll meet her."

After dinner, we settled on the big gray sectional and flicked through the TV guide. When I saw *Dateline*, I said, "Ah, eso."

Mateo glanced at me, brows raised. "Since when?"

I'd never much been into "true crime." Even the name was ridiculous. A crime was a crime. It was only in the retelling that it became true or false, and I bet mostly false, because everyone had an agenda. But I was curious now. Cassie had told me she used to watch this show with her mother. I wanted to see if I could feel what she felt back then.

The episode started with an aerial view of a mansion on acres of green land. The teasing of "explosive fights, torrid affairs, deadly secrets—and a wicked plot." Then the blond reporter started interviewing a doctor about the woman he'd married. There were black-and-white college yearbook photos. The doctor calling her "caring and supportive of me. She was there when I had to study very long hours."

I snorted.

"What?" Mateo was half smiling, like he was ready to be in on the joke.

"Nada," I said. "I just hate it when men describe their wives in relation to themselves."

The reporter was going on, talking about the wife eventually earning her own PhD.

"¿Ves?" I said. "Did you hear him call her smart or ambitious?"

Mateo laughed. "It was a two-second clip, Mom."

The reporter, dressed in a fuchsia lace dress, asked, "When you said your I dos, did you both feel it was right?"

The doctor looked down and to the right. Did that mean he was about to tell a lie, or that he was thinking? I could never remember.

"I did," he said.

The couple got rich, apparently, and the wife "developed quite an appetite" for the finer things. Forty thousand dollars on her monthly credit card bills. A stay-at-home mom of three with a full-time nanny, who started book clubs and cooking clubs and was out four nights a week, while the doctor apparently worked day and night to support them, aunque I'd never heard of a podiatrist who worked nights before. Eventually, he started having an affair.

"Ah, pues, qué bueno, he found some time after all," I said, enjoying myself.

Mateo stiffened—I'd stuck my foot in it. He tossed me the remote. "I'm getting up early for a run tomorrow. Night, Mom."

"Night, mijito." I stood and kissed him on the cheek. He held his body tight, and I knew he didn't want to be here with me anymore, thinking of Andres and me and Fabian, Cassie and the book. I paused the show, only resuming once he'd gone upstairs.

I watched the rest of the episode—qué bárbaro. They'd started out as if the doctor were the victim, and now he and his new novia were offering to pay a car salesman $100,000 to run over the wife and make it look like an accident. Apparently, money was making divorce proceedings messy. Pero the car salesman wasn't cut out to be a hit man. He went to the police and wore a wire for their next conversations. The doctor and the novia were arrested.

"Ándale pues," I said, satisfied. It seemed to me the whole thing was about punishing a woman who wanted too much, and I was glad they hadn't gotten away with it.

In bed later, I Googled the wife. I watched a press conference where she pushed for a bill that would impose stricter sentencing for conspiracy to commit murder. She was elegant and composed in a black belted dress with gold buttons, straight dark hair past her shoulders. The only time her voice shook was when she said the hit man was told that if the couple's oldest daughter, who had severe special needs, was in the car with the wife, so be it. But if the other two kids were there, he should not go through with the attempt. She said it was a struggle to get out of bed every day, but that she was doing it for the sake of her children.

The *Dateline* show was entertaining, I had to give it that. But the only thing that felt *true* was the shake in this woman's voice when she spoke about her kids, which to me seemed less like sorrow and more like rage.

On Saturday morning, before Gabriel and his family arrived in town, Mateo treated me to shopping at La Cantera. He bought an iced coffee and waited at one of those iron tables outside Nordstrom while I tried on and squirmed out of silky printed blouses and skinny jeans—those fashion designers must be laughing, no longer bothering to hide exactly who their clothes were meant for—before finally slipping into a red dress. The fabric was stiff on the bodice, supporting and tucking, and flared out softly from the waist down.

Qué vergüenza, that young salesgirl urging me to stand on a circular pedestal, to consider the fit from all angles. I tried to brush her off, saying, no, no te preocupes, it's fine. But she insisted. It had been so long since I'd really looked at myself, and now here we both were, bearing witness to my body in a red dress. It felt like saying: I am still alive. I am still a woman.

That night, Mateo arranged for a friend to babysit Michael and Joseph so that he, Gabriel, Brenda, and I could have my birthday dinner on the River Walk. I came downstairs—so many stairs in that pinche town house, three flights—feeling flushed and shy, the red jersey fabric swishing around my knees as I briskly grabbed my purse and phone. It was Michael, five years old and leche-quemada eyes wide, who said, "Güela! You look like a princess!"

I swelled with ferocious love. "No, precioso," I said, bending to kiss him. "I look like a *queen*."

It was still too hot to sit outside, really, but I insisted, hungry for the lights, the laughter, the languorous glide of red tour boats on the river. So we sat at a white-clothed table and ordered wine and I sighed, smiling, watching the cuates scan the menus with the same focus they'd had as toddlers.

They were no longer identical, Gabriel and Mateo. Mateo was

training for the Rock 'n' Roll Marathon in December, already running ten miles on Saturday mornings like a loco. He looked . . .
essential, nothing wasted. He was so handsome, like Fabian, though
it was Gabriel who was built like his father, with those bowling ball
shoulders, the wide chest and panza that still looked firm, though it
was far from flat. Coaching basketball wasn't the same exercise as
playing, and I bet he missed those days: sneakers squeaking on a polished gym floor, ball sailing into his hands. He'd wanted to play in
college, but after everything that happened—junior year hadn't been
an easy time for him.

"So how's it all going? With the reporter." Gabriel glanced at me
as he tore the middle of the sourdough bread from its crust and sank
it into garlicky hummus. Brenda—petite, controlled, opinionated,
the kind of person who only needs four hours of sleep each night—
watched him with an arched brow. A lo mejor she had him on a diet,
not that you could tell.

I smiled as I remembered that first day with Cassie. We'd ordered
sushi from Posh for dinner and she'd insisted on paying, aunque I
saw her hesitate when she opened her wallet, like if she was deciding which card to choose. I slipped a twenty in her bag when she
wasn't looking, the way I always had with the cuates when they left
for A&M after a weekend visit. She seemed younger to me, younger
than she probably felt, and it felt good to take care of someone.

Since then, I'd come to look forward to our nightly calls. Sometimes we FaceTimed over triste little dinners of leftovers or sandwiches. Marta owned a restaurant and did catering now. Sometimes
she brought over trays of fajitas or mole enchiladas that could last me
for weeks. Cassie said she lived on her fiancé's leftovers the same way.

"It's fine." I felt protective. The past had just been waiting there,
a sliver of light beneath a closed door, and it was mine.

"She hasn't asked you to sign anything, has she?" Mateo asked,
clipped.

I took a sip of Chianti. White lights in the trees, windows lit
across the river. I wondered who was inside, what lies they were

telling the people they loved. I thought about Cassie and her mother. Mami and me. The earth rich with mothers' secrets and daughters' unanswered questions. I remembered the bookshelves in Andres's apartment in Tlatelolco, colorful spines out like fish in an aquarium. Imagine a book about me on a shelf like that.

"No, Mateo," I said. "I would tell you if she did. I'm not stupid." I couldn't help noticing that despite having all last night alone with me, he only asked this today, with Gabriel as backup. They were always like that. "It's actually been nice, though. Telling my story."

Gabriel scoffed. "Well, I sure as hell don't want to read it."

My chest pinched with disappointment, though not surprise. I didn't like to be sexist, but that's the difference between men and women. Women are detectives of the heart, constantly seeking, while men prefer not to see what's right in front of them.

Mateo spoke to Gabriel como si I wasn't even there. "Look, realistically, it'll probably never get off the ground."

What, like my story wouldn't be *interesting* enough to publishers? "Well, for all our sakes, we'd better hope it does," I snapped. "Otherwise, that other writer might come into the picture again."

I'd called the New York gringo back after that first weekend with Cassie. He'd sounded so smug, as if he'd known I would change my mind. His voice had thinned when I told him I'd decided to talk to someone else. "I'm sorry to hear that," he'd said, then wanted to know who it was. Afterward I imagined him like a dog, licking his wounds, unable to resist one last snap. "Best of luck going with a nobody."

"I told you," Brenda said unexpectedly, looking at Gabriel.

He flushed, dark and blotchy. "Brenda," he hissed.

Brenda looked from him to Mateo, who suddenly couldn't keep his eyes off the ducks waddling between the tables in hopes of scraps. Something dawned in her expression. "Shit," she said, and while normally, just out of habit, los regañé for swearing, this time I let it go.

"What?" I focused on Mateo. "Dime."

He pushed his bread plate aside, taking a sip of water. "We——"

His *we* always included Gabriel. Sometimes it *only* meant Gabriel. "I offered to pay the writer to drop the whole thing. I assumed she would've told you."

"I told Gabriel it didn't make any sense." Brenda swept a hand over her already-smooth ponytail, not a single flyaway, even in this humidity. "Then what, the other guy swoops right back in, and you didn't like him, right, Lore?"

"That's right." I was surprised at how steady my voice sounded, because inside I was quaking with rage. I could feel it rolling off Gabriel, too, so I knew it must have been his idea, inelegant and crude, but maybe, they thought, if presented by Mateo, it stood a chance. Only Cassie had said no. I felt a warmth toward her, tempered with irritation that she hadn't told me. "That was stupid," I said, directly to Gabriel. "And how dare you go behind my back like that?"

Gabriel snorted. "That's rich coming from you, Mom. Really."

"I talked to Dad," Mateo said, an abrupt subject change as our waitress came to settle our plates before us. She smiled apologetically at the interruption.

"Should we say grace?" Gabriel asked once she left. He and Brenda went to some megachurch in Dallas, but they still said Catholic grace. Apparently you could pick and choose. We clutched hands grimly and bowed our heads.

"I talked to Dad," Mateo started again after the prayer. He twirled a fork in his pasta primavera. Todavía vegetarian, after all these years. "He says she's made a couple of interview requests with him. She's pretty persistent, isn't she?"

I cut a shrimp in half, speared it, wrapped it in a layer of spaghetti. Si tuviera una hija, I would have liked for her to be called persistent. "She told me," I said curtly. Eso, at least. I didn't like it, though I knew Fabian would say no. "And a woman needs to be persistent, in this world."

"Oh, so you're a feminist now, too?" Gabriel rolled his eyes.

Brenda smacked his shoulder. "We should all be feminists."

"Ustedes dos," I said to the cuates. "Look at me."

They did. They were men, yes. But I was their mother. They would listen to me. They had no other choice.

"Just remember," I said, recalling something Cassie had told me about her mother, "whoever tells the story has the power."

"There's power in withholding as well," Brenda said, pinche devil's advocate.

¿Tú qué sabes? I wanted to ask her. But I let my gaze slide over her, back to the cuates.

Gabriel took a reckless swig of wine. "What, you're saying to talk to her? No. No way."

"Solo estoy diciendo," I continued, "I haven't talked about any of this, either. But maybe it's time."

Gabriel stopped short of slamming a palm down on the table. "What, like this was all something that happened *to* you, something you need to 'process'? Must be nice to be treated like a victim instead of—"

"I have never made myself out to be a victim," I said, each word crystalline sharp, blown glass. "¿Me oyen? And I am not starting now."

CASSIE, 2017

A few days after my conversation with Mateo Rivera, I opened Facebook, searching for Gabriel. It had become a habit, as perversely comforting as my favorite subreddit. Gabriel and Brenda refused to speak to me, and yet they'd show their home and children and inner lives to complete strangers on the internet. Sometimes they posted from the same park or restaurant, and I saw the world from both their eyes simultaneously. Brenda preferred filters that heightened contrast, making the world seem hyper-real, almost harsh. Gabriel often used black-and-white or sepia on his sons, captioning them with things like "Everything I learned about being a dad, I learned from my dad," and "There is no love like a father's love. Thanks for everything, Dad." Sweet, although I doubted Fabian had access to Facebook in prison.

Fabian's case file included half a dozen videotaped interviews. I had rented a VCR online for two dollars a day, far cheaper than any option I'd found to convert them. On Duke's night off, I held the first tape aloft.

"Police tape and chill?" I asked.

Duke glanced up from his Fantasy Football group chat. He looked bewildered for a second, then comprehended. He made a face. "You know that's not really my thing, Cass."

"Oh, come on." I fed the tape into the VCR, and the click and whir spun me back to a million moments in my childhood. "It'll be fun." The word *fun* was clanging and out of place, but I wanted to make him understand why I cared, to see this part of me. So I opened a bottle of wine and even, with a curdle of shame, made popcorn. Finally, he shrugged and set his phone aside. We settled in together, our butter-slick fingers sliding against each other in the stainless steel bowl.

The footage was instantly familiar: the gray-box room, the two-way mirror, the clattering metal chairs. How many rooms like this had I seen on TV over the years, starting with those Friday nights with my mother? There is such comfort in feeling that soon you'll know everything; that for an hour, certainty exists. Though this was different—raw, unedited, *unpackaged*—I felt a Pavlovian sense of pleasure as the interview began.

In the tape, Detective Ben Cortez was skinny, with a Tom Selleck mustache. The other detective, Manuel Zamora, was soft-spoken, with a gray ponytail and white sleeves rolled right below the elbow. Zamora was clearly the lead. He had a presence.

Then there was Fabian, brought to life before my eyes. "He's so young," I murmured, glancing at Duke, with his boyish mop of blond curls. Duke and video-Fabian were only a few years apart. How would Duke react if a stranger knocked on the door, claimed to be my husband? If he actually *was* my husband?

The interview began with Zamora establishing names, dates, and Fabian's relationship to Lore. When he got to Andres, the tone shifted.

"I can tell you're a smart guy," Zamora said. "You must have known about the affair. Dime, when did you find out?"

Fabian rubbed his black beard, slightly unkempt. "Friday."

"When Russo knocked on the door," Zamora supplied.

Fabian nodded.

"That'd be around what time?"

"I don't know. Four. Five. I wasn't keeping track."

"Easy to lose track without a job, right?" Zamora said sympathet-ically. "This fucking recession, te digo."

Fabian crossed and uncrossed his arms.

"All right." Zamora leaned in. "So Russo knocked on the door around four or five on Friday. But that's not when you *found out*, right?"

"Yes. It is." Fabian turned to look at Cortez, who was pacing ca-gily behind him. "Look, I'm still trying to wrap my head around it."

Cortez shook his head. "Puro pedo, güey."

"¿Tú crees?" Zamora said.

"What are they saying?" Duke asked.

"You think I speak Spanish all of a sudden?" I said with a laugh. "But they obviously think it's bullshit."

"I mean, it *is* kind of unlikely he wasn't even a little suspicious," Duke said. "Don't you think?" He looked at me with something like hope.

"Probably," I said, aching a little. I pressed pause. "What would you do?" I blurted.

Duke's arm brushed mine as he reached for his wineglass. "If you were secretly married to someone else?"

"Yeah."

"Might explain why we haven't planned anything for the wed-ding." He was teasing, though I still felt the barb, the question, be-neath his words. I swatted his shoulder.

"Seriously."

"Seriously?" He took a sip of wine. "Well, I don't think I would kill anyone, if that's what you're asking."

"But how would you *feel*?" I pressed, searching for something, though I couldn't say what.

Duke set his glass back on the coffee table and shifted on the love seat so one knee pressed against mine. "How do you think I'd feel,

Cass? If you could keep something like that from me—*do* something like that? I'd feel like you'd torn out my fucking heart."

I nodded. I guess I'd just needed to know it would hurt.

Then I thought of something. "Let's say I did, though. And you found out like Fabian did. Who would you be angrier at—me or the other guy, who clearly didn't know about you, either?"

"Assuming you're not trying to tell me something here . . ." Duke trailed off. "You. But maybe it would be easier to take it out on him. Someone I didn't love. You know?"

"That makes sense." Andres as a surrogate for Lore. I intertwined my fingers with Duke's and squeezed, then pressed play.

"Come on," Cortez said to Zamora, as if they were arguing about a football play. "¿Cuántos años has estado casado?"

"Veintitrés," Zamora said.

"Me, last year," Cortez said. Back to Fabian, "So here we are, this guy with twenty-three years of marriage, me with one, both ends of the spectrum, and"—to Zamora—"can you imagine not knowing if your vieja was taking up with someone else? And I'm just talking cheating. Not even the rest of it."

Zamora shrugged. "Women," he said to Fabian, "are much craftier than men, ¿verdad? They run circles around us."

Fabian said nothing.

"Tu esposa es bien inteligente, ¿verdad? Must've been nice having her paycheck to count on in these times."

"Ouch," Duke said.

"Pero all that travel," Zamora said. "That never got to you?"

"Of course it did," Fabian snapped. "Like losing my business got to me. Like not being able to find work got to me. That doesn't mean I killed someone."

"No, no," Zamora said with a laugh, pushing back into his chair. "No one's saying that. We're just trying to figure out what happened here."

They questioned him for the next hour, harangued him about the timeline—Fabian was still saying he was home all night, after returning at eight from his brother-in-law's ranch—before eventually returning to his knowledge, or lack thereof, about the affair. They told him a neighbor had witnessed him shouting at Andres.

"Fuck yes, I shouted at him!" Fabian swiveled his head from Zamora to Cortez, fists clenched. "Wouldn't you?"

Cortez said darkly, "Al chile que sí. I'd do a hell of a lot more than that."

Zamora said, "This güey would get his badge taken, for sure. ¿Y sabes qué?" He shifted, lowered his voice. "I wouldn't blame him."

"I told him to get the hell off my property," Fabian said through gritted teeth. "He did. That's the last time I saw him. Can I go?"

Zamora sighed, closing his notepad. "Fabian. We dusted all over that room for prints. Everywhere you can think of and probably a few places you can't. So if you were there, se va a ver muy mal if you don't tell us about it now. If you went to talk, things got out of hand, maybe he came at you—this is when we can help you. Fabian," he said again, lower. "We *want* to help you. You didn't deserve this—what she did."

I watched Fabian closely. His back was rigid, his chest pulsing with shallow breaths. It wouldn't take much more to make him explode.

"I had nothing to do with that man's death." Fabian spoke evenly, but the effort it took—all the muscles in his face strained—was exhausting to watch. "Neither did Lore. She was with the cuates all evening, and then we were all home together the rest of the night."

I grabbed the remote, rewound the tape.

"What?" Duke turned to me, startled. He'd been watching as intently as I had, I realized.

"I don't know. Probably nothing." I pressed play.

Fabian: "I had nothing to do with that man's death. Neither did Lore. She was with the cuates all evening, and then we were all home together the rest of the night."

I hit pause.

Duke looked at me quizzically. "Yeah?"

"Just the way Fabian volunteered, 'She was with the cuates all evening' before saying they were home together the rest of the night." I stared at Fabian on the screen. His fingers curled around the edges of the metal table, shoulders curved forward, as if about to launch himself to his feet. "Everyone says she alibied him, but doesn't it kind of sound like . . . he's alibiing her?"

Duke frowned. "It could go either way. Why?"

I set the popcorn bowl aside, wiped my hands, and grabbed my laptop from the coffee table. "Well, I made a timeline of that last day," I said, opening the document. "See? If I'm right, there's this weird gap in Lore's alibi that doesn't show up on the police report. When it counts, her alibi is solid: Wendy's with the twins for Frosties, then a movie, then a call with her sister."

"Okay . . ."

"Andres left a note for her at the bank that afternoon," I continued, "which was never found. She claimed it said 'I'm sorry I missed you.' He'd just found out she was married to someone else, so maybe he wanted to leave her on edge with this cryptic-ass message. But it doesn't *feel* right to me. If you were him, wouldn't you be desperate to talk to her? Hoping it's all a mistake? And if you didn't know where to find her, wouldn't you make damn sure she could find you?"

Duke rubbed the joint burn on the arm of the love seat, left over from a party years ago. "I guess so. I mean, unless he decided to bounce after that, go back home."

"But he *didn't*. He still had a room at the Hotel Botanica. I'm guessing maybe he went back there and looked up the Riveras' address in the phone book—you know how hotels always used to have phone books—then went to their house to confront her."

"Okay, so maybe that was his plan." Duke shrugged, as if this solved everything. "To find her. So that's why he didn't leave his contact information."

"But the thing is, how did Fabian know what *room* he was in?" The more I talked about it, the stranger it seemed. Pieces that almost fit together, but not quite. I stood up, started to pace. "The neighbor overheard Andres tell Fabian which hotel he was at, not what room.

The hotel clerk said Fabian never came to the front desk to ask. No one else at the hotel claimed Fabian knocked on their doors looking for someone. So how did he know?"

Duke looked stumped. "Well, what does Lore say about it?"

"Nothing! She shuts me down hard every time I ask. So, let's try this—what if Andres told Lore in that note where he was staying, and she went directly to see him after she left the bank? And then later, intentionally, or not, she told Fabian how to find him?"

It was the first time I'd said the words out loud. It felt like opening a treasure chest, the creak before a possible glimmer of gold. My heart thrummed. Duke was looking past me at TV-Fabian, as if he might turn to us and explain everything.

"Even if that happened," Duke said, slowly, "this Fabian guy confessed, right?"

"Yes, but the confession was a condition of his plea deal. And minus his print, the evidence is more circumstantial than anything."

"What are you saying, Cass?" Duke yanked a paper towel from the roll I'd brought to the coffee table, wiping his hands almost aggressively. "That he didn't do it?"

I thought of all the crime books and shows and podcasts that had exposed wrongful convictions over the years, and something animal stirred in me, a sniffing nose and wide-open jaw, a hunger. But then I saw the crime scene photos in my mind: the sheets and coverlet rumpled on only one side of the bed. Two mini bottles of Scotch, only one glass. Fabian's print the one left behind. Fabian seen at the hotel after ten, precisely within the window for Andres's time of death. No trace of any other suspect, including Lore, in the room.

I bit the inside of my cheek, dropping down beside Duke. "I don't know. I just feel like there's more to what happened than police records and court documents show."

Duke shifted away, almost imperceptibly, but I noticed. "Okay, but if it doesn't change the outcome, and Lore doesn't want to talk about it, why is it any of your business?"

Because it's a kind of honoring, I wanted to say, uncovering step by step exactly how someone's life ended. Duke might see it as an unnecessary exhumation, an exploitation of what should be private, entombed. I saw revealing the truth about someone's death as a way of saying their *life* mattered.

"This isn't the blog, you know?" Duke gestured pointedly at the TV, as if to remind me that Fabian, that all of them, were human beings, unlike, I suppose, all those other human beings whose tragic ends I served up as entertainment. "You're writing a *book* about this woman's double life with her permission—and that's fine. Good for you. But to start shaking things up about the murder when everything points to him *and* he confessed? It seems like it'd bring a lot of pain to a lot of people, and for what?" He paused, catching me in his steady gaze. "For what, Cass?"

I clutched the VCR remote. There was no mistaking his meaning. He thought I was willing to hurt two families for the sake of my career, a career he'd never understood and had probably secretly hoped would never go beyond writing for some blog. *Good for you.*

"I have a duty to find out the truth," I said.

And if duty felt quite a bit like excitement, there was nothing I could do about that.

LORE, 1983

Lore meets her potential customer, David de la Garza, at Hostería de Santo Domingo, a sun-scorched pink building in the Centro Histórico. The cheerful, modest bottom floor is bustling, with paper flags waving from the ceiling, while the second floor salón is all polished wood floors and stained-glass ceilings. This is one of the oldest restaurants in Mexico City, Mr. de la Garza tells her, somewhat unnecessarily, since the year it opened—1860—features prominently on the paper menus.

"You must try the chiles en nogada," Mr. de la Garza says, with endearing boyish eagerness. Like most of the bank's Mexican clientele, he clearly considers it important to be a good host.

They both order the chiles en nogada and Gusano Rojo mezcal, and when Mr. de la Garza offers her a cigarette, she accepts. His fingertips are stained yellow, though the teeth below his dark mustache are strong and white.

"I only smoke in DF," Lore admits with a laugh, taking her first drag. God, that feels good. A burning path back into herself.

"What a coincidence," says Mr. de la Garza. "Me too."

They laugh and toast when the mezcal arrives, and an hour passes before they even begin to talk business. Mr. de la Garza speaks of his company with an owner's pride, the same pride in Fabian's voice, the same pride she grew up hearing in her father's voice. She hears something else, too: worry.

"You're wise to consider depositing in a U.S. bank right now," Lore says, swirling the last bites of her stuffed pepper in creamy sauce. "We're predicting an annual devaluation of thirty percent next year. I'm afraid things are going to get worse before they get better."

"U.S. banks are in trouble, though." Mr. de la Garza pushes away his plate and reaches for his pack of cigarettes. He offers it to Lore, and she accepts. "Am I right?"

He's referring, of course, to Mexico's debt. As of last year, Mexico would need more than $8 billion a year to make its interest payments to U.S. banks. Thirteen of the biggest banks have $60 billion— almost half their total capital—to lose if Mexico collapses, and if Mexico collapses, the rest of Latin America will follow, toppling the whole international financial system.

"You must know we're not a big bank," Lore says. "We're a community bank, a border bank—forty percent of our deposits come from Mexican nationals. Should the peso continue to fall while the dollar holds steady, your hundred thousand will multiply significantly in value. It's a low-risk, stable investment in your business—and you don't need to worry about us going down with the big boys."

"Mmm." Mr. de la Garza studies her thoughtfully.

Lore takes a sip of her second cocktail. "But if that doesn't convince you, you also get me as your banker. And what that means is you have someone who cares about your business and who is dedicated to serving you. I think of my customers as family. And family is everything. Don't you agree?"

Mr. de la Garza leans back in his seat, blowing smoke toward the ceiling. Lore smiles at the waiter who collects their plates with practiced discretion.

"Well, then." Mr. de la Garza talks around his cigarette, leaning forward to outstretch his right hand. "I still believe in sealing a deal with a handshake."

Lore takes his hand. "Welcome to the family."

I᷀t's a short walk from the restaurant to La Opera Bar. Giddy with her success and the glowing beauty of the Zócalo, Lore thinks of Andres's voice on the hotel phone earlier: "No veo la hora." Somehow, in Spanish, "I can't wait" felt true and urgent, as if the waiting might kill him.

She can't remember the last time she felt such exquisite anticipation, everything around her rendered sharp and luminous—the perfumed swirl of pedestrians, the golden arched windows of the Palace, the neon FELIZ NAVIDAD sign pulsating with early holiday madness. She can hardly catch her breath. Her chest is a music box whose key has been wound again and again and will wind no more.

Last night, she'd asked Fabian on the phone, "When are you coming home?"

Fabian sighed. "I don't know, Lore. I'm doing my best here." And he is—he's bringing in sales, and as of this week, stopped paying himself so he won't have to let anyone else go so close to the holidays.

"It's been a month," she said.

"And it may be another six," Fabian snapped. "What's the alternative?"

Lore thought of her parents, the risk they took with the loan, the GOING OUT OF BUSINESS SALE sign on the door. Now she was the one who sighed. "You're right. I'll hold down the fort."

A moment of silence, a bud opening. "Thank you, partner," Fabian said softly. "I know I don't say it enough, but I appreciate everything you're doing. I appreciate you."

Fabian hadn't said he appreciated her in so long. Years, maybe. She was like a good soldier, who kept their lives regimented and smooth, and good soldiers don't get acknowledged until, maybe, their leg gets blown off and they get a medal to pin on their lapel, too little, too late.

That night in the shower, she shaved her legs. She shaved her bikini line. She packed her nicest bra and panties, the black lace she bought at Bealls a few Valentine's ago. She was only a body performing motions that wouldn't mean anything unless her mind gave them meaning, and her mind refused to give them meaning. She was a woman shaving in the shower, packing nice underwear. That was all.

You can still turn around, she tells herself as the bar comes into view. Windows like closed eyes, the interior concealed by scarlet curtains. It's not too late.

She reaches for the door handle.

Inside: red velvet booths, damask wallpaper, ornately carved wooden arches and ceilings. She stands in the doorway, and for a few mortifying seconds she's sure he stood her up. She almost hopes he did. Then she thinks again of the low sandpaper rub of his voice, and it's as if she summons him: he lifts an arm from the bar, and she can tell by his smile that he's been watching her since she walked in.

Here we go, she thinks.

"Hello, Doctor," she says, trying to keep her voice light as she nears him. He's wearing dark slacks and a slightly wrinkled linen blazer, though they're well into fall, and in the dim, his green eyes are all pupil. His hair is tucked haphazardly behind his ears. A shadow of stubble frames his lips, which are as precise as if they're drawn in felt-tip. His features had faded in her memory. Now they are shockingly vivid.

"Hello, Ms. Crusoe," he says, and there is that voice, familiar yet strange. "I was beginning to wonder if you were going to make it."

"Sorry." Lore slides against the dark lacquered bar. The lapel of his jacket brushes her chest. "He wanted another drink to celebrate."

"You got the deal?" Andres's voice lifts, and Lore laughs, gratified by his excitement.

"Yes, short of seeing the deposit hit the bank."

Andres smiles. "Can anyone resist you?"

"Not so far," Lore quips, and she orders a dirty martini, something as glamorous as she wants to feel. "How was a part of your day?" she asks with a small smile.

"Actually," he says, holding his Scotch, "my daughter—Penelope—she went into the hospital this morning. Appendicitis. You know my dad was a surgeon, so I grew up around hospitals—but when it's your child in that bed . . ." He shakes his head.

Lore opens her mouth to tell Andres about the car accident she and the cuates were in when they were four—when she *saw* Gabriel's head whip to the left in the rearview mirror, certain his neck would be broken when she wrenched open the door—and then realizes what she's about to do. "I can only imagine," she says instead, hoping he can hear the feeling in her voice, the way she'd grieved for a million years in those moments before discovering both cuates were okay. "Andres, what are you doing here? You should be with her!"

He smiles, touches her hand. "Thank you, but Rosana is spending the night there. Carlitos is home with his stepfather."

"I didn't realize Rosana had remarried." Lore takes a sip of her martini, enjoying the bitterness. "What do you think of him?"

Andres stares at the mirrored alcove built into the wooden bar, where their reflections hide behind dark bottles. "He's good to her and my kids. That's all that matters."

Men don't want to talk about their exes—even she, who has only been with one man, understands this—but she needs to know how real this is, how real it could have been, if things were different. (*If things were different.* Her mind's careful phrasing.)

"What happened between you all?" Lore asks. "You and Rosana?"

Andres doesn't look surprised by her question. He leans an elbow on the bar, absently tearing a wet cocktail napkin. "You don't mind talking about this?"

"If I did, I wouldn't be asking."

He nods. "I told you we married young, twenty-four, and we had Penelope the following year. I was still new to DF, I was getting my maestría, I felt like there was so much life still to be lived and like I had . . . given it up. That's how I saw it. That marriage and kids were a sacrifice, instead of a gift."

Lore swallows, shame slick at the back of her throat.

"I was not a good husband," he continues, tapping the edge of his glass on the bar. "I used every excuse not to be home: I was studying, I was working. Then I started going out with friends from the UNAM. We went to the oldest, shittiest, most wonderful cantinas, drinking tequila with the viejos from afternoon until close, all of us trying to escape something—wives, kids, boredom, memories. We went to speakeasies hidden in basements and behind restaurant freezers. We went to clubs and danced until the sun came up. And all the while, Rosana was home with Penelope. The baby would be crying when I left and crying when I got home. The pitch of that damn cry, it made me want to scream."

Lore winces.

"I know." Andres's jaw is clenched. "On top of it, Rosana was struggling with breastfeeding, and Penelope wouldn't take the bottle. So Penelope was hungry and miserable, losing weight, and there's Rosana, no sleep, recovering from a C-section. Then one day, I get home, and they're not there. It turns out Rosana had been in the hospital for half a day already. Mastitis. The infection had gotten so bad she was in there for a week, on heavy-duty antibiotics. And I'd never even noticed."

"Oh, God," Lore says, feeling for Rosana. She thinks of how dutifully Fabian woke up with her for those early nighttime feedings, how he always helped position the boys at her breasts, and how, once she was settled with pillows beneath both arms, he'd make her warm buttered tortillas to keep her energy up. When her nipples cracked and bled, he pressed Vaseline into them with the tip of his pinkie finger. They were both so tired, but she remembers those first few weeks with a blurred warmth, the sense memory of skin on skin. This was before Lore's anxiety set in, all the terrible fantasies of loss.

Before the power of watching her give birth had faded from Fabian's memory. Before the cruel banality of motherhood set in.

"I know," Andres says. "Her father told me it was time to step up. But I didn't know how to do that." He takes the final sips of watery Scotch. "It took two years for me to finally come to my senses. By then it was too late. Rosana never saw me the same way again."

"But—how long were you married after that?"

Andres smiles wryly. "Ten years."

"And in all that time . . . ?"

"We were good to each other." Behind them, a sudden burst of laughter. Andres waits for the group to settle down before continuing. "But there was never that intimacy again, even when she became pregnant with Carlitos. I thought a new baby could be our chance. By then she didn't need my help. You have never seen a more capable mother," he says, with unmistakable pride, and for the first time, Lore feels a dart of jealousy, right to the heart.

"So why did it finally end?" she asks.

"She found someone she could see with fresh eyes."

Lore forces herself to look at him, instead of the olives in her empty glass. "She had an affair?"

"Looking back, I'm surprised it didn't happen sooner." Andres waves the bartender over, and they order another round. "I don't blame her anymore. But I'd be lying if I said I didn't hate her for a while. I'd spent so many years atoning, and for what?"

Lore feels a slow crumble in her chest. He deserves better than what she is doing. If they continue, she is going to hurt him. She is going to hurt everyone. She feels this, the way a dormant volcano must sense its own potential for destruction. Though right now, the heat is a smolder, contained. She can control it. She *will* control it.

Andres laughs awkwardly. "Well, if you didn't think I was a catch before . . ."

Lore slides a hand to the back of his head, and before she can think, before she's even decided, she's drawing his mouth to hers. His lips part as he rests a hand below her hips, where she wills it to touch, to squeeze, to drag her closer. After a few moments, he lifts that hand to stroke the hidden nape of her neck instead, a touch so intimate it makes her shiver. There's a dull roar in her ears, and something falls away, some piece of her, right as a different piece is revealed.

"Mmm." Andres sighs, smiling, as they pull away. "I've been thinking about that for three months."

"Me too." Lore reaches, shaking, for her martini, not noticing when it had been replaced. She blinks hard against the rise of tears, forcing them to recede.

"And what about you?" he asks, as softly as the noise of the bar will allow. "When was your last relationship?"

Lore freezes. She hasn't yet told him an outright lie, other than the one about her home phone line having issues receiving calls, and she doesn't want to start. Once she does, she sees how the lies will build, brick after brick into a fortress designed to protect, but protection means separation, means they will never be as close as he thinks or she wants, and one mistake, one misremembered detail, will be enough to take down the whole thing, burying them both beneath its rubble.

"Last year," she says, thinking it's true, after all; she and Fabian were together last year, just as they have been every year since she was seventeen.

"How long?"

"We were high school sweethearts." Lore hates herself for talking about Fabian in the past tense, for talking about him at all. He doesn't belong here, with this version of her. She touches her locket, a silent apology. Dangerous to be wearing it, but important, too, keeping this piece of Fabian and the cuates close. Her wedding ring is zipped into the inner compartment of her purse.

Andres raises his eyebrows. "So, you were together for as long as Rosana and me."

Lore nods.

"What happened?"

When Lore thinks back on this question many years later, she will understand it wasn't the recession or loneliness that brought her here. It wasn't that she no longer loved Fabian or wanted their marriage to end. It was a different kind of yearning. A nameless suspicion that there was more to herself than she'd ever accessed, and only by falling in love could she discover it, for only then do we become new to ourselves again.

"I'm not really sure." Lore traces a fingertip along the rim of her glass, trying not to imagine Fabian right now, tossing and turning in Joseph Guerra's guest room. "Maybe we just grew away from each other."

"Grew apart, you mean?" Andres asks, and after a moment, Lore nods, though this wasn't actually what she meant.

They stay at La Opera Bar for one more round, until Andres takes Lore by the hand and they bump, laughing, through the midnight crowd so he can point out a hole in the plastered ceiling, a souvenir, supposedly, from one of Pancho Villa's bullets. By the time they're wandering the Zócalo hand in hand, Lore is kinetic with martini-soaked happiness. At some point, despite Andres's laughing objections, Lore removes her patent leather heels and stuffs them in her purse, choosing the grit of the street over the swelling blisters.

"Did you bring your bike?" Lore asks finally, glancing up at him. In bare feet, her head falls right at his shoulder. The moonlight softens his features, though his profile maintains an aristocratic seriousness.

"Yes, but I'm not sure you're in a state to ride," he says, nudging her playfully.

Lore laughs. Back home, people refer to driving times by the number of beers you can drink from here to there: Laredo to San Antonio is a three-beer trip if you're taking it slow; Laredo to Houston is a six-pack.

"All I have to do is hang on, right?" Lore asks.

"Well, yes." A gleam comes into his eye. "Tightly."

"I'm pretty sure I can handle that."

"I'll . . . drop you off at your hotel, then?"

"I thought you wanted to show me the view from your apartment."

And then they are hurrying, as if they both know she could change her mind at any moment. Her hands tremble as they redo the ankle straps of her shoes, and she is pressed up against him, squeezing her thighs around his, her fingers clasped at his waist. He's given her his helmet again, and any time he slows, the weight of it pulls her head forward to bump his slightly. She can see his smile in the side mirror. She stares at his hands curled around the handlebars and imagines them sliding up her rib cage, encircling her breasts, brushing his thumbs across her nipples, and by the time they get to Tlatelolco, a housing complex so big it's like a city within a city, she is desperate to know what he will feel like inside of her.

They park and take the elevator to the tenth floor of Andres's building, where they stand in the back, tension crackling between their bodies until the doors open and Andres leads her to his apartment, fumbling with the key, laughing.

"Here we are." Andres steps aside so she can glance at the small brown couch and creased leather chair, the crammed bookshelves taking up an entire wall. She can see several framed eight-by-ten photos, his kids, surely, though she can't make out their faces from here. There's a boy's blue backpack in the corner, a copy of *Pedro Páramo* open on the condensation-ringed wooden coffee table. The carpet is worn thin in places, and the pale blue walls could use a new coat of paint—but the view! From three large windows in the living room, a spray of lights shines before them.

"It's beautiful," Lore murmurs.

"Yes," Andres says, though he's looking at her, and then she's pushing off his jacket, his hands running from her back down to the curve of her ass, cupping its weight in his palms. He lifts her, and she wraps her legs around him as he half stumbles toward a short hallway, shoving open a door with one free hand. Then they are on his simply made bed, absent the half dozen throw pillows that indicate a woman's touch. Lore wants him to hurry, to plummet them past the irreversible. He takes his time, pushing fabric aside inch by inch to press his hot lips to each new slice of skin. She's squirming beneath him, moaning, and he chuckles gently, teeth on his lower lip as he looks up from undoing her zipper. "Everything okay, Ms. Crusoe?"

"No!" She shoves her thumbs in the waistband of her pants, tilting her hips to pull them off, and he catches her wrists and holds them to the bed.

"What's the rush?" Andres asks, with that wicked tone he sometimes gets on the phone, sexier for the surprise of it and even more so in person, with the matching glint in his eyes.

He kisses her legs as he slides her pants down—the inside scoops of her knees, the marbles of her ankles. He maneuvers the pants around her shoes, then takes a moment to just look at her. In the hotel before dinner, she'd done the same, studying herself in the mirror. Her black hair sprayed gently into curls from her electric rollers. Her eyes smoky and eager for the night to unfold. Her body, demure in a white silk blouse tucked into black pants, her favorite gold belt winking in the light. But beneath all that? She'd stared at the swell of her breasts in the black lace bra, knowing how without its support, they'd hang lower than before the boys' hungry mouths had found them, her nipples large and dark as bullseyes. The sturdy width of her hips and softness of her lower belly, the silky white stretch marks curling like measuring tape from her thighs to her ass, an ass too big, really, for the tiny swatch of fabric pretending to cover it. Would he—if he were to see her like this—would he be able to tell she is a mother?

She holds her breath now, waiting for him to see all this history on her body. All he says is "God, you're beautiful." And she *feels* beautiful, not just beneath his gaze but her own. She appreciates the deep golden glow of her skin in the moonlight, her body's womanly softness, the strength beneath her curves. Then he unstraps her shoes and takes them gently from her feet, and she remembers her burgeoning blisters and the black dirt that must be caked onto her soles. He laughs, confirming her fears.

She laughs, too, lifting her ankles. "I'm going to get your bed dirty."

"Do you really think I care?" Then his lips are on her inner thighs. She gasps as he kisses her through black lace, the teasing heat of his breath, the stroke of one finger against fabric that is cool against her with its own wetness. She moans, lifting her hips again, rubbing against his open palm as he slides over her body, tongue in her mouth, lace pushed aside, one finger, then two, sunk deep into her, bucking against his hand, already so desperately close when those fingers recede, pulling the panties with them, leaving her breathless with reality: this is it.

She looks into Andres's eyes, the ferocity of his desire, and sweeps his pants and boxers over his hips. He pulls a condom from a bedside drawer and rolls it on with quick, fevered expertise, making her wonder who was last in his bed and when, and then, with a question in his eyes she answers by wrapping her legs around him, he slides inside her, swallowing her gasp. Their bodies swiftly find a rhythm together, another, and another, and there is no room left for doubt or recrimination. His sweat smells like damp cotton, and she kisses it from his skin, licks it from her lips. It's exactly as she imagined, except for one thing: Fabian, watching from the corner.

Why? Fabian asks. *What did I do?*

Nothing, Lore tells him, wanting him to look away, but also wanting him to keep looking, to really see her. *It's not about you.*

Afterward, Andres rests his forehead against hers, breathing hard, and Lore isn't sure what should come next. At home, Fabian would extract himself, kiss her, and immediately fall asleep, while she would slip from bed to clean off and pee, lest she get a bladder infection. At home, sex is casual and seamless, like any other necessary but mundane physical activity. Afterward, life just resumes. And that isn't bad. That kind of comfort and familiarity, it's hard won.

The ability to laugh at the sounds their bodies make—the slaps of soft flesh, the gurgle of a full belly—to have sex in the daylight (not that they often do, with two almost-teenagers and so much going on in their lives, but still), where every bulge and scar and stretch mark has a history they both understand.

But is it enough?

Later, Lore will see this is when the thought first occurred to her, shapeless and half-formed. That perhaps not every affair is about lack in the primary relationship; perhaps some are about a complement. Perhaps multiple relationships can illuminate different parts of the self, like a prism turned first this way, then that, toward the light. Perhaps to love and allow love from only one person at a time is to trap the self into a single, frozen version, and it's this that makes us look elsewhere.

"How about a shower?" Andres kisses Lore's jaw, and she shivers, hypersensitive.

"Okay," she says, smiling. As they disentangle, her self-consciousness returns. Andres is still looking at her with naked appreciation, and she tries to see herself that way again.

In the bathroom, Andres turns on only the dim light. He runs the taps, tests the water, and before he pulls the lever to switch tub to shower, he takes a washcloth from beneath the sink.

"Sit down," he says, with a smile, gesturing to the far lip of the bath.

Lore obeys without understanding, surprised by the eroticism of her uncertainty. Then Andres kneels by the bath, dips the washcloth in warm water, and gently begins washing her feet.

CASSIE, 2017

Andres's two children, Penelope and Carlos, were forty-nine and forty-six. Penelope was a psychology professor at the UNAM, the same university where Andres had taught. Carlos, according to Facebook, was a drummer in a band, though their events page was rarely updated. His profile picture—head down, drumsticks in hand, sweaty hair in his eyes—was two years old. Penelope hadn't returned my calls or emails, and I couldn't be sure Carlos had seen my Facebook messages.

Lore's sister, Marta, who had been on the phone with Lore while Fabian was spotted at Hotel Botanica, didn't want to talk. But with some Googling, I reached her husband, Sergio, at work, and he told me he'd call back when he had a chance. If it got back to Lore that I was doing outside research about Andres's last day, I'd tell her I was fulfilling my end of our agreement—not asking her about it, since she refused to answer anyway.

The week after watching Fabian's police tapes, I got lucky with Lore's former colleague, Oscar Martinez. Oscar, who was the only one besides Lore who *may* have seen Andres's note, was now an executive vice president at the same bank where he and Lore used to work together. He answered his extension with a rough smoker's bark.

"Oscar Martinez."

"Oscar, hi." I shifted on the love seat, the early-fall sun casting shadows of moving leaves on my keyboard. "My name is Cassie Bowman. I'm working on a book with Lore Rivera, about her life back in the eighties. I know you two worked together. Could I ask you a few questions?"

"Her life in the eighties," Oscar repeated. "You mean that *LMT* article that came out a couple months ago."

"I have nothing to do with that piece," I said. "In fact, that's why Lore agreed to work with me—so we could tell her side of the story."

"Uh-huh." Oscar sounded skeptical. But he didn't hang up.

"So, were you two friends back then?"

"Sure," Oscar said. "It was a small department."

"How many were you?"

"Well, let's see—one branch, about sixty employees. International was maybe . . . five of us?"

"Did you travel together often, you and Lore?"

"Every few months. But we each had our own clients, with their own needs, so we traveled on our own more regularly."

"Were any questions ever raised about her travel?" I asked. "How often she went, how long she stayed, that kind of thing?"

Oscar let out a thoughtful exhale. "Pues . . . not that I can remember. I think at one point she had a sick grandmother—" He cut himself off. "Or said she did. I never did find out if that was true. But I think she went more because of that."

"It can be hard after the fact," I said. "Trying to figure out the truth among the lies. Were you two friends outside of work?"

"There wasn't much 'outside of work' during those times. There were years I don't remember anyone socializing. You went to work, if you still had a job, and you went home to your family. Eso era todo."

I was used to untranslated Spanish words and phrases by now. I

Googled them later. "But you knew she was married to Fabian, had the twins, all that?"

"Of course."

My heart rate picked up. "You must have been surprised to meet Andres Russo, then."

Oscar didn't respond.

"What were your impressions of him when he came to the bank?" I pressed.

"Look, I really don't know if Lore would want me talking about that."

"Oscar, Lore is telling me every aspect of their relationship. You don't need to worry." It was the first time I felt guilty.

"Okay . . ." Oscar sounded like a man who wanted to believe what he was told.

"How did Andres seem to you?" I asked. Quiet, calm. Trying not to spook him. "What was his emotional state?"

"Well," Oscar said, slowly, "he was nicely dressed, polite. Smiling, at first, when he introduced himself."

I winced, feeling for Andres, for everything that was to come. "Did he introduce himself by name, or as Lore's husband?"

"Both." His voice lifted with incredulity, even now, though with an odd curl of scorn. "Obviously, at first I thought it was a mistake. Then, when he showed me the picture, I was like, chinga—I didn't know what to think."

I looked up from the computer screen, where I was typing notes. I couldn't remember seeing anything about a photo being found on Andres's body. "Picture? Of the two of them?"

"Yeah. Supposedly on their wedding day. But look, after Lore told me how he was bothering her—I mean, we all make mistakes. I just wish—" He cut off.

My questions split off in three directions at once. "Wish what, Oscar?"

"I don't know—that I would've done something to help. But Lore was very independent like that."

"Let's go back. She said Andres was *bothering* her? Bothering her how? When did she tell you this?"

"When she came back to the bank that afternoon, after I gave her the note he left." Oscar sounded harried. "She didn't go into detail. But again, that's Lore. You could tell she was rattled, though."

"How so?" I asked. The woman I knew was always in control.

"She was looking for her keys to lock up her office. Ended up dropping her whole purse on the floor. Everything spilled out." Oscar's voice shifted, halting. Worried he was saying too much. "You know, maybe I should call her first. Just to make sure she wants me talking to you."

"Of course," I said. "Quickly, though—did you happen to read Andres's note?"

"No, she threw everything in the trash right after she read it."

My breath caught, like a fingernail snagged on a thread. "Everything? What's everything?"

Silence.

"I'm going to call Lore now," Oscar said.

LORE, 1983–1984

Four times. Four times Lore had sex with a man who isn't her husband. And then this morning he made her café de olla, telling her, "Stay in bed, I'll bring it." Andres had looked so happy and light, she could hardly meet his eyes. Now, as she drives to Marta's house to pick up the cuates, her body feels tender and sore, a keeper of secrets.

When Marta opens the door, the house is quiet. It smells like the morning's bacon and chorizo.

"I guess you haven't been home yet," Marta says, hugging Lore.

"No, I came straight here." Lore takes a step backward, irrationally afraid Marta will feel something different about her. "Why?"

Marta smiles mischievously. "Well, go."

Three turns, and Lore is in her neighborhood. Only a few years ago, all the FOR SALE signs would have brought a surge of excitement. It's a buyer's market, she'd have said to Fabian. Now every sign is a glimpse of the desperation behind those curtained windows. She once thought owning a home meant you had made it. Now she understands you never own anything. These rambling ranch-style houses are little more than stage sets; they can be bustled off into the wings while you're still brushing your teeth in the morning.

She sees it from half a block away: Fabian's truck. It's parked in their narrow driveway, where Lore usually parks. Her fingers fly to her swollen lips. What is he doing here? He isn't supposed to be back until Thanksgiving, almost two weeks from now! She isn't ready. Her Mexico City self—her Andres self—is half-exposed. She can still feel Andres's hands on her from when they awoke this morning. Running from her ankle to the curve of her hip, her ribs, her breast, then back down, their legs intertwined. The strong, rhythmic way he moved. Her chin and nose reddened by stubble.

How will she be able to look at Fabian? How will she be able to look at herself? Yet, she doesn't regret it. She can't. And how can that be? How can shame exist without remorse?

She inches the car around to the carport, but the gate chain is loose, the wrought iron stuck a third of the way open. Before circling back to the front, Lore lowers her visor mirror and reaches for her purse to apply makeup. But the back door swings open. There he is, Fabian, grinning tiredly as the cuates push past him, sliding their baseball mitts on. Lore parks in the street, turns off the ignition.

"Mom!" Gabriel calls, surprised, as she steps out. "You're home."

Lore is grateful for the delay of pulling the cuates' reluctant, distracted bodies close. When they were toddlers, they used to sit on her feet and she'd lug them around their small living room calling, "Mateo? Gabriel? Where are you? And why are my legs so *heavy*?" They would muffle their squeals against her knees, as if their laughter would give them away. Lore feels that way now, her attempts to hide unbearably obvious.

"Sorry for stealing your spot." Fabian gestures at the loose chain. "Got to fix this gate—not very good advertising, is it?"

Lore laughs weakly, and in a few long steps, he crosses to meet her.

"Surprised?" Fabian asks softly, pulling her close.

. . .

Lore sits on one of their hard plastic lounge chairs, watching Fabian throw the baseball to Gabriel and Mateo. The grass is dry and patchy. She keeps forgetting to turn on the sprinklers. She's embarrassed Fabian is seeing it this way. It feels like a failure. She almost laughs. The *grass* feels like a failure?

The fall sunlight is waning, the temperature cooling, when Gabriel shouts to her, "Pizza Hut?"

"Sure!" Lore is already standing, relieved to go inside, to let her expression settle without fear of what it might reveal. She makes their familiar order and is sorting laundry when Fabian comes into the small space fifteen minutes later, arms around her waist and chin on her shoulder. She tenses, then forces herself to relax.

"I missed you guys," he says, warm lips to her neck.

She closes her eyes. "We missed you, too."

That night, after pizza, Fabian lights a fire in the fireplace and the four of them toast marshmallows, the edges darkening, caramelizing, melting sticky and sweet in their mouths. In bed later, Lore and Fabian don't talk about the store, Austin, or the recession. She expects not to want him, not the same day as Andres. But she's happy Fabian is home, happy he missed them, and her desire to be close to him feels simple and animalistic. She straddles his waist, and her hair sweeps his face until he holds it behind her neck with one hand, and they come within moments of each other, the most in sync they've been in many long months.

The guilt rushes through her later, like an aftershock, her stomach heaving so violently she jolts from the bed and runs to the toilet. The nausea fades as suddenly as it came. Gripping the edge of the counter, she stares at herself in the mirror. "Who are you?" she hisses.

That first weekend, there are so many slivers of moments when the secret nearly slides wild from Lore's throat before she swallows it back down. Then on Sunday night Fabian leaves for Austin again and the secret seems to curl and circle and settle in her belly, content to remain hidden. It's over, she keeps telling herself. It's over.

Her resolve lasts until Monday, when Andres calls her at the bank. Soon she's like an addict, promising herself this is the last call, no, this one. Then Mr. de la Garza opens his jumbo CD and Lore is sent back to DF.

Once again, Marta and Sergio watch the cuates while both Lore and Fabian are gone. This time Lore is in DF for three days and two nights, neither of which she spends in her hotel bed.

Before her third trip, Andres asks if she'd like to meet his kids. "It's my weekend with them," he explains.

Lore's house is midnight quiet. She thinks of the cuates, sleeping down the hall as she talks to Andres. Imagine the faith—the hope—it takes to bring someone new into your home, to introduce them to your kids knowing that person could break their hearts. Lore doesn't want to be that person.

"You don't think—it doesn't feel soon?" she asks, wincing.

"Not for me," he says. "But I understand if it does for you. I know it's a lot. But, you know, we're sort of a package deal."

Lore exhales slowly. "Of course," she says. "Of course."

In DF, Lore goes straight to her lunch meeting before taking a cab to Tlatelolco. Her mouth is dry, and she unwraps a stick of Big Red before knocking on the door. Andres answers right away, as if he's been standing there waiting, and pulls her into his arms. She can feel his pounding heart beneath his dark blue sweater. "They just got home from school," he says in her ear. "I'll get them."

Lore doesn't know what to do with herself, so she stands there until Andres leads the kids out. Penelope is fifteen and Lore's height. She's skinny, the way the cuates are when they've emerged from a growth spurt, and a red headband holds her thick black hair away from appraising dark eyes. Carlitos is exactly the kind of boy Gabriel picks on at school, nothing terrible, but Lore isn't blind: if Mateo weren't his twin, if he looked like Carlitos, with those glasses and unruly curls, Gabriel would probably pick on him, too.

"Penelope, Carlitos," Andres says, smiling. "I want you to meet Lore. My . . . girlfriend." He looks at Lore, uncertain and apologetic, as if realizing it's the first time they've used a title out loud. It's all happening so fast, but what can she do in this moment except smile and shake the kids' hands? Andres's relief is palpable as they decorate the tree, and at one point he slips an arm over her shoulders and dips his head to kiss her. "Novia," he whispers. Lore catches Penelope staring, in a way that seems to see right through her, and she turns her face at the last minute.

The next day, they go see *A Christmas Story*, and Lore cries in the dark theater because she and Fabian had planned to take the cuates and somehow this, this, feels like cheating. It's too much. A whole other family. But she can't walk away, because soon she's in love with them, too. She loves the way Penelope and Andres talk about books, cheeks flaming, arms waving, "No, no, *¡escúchame!*" Andres sneaking quick smiles at Lore as he teases Penelope into debate before laughing, admitting she was right, and did she know . . . There's always more he knows, that curious, professorial mind, and Penelope listening eagerly, nodding, while Lore and Carlitos grin at each other, co-conspirators in their unspoken agreement to be the audience, to enjoy the Andres-and-Penelope show.

In the spring of 1984, the trips become more regular, scheduled: Lore in DF one week of the month, the cuates with Marta and Sergio during that time. Sometimes, after dinner, Penelope sprawls on the couch with her head in Lore's lap, her feet in Andres's. "Play with my hair?" she asks, smiling up at Lore, and Lore's heart seizes— imagine, having a daughter, after all.

When Carlitos struggles with his math homework, she's the one he asks for help, and she wants to laugh, thinking here she is, in a different country, with a different man and two different children, still solving for x, as if any choices she could make in this life would end with her at a kitchen table beside a twelve-year-old boy smelling newly of body odor beneath the childish scent of pencil shavings. Does she mind this? No, because she is not Penelope and Carlitos's mother. She is free to enjoy them without being the one charged with maintaining the grinding gears of their days.

Then it's back home to the whispered phone calls, Andres telling her where he'd like to touch her, where to put her own hands; the daytime fantasies, the places Lore can retreat to inside herself when the cuates are fighting over the TV control or dribbling a basketball inside the house, leaving black scuff marks on the floor she's just mopped.

But also, every six weeks: the slam of Fabian's truck door on a Friday night. Ranch days, the four of them with Marta and Sergio, taking turns shooting the .22 at cans of Schaefer Light—Chafa Light, Sergio calls them, only good for target practice, and yet the adults all drink them anyway—the cuates passing out slumped and pliant as toddlers on the way home. Lore and Fabian holding hands, the truck smelling like mesquite, their skin covered in dust fine as powdered sugar.

Inevitably, the lies become uglier and more complicated. She tells Andres her parents died in a car crash and that she and her siblings don't get along; it's hard to even force out the words, and she knocks on every piece of wood in Andres's bedroom when he goes to take a shower. She can't spend Easter with Andres and the kids, she says, because she has to work that Saturday and Monday. It's too much to spend on a plane ticket for one day. Really, the whole family goes out to the ranch, a day of water balloons and four-wheeler rides and cascarones, coming home with their sweaty skin polka-dotted with confetti dye.

When Andres suggests coming to visit her, she tells him to save his money. There's nothing for them to do in Laredo. She'd rather stay longer in DF next time, spend a dizzying afternoon at Merced, or maybe play tourists (which she is, of course) and take Penelope and Carlitos on a trajinera at Xochimilco. Lore has only been on a boat once, at Lake Casa Blanca, and she's hungry to float through the canal system in a part of Mexico that supposedly most resembles its precolonized past. Lore is hungry for so much, an appetite that seems to yawn and yawn and never be filled.

Andres says, "It's not about what we *do*. I just want to see where you're from. Meet your friends. Or are you embarrassed of me?" he teases.

What friends? she wants to say. She has plenty of friendly acquaintances, but the last twelve years have been so consumed with family and working that that's all there is: family and work. Marta is her best friend and Sergio is Fabian's. Their social lives revolve around children's birthdays and Sunday lunches at Mami and Papi's house. But she's supposed to be a single thirty-three-year-old, and what single thirty-three-year-old doesn't have friends?

"More like embarrassed of them," Lore jokes. Then, more seriously, "You will meet them. But trust me. Everyone is so stressed out right now, myself included. I'd rather be over there with you all. Okay?"

Even through the phone line, she can feel Andres's smile. "Okay."

Eventually, if this continues, she'll have to figure out a way he can come. The bank recently repossessed a condo it's now using as occasional corporate housing. That's probably the best option. She can say a customer from DF is visiting to evaluate a potential site. She'll ask Marta and Sergio to watch the cuates for another DF trip. Then she'll cart over an armful of throw pillows, her bedsheets, which smell like her, and as many of her clothes as she can fit in the tiny trunk of her Escort. She'll fill H-E-B bags with canned corn and spinach and asparagus, things from the pantry the cuates won't miss, grab a few trinkets and childhood photo albums. Then, when Andres is here, she'll come down with food poisoning, something that will keep them in the condo all weekend, no chance of bumping into anyone Lore knows. She wants to laugh, thinking of how incomprehensible such a scheme would have been to her only six months ago, but now she can hardly remember a time before, when there was only one family.

Still, until Día de los Muertos, she almost convinces herself no one will get hurt.

That day, Rosana has the kids, and Andres suggests that he and Lore go to Mixquic to honor their parents—his, buried in Buenos Aires, and hers, as far as he knows, in Laredo. So they take the bike, an hour plunging toward darkness as the sun sets in miniature in the mirror.

Ever since their first ride together, the bike has been magic, the only way Lore knows to be both exquisitely, impossibly present, and also outside herself, with the serene understanding that she is as close to death as ever. Andres was surprised by how much she loved it. At best, she gathers, Rosana had tolerated it, but never completely shirked her resentment that, even with two children, Andres took such unnecessary risk, no matter how safe he was while riding. And he is safe. He needs to be. On the bike, Andres must account not only for himself but for every other Mexican who might veer into his lane without checking their blind spot, who might stomp on the brakes to piss off the driver behind them, who believes it is their right of way, always. When it became clear Lore would ride with him, he bought her a helmet, a perforated leather jacket, and riding pants and ankle boots reinforced with Kevlar. Holding their form, they're like armor in her otherwise sparse half of his closet.

Their first trip outside the city was to the Sierra Gorda. Before they left, he repeated to her: "Remember, lean with me—don't resist the curves." And she wanted to say she'd been leaning with him, she hadn't resisted a single curve yet, had she? Instead, she wrapped her body around his, armor to armor, as the highway to Jalpan de Serra eventually cleared and the views cracked open to prehistoric hulking mountains hewn in rough brushstrokes of jade and rust, and there were those curves. Low in her helmet, Lore said, "Whoa," as if calming a spooked horse, while Andres lowered them to the rushing road, then lifted again. In Lore's helmet, the wind compressed into a distant roar, reminding her of holding a conch shell to the cuates' ears when they were little, asking if they could hear the ocean. The wind flooded the space between her and Andres, pushing and pulling, and she could nearly feel the disequilibrium of tires losing traction, the slide, the roll, the fall. It reminded her of standing on the tracks as a girl, waiting and waiting until she could almost feel the hot breath of the train like a dragon's roar, and thinking maybe this was the secret to fully inhabiting a life. And if you could do that, if you could be the fullest version of yourself, then surely you had more of yourself to give. When she thought that way, the guilt—a constant presence, an extra limb—unfurled behind her like a cape.

She can smell the incense even before they reach San Andres Apóstol. They buy buckets of marigolds from a street vendor, wander into the cemetery hand in hand. Floating candles and golden smiles soften the winter darkness. Children with serapes over their shoulders, graves draped with marigolds and roses, green apples and sugar skulls. Chocolate and aniseed sweeten the air as they lay marigolds on undecorated graves.

"Bringing back memories?" Lore asks, with a small, private smile. Reminding Andres of their early days, how he'd told her about retreating to La Recoleta's cemetery as a boy, hiding from his mother's love in the shadows of mausoleums.

He smiles back, squeezing her hand. "I was alone then."

The church bells ring, solemn and triumphant. Eight o'clock, and the Alumbrada is beginning. Lore can sense the souls of the dead, their joyful rise. She can feel their ephemeral sweep as they search for their loved ones.

"My parents would have loved you," Andres says.

"Even though I'm Mexican?" Lore teases.

He grins back. "We could have worked on your accent."

Someone nearby is playing a guitar. Lore and Andres stop for a moment, listen, sway. In the golden darkness, Andres's eyes shine. He sets his bucket down and gestures for her to do the same. Then he takes both her hands.

Something is coming. The spirits pause, waiting. Whatever it is, she wants to stop it.

"Lore," he says, "I never thought I would feel this way again. I never *have* felt this way. You are everything I never dared to think I could have, after—" He shakes his head, as if bewildered by this clumsy reminder of his failures as a husband and father.

The panic in her chest is like wild hoofbeats, a stampede of animals kicking up dust in retreat. She wants to be back on the bike, where all they ever have is the single wordless moment they're in. It's all she can give him. But Andres continues, his eyes soft.

"Lore," he says, "I want to spend the rest of my life with you. If you'll let me."

As he opens a small crimson box, Lore is twenty years old again—Fabian's face open and earnest in the twilit blind, his hands shaking, *I was going to wait. I'm sorry, the box is all dusty now. I should have waited, but Lore, will you marry me?* She had shrieked, and the monte had shivered, birds startled to flight. She'd thrown her arms around him and cried into his neck, and they'd both been laughing and talking over each other when Fabian slipped the gold band with the tiny diamond onto her finger. *Yes,* she'd said a few minutes later. *I forgot to say yes!*

"Lore?" Andres is smiling at her, though his eyes are questioning. She feels frozen, as if she might be found a thousand years from now still in this graveyard.

Finally, she crashes back into herself. "Oh, Andres." She reaches a tentative finger for the box, touches the emerald. "It's so beautiful. But I—I can't."

A family edges past them, sidelong looks and arms laden with candles and pan de muerto. Andres stares at her as though he's misheard.

"I love you." Lore clutches his elbows, urgent. "And I want to be with you. It's just—how would it even work? My job—the recession. And I would never ask you to move to Laredo and leave the kids. It's just—it seems—"

"You're not ready." Andres's voice is flat, disappointed.

"I don't know. But I love you. You *know* I love you. Can't that be enough for now?"

Andres looks toward San Andres Apóstol. A low, thick fog of incense obscures the monastery's ancient stone. A baby cries, disembodied, and strangely, Lore feels a needle-sharp prickle behind her nipples, the way her body used to respond, leaking warm sweet milk, when one of the cuates cried. How far she has come since those days when her dreams, her ambitions, her desires were all subsumed, stamped out like a campfire in the morning.

Andres is still holding the box. The emerald glows, candlelit. Without looking at it, he snaps the box shut and slips it back inside his jacket.

"That's the thing about love," he says, with a wry, sad smile. "It's irreducible. I can never know what your love for me feels like to you and you can never know what my love for you feels like to me. I suppose this"—with a touch to his jacket—"was an attempt to show you, which is irrational, and also not fair of me to assume—"

"No," Lore interrupts, taking his hand. "It was fair to assume." She can imagine their life together, a life filled with books and conversation and adventure. Café de olla in bed, ears ringing with the wind. Penelope and Carlitos.

Then, as it so often happens, a wave of nausea nearly sweeps her sideways. Fabian still working twelve-hour days in Austin, desperate to keep the store alive; how he surprised her two weeks ago, coming home and immediately taking her to the Tack Room, a steak dinner she didn't dare say they couldn't afford. Gabriel and Mateo, how their faces have recently taken on the quality of a magic trick: now you see me—childish roundness, echoes of the babies they once were—now you don't, transforming in her peripheral vision to the faces of men she doesn't yet recognize. She *has* a life.

But that life is better now that she's with Andres. It's better because *she* is better. When Fabian told her at the Tack Room—more than a year after he first left for Austin—that he wouldn't be moving home anytime soon, she could accept his decision without resentment, because she knew it was for their family, yes, but also for Fabian himself, for his idea of himself as a man; even if he's biding time before the inevitable, working is necessary for his survival, and she can give that to him now. Her love for him has become more expansive and generous, and he can feel it. In the small, dim restaurant north of the river, she'd said she understood, and he'd stroked the lines of her palm, making her shiver.

And she is a better mother, too. When the cuates were babies, she'd been forced to become an efficiency expert. She learned to feed one while changing the other's diaper, one-handed; managed to shower, dress, and pee in under five minutes; timed grocery shopping with their naps, Crock-Pot dinners she could start at noon and not touch again until six. As they grew older, she became a kind of drill sergeant: Time to wake up! Time for dinner! Time for baths! And older still: Have you finished your homework? Gabriel, Mateo, in the car, *now*, we're going to be late! Fabian a benign background presence, a reliable copilot who has long since ceded control of the plane. Without her at the helm, it would crash.

Only it won't. She can see this now that she's away one week a month, and she can see, too, that while her regimenting was once necessary, perhaps it isn't anymore, at least not to the same extent. And more, it's keeping her from simply enjoying her boys, the way she can enjoy Penelope and Carlitos. And so, thirteen years after their birth, she is beginning to squirm loose of the bindings that once felt so essential—that once *were* essential—but now only trap her in a role she despises.

Sometimes she wishes Gabriel and Mateo could see her, leather and Kevlar on the back of a motorcycle, pointing at cloud-studded sierras, hidden waterfalls, the phantasmagoric midflight blur of a macaw. She wishes they could see her and know she is more than who they've always known her to be. Maybe one day, when they're older, but for now she can stop nagging them, allow them to make their own mistakes, grab the Atari controller and let them teach her how to play.

Could she give up Andres and this life, here, and still be the wife and mother she wants to be there? Could she continue to explore the parts of herself—adventurous, curious, relaxed, open—she's discovered, or would they eventually shrink within her again, obliterated by the unyielding demands of one life? She doesn't know. She doesn't want to know.

"I want to marry you," she says softly. "But it's not the right time."

Around them, the cemetery pulses and flickers with collective grief, collective hope. She sees herself sitting at a spinning wheel, turning straw into gold—something as ugly and ordinary as an affair into something precious. But is she the imp, demanding more and more in exchange for the magic, or is she the girl trapped in a room, making promises she can't keep to save her own life?

As always, she is both.

CASSIE, 2017

Andres's proposal meant things couldn't go on indefinitely," I said to Lore on the phone. Mid-September, the evening humid and heavy as I sat at our small iron patio table out back. Iron reminded me of Fabian now. "How long did you think you could sustain the affair?"

On FaceTime, Lore winced. She didn't like that word, I could see.

"The constantly sinking land," she murmured.

"Sorry?"

"That's what Andres called DF that night in Chapultepec. Because it was built on an ancient lake bed, and just the way we can't feel the Earth rotating, you can't feel the city falling deeper into the ground. That's how it was for me. I didn't recognize the shifts as they happened. It was probably six months before I even admitted to myself that I was having an *affair*, como tú dices." She did one-handed air quotes around the word.

"How did it feel to admit that?"

"How do you think it felt?" Lore snapped. "Do you think I was proud?"

"I don't know, that's why I'm asking."

I had come to enjoy these beats of tension, moments of pushing up against a door Lore didn't want to open. Behind those doors, that's where the true story was hiding.

"You know," Lore said, "in other cultures, other times, a person—a woman—wouldn't be demonized for loving two men at once. Only a tiny percentage of mammals practice monogamy, and we're the only ones who try to regulate it through marriage."

"But that's not what we're talking about, is it?" I asked. "We're not talking about three adults consenting to a polyamorous relationship. We're talking about one person deciding for all three. One person thinking she could have it all."

"I didn't think that way," Lore said. "I just knew I loved them both."

"But something had to give." I thought about what Oscar had told me about Andres bothering Lore. What did that mean?

"It did," Lore said. "With the temblor."

The next day, Lore called me right as I was leaving Andres's daughter, Penelope, another voicemail. I'd sent Carlos another message on Facebook, too. Maybe they would know if, toward the end, Andres and Lore's relationship wasn't as ideal as she made it sound—perhaps as ideal as it would become in her memory.

"Lore, hi." I looked at the time on my laptop: one thirty. "I wasn't expecting your call. Everything—"

"Turn on the news!" Lore interrupted. "Apúrate!"

"Why, what's happened?" I dug for the remote between the love seat's saggy cushions. "What channel?"

"Any channel!"

I flipped to CNN. A 7.1 magnitude earthquake had rocked Puebla, near Mexico City. Newscasters spoke over a chaotic montage of cell phone videos—people shouting in the streets, buildings collapsed, dust billowing. Police, fire trucks, ambulances. Long lines of men climbing like ants on the ragged hilltops of toppled apartment complexes, women with their arms around dusty open-mouthed children. Enrique Peña Nieto in a somber gray suit, reminding Mexicans they'd been here before, they'd come together in a spirit of solidarity and they would do so again in this tough time.

"Oh my God," I murmured. I put us on speaker, began recording on my laptop.

"It's thirty-two years to the *day* since the one in 1985." She sounded as unraveled as I'd ever heard her. "All this talk about the past. Es como . . . es como que . . . we've brought it back to life! All that dust." Her voice was strangled. "It feels like it's choking you."

Goose bumps rose on my arms. She had started telling me about the earthquake only yesterday. On September 19, 1985, nearly a year after Andres's first proposal, an 8.0 magnitude earthquake had devastated Mexico City. The number of dead was estimated between five and thirty thousand, depending on the source; a third of the living space in the city destroyed, much of it in Tlatelolco—where Andres had lived and where they'd both been when the earth cracked open. For a moment, it seemed possible we had that kind of power, to exhume the past and reanimate it.

We watched the news together for the next two hours, as Lore overlaid the devastating images with her own memories. It was as if she had a foot in each world, thirty-two years apart, and might disintegrate any second, her body turning to dust, more dust. While we talked, I pulled up old photos and news clips of the 1985 quake. I read about the "Miracle Babies" of Hospital Juárez, who had survived for seven days without milk, formula, human contact. I pictured Andrew the day he was born. Eyes swollen and disconcertingly alert, his wrinkled crimson limbs twitching in the plastic bassinet. I imagined the horror of the hospital collapsing around him, a mausoleum of babies squalling for mothers who would never come.

At 2 A.M., the curve of Duke's back beside me was like a boulder in the darkness. I watched his shoulder rise and fall as he snored. I wanted to shake him. Instead, I put on my headphones and listened to a podcast by an investigative reporter who'd spent more than a decade trying to find answers about a string of missing girls he believed were connected. They'd lived in rural America, where "things like this don't happen," and yet once the reporter dug deeper, he discovered a scourge of domestic violence the girls had endured inside their own homes. I wasn't prepared to hear the 911 call from a screaming six-year-old begging for help as her stepfather beat her mom and siblings in the background. I ripped out my headphones, breathing hard. Just like that, I was nine again, crotch of my purple jeans soaked with urine, only I hadn't made a sound. I never made a sound. Never called for help. I only ran to my room, where I wouldn't have to see it.

I opened my texts. *How's it going, buddy?* I messaged Andrew. *FaceTime soon?*

He responded with a thumbs-up. Like a loser, I sent a heart emoji, which he didn't acknowledge. For the last few months, his messages had been particularly short. Andrew was twelve, though. Duke was right—with so many years between us, what did we have in common? What did we have to say to each other? My body reverberated with sadness, loss.

At three, I popped some Tylenol PM and opened Gabriel's Facebook page. I scrolled aimlessly, stopping at a photo of Mateo with his nephew Joseph on his third birthday. Mateo was helping Joseph swing a stick into a piñata shaped like a car, both taking a batter's stance with near-identical looks of concentration. *Think of my nephews*, Mateo had said. It had been a couple of weeks since we'd met. I thought of his attempted bribe. His kindness with the euthanasia. How he'd managed to forgive Lore and maintain a relationship, despite everything she'd done. And my desire, however fleeting, to match his pain with my own. The conviction that we weren't all that different.

Maybe he'd be willing to talk to me again.

I opened an email draft on my phone. By the time of the earthquake, Lore had been with Andres for two years. Soon, they would be married. Less than a year later, he would be dead. What had the twins noticed about her during this midway point?

Hi Mateo,
I know you said you're not interested in being interviewed
for your mother's book, but I was hoping you'd reconsider. I
spoke with her today about the earthquake in 1985. It sounds
completely terrifying. What do you remember about that time?

To my surprise, I received a response within minutes: *You're burning the midnight oil.*

A grin tickled my lips. There was that unexpected humor again.

Someone has to, I wrote back. Maybe Lore had softened him to the project. Or maybe he'd felt a similar connection with me. *So, where were you when you found out about it?*

School, he said. *My dad heard about it on the news in Austin. He couldn't get ahold of her, so he drove straight down and took Gabriel and me out early.*

Did you know right away that something was wrong? I asked.

No. We were excited at first. But then we saw his face in the office. He looked so bad we knew it was about her. We thought she was dead, even before we heard about the earthquake.

I imagined the boys, only two years older than Andrew was now. Only a few years younger than I was when my mother died. I could still feel that punch of shock, the strange numbness in my hands and feet, the magical thinking, willing to strike any sort of bargain if it would turn back time.

What happened next? I asked.

Duke's snore caught and dragged. I turned my back to him, curling around the phone.

Dad told us about the earthquake and said no one had heard from her. Which made sense—the phone lines were down. But still, we were all thinking the worst. My dad was a wreck. He took us home and we were basically glued to the news.

Now that he was talking, it was a gamble, what I was about to ask. But it felt important, even necessary, to hear his voice as he told the story.

Mateo, can I call you? I wrote. *It can be off the record if you want . . .*

Nothing. I bit my lip.

Now? he wrote.

Unless you have something better to do? I sent the message without thinking, then flushed. God, that sounded inappropriate. One minute passed. Two. Then:

Okay. He included his cell number.

I slunk from bed, closed the door quietly behind me. Leaving the room was only a formality. There was no such thing as privacy in seven hundred square feet. Of course, I wasn't doing anything I needed to hide.

"Hi," Mateo answered, low, as if he, too, were trying not to wake someone. He was divorced, I knew from Lore, but maybe there was someone in his bed.

"Hi." I felt suddenly awkward, almost shy.

"So," we said at the same time, then laughed a little.

"You were saying," I started, leaning against the kitchen counter. "Your dad was a wreck. Can you tell me more about his reaction?" I wanted a sense of how Fabian acted under pressure. Was his instinct to be methodical, to plan? Or did he boil over?

"He's one of those people who has to take action," Mateo said. "The only thing he could do was call people. The bank, my tía Marta, anyone who might somehow know what had happened to my mom's hotel—because we figured she'd probably been there, just after seven in the morning. The news kept showing the St. Regis, destroyed, and I remember thinking if it could happen somewhere that fancy, it could happen wherever she was staying. I kept imagining her buried and burning at the same time. But instead." He cut off.

"She was with Andres," I finished.

He didn't respond.

"While your dad was in Austin and your mom was traveling frequently to Mexico, did you notice anything different about her?" All the secrets Lore was keeping. Surely something must have slipped through the cracks.

"You want to know if she's a master manipulator. Like that article implied."

"Actually, I think very few people are," I said. "When we're shocked someone isn't who we thought they were, it's usually not because they hid it so well—more like, the closer we are to a person, the less clearly we see them."

"Speaking from experience?" Mateo asked.

It felt like an invitation, a test. He was not dissimilar from Lore in that way. I swallowed. "My parents weren't who I thought they were, either."

A soft, companionable silence.

"Do you talk about it?" he asked. "Maybe with your husband?"

What an unexpected, intimate question. And *husband*. The word gave me a frisson of—something. Had I mentioned Duke that day at Mateo's clinic? He must have noticed my ring.

"We're not married yet," I said. "But no."

I thought he was going to use it against me, ask me again how I got off on demanding other people's stories when I couldn't even divulge mine to the person closest to me. Instead he said, "Word of advice?"

"Sure."

"It's not easy to live with someone who keeps secrets."

He could have been talking about Lore, though something told me he wasn't. I imagined his ex-wife asking him questions about his father, imprisoned for murder. "You can talk to me," she'd say, stroking his arm. And Mateo kissing her forehead and saying, "There's nothing to talk about." He'd say it wishing it were true, while the weight of the past buckled his knees, a weight he'd grown so accustomed to that he might fall without it.

LORE, 1985

Years later, Lore won't remember exactly what she and Andres were talking about in the kitchen on the morning of September 19, 1985. She'll remember earlier, in bed. She'd taken to selecting one of his classes and reading along with the syllabus. Kant and Nietzsche, Otto and Kierkegaard. They'd been talking, lately, of Otto's concept of the numinous, a word Lore loved for sounding exactly like what it meant.

"It's wholly other," Andres says in bed. Even this early, the apartment is honeyed with summer. They lie naked on a mostly naked bed, any unnecessary fabric hurled to the corner of the room. Through the open windows, music and yelling and the blare of honking horns float up from the Paseo de la Reforma.

"Wholly other," Lore repeats, her fingertips grazing his chest, his hips, his inner thighs, stroking him.

"Unlike"—Andres struggles to speak, hard in her hand—"anything we experience in our day-to-day lives."

"Anything?" she murmurs against his neck.

"Mmm." He closes his eyes.

She removes her hand. "Go on, Doctor."

He groans. "Lore . . ."

"Tell me."

"You know. You've read," he says, but he continues, brisk, hurrying through. "It's the experience that is meant to underlie all religion. *Mysterium tremendum et fascinans.* Mysterium is the mystery, the unknown, the impossible-to-know. When you feel it, the only possible reaction is silence."

"Silence," Lore says, and it sounds like a command. So they're silent, eye to eye, and when they do this, when they look into each other, Lore wills herself open, nothing hidden, nothing untrue. She wills him to see her.

"The numinous provokes awe," Andres says, not breaking their gaze, "but also terror, because of its overwhelming power."

Lore has been trying to get through Kierkegaard's *Fear and Trembling*, which Andres's Philosophy of Religion class is reading. The whole book explores the story of Abraham, whom God commanded to sacrifice his son as a demonstration of his faith. Lore has always hated that story, God so petty and cruel, so desperate for human affirmation he would inflict upon a parent the greatest suffering one could endure—and Abraham? What kind of father raises a knife to his son before sacrificing himself? Kierkegaard calls Abraham a "knight of faith" for being able to hold such a contradiction in his heart—that the God who would ask such a terrible sacrifice was also a God who loved him, that this is the essence of faith, but when Andres asked her what she would do in that circumstance, she was indignant: "I would never sacrifice my child. Not for anything. And any God who asked me to can go fuck himself." Andres looked startled, and she understood why: she sounded like a mother.

"But the numinous is also merciful," Lore prompts him.

"Yes," Andres says. "Fascinans. Merciful and gracious."

She closes the small distance between them, her warm mouth to his, and soon they are so slick with sweat they need to take a second shower.

So in the kitchen afterward, maybe they're still discussing the numinous. The foundation of Abraham's terrible faith. Or maybe they're talking about nothing at all. Not every conversation between them is important.

This is what she'll remember: Perching on the countertop beside the stove, drinking her café de olla as Andres scrambles eggs. *Hoy mismo* on the little living room TV. Wilted chives on the cutting board. She'll remember that if they didn't eat quickly, they'd be late, or at least Andres would be for his eight o'clock class. Lore has until nine to meet with Mr. de la Garza, the customer she won the night she and Andres went to La Opera Bar. She's still wearing only one of Andres's T-shirts. That will be impossible to forget.

The first tremors come hard and fast—Lore is on the counter and then she's on the linoleum, sharp, shooting pain in her tailbone. Andres stumbles backward, knocking over a dining chair. The pot flies from the stove, spilling half-scrambled eggs at their feet, the hot metal missing Lore's ankle by inches. On *Hoy mismo*, the light fixtures shake, and then the cameras. The anchorwoman tries to laugh. Then the floor is bucking, swelling, like a ship on a violent ocean. Lore screams, reaches for Andres, grasps his fingers before she is thrown back again. The walls shriek as wood splits apart. A monstrous crack shoulders its way through one of the living room windows, and then the window explodes. Lore screams again and Andres grabs her arm and wrenches her with him to the door. They're both barefoot.

"Wait, shouldn't we—" And what is she about to say, that they should hide below the breakfast table, clutch the bedroom doorframe? This is a fucking earthquake. Lore doesn't know what to do.

"No!" Andres grabs her arm and pulls her out of the apartment. The floor is still wild, jolting them straight up and down as they run toward the stairwell. "We're on the lake bed!"

Mexico City, the constantly sinking land . . . Do you feel it?

Lore feels it, she hears it, roaring and shattering, and she thinks they've done the wrong thing, because in the stairwell it's like they're in the throat of some giant beast, already half-swallowed. Andres is crushing her fingers, his other hand between the shoulders of the man in front of him, pushing, shouting, "¡Corré, corré!" and the walls are shaking, cracks shooting up below their feet, the stairwell smelling like cigarette smoke and piss and the sulfur of their terror.

"Han visto—"

"Madre de dios—"

"Muévanse, muévanse, ¡apúrense!"

They burst out the heavy metal double doors and into a morning of screams and sirens. They run through the noise of the world ending. Finally, Lore gasps, "Stop, I can't—" She leans on her knees, panting, and turns around: the bottom few stories of their building are intact below top stories that are half-collapsed, rotated sideways. There's glass everywhere, an angry tangle of steel, and which one was their window? Lore doesn't know, because it's gone. Gone, and they were just inside. What if Andres hadn't known to run? They would both be dead, and how would Fabian have found out? *Would* he have found out? Or perhaps her body would never be excavated, and she would simply be lost, and when he blamed the bank for sending her so much over these last two years, Raúl, the president, would accept responsibility but secretly he'd be thinking: Wasn't it Lore's sick abuela who had made her business trips more frequent, and wasn't he doing her a favor by letting her extend those trips to take care of her? And they would have a service, and the cuates would heft the weight of an empty coffin, and they would lower it into the traitorous earth and visit a spot she'd never been, never would be, and they'd never know she'd died in a kitchen beside a man she loved who was scrambling eggs for breakfast, and now she's on her knees, retching, prostrated before the unfathomable wreckage.

"¿Cómo . . . cómo?" Lore wipes her mouth. Andres pulls her against him. There are people who don't seem to know they're bleeding. Babies with wondering tear-filled eyes. Dust graying their hair, coating their teeth, and Lore feels all the terror of Abraham's God and none of the mercy of the numinous.

Andres repeats her name. He asks if she can hear him, and finally she nods. His eyes are wild, sweat beading on his forehead. "Penelope and Carlitos," he gasps. "We need to get to them."

Andres pulls her to her feet, and they begin to run. Normally it would take a little over an hour to walk from Tlatelolco to Rosana's house in La Roma. But everywhere they turn the roads are blocked, buried. The city is ashen, covered in cement dust, the air thick with smoke and soot. Some multistory buildings are toppled as if by giant hands. Others seem to have crumbled from the inside out. There are awnings and glass and shattered marquees on the sidewalks, isolated letters like oversize children's toys. Cars crushed, crumpled hoods peeking out from beneath hunks of concrete. And everywhere, people screaming.

At some point, Lore and Andres pull the glass from their feet, and Lore is shocked by how much they bleed and how little she feels the pain. Andres tears strips of his shirt for makeshift bandages. They can't speak. They cough with every breath. The city is shrieks and wails and sirens. Everywhere they look, every building that has fallen, Lore thinks, There were people in there. Dizzily she thinks of Teotihuacán, where she and Andres took Penelope and Carlitos early on. The kids had run before them down the Avenue of the Dead, racing to the Pyramid of the Moon as if this were a giant playground. She and Andres had walked quietly, holding hands. The Aztecs had named Teotihuacán—the City of Gods—but it had first been inhabited by farmers and artisans who'd mined obsidian, sharpening the dark rock into blades and trading it across the Americas. They'd been thought to be a peaceful people, a hundred thousand or more who fled mysteriously around 300 BC. But just recently, the remains of 137 bodies had been found in mass graves near the temple. Their beaded shell necklaces had been carved into the shape of human teeth, hands bound behind their backs. Unwilling sacrifices. How much could you ever know about a people who disappeared?

Even in the swell of panic and devastation, news travels fast: Hospital Juárez has fallen. The ambulances were all crushed within the parking garage. Hundreds if not thousands were trapped inside, including the dozens of babies unlucky enough to be born into a world right before its destruction.

Lore looks at Andres, her heart lurching. "Wasn't Penelope going to—"

"Not until this afternoon," Andres says, and though his voice is sure, tight, his green eyes turn nearly black with fear. Penelope's friend Leslie had just had her tonsils out. Penelope was supposed to visit her with mango paletas. "They should still be at home." He adds, a furious, hissed prayer: "Dios, por favor, let them still be at home. Let them be okay."

They run when they can, shaking off people who tug at their elbows, grab at their shirts. Lore wants to shut her eyes against the need, against the strange collections of belongings in people's arms: flowered sheets, twelve-inch TVs, ragged collarless dogs. What can she do? She is powerless, they all are.

They stop only once, when a heavy-breasted woman with a thick unraveling braid thrusts her newborn into Lore's arms. The woman is weeping, begging Lore to hold her daughter while she looks for her boy, who'd gotten separated from her in the stairwell of their apartment building. And then the woman is shoulder to shoulder with the dozen men digging by hand, a task that seems unbearably futile. A man yells, "¡Silencio!" and everyone hushes, straining their ears, and sure enough, there is a high keening cry coming from somewhere, everywhere. Andres says, "Fuck," and runs to join them, leaving Lore alone with the baby, who can't be more than three weeks old. The mother in the middle of the cuarentena, the forty-day cocoon in which Lore had felt trapped, literally eaten alive, but now, with the tiny wrapped bundle in her arms, the closed eyes and milk-dreaming lips, she would give anything to be back there, safely in bed with the cuates in her arms and Fabian feeding her freshly buttered tortillas.

"Shh," Lore says, the swaying bounce returning to her as if no time had passed. The sun is in the baby's face, and Lore turns slightly to offer her shadow.

"¡Silencio!" the man on the highest point of the rubble shouts again.

The cry comes, weaker now, and someone yells, "¡Aquí, aquí, miren! ¡Ayúdenme!" Andres is on his knees among the rest, and the mother is screaming for them to hurry, please, hurry, and Andres says something to her, and she clasps a hand over her mouth and nods, waiting.

In Lore's arms, the baby jolts, loosening the thin pink blanket. Her eyes open abruptly, and her face reddens, and she wails. The mother whirls around, and Lore wants to weep for the two patches of wetness forming at the woman's breasts, and for the way she turns from the baby to the rubble and back again.

Lore waves, shouting, "¡Estamos bien!" She puts the baby on her shoulder and pats her back, and the mother touches her heart, tears streaming. She turns back to the wreckage and shouts something Lore can't hear—that everything is going to be okay, maybe, that Mami is here, he just needs to be brave, and patient, and it will all be okay.

Finally, finally, there is a great commotion, dust pluming around the curved backs of the mother and the men, and then a vast, disbelieving cheer rises up. When the mother stands, she is cradling her son like a baby, his skinny toddler legs dangling, and then she shifts him so that his arms wind around her neck, and for a few glorious moments, they are all a part of the miracle.

Andres and the mother walk back to Lore together. The mother is thanking him, turning back to the others, thanking them, but already they are digging again, and Lore thinks *this* is faith, men's hands against thousands of pounds of rubble, searching, believing. The mother adjusts the boy so that he sits on her hip, and he's dirty and scuffed, but his tearstained face is bright as he looks around with uninjured curiosity.

The baby has drifted into sleep again, and Lore and the mother giggle as they shuffle her into the mother's waiting arm. The toddler looks at his sister with casual indifference, starting a stream of chatter: "How did you know where to find me? Mami, I was buried! I couldn't move!"

The mother looks at Lore, her dark eyes brimming. "Ya sé, mijo," she says. "I know. It must have been so scary." To Lore, she says: "Madre a madre: gracias." And Lore leans forward to embrace the three of them, the one unwieldy body they have become, the way mothers always become with their children.

"Que Dios te bendiga," Lore whispers.

CASSIE, 2017

The Saturday after the earthquake, Duke convinced me to leave my work on the book for brunch at La Condesa—market research. We sat in a saddle-leather booth beneath a bright mural that looked like a decoupage of Mexican street signs. In my mind, I saw kaleidoscopic flashes of toppled buildings, Lore and Andres running in bare feet. Her story was alive inside me, practically writing itself now.

"So I was thinking," Duke said. "For the wedding, instead of a sit-down dinner, why don't we do hors d'oeuvres? And we could make custom cocktails or even infusions—like, vodka infused with fresh citruses—to pair with them. Maybe something like mini flights."

"Sure." I was only half listening as I poured coffee from the small French press on the table. "That all sounds great. Expensive, probably, though. The food and drinks, I mean."

A shadow crossed his face, deepening when my phone rang. He probably thought it was Lore-related. The book had been an unspoken source of tension between us since we'd watched Fabian's police tapes together. But it was Andrew. Normally I wouldn't answer around Duke, just in case. But it had been so long since we talked.

"Hey!" I answered. "I was going to FaceTime you later!"

"Wouldn't have worked." Andrew's voice was changing—not yet a teenager's but no longer a little boy's. An in-between phase I hardly recognized. "The internet got cut off."

The first flicker of alarm. "What? Why?"

"I guess Dad didn't pay the bill."

My mouth went dry. I whispered to Duke, "Be right back," before slipping out the patio doors onto Second Street.

"Andrew, what's going on?" I asked.

All I heard was breathing, shallow and raspy. A quicksand feeling in my chest, slow sinking. I knew, somehow, that these were the final moments of pretending.

"Andrew?"

"He's drinking again." Andrew said it so matter-of-factly that bile rushed up my throat.

I turned away from the patio diners. "What do you mean?" I said, almost a gasp. Sun like a spotlight. "Again. What do you mean?"

"Dad's an alcoholic," he said. "You didn't know?"

I sank to the curb, elbows on my knees.

"When did it start?" I managed, instead of answering his question. "This time, I mean."

"I don't know. June, July. He forgot me at karate last night. My sensei took me home. Dad was passed out on the porch. He'd locked himself out. My sensei had to call a locksmith." The sentences came quickly, stacked like coins. "It was so embarrassing. And, Cassie, he's gotten—" Andrew stopped.

"What, Andrew?"

"Mean."

The sidewalk seemed to tilt beneath me, knocking me off balance, even though I was already on the ground. This was it, the reckoning some part of me had been expecting for the past twelve years. I saw myself handing Andrew to my father in the driveway after months of wearing him like an extra appendage, nights of setting him on the mattress beside me after a feeding, pushing pillows and blankets away so there was nothing that could smother him, my face so near his that I breathed in the air he breathed out. It smelled like nothing. I kept thinking of the flower, baby's breath. I finally understood why it was called that.

An infant passed from one set of arms to another in an ordinary suburban driveway. The chance I had taken with his life, in exchange for mine.

"What do you need?" I asked. "What can I do?"

"I don't know." He sounded exhausted, a child hoping I could solve a problem he'd been dealing with in secret for God knew how long. He was braver than I was, asking for help. But he'd come to the wrong person.

"Okay," I said. "Does Dad still have his job?"

My father had lost it when I was nine, right before getting shit-faced at a bar and coming home to hit my mother in front of me for the first time. He could've been fired again, triggering a relapse, or maybe the relapse had gotten him fired, and now he had no money to pay the internet bill. I could feel myself spiraling.

"I guess," Andrew said. "He still leaves in the morning and comes back at six."

"Okay. Is he behind on any other bills that you know of? Do you need money? I can Venmo you . . ."

I trailed off, thinking of my account. No, I couldn't. Not any sum that would make a difference, anyway.

"I don't know." Andrew sounded frustrated. "How am I supposed to know that? He pays everything online."

"Right. Okay. Well, if nothing's gotten turned off besides the internet, that's a good sign."

He didn't say anything. I could almost hear him wondering why he'd told me, realizing just how pathetic and useless to him I was.

"I'm going to talk to him. Okay? I'll call him tonight." The idea made my gut twist. I took a slow, steadying breath. "Andrew. Are you—do you feel safe? With Dad?"

A beat passed. "I guess."

I closed my eyes. Of course, over the years, I'd thought about what I'd do if I found out my dad was violent with Andrew. I'd imagined myself flying into Enid on wings of righteous fury, spiriting my little brother away. But then what? I barely made enough to support myself, let alone a kid. And preparing meals, doing school drop-offs and pickups, helping with homework, seeing him through puberty, dating, SATs, college applications, his needs before mine, always. If Andrew needed to live with us, what would happen to the book? To my career? What would happen when Duke found out the truth?

None of that mattered. I told myself to push harder, to make Andrew tell me. But the words that came out were: "If you ever don't feel safe, go straight to a neighbor's house and call me. Okay?"

He let out a sound that was almost a laugh. "Yeah. Sure."

"I'll call Dad tonight. We'll get this figured out."

He sighed. Then, softer, younger: "Thanks, Cassie."

Inside, our waiter appeared before Duke could ask any questions. After a hasty glance at the cocktail list, I ordered La Bruja: tequila and gin, lemon, and angostura and fresh Fresno pepper. Make it hurt, I wanted to say.

"Everything okay?" Duke asked. His blond curls were springy, freshly washed. His green button-down brought out the hazel in his eyes. He looked wholesome, untarnished.

Tell him, I thought.

"My dad forgot to pay the internet bill." I managed a weak shrug. "Andrew was upset."

Duke stared at the light installation that looked like hanging vines. "You know, I've been thinking about what we talked about a couple of months ago, about meeting your family." He met my gaze again. "Maybe we should go out there soon—maybe for Thanksgiving? Doesn't your dad at least want to meet the guy you're marrying?"

His tone was teasing, all wrong, and I felt choked with rage I knew Duke didn't deserve. He couldn't know what I'd never told him. For the first time, I understood the blinders Lore had forced herself to wear as time marched toward its inevitable reveal.

"Maybe." My drink arrived, and I took a deep, burning gulp. "I'll think about it."

"Let's just do it." Duke had his phone in his hands, opening the calendar app. "We were going to close the truck anyway and—"

"Duke!" I snapped. "I said I'd think about it! Jesus."

Duke gave me a long, unsettled gaze as he set his phone down, and I knew—the way Lore must have known—I couldn't keep my secrets much longer.

LORE, 1985

Rosana lives in a second-floor apartment of a century-old Art Nouveau building in La Roma. The colonia was modeled after Parisian neighborhoods, with broad tree-lined boulevards, plazas, and parks. The first time they went, Andres told Lore she should have seen it before the commercial developers descended in the sixties, tearing down or gutting hundred-year-old mansions; before General Gas and Woolworth moved in and office buildings went up, and before the new road system connected La Roma more easily to the rest of the city, making it less isolated and exclusive. There was a total lack of urban planning or zoning regulations, Andres had griped. It was an epidemic in DF. But Lore didn't care. She loved the graceful plaster facades of the old mansions, the classic brownstones, the jewel-tone apartments like Rosana's. She fantasized about living here.

Now she clutches Andres's arm. Her right foot throbs like a heartbeat. "Andres," she manages. La Roma is ravaged. Old mansions crumbled, new apartments wrenched off their foundations, ancient trees draping thick roots across the roads.

"Fucking Christ," Andres says, and then, "Lore, get on my back, hurry."

He turns, offering himself to her. She says, "I can run."

So they run, shoving through the crowd gathered around the circular fountain in the Plaza Río de Janeiro, women in robes, men in underwear, the intimacy of morning routines made public. Rescue workers are arriving now, men in hard hats, the Red Cross. Finally, they're in front of Rosana's building, and a ragged cry escapes from Andres's throat: the roof looks askew, like a hat on sideways. Windows broken, plaster cracked. But the building stands. And outside it, mere feet away, are the kids, standing with Rosana and her husband, Pedro.

Penelope sees them first, cries out, "Papi! Lore!" and runs to them. Carlitos follows, and they laugh and cry, touching each other's faces and saying "Gracias a Dios" and "Are you okay, are you hurt, who's bleeding?" Lore sobs into Carlitos's untamed curls, and suddenly, fiercely, she wants her own sons in her arms, and that makes her cry harder. Has Fabian heard by now? Has he tried calling her at the hotel where she'd told him she was staying? Is the hotel even still standing? The thought of Fabian in Laredo, not knowing whether she is dead or alive, tears at Lore's heart.

After the initial reunion, reality descends: The street looks like the photos of the Beirut bombings two years earlier. The air thick with dust, buildings gutted, their incomprehensible innards exposed. People sit on chunks of concrete or half-crushed cars, dazed and desolate, no idea what comes next.

"What are we going to do?" Penelope pulls at her dark ponytail. Her school uniform is twisted, the seam of her skirt aligned with her knee instead of her hip. Her left shin is scraped.

Rosana, tall and elegant and bookish, pulls Penelope into her side. "There won't be power, but we should get the radio." Andres nods, and Lore feels a sharp prick of jealousy: Rosana and Andres are the parents, Penelope and Carlitos, their children. They are the family. Lore and Pedro the interlopers.

"I'll go," Andres says. "Where is it?"

But Pedro is already walking briskly up the three stone steps leading to the mint-green front door. Lore blinks back more tears. There used to be so much color on this street. Now everything is brown and gray, decomposing.

"Do you think it's safe to go back inside?" Rosana asks Andres. "Tonight, I mean. Where will we sleep otherwise?"

They look at the roof, half of which seems intact, the other half badly battered. Andres, Lore knows, is not handy. When the toilet backed up one time and ten minutes of plunging didn't work, he called a plumber. When he needed new brakes on his bike, he took it to the shop. Fabian would be able to tell them whether the building was structurally sound. He'd know what needed to be done if it wasn't. She misses him the way she'd missed Mami when once, as a child, she'd gotten lost in a department store downtown. She couldn't see over the racks of clothes, kept running into unfamiliar hips, the world from that angle strange and uninhabitable; she wouldn't survive it alone.

"I don't know," Andres says.

Lore's arm is around Carlitos's arrowhead shoulders, and she feels a surge of love for Andres, that he can admit what he doesn't know.

"We could—your parents—" he starts.

Rosana shakes her head. "How would we get there?" And once again, Lore is on the outside, because she doesn't know where Rosana's parents live, far enough away to be presumed both safe and unreachable.

"There will be shelters—"

"'Shelters,'" Rosana snaps. "You mean tents. With thousands—"

"I know." Andres looks at Penelope and Carlitos.

"Your apartment?" Rosana asks, as if it just occurred to her.

Lore speaks for what feels like the first time since they got there. "Gone."

Rosana's hand flies to her mouth. Her diamond catches the sun, and Lore gasps, looking at her own bare finger. Her wedding rings zipped into the interior compartment of her purse, now buried beneath tons of rubble. And the emerald Andres had tried to give her. She knew he'd put it in the small metal safe in the closet. It, too, is lost. She closes her fingers around her gold locket, brings it to her lips for a kiss. A dangerous thing, to continue to wear it here, but it's her way of honoring Fabian and the cuates, and she never takes it off. Now she is desperately glad, as if the locket is a magical item, able to transfer the brush of her lips through the miles.

"Gone?" Rosana repeats. "Completely?"

Andres nods. "We barely made it out." When Penelope pales, bluish half-moons darkening beneath her eyes, Andres says hurriedly, "No, mija, tranquila, I'm only being dramatic. We were already half out the door when it happened."

"Then why are you only wearing a T-shirt?" Carlitos asks, and they all look down at Andres's T-shirt, hanging to Lore's thighs, her legs bare and dust-gray. "And no shoes?" Their feet are chalky and filthy, Lore's makeshift bandages soaked through with blood.

"Jesus." Rosana looks at Lore with new respect. "Pedro should take a look. Where is he, anyway?"

As if on cue, Pedro appears in the doorway, triumphant, Penelope's boom box in hand. They can hear the low tones of the emergency broadcast, and it draws half a dozen other people standing nearby.

"Pedro," Rosana says, touching his elbow. "Andres and Lore are hurt."

Pedro is a doctor, ten years older than Rosana and Andres, with a thick shock of white hair and a dark beard. "Where?" he asks, as if affronted. When she points toward their feet, he says, "Ah, yes, of course. Look, we should all go inside. It seems stable enough in there and better than . . ." He looks around.

There is a small crowd surrounding the boom box—a paunchy-thin viejito in a guayabera; a Middle Eastern couple with three young children; a twentysomething woman in tight jeans and a rhinestone top.

"Por favor," says the viejito. "Leave it if you're going inside. We need to know what's happening."

Pedro is still gripping the handle. The boom box is red, the speakers yellow. It's from another time. "We need this as much as anyone."

"I have one, too," Carlitos says. Lore squeezes his shoulder.

"Pedro, honestly," Rosana says, impatient.

"Fine, fine." Pedro gives it to the viejito, who says a somber thank-you.

"Yes, but are you sure we should go back in?" Andres squints up at the roof. "I'm not sure that—"

"Excuse me, are you an engineer?" Pedro snaps.

"Are you?" Andres shoots back.

"Why don't we go take a look?" Lore suggests. "If nothing else, we can put some things in suitcases, make a plan."

Rosana nods. "And we can take care of those feet." She leads the way, with Penelope under her arm, and Lore follows, with Carlitos under hers. Now Andres and Pedro are the interlopers.

Inside, Pedro cleans Lore's feet with hydrogen peroxide and spackles them with butterfly stitches before bandaging them. Andres rebuffs Pedro's efforts, wiping his own feet, covering them with Band-Aids. Then Lore and Penelope begin sweeping the parquet floors free of glass and plaster and the concrete dust that seems to be everywhere. Pedro and Andres heft up Rosana's heavy bookshelves, and Lore and Penelope pick up the dozens of fallen books. Lore asks Rosana whether she likes them organized in any certain way. After a moment, Rosana laughs. "DF may be destroyed, but goddamn it, my books will be alphabetized!" They laugh until it isn't funny anymore.

On the radio—Carlitos's boom box, silver, with a Luis Miguel cassette in the deck—they learn that the Secretaría de Comunicaciones y Transportes, on Eje Central and Xola Avenue, the southern end of the lake bed zone, has failed, cutting off communication between DF and the rest of the world. If Fabian has tried to call the hotel, he wouldn't be able to get through. Lore is desperate to hear his voice, to let him know she's alive, but how?

In the kitchen, Rosana is assembling lunch, or is it dinner by now? Lore looks out the window: all she can see are treetops, swaying. For a moment she panics, though it's only the breeze. Yes—dinner. The sky, from what Lore can see, is a dusky pink.

Pedro and Andres are looking for candles and flashlights and extra batteries, discussing what they'll do when they run out of drinking water. Lore swallows a dart of panic. She's booked on a flight back to San Antonio in two days. Will planes still be flying in and out? How can she leave? How can she stay?

As the apartment dims into evening, Rosana and Lore set out plates on the blond wood dining room table. They're serving all the cold food: roughly cut chunks of cheese, slices of ham, small bowls of leftover picadillo. Rosana pours generous glasses of red wine for the adults and Penelope, who is close enough, and Andres lights candles—"Better to reserve the batteries," he says—and despite the surreal drone of the radio and the lacerating pain in her feet, dinner feels strangely festive, almost giddy, and Lore realizes they're all on the verge of hysteria, because how do you process how quickly everything can be taken, including your own life?

That night, on blankets and pillows spread out on the living room floor, Lore's tears come fast. She's thinking of Fabian and the cuates, a deep, physical ache, but she's also thinking of how things could have been different, if she had still been in Laredo, if Andres had been on his way to the UNAM without her making him late. She imagines him on his bike, the earth's shudder sending him flying, the final crack of his skull.

"I'd die if I lost you," Lore whispers, and the tears come harder.

Andres kisses her, the wine soured on his tongue and the smell of his sweat sharp and essential and alive. Lore pulls him on top of her, her hands on the waistline of his borrowed pajamas, with an urgency that borders on panic. They cover each other's mouths—the bedrooms are all right beyond this room, anyone could walk out at any moment—and tears mingle on their faces as they move against each other, harder and harder. Lore wants to feel him everywhere, she wants to feel everything.

"What are we going to do?" Lore whispers afterward. Andres is still inside her. "What happens next?"

"You marry me," Andres says.

Lore laughs. "What?"

"Marry me, Lore." He touches her face, and a silvery streak of moonlight illuminates his eyes. "These are the times you realize what's important, and that's you and my kids. That's it. I don't care what happens next as long as they're safe and you're with me."

And what can she say to that? How can she deflect the question again, here, now, after what they've just been through? She can no longer imagine life without him. She can no longer imagine *herself* without him. And what is marriage, really, but making official, on paper, what is already in your heart? So she says what she wanted to say almost a year ago, even though it's destined to end in pain, though whose pain she cannot bear to imagine:

"Yes."

CASSIE, 2017

Before I gave up on my mother, I used to fantasize about the two of us running away together. It was always after one of the bad nights—heavy things knocked off shelves, the unmistakable dull thud of my mother hitting the wall—when I could hardly catch my breath in my dark bedroom, listening, some primordial reflex to remain vigilant. I'd imagine my mother and I meeting in the hallway, carrying only the most important things: our favorite crystals we'd dug up from the Salt Plains, my Tweety Bird journal with the little silver key, her wedding rings to pawn. We would pause outside her bedroom door, listen to the harshness of my father's snores. In the dim, her bruises would look like war paint. She would grab my hand tightly enough to hurt. She would say, "He won't wake for hours." And we would exchange grim, knowing smiles, because she'd have slipped something into his drink. We'd like knowing that if we wanted to, we could do anything to him.

After that, though, the fantasy lost its shape. The edges blurred, fading out. I never knew what would come next. I felt that way now, with Andrew. We'd reached a tipping point of some kind, but where would it lead?

Once Duke left for the food truck after our brunch at La Condesa, I rehearsed what I'd say to my father. I'd be firm but nonconfrontational. I couldn't risk him taking his anger at me out on Andrew. I'd call him at five, before my nightly call with Lore and before, I hoped, he'd be too wasted. At 4:45, though, my phone rang with a long international number. "Cassie Bowman speaking," I answered, dropping the laundry I was folding in an effort to distract myself.

"Ms. Bowman. This is Penelope Russo." The voice was husky, mellow. "You've left me several messages. I wasn't sure I wanted to get involved, but—well—I'm intrigued. You're working on a book about Lore?"

"Dr. Russo." I shoved aside the clothing on the bed to set up my laptop. "Hi. Yes. As you can imagine, the *Laredo Morning Times* story caught my attention."

Penelope gave a hard laugh. "Oh, I'm sure. Did Lore read the article?"

"She did."

Penelope was silent, waiting for more.

"I don't think she expected it all to come back into the public eye," I said carefully, not wanting to alienate her by sounding too sympathetic toward Lore.

"Well, if you do something like that, you should be prepared for the consequences, whenever they occur," Penelope said. "Don't you think?"

"I do," I said, both because it was what she needed to hear, and because it was true.

"I'm glad we're in agreement," she said. "So. What do you want to know?"

"Well, to start, I'd love to hear about your father. How you'd describe him, any special memories . . ."

Penelope sighed. "Thank you. That other reporter hardly asked about him. Everyone wants to know about Lore. It's like he just gets lost."

"That must be so hard," I said, with a pinch of guilt.

"I'm older than he was when he died, you know. No parent should outlive their child, but outliving your parents—I mean literally accruing more years on earth than they did—it feels wrong in its own way."

"I know what you mean," I said. A part of me dreaded turning forty.

"Have you lost a parent?" Penelope asked.

"My mother," I said. "I was seventeen."

"I was eighteen."

We were quiet, and I remembered how Lore and I had connected in this same way during our first interview. Penelope wouldn't like that they had this in common.

"What was he like, your father?" I asked again. "Do any stories about him come to mind?"

"Memories change over the years, don't they?" Penelope murmured. "Become less specific. Let's see. After he and my mother divorced, he told me the most important thing in a relationship is mutual respect. He said once respect is lost it's gone for good, and then—" Penelope laughed. "He panicked and said, 'I'm not using *respect* as code for *virginity*!'"

I laughed along with Penelope.

"We were both so embarrassed. But then he turned serious again. He said I would always recognize the lack or loss of respect by the feeling in the pit of my stomach. He said if I ever got that feeling, I could call him, day or night."

"Did you?" I asked.

"Luis was a hot-blooded sixteen-year-old Mexican boy," Penelope said, with another easy laugh. "I got the feeling exactly two weeks later, when a friend told me she'd seen him making out with someone else at a party."

I held the phone between my ear and shoulder as I took notes. "And did you call your dad?"

"I did. In the middle of the night, sobbing. After he figured out that I was safe, he just let me talk. He didn't interrupt, didn't give advice. He listened. He made me feel like it was important. Like *I* was important."

An ache spread through me like a stain, brutal and unforgiving.

"He sounds like a great father," I said.

"Not at the start, apparently," Penelope said. "That's how he lost my mother's respect. But for all the years I can remember—yes, he was."

I felt the small give of opportunity. "Did your parents argue?"

Penelope seemed to think about this. "I'm sure they did. But what we saw was worse, somehow. They were so civil to each other. Like strangers. Until the end, when— Well, anyway. I don't want to air my mother's dirty laundry, and she and Pedro have been married for more than thirty years now, so."

Lore had told me about Rosana's affair. A history of betrayal she knew would make it even more painful for Andres if he ever found out about Fabian.

"Can we talk about Lore?" I asked Penelope. "The *Laredo Morning Times* piece said you liked her immediately. Is that true?"

Penelope sighed. "Yes. Carlos and I both did. We *wanted* to like her. We worried about our dad being lonely when we stayed with Mom and Pedro. I remember he leaned in to kiss her that first day, and she turned her head so that it landed on her cheek, and she smiled at me as if . . . trying to include me in the moment. I felt her concern for my feelings." Penelope sounded strained, stiff, the challenge of parsing out the good in someone she'd spent years despising.

"In the article, you said she used you and threw you away like trash." The quote had been one of the reasons Lore agreed to talk to me. To make herself understood. "The piece spent a lot of time trying to diagnose her in some way—in your opinion as a psychologist, do you think she was a narcissist or a psychopath? They share characteristics, don't they?"

"Yes," Penelope said, her tone turning academic. "Grandiose sense of self, an entitlement that justifies, among other behaviors, pathological lying. Inability to feel remorse, shame, or guilt. You know," she said, interrupting herself, "other than my father's death, that's what hurt more than anything. We just never heard from her again." Even now, Penelope sounded puzzled, wounded. "She didn't come to his funeral, of course. But she never called us, never wrote. Never apologized."

That was why Penelope was talking to me. Thirty years later, she was still a hurt child who wanted an explanation.

"Actually," I said, "she did."

"Excuse me?"

"She wrote to you, supposedly. Multiple times. You never received those letters?"

"I . . ." Penelope trailed off. "No. We didn't."

"Could they have been intercepted? Maybe your mother saw them first if she checked the mail?"

The silence was fraught. "Yes, I . . . maybe." She trailed off. "Listen. I assume you've tried to reach my brother?"

"Yes," I said, surprised by the turn in conversation. "I've left him a few Facebook messages, but no response. Do you have a good phone number for him?"

Penelope gave it to me. "He had some tough years, just like I did after—you know, drugs and alcohol. Only he never quite pulled out of them." She hesitated. "If you talk to him, tell him my offer still stands."

"Of course," I said, wondering what the offer was. Rehab?

The conversation was winding down. I could feel her emotional reserves faltering. I needed to bring us to Andres's death. "Penelope, was there a specific reason your father went up to Laredo that weekend?"

She quieted. "The police asked that at the time. I wish I knew.

We'd been staying with him that week. We were still supposed to be there over the weekend. But then suddenly he said he was going to see Lore, and we went back to my mom's."

A deep, discordant chime rang through me: something, a definitive *something*, had prompted the trip.

"So he and Lore were still together at the time?" I asked carefully. "You didn't get the sense they'd broken up recently?"

"No," Penelope said. "Why?"

"Just an angle I'm exploring." I'd read through my notes from the call with Oscar so many times I'd memorized his words, including Lore's alleged claim that Andres was "bothering" her. If that was true, the only way I could see it making sense was if she'd tried to end their relationship and he hadn't taken it well. "There wasn't the slightest hint of conflict between them?" I asked.

"No." Her voice took on a hard, protective layer. "Why? What is she saying?"

"Like I said, it's an angle I'm exploring."

"Exploring for *what*?" Penelope's fury was laced with tears. "Hasn't she done enough? Now she's trying to damage my father's name?"

"I just needed to be sure," I said.

But was I? If I'd been asked, I probably would have defended my father just like this. We talk about needing to believe women when they come forward about abuse—but what are we supposed to do when they deny it?

"Don't forget," Penelope said, "Lore is a very good liar."

How could I forget? For months, Lore and I had been demanding honesty from each other, and here I was, investigating the day I'd promised her the book would not revolve around. It would be naive to assume Lore had never lied to me, no matter how intimate our conversations often felt. The question was—what had she lied about?

LORE, 1985

The power comes back the day after the temblor, and goes out again that night, when an aftershock sends them racing back outside, expecting Rosana's apartment building to collapse. Still, it remains. Once they go inside, they sit in the dark, dusty, hot living room, too nervous to talk, all their notions of safety stripped away. They could all be in their coffin right now, so accommodating, waiting for the walls to close in on them.

A third of the city is without electricity. Millions without running water, shitting in buckets. Flights to and from the United States have been canceled. Early reports estimate that a third of the city's buildings were damaged, with up to half the older architecture destroyed. The hospitals, the ones left standing anyway, are full. The army deployed. A curfew enforced. Gas leaks and fires and only one radio station coming through on Carlitos's boom box. Everywhere, men are digging by shovel and pick, tiny handheld tools, trying to unearth people whose screams grow weaker by the hour. They work around the clock, guided by car headlights at night. The women hand out soup and tortillas and take turns digging with their hands, all while the pinche government rejects foreign aid, specifically from the U.S., at least until the day following the aftershock, when the collective roar of the people becomes too loud to ignore and finally the heavy equipment starts to descend, along with talk of Nancy Reagan coming to tour the disaster, a pointless gesture even with the million-dollar "down payment" on aid she's rumored to be bringing with her.

A few days later, they're finally able to make long-distance calls again. In the middle of the night, Lore slips from the nest of blankets on the floor and into the kitchen. She stretches the avocado-green cord as far as it will go, snaking it into the tiny laundry room. Her stomach curdles with fear of getting caught. She needs to do this.

The phone rings one and a half times before Fabian rasps hello. For a moment, Lore can't even speak. He was sleeping. *Sleeping,* when he didn't know whether she was dead or alive. In a flash of pettiness, she wants to punish him by hanging up. Instead, she whispers, "It's me."

And then he is awake, voice ripped open with relief. "Lore? Oh, thank God! Are you okay? Where are you?"

Her throat closes. "I'm okay."

"God, Lore. They've been saying on the news that three Americans— I haven't known what to think."

"I'm sorry," she whispers, and then she's crying, trying to be quiet, though a sob is trapped in her chest. "I'm so sorry, Fabian."

"Ay, Lore, it's not your fault," he says, rough and tender. "Where are you? Why are you whispering?"

"I'm—" She hesitates. "Staying with friends. Everyone is asleep. It's been so hard to know anything about what's happening. There's only one radio station. The airport is still closed, I think."

"No," Fabian says urgently. "No, it's open. The runways weren't damaged. The UN is sending aid and everyone here is putting together packages, so—okay. Don't worry. I'll take care of everything. Just give me a phone number where I can reach you."

"Oh, uh—" The phone number is written in blue ink on a piece of paper taped to the handle. "I don't know it. I'll have to call you back when I can."

"Tomorrow. Today," Fabian says. "Call me later today. I'll have everything figured out."

Fabian has never sounded so capable, so determined. Lore closes her fingers around her locket, presses the sharp tip of the heart into her thumb. "Okay. Thank you. Wait—Fabian."

"What is it?"

"My purse. I lost it. I don't have my wallet, my passport, anything."

"God, Lore." Fabian's voice shakes, as if imagining how she'd lost her purse and how she could have been lost, too. "Just hang on. I'll get you home. I love you."

"I love you, too," Lore whispers. She creeps back into the kitchen and sets the phone in its cradle. Then she gasps. Carlitos is standing near the pantry, a straw punched in a box of mango Boing.

"Carlitos!" Lore says, a hand on her chest. "You scared me."

He lifts his drink. "I got thirsty." His eyes are wide without his glasses. "Who were you talking to?"

Lore's mind races. How much did he hear? "My sister. Come on. Let's go back to bed."

Carlitos lets her lead him out of the kitchen, a palm on his back. He slips into his room with a quiet goodnight, and she returns to the living room floor, heart pounding. Andres murmurs, folds himself around her. They will be married tomorrow.

Lore and Fabian were married at San Martín de Porres Catholic Church on December 12. They chose the date because the church, where they'd both grown up attending Mass, would already be decorated for Advent, the altar draped with aubergine cloth (so Lore's bridesmaids wore purple). The scarlet blooms of poinsettias shivered when the heater kicked on. They smiled at each other while Marta read from Corinthians.

Lore had chosen the reading not for the lines everyone read but for these: "For now we see in a mirror, darkly, but then face to face. Now I know in part, but then I shall know just as I also am known." Lore wanted to know Fabian, and she wanted to be known by him. She wanted to know everything she did not yet know. Her desire for the world was vast and dark and dizzying, and what was marriage if not a crucial part of that unknown world? What was love, Corinthians love, a love that transcended everything, even knowledge of itself? She wanted that.

But Corinthians didn't tell her about the *work* of love, a work as endless as mining the earth for obsidian, transmuting it from rock to blade. If you didn't kneel, if you didn't take your tool in hand, if you didn't search, you would have nothing. The obsidian of love would stay buried, and you would only half know, and you would only half be known.

As she limps beside Andres, with the ruins of the city momentarily obscured, Lore thinks there should be a word for the love that remains when the other love becomes unreachable. She and Fabian, their bodies monuments to the time they've spent together, the experiences they've shared, the lives they've created. Their bodies are like trees, branches separating even as their roots grow more deeply intertwined. Lore never wants those roots to untangle. She won't let them untangle.

But with Andres, she has a chance again at that other love. The obsidian kind.

And yet—it's crazy, what she's about to do. How had one dance come to this? But she's not willing to give him up, and if she'd said no to his proposal again, he would wonder why they're together at all, why he's wasting his time with a woman who doesn't see a future with him and his kids. From moment to moment, Lore veers from a trapped kind of panic to a hyper-rational calm, a low internal voice reminding her that as long as neither man finds out, they won't be hurt.

On their way to the UNAM's Jardín Botánico, Lore, Andres, and the kids pass handwritten lists taped to telephone poles—the names, ages, and descriptions of people who are missing. They pass mass immunizations and temporary shelters made of sheets and plywood, the newly homeless gathered on a torn sofa or a seat ripped from the back of a totaled car. They pass protests, people with signs saying NO BURNING BODIES, and WE WANT THE BODIES.

"Do you think it's wrong to do this now?" Lore asks Andres. Penelope and Carlitos walk ahead of them cautiously. They know now that the earth can devour them.

Andres squeezes her hand. "This was your idea," he reminds her.

"I know." There was no way she could actually plan a wedding. Who would she invite? It's not like she could ask Marta and Sergio to be the padrinos de lazos, the way they were for her wedding to Fabian. But now Lore's chest is tight, her breathing shallow again.

"Just, with everything that's happened . . ." Lore says, trailing off.

Up ahead, Penelope is daring Carlitos to touch one of the talon-like thorns on a cactus labeled *Myrtillocactus geometrizans.* "Penelope!" Andres shakes his head once, sharply, and Penelope gives a wry half smile. Turning back to Lore, Andres says, "Like happiness shouldn't be allowed in the midst of so much unhappiness?"

"Yes, I guess so."

"Who deserves happiness?" Andres asks. "When should it be allowed or not allowed?"

Lore smiles. "Is class in session, Doctor?"

"Come on." Andres smiles. "I want to know what you think."

Lore loves his interest in her opinions, her beliefs, his questions prying open parts of herself she'd never known. She feels herself relaxing as they walk, in the middle of that thorny jungle.

"Everyone deserves happiness," Lore says, but that's not quite right. "Unless you've hurt someone—really hurt someone. Torture, rape, murder. After that, I don't think you deserve happiness anymore."

"So only those who are moral deserve happiness?" Andres asks.

Lore considers. It seems like a trick somehow. "I guess so."

Andres laughs. "Well, Ms. Crusoe, you're in good company. The ancient Greeks believed, first, that happiness is a worthy pursuit—in some cases, the only worthy pursuit—and that it can only be found by those who understand and live into certain virtues and values. So," he teases, "do you consider yourself a moral person?"

Lore's first thought: *No, I am not a moral person, and I told you this the first night we met, look at what you call me, for fuck's sake—Ms. Crusoe. I told you everything you needed to know about me, and you weren't listening.*

But what if she believes that everyone is entitled to love, to giving it and receiving it, as much and as often as they can? How can love be immoral? Just look at Corinthians: Faith, hope, love. And the greatest of these is love.

If love is her moral center, and she is living into it, how can that be wrong?

"Yes," she says, finally, with a jut of her chin. "I think so."

Andres's guayabera—bought at the nearest open mercado along with Lore's dress, their simple silver rings, the arras, and the lazo—flaps a little in the breeze. "I know so. Look, we'll make mistakes. But if we are moral people and we believe that moral people are deserving of happiness, then what is happening outside of us in this moment"—he gestures toward the invisible fallout—"is just that: outside of us."

"So, in other words," Lore says in English, with a slow, playful smile, "fuck 'em."

Andres laughs. In English, he repeats, "Yes. Fuck 'em."

They walk a few more steps before he takes her hand and turns her toward him. Lore squints into his face, the sun in her eyes.

"Seriously," Andres says, "we don't have to do this now. But—you do want to marry me? Because—"

"Yes," Lore says, with a little shove to his chest. He catches her wrists, pulls her close, lowers his hands to her waist. She can feel their heat through her white sateen shift. Her heart catches at the intensity in his eyes, and she does what she always does when he looks at her like this: she tries to unshutter every hiding place, to let all her dark corners show.

"Good," Andres says, his breath against her lips.

And so, five days after the earth bucked below their feet, they stand at the base of a saguaro cactus that looks like a massive hand stretched toward the sky. Penelope at Lore's right, Carlitos at Andres's left—their maid of honor and best man. Andres's friend Jorge, a small, almost dainty man with an unexpectedly baritone voice, speaks words Lore will remember so many years later: "In this time of crisis, collapse, and separation, the two of you are forging a union—and amid all the rebuilding yet to come, the foundation of your union will be your starting point."

Later, of course, they'll need to get married at the Registro Civil, once they fill out the paperwork and Lore has a copy of her birth certificate translated to Spanish and they have their prenuptial blood tests done and Lore acquires the permiso to marry Andres. Legally, that's the only wedding that counts in Mexico, and Lore is hoping to put it off as long as possible, though what's the difference, really, when it's *this* wedding that will count to Andres? But for today, they've chosen their favorite parts of the traditional Catholic ceremony to be performed in the botanical gardens, nature as their church, no roof that might cave in on top of them.

Jorge has brought two small white kneeling pillows embroidered with lace, his gift to them as not only their minister but a padrino.

And now the time has come.

"Lore and Andres, have you come here to enter into marriage without coercion, freely and wholeheartedly?" Jorge asks.

Andres's hands are warm on Lore's. In the sun, his eyes are the color of shallow river water. "I have," he says.

Lore takes a deep breath. "I have."

"Are you prepared, as you follow the path of marriage, to love and honor each other for as long as you both shall live?" Jorge asks.

"I am," Andres says.

A flickering image of them as viejitos, Andres's lean limbs age-spotted, his hands gripping the rubber handles of a walker; her in a rocking chair, a crocheted blanket on her lap. She feels tears on her cheeks, she alone aware of the impossibility of her promise.

Her voice trembles. "I am."

"Repeat after me," Jorge says to Lore. "I, Dolores Rivera . . ."

"I, Dolores Rivera . . ." (Is claiming Fabian's last name a kind of thievery? Or an honoring, an inclusion of him in this day?)

"Take you, Andres Russo, as my lawful husband . . ."

"Take you, Andres Russo, as my lawful husband."

"To have and to hold from this day forward . . ."

"To have and to hold from this day forward." (As long as I can.)

"For better or worse . . ."

"For better or worse." (I'm sorry.)

"For richer or poorer . . ."

"For richer or poorer." (Fabian, in Austin.)

"In sickness and in health . . ."

"In sickness and in health." (The way Andres washed her feet the first time they'd made love.)

"Until death do us part."

Lore's armpits prickle. Would Andres still be alive if she'd walked away in this moment? Impossible to know, of course, which vagaries of life he would encounter without her, but at least he would never open that door at the Hotel Botanica. He would not lie on blood-wet carpet, waiting to be found by a stranger. But they are living in innocence now, as everyone is of the future.

"Until death do us part," Lore says.

Andres gives Lore the arras, thirteen gold coins tucked inside an ornate gold box. Their symbolism—a man's promise to support his wife—reminds Lore of Fabian and his endless labor, and she wishes they'd left this part out.

Then Penelope and Carlitos drape the lazo over their shoulders, smiling. The pearl beads of the oversize rosary are cool on Lore's skin. Somehow, she'd expected them to burn.

Jorge smiles as he begins the nuptial blessing. "O God, who by your mighty power created all things out of nothing, and, when you had set in place the beginnings of the universe, formed man and woman in your own image, that they might be no longer two, but one flesh, and taught that what you were pleased to make one must never be divided . . ."

Not divided, Lore thinks. Multiplied. Love, multiplied.

And soon after that, they are married.

CASSIE, 2017

I was a coward. Just like my mother, who'd done nothing to get me out of that house. I'd told Andrew I'd spoken to my father when I'd actually hung up after the second ring. The next day, though, Andrew told me the internet was back on. The following evening, he said he thought Dad was going to meetings. "Whatever you said to him must've worked," Andrew said, and I hated myself for taking credit for what was, at best, a temporary improvement. *Dad's an alcoholic. You didn't know?* Andrew's voice chimed through my mind at odd hours, waking me in the middle of the night. The way he wasn't surprised when I asked whether he felt safe.

I threw myself into working on the book. I had hundreds of pages of interview transcripts, and my proposal was nearly finished. Recently, I'd started writing some sample chapters—Lore arriving in Mexico City, meeting Andres, their midnight walk at Chapultepec. I'd begun this project wanting to understand Lore, to dissect her, to lay bare her choices. Now, in writing, I was *inhabiting* her. It unnerved me, how easy it was.

Over FaceTime a week after the Andrew call, as I'd come to think of it, Lore gave a small laugh. "They all thought we were crazy, getting married five days after the temblor, but it made sense in a way: the city was rebuilding; we were rebuilding. The 'foundation of our union'—I loved that, something the minister said—the 'foundation of our union' would be our starting point."

"And what *was* the foundation of your union?" I was crabby today. Not in the mood for her romanticizing. "What could it be, considering you were already married?"

Lore straightened up on her living room couch, adjusted the angle of the phone. "They were independent of each other. They were like neighboring houses."

"Yes, but—" I clicked between articles, found what I was looking for. "Take the earthquake, for instance. Take Roma."

"La Roma."

"La Roma. Some of the old mansions were destroyed because of cracks in their foundation caused by the construction of those newer office complexes." Lore made a murmur of possible acquiescence, and I built on her silence. "I don't think they could have been as independent as you thought. You say you brought a wholeness into each relationship, but there were things you couldn't give to them both. Andres never knew you as a mother, for example. You must have felt that. It must have been hard."

"He saw me with Penelope and Carlitos."

"That's not the same."

Lore was quiet, then said, "You know, when we stopped to help that toddler in the temblor, the mother thanked me—'Mother to mother,' she said. She could tell."

"Are you suggesting that you think Andres could tell, on some level? And that was enough?"

"I think there are things we carry in our bodies and in our souls that don't need to be explained to be known by others."

"I think," I said to her, to both of us, "that might just be a justification you told yourself."

"Okay, what do you think I didn't give to Fabian?" Lore asked, a challenge.

"Fidelity. Honesty. Time," I said. "To start."

"Yes, but I was more there, more present, in our time together than I had been before. That matters, doesn't it?"

"I don't know," I said. "Do you think Fabian would agree? Do you think if he'd had the choice, this is the one he would have made?"

"Fabian," Lore said, "made his own choices."

"You mean killing Andres?"

"I don't want to talk about that."

I took a risk. "Oscar Martinez told me you said Andres was bothering you. What did you mean? Did you see Andres that day?"

"Oh, yes," Lore said. "I was wondering when you'd tell me you talked to Oscar. That was very sneaky, Cassie."

"Not sneaky," I said. "My *job*. We can't pretend it didn't happen, Lore. If you refuse to talk about it, I need to get my information elsewhere."

Lore looked away, toward her back doors, but not before I caught the flash of hurt in her eyes. "Is that all this is to you?" she asked quietly. "A job?"

I heard a different question: *Is this all* I *am to you?* I didn't know how to answer.

Lore turned back to the screen. After a moment, her lips curved into a self-satisfied smirk that suggested she was about to strike where she thought my flesh was soft. "Tell me," she said, "what's really holding you back from marrying your fiancé?"

I glared, cheeks flushing hot. Duke wasn't home, but she didn't know that. "Money," I hissed. "That's it."

Lore chuckled. "Whatever you need to tell yourself, mija."

When it came to Andres's last day, I was getting nowhere. Oscar now refused to take my calls. Fabian continued to decline my prison interview requests. Carlos Russo hadn't responded to my Facebook messages or calls, and Lore's brother-in-law, Sergio Muñoz—who had been Fabian's alibi until 8 P.M.—had never returned my call as promised. Finally, on a Thursday in mid-October, I tried him again and he answered.

Sergio was garrulous, the kind of man who could extend a simple anecdote to twenty minutes. Retired from banking, he was now a competitive skeet shooter. He was eager to talk about everything except Lore and Fabian—especially the ranch, 175 acres south of Encinal, which he and Lore's sister, Marta, had bought in the 1970s, when they were just "little chavalitos." They'd thought they'd be able to sell some or all of the acreage to pay for their kids' college education, only "we were never blessed in that way." It took forty minutes to build up to the day of the murder. Then Sergio's voice became heavy, like wood swollen with water, warped.

"We usually went on weekends," he said, when I asked if the ranch trip was planned. "Unless it was hunting season. I think he probably wanted to go by himself, but he didn't have the key to the padlock at the gate."

"Why go at all?" I asked. "You didn't think the call was strange? Random?"

Sergio laughed. "Fabian and I were in school together since we were chiquitos. We used to sneak into other people's ranches when we were teenagers. Could've gotten our brains blown out, two little idiots hiding in the monte, but that's how much we loved being out there." He chuckled again, melancholy now. "No. It wasn't strange."

"How did he sound over the phone?"

"Not good."

Interesting. In his witness statement, taken several days before the arrest, Sergio had told the police Fabian sounded normal. I also hadn't realized he and Fabian went so far back. Sergio must have wanted to protect his friend.

"Not good, how?"

"Just—stressed out. Like he needed to get out of the house."

"What happened next?"

"It's been a long time," Sergio said. "But I had just gotten home from work. I basically changed, got my guns, and went to pick him up. He was standing in the middle of the empty driveway, looking almost like he didn't know where he was. That always stuck in my memory."

I pictured Fabian as he'd been in his police tapes—disheveled, frustrated, a man who didn't know how to act in a place he'd never expected to be. The image of him dazed in the middle of the driveway was striking and sad. "Did he tell you about meeting Andres?"

"No." Sergio sighed. "I wish he had. I wish I'd asked what was going on."

"What did you talk about?"

"Oh, you know, all the usual pendejadas of the times. Reagan and NAFTA and the whole multibillion-dollar package of loans and credits the U.S. had pulled together, supposedly to bail out Mexico but really to save the U.S. banks from themselves. Credit unions were shutting down right and left. I lost my job a year later. Gracias a Dios, Lore was able to talk her boss into hiring me."

"How did you feel about her at that point?"

"Fabian was in prison because of her," Sergio snapped. "But I couldn't turn down work, could I? And she was still family."

Instinctively, I wanted to correct him: Fabian was in prison be-cause of an action *he'd* taken—at least, allegedly. Detective Cortez may have wanted to lock Lore up for what she'd done, what she rep-resented, but that wasn't how the law worked.

"On the day of the ranch," I said, "Fabian's store had already closed, right?"

"Yeah, but Fabian—he was a hustler. Didn't let his pride get in the way. There he was at Dr. Ike's looking for construction work with all the mojados."

Mojados. I knew what that meant: wetbacks. The slur surprised me, considering Sergio's own ethnicity. I didn't pause on it, though.

"So Fabian's mood that day, it was nothing out of the ordinary for the times?"

"I didn't say that. I just said we didn't talk about it. No, it was out of the ordinary. But I figured it was related to the crash, like Lore was losing her job or something. I even thought maybe . . ."

"Maybe what?"

"That maybe he and Lore were splitting up." He rushed to add, "It was nothing he said. I mean, most of the time they seemed pretty good, better than most couples we knew. That's why the whole thing with—you know, the other guy—was such a damn shock. Anyway, I suggested target shooting so Fabian could blow off some steam."

"Was he using the .22?" I asked, flipping through the case file. I didn't need to specify which .22. We both knew what I meant.

"Oh, I don't know about that," Sergio said. "They owned a few handguns."

"They?" I repeated. "Lore owned a gun as well?"

"That's not unusual down here," Sergio said. "But, yes, Fabian bought her one. He thought she should carry for protection."

There was a buzzing in my ears, a low whine. "And she definitely did? Carry, I mean?"

"Well, I can't say for sure. I just know Fabian wanted her to."

I paused, regrouped. If Lore had a gap in her alibi, and if Andres's note had told her where he was staying, and if he'd been "bothering" her—and she happened to be carrying a gun, possibly the murder weapon . . .

Guilt is a terrible bedfellow, Lore had told me once. *I couldn't look at mine, either.*

But it was all speculation. And, more to the point, it still didn't make sense. Or, rather, it didn't change anything. She could have been carrying the .22, seen Andres, and then gone home, where Fabian would have confronted her about her double life and later left to—intentionally or not—kill Andres.

"Did you hear from Fabian again that night?" I asked Sergio.

"No," Sergio said. "Marta got on the phone with Lore later on— they were always on the phone, those two. You'd think they never saw each other. I assumed Fabian was there."

"Could you hear what they were talking about?" Lore's double life had been exposed by that point—how could she have been acting normal? There was nothing to preserve anymore. But maybe lying came naturally to her by then.

"I was watching TV," Sergio said apologetically. "Marta took the call in the kitchen. I told her to go into the bedroom. I didn't hear anything."

"Were you surprised, afterward, to find out what Fabian had done?" I asked. "Did he normally have a temper?"

For the first time, Sergio sounded angry. "Of course I was surprised! It's not like Fabian was some gangster. But look, if Marta had done what Lore did . . . I mean, who's to say how you'd react?"

Sergio was saying something I'd learned from consuming crime my whole life: under the right circumstances, everyone has the potential for violence.

"You didn't quite answer the question, though," I said. "Did you ever know Fabian to be aggressive or violent?"

"No. Before this, he'd never hurt a fly. Well—maybe a fly, if it was hunting season. Here's the thing, though." Sergio's voice lowered, drifted into timeworn regret. "He wanted to stay."

I frowned. "Stay where?"

"At the ranch. He wanted to spend the night. That's why I thought they might be splitting up."

"So why didn't you?"

Sergio exhaled. "It had rained earlier, when we were driving out there, and the pinches zancudos were biting something fierce. We were dripping sweat, no meat to cook, we'd drunk the beer. Fabian was pissed off, not good company. I just wanted to take a shower and watch TV in the air-conditioning. I always think—what if the cabrón was trying to keep himself away? To talk himself out of it? And I drove him right back."

Sergio's words had the sense of coming unglued, as if they'd been caught in his throat all these years and it was a relief to push them out.

"Do you remember the last thing he said to you that night?" I asked softly.

Sergio's laugh was a puff of breath with a sound attached. "Pointed to his truck and said of course it had rained—he'd just washed it. That was exactly the kind of day he was having."

LORE, 1985

Fabian was true to his word. The U.S. Embassy was chaotic but miraculously undamaged, and he coordinated with them to get Lore a new passport, then sent her some money through Western Union and made her an airline reservation.

By her gate, she clings to Andres. "I don't want to go," she says, her voice muffled in his shirt. She's desperate to see Fabian and the cuates. To take a hot shower. To flush the toilet. To sleep in a bed. But how can she leave him here, like this?

Andres rubs her back, pressing a kiss to the top of her head. "DF is no place to be right now. By the time you return, I'll have a new apartment for us."

Lore's smile is wobbly. Andres is being optimistic. Tens of thousands of people—more!—lost their homes. She understands supply and demand.

"I love you, Mrs. Crusoe," Andres says in her ear. It's only then that she realizes how close it sounds to Mrs. Russo, and she laughs, on the verge of tears.

On the plane, Lore kisses her silver ring before zipping it into the interior pocket of the cheap purse she bought at the mercado. The canned air is thick with cigarette smoke and hushed, fervent conversations. As they taxi down the runway, picking up speed, the passengers meet each other's eyes guiltily—what right do they have to be going where bodies aren't being stuffed into plastic bags, arranged in wooden coffins at the baseball stadium, the unidentified ones thrown into mass graves?

And then they're airborne. She can't believe how quickly DF disappears beneath the clouds. It's as if it ceases to exist. And with it, what she's done. The man she's married.

Once the plane lands, she follows the slow cattle trail of passengers through the oven-hot Jetway and into the San Antonio airport. A blast of air-conditioning hits her, and before she even begins to look for her family, Fabian's arms are around her, followed by Mateo and Gabriel, their skin hot and summer-dark and smelling like the Irish Spring soap they use until the bars are translucent and sharp. Lore's knees buckle.

"Mom, are you okay?" Mateo holds her elbow, supporting her.

"Is it true?" Gabriel asks. "How many people died?"

They stare at her with wide, dark, almond-shaped eyes, the eyes of her grandfather in the black-and-white photo in her childhood home. They both need a trim, their thick black hair falling below the collars of their shirts, Gabriel's growing into a rat's tail. They are a head taller than she is now and need jeans that aren't too short. When she tried to take them back-to-school shopping last month, Gabriel said, "Mom, you can just drop us off." Trying to hide the sting, she'd told them to be at the food court doors at three or she'd go looking for them. Even Mateo had grimaced.

Fabian isn't letting Lore go. Even after the boys begin peppering her with increasingly morbid questions (Gabriel: "Is it true there are stacks of bodies in the streets?"), Fabian holds Lore close. She can hear the reassuring, slow beat of his heart. He rests his chin on her head, a perfect fit. When he finally pulls away, his eyes shine with tears, a sight so rare the cuates stop talking.

"I was so afraid," Fabian says. She can't remember ever hearing these words from him.

"I'm so sorry." Her throat closes. It feels good to apologize, even if he doesn't know for what.

"It's not your fault," he says, with a choked laugh. "I'm just so glad you're home. Do you have anything? Any bags, or . . . ?"

Lore hefts her purse. "This is it." She left what little clothing she'd bought with Andres. "Did you remember the spare key for my car?"

Fabian taps his pocket. "So—" He hesitates as they walk toward the escalators. "You lost—everything?" His voice croaks again, as if realizing that wherever she'd been staying was gone.

Lore nods. She looks at her bare ring finger. "Fabian, I'm so sorry—I took off my ring before bed. I was running late for a meeting. I left it there." Lore didn't know how difficult this particular lie would be to tell. Her life is one erasure after the next, because all of it—all of her—can no longer exist at once.

Fabian pulls her close. "You're the only thing that matters."

For a moment, guilt is a boa constrictor tightening around her, its cold muscular body emptying her lungs. She almost has to gasp for breath, pushing away from Fabian.

"Are you okay?" Fabian's arm is still around her waist, ready to catch her if she falls.

Overhead, in English and Spanish, a woman's measured voice welcomes them to Military City.

"I—yes." Lore blinks hard, fighting off a wave of dizziness. What is happening to her? "Sorry. I just want to get home."

"Of course." Fabian is suddenly brisk and efficient, pleased to lead them where she remembers parking. "Are you okay to drive? We could always—"

"I'll drive!" Gabriel says, and Lore laughs.

"Nice try," she says. Though she and Fabian have been practicing with them, they won't take driver's ed until spring.

"But I could—"

"I want to get home," Lore says again, though right now she can't picture home at all.

Fabian returns to Austin several days later. He might not be back until Thanksgiving. He's been bidding on jobs large and small: wrought iron gates for a restoration in Travis Heights; an altar railing with gold-leaf Trinitarian emblems for a Lutheran church; exterior stair railings for two medium-size business parks. The small jobs he forges himself in the warehouse space he rented. The larger ones are fabricated down here. Altogether, they usually cover payroll. But Fabian had to let go of the bookkeeper last week, meaning now the job is Lore's, and for the last six months they've been making loan repayments out of their own dwindling savings account.

Over the next few weeks, Lore keeps jolting awake at odd hours, heart racing, sure the house is shaking. At the first Sunday lunch at Mami and Papi's house, it's all anyone talks about, ten pairs of adult eyes on her, and Lore tells as much of the truth as possible—that she was in Tlatelolco, that she saw the apartment buildings fall, that she stayed in La Roma for two weeks after. It's as if she's talking about a nightmare, something only she experienced, the horror of which is impossible to convey, and then suddenly, right in the middle of her telling, she remembers marrying Andres, the words they spoke, the lazo around their shoulders and the saguaro pointing up toward the sun, and she feels a different kind of terror, like a spider who's stuck in her own web.

She consumes the news helplessly, voraciously. The count of the dead goes up to five thousand, then seven thousand. President de la Madrid refuses to cut foreign debt payments to help with the recovery, which must include demolition and clearing and the reconstruction of some thirty thousand housing units. Community organizers from Tlatelolco and La Roma are organizing marches for a more democratic reconstruction process, demanding meetings with the president.

But the story that destroys Lore comes from Andres. She calls him during the day, from her office, and he tells her about a nine-year-old boy who was sleeping in an eighth-floor apartment with his grandfather when it collapsed. For ten days, rescue workers tunneled in with shovels and their bare hands while the boy's family kept vigil on the street. The cries grew weaker. Finally, sensitive sound equipment was brought in, listening for breathing and heartbeats. Sixteen days after the temblor, the workers were still convinced they could hear him knocking in reply to them. On the seventeenth day, heavy construction equipment was brought in. But by then, the sound equipment picked up only silence.

Three days later, the grandfather's body was found.

"But what about Luis Ramón?" Lore asks at her desk. Everyone knows the boy's name by now.

"Nothing," Andres says, and Lore lowers her head and weeps, thinking of the mother they'd helped, Carlitos, the cuates at nine, their satin skin and rabbit hearts and the way they still hugged her with all their force. A nine-year-old boy buried alive for more than two weeks, a grotesque hide-and-seek, before eventually succumbing to entombment. It's more than her heart can bear.

"Give the kids my love," Lore says, getting control of herself. She doesn't want Andres to feel responsible for her sadness.

"I will," Andres says. "I love you, Lore."

"I love you, too."

When Lore has been married to two men for a month, Mateo comes down with the first cold of the season. Well, Lore hopes it's a cold and not a throat infection, which is why she's taking the morning off to take him to the doctor.

You aren't supposed to have favorites as a mother, and yet she'd always known her own mother's favorite was Pablo. Artistic, emotional, hypochondriac Pablo, who had painted over the white walls so long ago to "fix" them. With the rest of them, her mother's love was brusque, matter-of-fact. When they misbehaved, punishment was a wooden spoon to the backside, the spankings measured and disciplined. But with Pablo, there was tenderness. That time he'd fallen from the high branch of the pecan tree, Mami had run outside and scooped him up, kissing his scrapes and singing, "Sana, sana, colita de rana," while she dabbed Neosporin on the wounds. And when she had to spank him, tears shone in her eyes. Maybe it was because he was premature, ejected from Mami's body before he could survive without lights and tubes doing the work of her womb. In any case, he was her Pablito. The favorite. And they all knew it.

Lore always promised herself she wouldn't have a favorite. And what better chance does a mother have of loving equally than with identical twins? Conceived together, grown together, born minutes apart. Indistinguishable, until they are.

And maybe that's the problem. When two boys start life at the same time, identical down to their eyelashes, their individuation is stark, and one is bound to fall short. And that one, God help her, is Gabriel. A whirlwind on the basketball court, the one with the quick smile girls are drawn to, but moody, prone to snapping and slamming doors. Just yesterday she was trying to talk to him about his grades, which she was shocked to see were all C's on his first report card after a lifetime of A's and B's. He didn't even bother looking away from whatever video game he was playing, as he muttered, so full of scorn, "Fuck off, Mom." The rage inside her was like vines climbing from her stomach to her throat, thorns pricking her ears. She said, trembling-quiet, "Dímelo otra vez." They glared at each other, breathing hard, and Lore wanted to hit him. Instead, she ripped the controller from his hand, yanked the console out from under the TV, and said, "I'm donating this—you have no idea how lucky you are! None! ¡A tu cuarto!" He stormed off, slamming the door behind him, and she heard the sound of things breaking. She didn't trust herself to check.

Mateo, though, he's never spoken to her that way. And maybe

that's the terrible truth: that mothers love best the children who best love them.

Or maybe she's simply not as good a mother as she'd like to believe. Maybe that's what is really happening with Gabriel. Can she blame him for acting up, with two parents he hardly sees?

In the car, Mateo is sneaking glances at her, his profile sharp and worried as they turn down Saunders. Finally, he stabs the volume knob. Dire Straits, "Money for Nothing," goes silent. How appropriate.

"Mom," Mateo says. "We need to talk."

"Okay . . ." It comes out like a question. "What is it?"

Mateo swallows, his still too-big Adam's apple wobbling in his long, graceful neck. He isn't looking at her. Oh, God. Did he find Andres's letters, the two or three she hasn't yet taken to her parents' house and tucked beneath that loose flap of living room carpet? Is it something else? Did he overhear a phone call, did she slip up some other way?

Lore focuses on her hands on the wheel, her chipped red nail polish. "Mateo? What is it?"

Silence. Then: "It's about Gabriel."

The pinhole of Lore's vision widens, then narrows again. A different kind of dread rises within her. "Gabriel? Tell me."

Mateo sucks the inside of his cheek, the way he used to as a toddler. "He wouldn't want me to say anything. But you're going to find out anyway. Don't freak out. Okay?"

"Mateo," Lore says sharply.

"He was caught cheating in Chem," Mateo tells her in a rush, evading her gaze.

"Cheating." The first wisps of relief are settling. Okay. She can deal with that. "God, Mateo, you scared me!"

Mateo's cheeks flush. "Oh, I'm sorry that's not bad enough to get your attention."

Lore nearly rear-ends the car in front of her, she's so surprised by his tone. She parks across the street from the pediatrician's office. Next door, a young boy and girl play basketball in a dirt front yard, the net long since torn from the hoop.

"That's not what I meant," Lore says. "Okay. Cheating. Off who, exactly?"

Mateo doesn't answer.

"You," Lore says. Mateo, who aces all his science classes.

"It's just that if he fails, he'll get kicked off the basketball team!"

Lore digs a thumb between her eyebrows, where lately the frown lines have been etched each morning. "So you're not worried about the failing, per se. Or the cheating, or the fact that you're both in trouble. You're worried about his basketball status?"

"You don't understand. He—" Mateo cuts off with a rough cough, wincing. "He can't get kicked off. He needs it."

"Needs it? For what?"

"Well, who do you want him hanging out with?" Mateo stabs the button for his seat belt. "The team or those other chucos?"

"*Chucos?*" Lore says. "What chucos? You two have had the same friends forever!"

Mateo snorts, and his derision shocks her. What has she been missing?

"What chucos, Mateo?"

"Rudy and Wayo. You know what? Forget it." Mateo yanks the door handle. "You obviously don't give a crap."

"Mateo!" Clearly, it isn't only this he feels she doesn't care about. Has she been fooling herself all this time, thinking being with Andres has made her a better wife and mother here, when all she's really been is gone? "Of course I do. Mateo, look at me."

He does, hair falling into his eyes. He has one leg in the car and one leg out.

"I care about you two more than you will ever know." Lore thinks of the boy, Luis Ramón, buried alive while his mother could do nothing except stand on the street, hoping her voice might bring him comfort. She wonders if the woman tried to lift away the rubble herself, convinced her love would give her superhuman strength. She wonders if the woman felt the moment her boy stopped breathing. "Do you understand me?"

A one-shouldered shrug.

"We need to sit down, all three of us, and figure out what's going on," Lore says. "But you did the right thing."

Mateo grimaces. "Don't tell him I told you."

"I won't." Lore grips his arm. "Mateo."

"Yeah?" The sun hits his eyes, making them glint amber.

She says again, "More than you'll ever know."

CASSIE, 2017

Everyone who becomes obsessed with a particular crime wants to discover something new about it. Some clarifying detail that will shift the whole thing, the way an image can look like a vase until the exact moment it becomes the profile of a woman's face. I'd wanted to investigate the crime—if you could call it that, which was, confusingly, less obvious to me than when I'd begun this project—of Lore's heart. But after talking to Oscar Martinez and Sergio Muñoz, I felt my focus being pulled in another, more familiar direction. One I told myself I'd been trying to resist, yet whose magnetism I'd felt since first holding the case file in my hands. I wanted to know everything about Andres's murder—and Lore's role in it.

"How about this?" I said to Lore in October. At six thirty, it was getting dark outside. The duplex next door glowed with orange lights, the trees decorated with stylish sugar skulls. I pulled my slubby cardigan around me on the front porch bench, adjusted myself so my face wasn't hidden in shadow on the phone camera. "Each call, I'll ask you one question about that day. One question, and we're done."

Lore sat in her usual spot on the living room couch. As always, she held the phone too low, so it caught the soft underside of her chin. "If this is my story, my book, shouldn't I get to say what goes in and what's left out?"

"We can't just *leave out* what happened to Andres," I said, trying not to lose patience. "It's part of your story. Not all, but part. I need to know the details from your perspective. Lore—do you trust me?"

As I asked, I realized—I really wanted to know. After months of exchanging some of the most intimate stories of our lives, *did* she trust me? *Should* she trust me? What did we owe each other at this point?

"Fine." Lore reached for something, a blanket, maybe, shifting on the couch. "But I get to ask you one question in return."

I rolled my eyes. "Aren't you already doing that?"

She laughed.

"Let's start from the beginning," I said. "I spoke to Penelope, and—"

Lore sucked in a breath. "You did? And you're barely telling me?"

"It was recent."

"Well, what did she say?" Lore brought the phone closer, her face pinched with strained eagerness.

"That's one question for you," I said, trying not to sound smug. "She said they never received your letters."

"¡Por eso!" Lore nodded once, indignant and also oddly satisfied. "No wonder she said those things in the article."

"Well, that's probably one small part." Sometimes it still shocked me, the way Lore didn't seem to see what she'd done as unforgivable in the eyes of those she'd hurt. How did she learn to judge herself so gently in a world that taught women to nail themselves to the cross for any tiny infraction? "She said she and Carlos were staying with Andres that week. They were supposed to be there that weekend, but Andres suddenly took them back to Rosana's and went to see you. My question is—why?"

If Lore was surprised by the new information I'd discovered, she hid it well. Her expression barely changed, a serene still frame. That was the tell. I was onto something.

"Honestly?" She sighed. "I wish I knew."

Bullshit. There was something *too* regretful in her voice, almost performative. *Don't forget*, Penelope had said. *Lore is a very good liar.* But I had an advantage over the people in Lore's life back then. I already knew this about her.

"You're telling me you have no idea why he made the sudden trip to see you?"

Lore flicked on a lamp as the room dimmed with sunset. Shadows gathered in the hollows of her face. "By all means, ask the same question a million ways. You'll get the same answer. My turn: When did you last talk to your father?"

She knew exactly how to knock me off balance. "I don't know. My birthday last year, I guess. What did Andres's note say?" I'd meant it when I said we'd be done after one question. Now Lore had made it into some sort of game, one for one, and I wasn't going to be the first to stop.

"Ay, Cassie, no sé." She huffed a breath. "Look in the police records."

My pulse quickened. "I have. You told them the note said, 'I'm sorry I missed you.'"

"¿Entonces? You already know, so why are you asking me?"

"Because I don't believe that's what it said, or at least not all it said—and I don't for a second believe you don't remember."

Lore said nothing as we stared at each other. A stalemate.

LORE, 2017

The furniture was covered in plastic, the far wall swatched with a dozen saturated colors: Gentleman's Gray, Salamander, Ebony King, Shadow. I already knew the dining room would be Dark Burgundy, and the casual den, bright with sunlight, would be Sea Star. I had thought Mami's white walls were so boring, so austere, ¿y luego qué hice? Taken an interior decorator's advice and painted the whole place white. But I hadn't cared back then. Andres was gone. Fabian was gone. The cuates were gone. There was no home to make here. It was a place to be when I was nowhere else.

That Monday, the day the police first came to the bank, a scream had built in my throat, as if before that moment there had still been a chance it wasn't real. Once they left, I rushed over to Marta's house, since she only worked mornings. Sergio was Fabian's alibi for the first part of the night, and Marta, though she didn't know it yet, was mine for the second. It wouldn't be long before the police interviewed them. It was better she hear it from me.

At first, Marta thought it was a joke. She'd laughed into her coffee cup, telling me to stop being stupid. Marta was wearing a Guess shirt. I remembered because I'd stared at the rhinestone-studded triangle—those three shining points, separated by equal distances. Once she realized I was serious, Marta had set her cup down so hard it broke. I reached for the secador, and she started yelling. "Get out, Lore! Get out of my house! I don't even know you. Get the hell out!"

I had cried, begged. But Marta couldn't understand. She refused to even try. The last thing she said to me before slamming the door was: "How could you do this? You had it all. Tuviste *todo*." But nobody could have it all, or at least not for long.

After the arrest, when Gabriel and Mateo were still too disgusted to even look at me, Mateo slipped a note beneath my bedroom door: *We're going to stay with tía Marta and tío Sergio. Don't try to make us come back.* I had felt engulfed with rage, a walking fireball. Marta had been jealous of me for fifteen years, ever since one careless night resulted in the cuates. I'd been able to do, without effort, what no amount of planning or prayer or potions had done for her. And now Marta had my sons. In those fevered moments after reading the note, I called my sister. "Are you happy now?" I shouted. "You win, are you happy?" Marta, rightfully, hung up on me.

But I needed to see my children, and Marta would never keep them from me. So, like some deadbeat dad, I dropped off cash for the cuates' food and basketball uniforms and field trips. I sat across from them in Marta's living room, watching *Miami Vice* and *The A-Team*, anything that would keep us in the same space.

Gabriel had been so angry. I had worried about them both, of course, though Gabriel more than Mateo, with his bad grades and skipping school and, as Mateo had feared, losing his spot on the basketball team. Once I'd forced them to move back in with me, all I saw of Gabriel was the sliver of light beneath his locked door. Terrible, angry music, the kind Mami would have called satanic. He refused to talk to me. Wouldn't eat dinner with us. I'd worry he never ate at all, except the plate I put in the fridge for him every night was in the sink by morning. I scrubbed at the hardened remains con ganas, con amor, because they were the closest I could get to my son, the closest he'd let me get.

Mateo's grief—because that's what it was, wasn't it, grief for the loss of Fabian and me, for the idea he had of us—was quieter, more restrained. Occasionally, he let me hug him. Then he'd slip away. Another shut door, another sliver of light.

And then, only a few months later, the hysterical call from Marta: "Papi's gone! He's gone!" For a wild moment I remembered the time the cuates had slipped away at H-E-B. I had shouted to anyone who would listen, "¡Mis niños! Please, help me find them!" They'd been playing hide-and-seek the way they did at Fabian's warehouse. Now, on the phone, I almost said to Marta, "Don't worry, we'll find him!" But she was sobbing, unable to speak, and I knew Papi was beyond finding.

Mami blamed me. All that stress on his poor heart, and I couldn't say she was wrong. She cut me out after that, and the rest of them—except for Marta, eventually, and occasionally Pablo—followed suit. I'd gone from two families to none. Sometimes, in the months and years after everything happened, I felt like a ghost haunting the wasteland of my old life. I sat in the living room in the dark, drinking Bucanas, flipping through photo albums of when the cuates were babies: there I was, smiling a stunned, aftershock smile, and Fabian, cupping one boy in the palm of each rough hand like some kind of god, though it was my body they'd ripped through on their way to the world. I stroked their cheeks and hair through sheets of yellowed plastic. I whispered apologies, regrets. I went to bed half-drunk and woke up feeling bruised. I went to the kitchen and dropped a curl of orange peel, a cinnamon stick, and piloncillo in a saucepan and drank café de olla, my fingertips smelling like Andres's. I wrote my useless letters to Penelope and Carlitos, and sometimes I caught myself driving to the cemetery. I wasn't sure why. I pretended it was to sit by Papi's grave, though I could still feel his disappointment coursing up through the earth.

Those were dark times. Now, at least, I had the cuates again, and my grandsons. If I didn't lose them.

The paint fumes were giving me a headache, so I went outside. It was one of those rare, perfect fall days, when the sky is heartbreak blue but the heat has finally broken like a fever, leaving only gentle warmth in its place. Since my retirement, gardening had taken up most of my time. Weekend mornings at Home Depot and Lowe's, plus countless hours listening to the *Gardening South Texas Radio Show*, and the springtime drives to Floresville for the South Texas Home, Garden, and Environmental Show. I was proud of my citrus trees, the fat lemons that smelled like oranges, the oranges nearly as big as grapefruits. The Braithwaite and Mary Roses and d'Urber-villes, all the secret knowledge that comes with trying to control the natural world.

Fabian was in a gardening program in prison. As I fertilized the broccoli, brussels sprouts, and cauliflower with ammonium nitrate, I pretended he was kneeling beside me. I could almost feel the brush of his glove on mine. We'd complain about our knees, laugh about what viejitos we'd become. We'd make sandwiches with rotisserie chicken from H-E-B, and on a day like this, we'd eat on the patio, sipping coffee and throwing a tennis ball for Crusoe.

Fabian was due for release in five years. He should have been out thirteen years ago, but his caseworker had said we didn't need a pa-role lawyer, that it was his job to help Fabian put together the packet. It was all so convoluted. Nadie nos dijo que we were supposed to start writing letters and pulling together a release plan *six months* before the hearing. Pero they had no problem letting Penelope and Carlitos know in time for Penelope to write that searing victim impact letter, and there went our chance.

Two years later, we hired a lawyer. Six thousand dollars, all our letters, family photos, Marta guaranteeing him a job at her restau-rant, Fabian's pinche high school transcripts. And he was a model inmate, part of all the programs, teaching other men English, or to read and write. But then out of nowhere there was a fight. After that second rejection, he waived the hearings. He didn't want the cuates and me to go through the disappointment again, he said. Spending half our lives hoping, como si hope were such a terrible thing. Well, now we'd be seventy-two before he was out.

If.

If Cassie's book didn't ruin everything.

After months of focusing on the double marriage, like she'd promised, now she kept chingue y chingue about the night Andres had died. Pinche Oscar. He was always kind of metiche. When he'd called me after his conversation with Cassie, he said he hadn't told her anything. He'd obviously let something slip, though, because Cassie was asking what else was in the envelope, what else the note had said. She wouldn't let it go. It felt like the past was literally loosening inside me, bolts and screws falling off hinges.

True to our deal, I had been answering one question, sometimes more, about the night of Andres's murder per phone call—though, obviously, not always entirely honestly. I'd told her the doctor's appointment that day was for my annual and that I'd gone back to the bank afterward. She'd asked why; it was nearly the end of the day, wasn't it? I made something up: a woman in a man's world during a recession needed to be seen putting in the hours. The truth was I'd had nowhere else to go.

Gabriel was still pestering me to stop talking to her. And I could. But that didn't mean she'd stop working on the book, especially now that she knew about the gap in my alibi, which the police either hadn't noticed or hadn't cared about after Fabian was ID'd. I kept insisting I'd gone straight home from the bank to pick up the cuates. It wasn't my fault no one could corroborate that.

No. If I stopped talking to her, I would forever be looking over my shoulder.

Besides, I liked our conversations. Our calls had filled my quiet evenings. I had been alone for so long that at some point the loneliness had simply settled inside me, like ten or twenty extra pounds over the years, something you only notice when looking at old photos.

Now, I liked knowing the phone would ring at six o'clock, sitting down with dinner or sometimes a glass of wine. I liked not knowing exactly where our conversations would lead. And I liked making her talk about the things that made her uncomfortable. There's no sense hiding from yourself, mija. There you'll be anyway. That's what I wanted to tell her.

Anyway, because of her, now I knew things I'd only wondered about for so long: of course Rosana would intercept my letters to Penelope and Carlitos. I could imagine her elegant hands ripping up the envelopes I'd lovingly addressed, burying them in the kitchen trash can beneath shriveled limes and wet paper towels.

Or had she read them first? Qué vergüenza, thinking of her reading my words. How I'd tried to explain—falling in love with their father, with them, wasn't intentional. It wasn't planned. But it was real. Maybe one day they might forgive me. Later I asked them questions, as if I were picking them up from school. I reminisced. I told them I missed them. How desesperada I must have sounded to Rosana. But I *was* desesperada, suddenly and catastrophically cut off from Andres, y los niños were all I had left of him, other than the things I'd stuffed beneath the floorboard at Mami and Papi's house.

Except now I had this. The story I was telling. The pleasure of reliving that time with their father. The best time of my life, honestly. And the truth is, I had always been a hedonist. A slave to the pleasures of the moment. Wasn't that how everything had started? Because, in a time of deprivation, Andres had given me his hand? How could I have said no? To the dance, to the wine, to that caged elevator, rising?

But Andres was not the only pleasure. Novelty is only one aspect to a relationship. There is also the velvet wrap of history, the bond of time.

There is loyalty. There is family.

CASSIE, 2017

In early November, I emailed Penelope, apologizing for upsetting her and asking—on an extreme long shot—whether she had any written memorabilia of Andres's from 1983 to '86, especially toward the end of his life. Calendar, journal, letters to or from Lore that might help explain his sudden trip to Laredo and his frame of mind when he arrived. I didn't expect her to respond, but it was worth a try.

Duke's mother called me right as I hit send on the email. She wanted to know how I felt about wildflowers—they were all over the farm in May, and they'd make lovely wedding decorations, unless I had something else in mind? I heard the question behind the question: We were six months away. Had we planned anything at all?

"I love wildflowers," I said. I didn't, really, but they were free.

"Great." I could hear the smile in Caroline's voice. "Listen, honey, I don't want to be *that* future mother-in-law, but if you need help with planning, I'm here."

I thanked her, going to the fridge to rummage through all the Tupperware dishes. I pulled out a container of potato salad and shoved a fork in it at the counter. What we needed was money, and we would never ask for that.

"One more thing." Caroline hesitated. A horse neighed in the background. "I know you're not close with your dad, and I'm not sure if you plan on inviting him . . ."

The potato salad became jammy and sour in my mouth, and I forced it down. "No."

"That's what I figured." Caroline didn't judge, didn't pry. "And of course, your mom . . . Well, I was thinking—*if* you want—honey, I would be honored to walk you down the aisle."

A knot of tears rose to my throat so quickly and violently it was as if it had always been there, waiting. "That is—" I swiped at my eyes. "Thank you. I would love that, Caroline."

Caroline's voice wobbled a little. "You're a part of our family. Remember that. You don't have to do things alone."

It was after eight on Wednesday, Duke's night off, and he would be home soon. We'd returned to seeing each other in short, uninspired stretches—groggy early-morning breakfasts before he left to start the brisket, reruns of *The Office* while I sat beside him with my laptop burning holes through my leggings. Since he'd been cooking all day, I thought I'd surprise him with dinner. There was chicken and broccoli in the oven, and the house smelled warm and nutty, edged with damp earth. I'd left the back door open earlier because it had been overcast and I'd wanted to collect the smell of rain, let it fill all the corners of this house.

I checked the timer on my phone, then called Andrew for our check-in, which had gone from nightly to weekly after it seemed like our father had gotten his shit together.

"Hey." His voice was dull and flat.

"Hey, buddy," I said, instantly on alert. "How's it going?"

Andrew said, "They shut off the power."

My heart skipped, a clumsy transition between beats. "When? Why didn't you tell me?"

Something crackled, hot, between us. "Three days ago, and I tried calling you. You didn't answer." He paused a beat, then muttered, "You never answer."

Shit. I remembered. I'd been talking to Lore and planned to call Andrew back right after. Then I'd gotten distracted transcribing and had completely forgotten. I thought of the calls I'd missed from Andrew this summer, the way his texts had gotten shorter and shorter in the last year. At some point, he'd stopped thinking he could count on me. And I hadn't even noticed.

"I'm so sorry," I said. "Three *days*? Does this mean . . ."

"Yup." Andrew's casualness did little to conceal his pain. "Off the wagon. Didn't last long this time."

Resolve slid into my veins, clean and smooth. "Let me talk to him. Is he home?"

"Yeah. But—"

"Now, Andrew."

My hand shook as I grabbed an open bottle of merlot, poured myself a glass that I drank in four long swallows—the fucking irony. I stepped onto the back porch. Across the street, another falling-apart bungalow like ours was being torn down to the studs, soon to be replaced, no doubt, by a new midcentury modern duplex. Its skeleton loomed in the darkness.

"Cassie!" My father's voice was slurred, a false edge to the joviality, like a trapdoor. So many bad nights had started this way— *Lisey!* when my mother walked into the room, as if her mouth weren't set in a grim, disappointed line, the presence of which would soon open that trapdoor, send them hurtling through the darkness. But he couldn't hurt her anymore. He couldn't hurt me. He could only hurt Andrew. And it was long past time to make sure he didn't.

My mouth was dry. "Dad, what's this about the power getting turned off?" No preamble. I couldn't lose my nerve.

"How am I? Oh, I'm doing great, thanks." My father laughed, and I flinched. "How are *you*? Been a while."

"What happened," I said, "with the power?"

"Jesus, I'm a few days late paying the bill, that's all." Thassall. "You're telling me you've never been late on a bill?"

"I've never had a kid at home depending on light and heat," I said.

"That's right," he said, and I knew I'd walked right into it, giving him a bruise to press. "You haven't."

We were both silent. Breathing.

"Look, it'll be back on by tomorrow," he said, sounding tired now.

"Okay, but what *happened*?" I tried for gentle, nonjudgmental. Like my mother. "Andrew said it's been three days. Did you lose your job? Do you need money?"

"Money?" A low growl. "What, you think I can't take care of my own house, my own son?"

"That's not what I mean." I ran my tongue over my teeth, tried to breathe, to slow my racing heart. "But you need to go to a meeting. Please. You can't do this to Andrew."

"Do what, exactly?"

"You're supposed to be taking care of him! You promised." I couldn't believe how hurt I sounded, how childish.

Behind me, the front door opened and shut. Duke called, "Smells good, Cass— Oh, you're outside." And then he was beside me, his smile fading as he took in my clenched jaw, the way I was shivering despite the mild temperature. *You okay?* he mouthed.

I nodded, willing him to go back inside. He didn't.

"Who do you think you are?" My father's voice simmered, and I felt all my younger selves inside me like nesting dolls, quivering. "Leaving at the first opportunity and then calling out of the blue with 'you promised.'"

I blinked against tears. "Either you get sober or I'm coming to get Andrew."

Duke's hand dropped from my shoulder. I'd gone too far. And not far enough.

"And I swear to God," I said, trembling so hard now I could hardly hold the phone. "You hurt him, and I will make you pay."

My phone timer went off as I hung up with my father. Neither of us moved.

"Cassie," Duke said, low. "What the hell was that?"

I sank into one of the Adirondack chairs we'd bought on Craigslist. It was a vulnerable position to sit in, belly half tilted up, exposed. I stood up again on shaky legs. "I'll tell you everything. Let me just—" I gestured to the house, the food that would burn soon.

Duke strode to the door. "I'll do it."

I was still standing there, clutching my elbows, when Duke returned. Above us, dusty-winged moths thrashed against the weak porch light.

I took a deep breath. "That was my dad."

"Yeah. I gathered. But . . . you told him to get sober. Is he . . ." He hesitated.

"An alcoholic. Yes."

Duke was standing close enough to me that I could smell the smokiness on his clothing. He didn't reach out to touch me. "Since when?"

"I was nine when I found out," I said. "I have no idea how long before that."

The emotions played out plainly on Duke's face—sympathetic eyes and clenched jaw, the desire to comfort me pitted against hurt that I'd kept this from him. I waited for him to ask why. All this time we'd been together, why hadn't I told him?

"Is he getting help?" he asked instead.

I sighed. "He's gone to AA off and on over the years. He was sober my last two years of high school. That was the longest stretch I can remember before Andrew was born."

Those were the days of him knocking on my door, beseeching: "How do you feel about dusting off those old fishing poles?" And my mother dog-earing recipes in *Better Homes and Gardens*, as if the perfect quiche might erase our memories. In the living room at night, it was the two of them who sat thigh to thigh beneath the blue blanket with matted tassels, their heads close in the TV's eerie flicker.

What did they whisper about in the privacy of those nights, when I slunk away because I did not—could not—trust the peace? Did they talk about me? Or were they too consumed with themselves, with the struggle of pretending, willing, believing things could be different?

"He relapsed right before my mom found out she was pregnant," I said.

It had been early fall. A weekend, because she was still wearing her mint-green robe with the faded coffee stain on one fluffy lapel. I was about to say something when my father shuffled in from the hallway. The defeated slump of his shoulders, the way he kissed the top of my mother's head, avoided my gaze entirely—the air went underwater thick. I hated myself for the pain of my disappointment, like a child who cried over not getting a Christmas gift she was never promised.

Duke was standing close enough to touch, still not reaching for me.

"He went back to meetings, but it was a struggle for a couple of months." He didn't hit her, though, I almost added. She was, apparently, protected by an invisible clump of cells. "I thought he'd been sober ever since Andrew was born, but"—I swallowed—"apparently not."

"Jesus." Duke shook his head, collapsed into one of the Adirondacks. "Poor kid. You're just finding out about this?"

"Yeah." My mouth tasted metallic, as if I'd bitten myself. I searched for blood with the tip of my tongue.

"But—" Duke looked up and I could see the hardening, like cement drying. "What was that about him hurting Andrew?"

This was it. My chance to finally tell him everything. *You don't have to do things alone.* But self-preservation is in our DNA, an instinct that outlasts the extinction of other species. Lore would understand.

"I meant emotionally," I said, stomach turning. "I just don't want him hurt by all this."

"And you going to get Andrew? What, like him coming to *live* with us?"

"Well, what am I supposed to do, Duke?" My voice rose, cracking. "Leave my little brother with a drunk who forgets him places and can't pay the bills?" The righteous anger of this role—the sister who would act in her brother's best interests, no matter the personal sacrifice—came as such a relief. I so wanted to be that person.

Duke cupped his hands over his nose and mouth, exhaling hard before removing them. "Were you even going to talk to me first? Was this going to be a conversation?"

"It is a conversation! We're having it now!" I glared down at him. "You're acting like he's packing his bags as we speak. All I said was—"

"I heard what you said." Duke batted away a moth, harder than necessary. "And would you have told me, by the way, if I hadn't?"

I didn't say anything.

Duke's eyes flashed. "Yeah. And what are the odds he gets sober for good this time?"

"I don't know."

"So then? Andrew's going to move here?" He gestured toward the house—the kitchen whose counter space I could touch end to end, our one bedroom, the bathroom with pedestal sink, our toothbrushes leaning against each other in a soap-scummed glass. "How would that even work?"

"He could sleep on the love seat until we find a bigger place," I said. "And—"

"A bigger place?" Duke laughed. "We can barely afford this one."

"But this book! Duke, I think the story is even bigger than I originally thought. I think Lore was somehow involved in the murder."

There it was, no caveats or disclaimers. Why else wouldn't she tell me why Andres was in town? Why would she lie about the note and not seeing him when, in my gut, I knew she had? Why had she alibied

Fabian if she'd loved Andres? What about the gap in her own alibi, the gun she may have been carrying?

Duke stared at me. "This again? That is a fucking serious accusation, Cassie. You do realize that, don't you?"

"Obviously," I snapped. "And if I'm right, everything will be different. For us, I mean."

Duke gave an aghast laugh. "Do you even hear yourself? You sound—"

My chest felt tight. I was breathing hard. "What, Duke? I sound what?"

I had the ugly feeling he was about to say *crazy*. That word you attach to a woman to dismiss her intelligence, her instincts, her ambition. If he said it, I wasn't sure he could ever take it back.

"Ruthless," he said, before walking inside.

LORE, 1985

Thanksgiving isn't celebrated in Mexico, of course, so there's no conflict in staying in Laredo, though Andres had asked her, kindly, with whom she'd be spending the day. It still startles Lore, the world she's constructed for him, in which she exists untethered by parents, supposedly dead, or siblings she doesn't talk to. She told him she'd likely go to Oscar's house; his wife, Natalie, is pregnant again and could use some help in the kitchen or wrangling their two-year-old. Lore has never been to Oscar's house and barely knows Natalie, but in this world, they're good friends, and Andres looks forward to meeting them both.

The meal this year is modest. Lore and Fabian made the turkey and mashed potatoes. Everyone else brought one side dish: creamed corn, beans, baked sweet potatoes. Mami made two pecan pies for dessert. Some of the kids are complaining—where are the hojarascas and chocolate chip cookies and Lisa's famous apple crumble? The parents all snap: "It's Thanksgiving—time to be grateful for what we have, not whine about what we want!" Lore wants to tell the kids to think about the children in DF who lost everything in the temblor, sleeping side by side on the streets like a platter of enchiladas. But children can't place the less fortunate in context with their own lives; they exist on different planes, unaffected by each other's existence.

The adults try to keep things cheerful. The men make plans for an early-morning hunt, and Jorge and Lisa share funny stories about the kids at their schools, though inevitably the conversation circles back to the economy. Lore's brother Pablo lost his restaurant job and is working in the warehouse of a transportation company for $3.35 an hour. His wife, Lisa, is still teaching, but she's pregnant now with their third, a surprise; when she broke down and cried over Sunday lunch in her first trimester—"How are we going to do it?"—Marta scraped her chair back and left the table. Lore found her in the living room, pretending to look for something in her purse while angry tears fell from her eyes. "She didn't think," Lore said softly, a hand on her sister's back. Marta flinched. "It's fine. I'm fine."

Marta still works as a physician's assistant and it seems inevitable that Sergio's savings and loan will fold, like so many others. Jorge's job as a school principal is safe, but his wife, Christie, was let go from the law firm. She's now a receptionist at a used car dealership with a reputation for cashing in on people's desperation. Beto and his wife, Melissa, have responded to the times with entrepreneurial zeal, using their home as collateral to buy a foreclosure, which they leveraged for the next foreclosure. They're buying up homes for pennies on the dollar, condos that were ninety thousand in 1981 now selling for forty. Recently they bought their first apartment complex, six units in El Azteca. One night, drunk at Lore's house, Pablo bitterly pointed out that they were turning into pinche slumlords, and where did they even get the money, anyway? His implication was outrageous. Lore gave him a Schaefer Light for the road and told him to sleep it off. Later, she would find out from Melissa that Pablo had asked them for a loan. He hadn't believed Beto when he'd said their assets weren't liquid.

And Lore's parents. Lore doesn't think they've recovered from having to close the store or, worse, rely on their children to bail them out of a bad loan. Papi spends most days out on Sergio's ranch, doing quién sabe qué—repairing fences, counting the deer, rehabing or disassembling old cars that Sergio's friends sometimes take out there. He needs to be doing something, Mami says. Mami, who spends her own days cleaning an immaculate house, ironing sheets that dried on the line. They don't know how to be still, how not to work. They live off social security and her father's VA disability checks, and though they're in their sixties—they're due some rest, they've earned it—they're ashamed. Over lunch, Papi struggles to meet their eyes.

"It'll turn," Beto says confidently, and Melissa nods. "We're seeing it already, with Mexico entering the GATT. Right, Lore?"

Lore nods, though she's careful not to offer too much hope. "Nothing will change overnight," she says, eyeing the hollowed-out turkey. She opts against seconds, in case any of the kids want some. "It'll take months for Mexico to negotiate terms of entry, and we're looking at probably ten years, at least, before its customs duties and regulations are comparable to other members'."

"But still," Lisa insists, "it's good, right?"

"Of course," Lore says.

They eat in silence, forks scraping against plates, drinks being refilled. Lore takes a sip of her chilled Carlo Rossi, sneaks a glance at Fabian. He's been quiet, withdrawn, though they had a good time in the kitchen this morning, goading Gabriel into pulling out the bird's neck and giblets while everyone, even vegetarian Mateo, laughed at his disgusted bravado. For a few minutes it had felt like old times, when the cuates were little and Gabriel would never dream of telling her to fuck off and Fabian had just opened the store and everything, every last thing, was promise and possibility.

Papi must have noticed Fabian's mood, too. "¿Y ustedes?" He's looking at Fabian. "¿Cómo les va en Austin?"

Fabian's shoulders jerk, and he compensates by holding them back proudly. "Actually," he says, "I've decided to come home."

Lore gasps. "What?"

It's been two years since Fabian's first trip to Austin. Two years of weekly phone calls and monthly visits, sometimes seeing each other only for a night before Lore returns to DF or Fabian packs up for the four-hour drive, with Marta and Sergio watching the cuates when Lore and Fabian are both gone. She misses either Fabian or Andres—or both—all the time. Fabian doesn't complain about her absences—how can he? He doesn't notice them as extraordinary, doesn't wonder about late-night phone calls. She misses him, wants him home, but she would be a fool not to know this will change things.

Fabian turns to Lore. "I've given it a lot of thought, y ya . . . llegó la hora."

"Time?" Lore shakes her head. "Time for what?"

There is a respectful silence, an acknowledgment from her family that this is a new discussion, and yet because they're all metiches, no one is going to step away and give them privacy.

"We need to close the store," he says.

Lore's eyes burn with tears. "Fabian, no. We've worked too hard—"

"¿Y pa' qué, Lore?" He shrugs, crossing his fork and knife over his empty plate, sad but resolved. He's already grieved, she realizes. "I told myself I would stay up there as long as I could keep the business afloat. But what, I'm going to drive us into the ground just to keep the sign on the door?"

"But Fabian—"

"I know. We still have the loan, the land, the building. There's more to discuss, but—" He sighs. "This is the right thing to do. It's the only thing to do."

"But," Melissa interjects, "what will you do for work?"

"Why?" Fabian tries to joke. "Are you hiring?"

"Don't even ask," Pablo says. "They don't believe in handouts."

The table erupts, and Pablo gives Lore a quick, conspiratorial glance that tells her he threw everyone into a tizzy on purpose to shift attention from Lore and Fabian. She smiles at him gratefully as Beto and Melissa raise indignant voices, Lisa issues mortified apologies, and Papi turns a solemn, suffering gaze to his plate. Marta gives Lore's back a quick rub.

If she had known this would be their last Thanksgiving together, maybe Lore wouldn't have excused herself from the table. Wouldn't have gone into the empty living room and taken Andres's last three letters from her purse, lifted the corner floorboard under the carpet, and settled them on top of the rest. Maybe, after lunch, she would have gone to the ranch with Papi, let him teach her something involving tools and oil in the muted winter sun. Maybe she would have talked with Mami until darkness fell, memorizing the cadence of her voice. Maybe she never would have let go of Fabian's hand.

Because next year at this time, everything will be different. They will be splintered and separated. Papi dead. Mami and Lore's siblings no longer speaking to her. The cuates living with Marta. Fabian in prison for murder.

But she doesn't know that. She's only thinking of how it's all going to work with Fabian home. She wishes she could read Andres's most recent letter one more time before sealing it away: *Querida Lore,* he had written, *our new home is waiting for you.*

CASSIE, 2017

Ruthless. The word still rang through me, louder and more blaring each time it crossed my mind. Duke may have been talking about the book, but what he had *seen* was the part of me capable of leaving Andrew behind. The part of me that could focus with single-minded intensity on one outcome, ignoring its impact on everyone but me.

He was right about one thing, though—my father might not ever get sober. We might have to make good on my hasty threat to bring Andrew here, in which case my career *mattered.* It mattered anyway. If caring about that made me ruthless, then so be it.

I reread the acknowledgments on all my recent favorite crime books, checked out a two-year-old edition of *Writer's Market* from the Austin Public Library, scoured Manuscript Wishlist and Twitter, and created a spreadsheet of twenty agents. In early November, I sent out my proposal to my top ten.

I knew I might be waiting months for even form rejections. Still, I pored over my mail tracker, refreshed, refreshed, refreshed. And only a few days later, Deborah Maddox—who had sold four of the six biggest true crime titles in the last five years—emailed me back.

Disbelieving, I stared at the subject line: *Offer of Representation.* "Oh my God!" I laughed, alone in our living room, and opened the email with shaking hands.

For one disorienting sliver of a second, I wanted to call my mother. Her absence hit me like a fist, grief made new all over again. I thought about calling Duke or going to the food truck to tell him in person, but I didn't want to see that spark of judgment in his eyes. I didn't want anything to take away from the joy I felt in this moment. The feeling, for the first time in my life, that I was getting close to everything I ever wanted.

I emailed Deborah back, and we set up a call for that afternoon.

"The fact that she's a woman!" Deborah said. Her voice was warm and broad, as if she'd moved to New York from the Midwest. "Now, there's a story we haven't heard before."

"I know! Exactly!" Her validation was like mainlining a drug. "I couldn't *not* pursue it!"

For the next half hour, we talked about the proposal, my interviews with Lore, how Deborah saw the book fitting into the market. "Any questions for me?" she asked.

I hesitated, thinking of Duke's reaction when I'd told him I thought Lore was involved in the murder. I didn't want Deborah to think I was a kook, a conspiracy theorist, or that I was suddenly pivoting from the kind of story I'd claimed to want to tell, about the secret lives inside women's hearts, how those lives can spin out into violence. But I couldn't ignore the questions I had—Andres's sudden, inexplicable trip to Laredo, the gap in Lore's alibi, my suspicion that Andres's note came with contact information, the possibility that Andres was "bothering" Lore. I ended with Sergio's revelation:

"Lore regularly carried a gun for self-defense. It may or may not have been the .22. That's not mentioned anywhere in the reports."

The line went quiet. I bit my lower lip hard.

"Well," Deborah finally said. "That could take an interesting turn. But we have to be sure before including any of this in the proposal."

I exhaled, dizzied by her use of the word *we*. I was part of a team now. "Absolutely. Yes."

"Keep digging," Deborah said. "And make sure you're keeping records of your process. Take photos of inconsistencies in the reports, maybe start keeping a journal, that sort of thing. We could use those artifacts later."

"Sure," I said, still so high on *we* that I almost didn't notice the shift in her tone: she was excited.

A tinny chime of misgiving rang through me. Maybe I should have waited before sharing my suspicions with her. Get a grip on the whole picture before showing part of it to someone else, let alone a high-powered agent with the experience to set something big in motion. I could lose control of it this way.

"Let me know right away if you have any new developments," Deborah said.

Solemnly, I promised I would.

The next night, Andrew called. My father was in the hospital. He'd been in a car accident.

Part III

LORE, 1985–1986

With Fabian now back at home, Lore has to stay late at the bank or invent some desperate excuse to talk to Andres in the evenings. Once, with a whispered "Discúlpame," she even pours half a gallon of milk down the sink so she can say they need more. Then she huddles at the pay phone outside the Maverick, counting the people putting gas in their cars, hoping not to see anyone she knows. When Andres is due to call her at "home," she races to the pay phone outside the bank. His letters go to a PO box she opened early in that first year, saying identity theft was becoming a major concern in this country. The home address she gave him is for the bank condo where they spent that one weekend last year, cooped up during Lore's sudden bout of "food poisoning."

The first time she returns to DF after the temblor is in December. Fabian and the cuates drive her to San Antonio first thing in the morning. Her flight is that afternoon, and Fabian thought they could walk along the River Walk or La Villita together. It's free and different, and maybe it'll help get Gabriel out of his funk.

"What's happening with him?" Fabian asked Lore recently, as she cleaned up after dinner. "How long has he been like this?"

Gabriel's C grades, his short temper, the fact that he and Mateo didn't seem as close lately—Lore felt defensive, as if she'd let something slip in Fabian's absence. She stacked the dishes in the drying rack harder than necessary. "Just teenage stuff. I'm sure it'll be better now that you're home."

Fabian nodded, and Lore felt guilty at how easily she turned the implication on him.

At the gate, she kisses Fabian and remembers how joyfully she fell into his arms when she last returned from DF. She's been feeling claustrophobic lately, ready to shrug off this part of her life for a few days. Before leaving, she gives Fabian the number to a random hotel, knowing he won't spare the expense to call her but having a lie ready just in case: they'd double-booked her room, so she checked in somewhere else. Mentiras, mentiras, mentiras. Exhausting but necessary. For how long can she keep this up?

On the plane, she slips the ruby ring—a gift from Fabian when times were good—onto her right hand, then slides the silver band Andres bought her onto her left ring finger.

At the gate, Lore sees Andres before he sees her, so she has time to conceal her shock: he's lost at least ten pounds, his face drawn, with dark ojeras beneath tired eyes. But when he sees her, he breaks into his familiar grin, sweeping her into his arms and swinging her around widely enough that her legs bump against other people. "Sorry, sorry," she says, laughing, as Andres kisses her. God, how she's missed him.

"Look at you," Lore says, as they walk hand in hand out of the terminal. "You haven't been eating!"

"No one here to cook for me," he says, and they both laugh, since he's the one who cooks for her. "There's been a lot going on."

The understatement of the century. Lore gapes at the ruined city, devastated all over again, as they take a cab an hour out to Ciudad Satélite, where Andres has found a tiny two-bedroom apartment.

The walls are roughly textured, clay red, and the only furniture so far consists of three beds and a small kitchen table. Sliding glass doors open out toward a back courtyard garden shared by the neighboring apartments.

"What do you think?" Andres asks, watching her expression.

She smiles. "I love it. I can't believe you were able to find something so quickly."

"Quick?" Andres jokes. "Did you forget how comfortable Rosana's floor was? I must have been there at least five years, according to my back."

"Pobrecito," Lore says, standing behind him and slipping her hands up his shirt. His skin is warm, his lean muscles tight beneath her palms.

The next day, they go to the Registro Civil to start the legal process for their marriage. A fountain out front lined with Talavera tile; a row of people leaning against bright yellow walls, waiting. The world could be ending, and people would still want to get married. She'd considered forgetting her birth certificate, delaying this part of things, but it hardly makes a difference at this point.

By the time Lore goes home four days later, she is legally married to Andres.

After that first spare Christmas—when she tells Andres she came down with the flu and doesn't want to get him and the kids sick—and the New Year's Eve when the cuates go to a party and Lore and Fabian sit on the couch and watch the ball drop, Fabian can't find even temporary work. Lore startles awake to his teeth grinding. His beard grows, threaded with silver. He inspects the H-E-B receipt every time she buys groceries, asking whether they really need bacon, griping about the prices of milk and eggs as if they'd been set to gouge him, specifically. Sometimes, while he sleeps, she imagines taking a tiny sharp blade to his sternum, a precise cut, releasing some of that toxic, impotent rage.

On top of all that, Lore's travel is wearing on him. "Lore, I'm supposed to be looking for work," he says to her Easter Sunday, crabby, as they get ready for Mass. "How am I supposed to find anything when I have to take the cuates to and from school and all their sports and shit? Not to mention making dinner every night."

"Making dinner takes you away from job hunting?" Lore replies archly, opening a tube of lipstick.

He sits on the edge of the bed to pull on his boots. "You know what I'm saying."

Lore steps out of the bathroom to look at him. "Fabian, what do you think I've been doing for a million years? Both when you were in Austin and before?"

"What, like I've never helped at all?"

She raises her eyebrows. "How much help is it when I get home after dinner?"

Fabian exhales, rubbing his beard. "Yes, but I was providing."

"So was I. So *am* I."

Fabian winces. It's not her fault if he feels like less of a man because she is the one keeping the roof over their heads.

"But do you have to be gone so much?" He walks over to her. Coils one of her still-warm curls around his finger. "We miss you."

She relaxes into his familiar shape. "I miss you, too," she says, kissing him.

Married to two men at once. Two families. When she thinks about it, it's with a suffocating squeeze, like waking up to remember someone you love has died. Or that, perhaps, you're being hunted. That you can never slow down, never relax. That there is no way out—at least not without hurting one of the people you love most.

CASSIE, 2017

My father had been T-boned running a red light. He had three broken ribs, a concussion, and whiplash. He also received a DWI and mandatory substance abuse counseling, and his license was revoked. The other driver had been in some jacked-up Ram, which totaled my father's Chevy while remaining more or less intact. If it had been a smaller car, or a pedestrian had been crossing the street, or my father hadn't been wearing his seat belt—safety first!—everything could have been different.

"It's my fault," Andrew said on the phone, miserable. "We were supposed to pick up burgers at Braum's. I was taking too long, and he left without me. If I'd been with him, I could've—"

"No," I interrupted, fierce. "Andrew, this is *not* your fault. Dad made his own choices."

So had I. There I was, playing the reassuring big sister, pacing the living room, muting myself so I could scream into a sofa pillow after hearing the Ram had hit the passenger side, which apparently folded in like an accordion. If Andrew had been there, he could have died.

I'd always thought the danger from my father's drinking was his anger. Now the other possibilities seemed so obvious—my father driving drunk, Andrew strapped in beside him, a child stuck on a broken carnival ride. It had probably happened a million times before, just as it had probably happened when I was a kid, and I was too goddamn trusting and self-absorbed to notice.

When I first told Duke about the accident and said we needed to bring Andrew to Austin, he looked momentarily dazed. "Isn't there anyone else?" he asked. In his family, there was always someone else.

"No," I said. "I'm all he has."

We made decisions quickly after that, the way you do when there's no other choice. Andrew would stay with a friend until we could get there. I bought an air mattress and sheet set with my emergency credit card. Duke made arrangements for the food truck, let his parents know we wouldn't be at the farm for Thanksgiving. We'd pick up Andrew, stay the night at a cheap hotel, and drive back the next day. We'd take Andrew to Kerbey Lane or Magnolia for a late holiday dinner. On Monday, he'd start school. On the phone, Andrew sounded stunned by the sudden turn of events, but also a little relieved, as if he was ready to let someone else take control.

Andrew couldn't sleep on an air mattress forever, of course. We'd have to break our lease, which wasn't up until June. Move south of Slaughter or, God forbid, up toward Pflugerville or Round Rock. But I'd warmed to the idea of him living with us. It felt that way, a warming, like long-dulled pieces of me regaining sensation. It felt like I was reclaiming my family, or making a new one: Duke, Andrew, and me. I could keep Andrew safe, make up for all the time we'd lost. I could do for him what my mother had never been able to do for me.

Outside the windshield stretched long driveways and big front yards, simple one-story ranch homes dwarfed by mature oaks, their leaves still green and shiny. All this openness should have made it easier to breathe, but the air itself felt weighted, my lungs like bags of sand.

My father had been discharged this morning. He and Andrew were waiting for us at the house, and I had no idea what to expect.

"That was my school," I told Duke, pointing at Glenwood Elementary. The "Little Red Schoolhouse" had started as a one-teacher school in a dugout on the old Glenn farm. In 1915, it was disassembled and transported by wagon a quarter mile east, where it would remain. As a child, I'd had trouble understanding that buildings weren't permanent, that they could be taken apart and stitched back together somewhere else. Sometimes I had nightmares of lying in a bed floating in vast empty space, nothing tethering it to a home, to the world.

"My mom taught third grade there. We used to decorate her classroom together at the start of each school year." I was babbling. I didn't care.

I'd loved sitting across from my mother at her desk, digging inside giant tin boxes of art supplies. One year we'd drawn and cut out characters from *Charlotte's Web*, hours of painstaking work because we wanted to be precise with the parts of Charlotte's legs, the way she named them for Wilbur: "the coxa, the trochanter, the femur, the patella, the tibia, the metatarsus, and the tarsus." We spent three afternoons drawing insects for the web, gluing sequins and glitter onto doomed wings. I liked to let the glue dry on my fingers and peel it off in one eerie film.

"That sounds nice," Duke said. Not quite chilly, but reserved. He softened. "I wish I'd gotten the chance to meet her."

"Me too." I hesitated, then reached across the console for his hand. After a moment, his fingers closed around mine. "Look, if he's drinking—"

"It's going to be okay," he said. So firm and confident, such easy certainty of favorable outcomes.

As I turned into my old neighborhood, nostalgia was the flap of a great wing. Here was where I'd first felt the wobbling freedom of a bike without training wheels, my mother's cheers floating like a kite behind me. Here was the Lowensteins' house, my old friend

Levi whom I'd once overheard telling another guy that screwing me would be like screwing a telephone pole. And here, before us, was my childhood home. The red brick that, on white winter days, stood out from sky and snow like a pulsing heart.

In the semicircular gravel drive, I clutched the key in the ignition. There was the pecan tree I'd climbed when I was eleven or twelve and had found the flask in my dad's boot. I'd tucked it high in the branches, thinking if he couldn't find it, he couldn't drink, and if he couldn't drink, he couldn't hit. Later I'd heard him yelling at my mom. Cabinet doors slamming, my mom's low, calm voice: "I don't know what you're talking about, John." I'd trembled in my room. How could I be so stupid? Of course he'd blame her. But I was too scared to tell the truth.

I took a deep, queasy breath. Duke turned to me. He wanted to keep punishing me with aloofness, I could tell, but it was against his nature. "You okay?" he murmured.

I gave a shaky half laugh. "Peachy."

Then Andrew stepped out of the house.

"Andrew!" I called, flinging open the door. "Look at you! You're so tall!"

"Not really," he said, as I pulled him in for a hug. His preteen body was a collection of bones growing too fast for clothes to keep up. His jeans were half an inch too short, revealing white Nike ankle socks. His shoulder blades were sharp under my palms, tensing like prehistoric wings. His feline face, all green eyes and cheekbones, looked so much like our mother's it took my breath away. He was wearing his straight blond hair longish, so it fell in a swoop to his eyes. When he pulled away, he flicked his head back like a member of a boy band.

Behind Andrew, my father winced with each step toward us. A thick white neck brace cradled his chin. A red-black scab covered the bridge of his nose. Glistening black bruises extended from the inner corner of each eye to below the frames of his glasses. I'd never seen him look so fragile. I wanted to take my fingers to those bruises.

To press him where it hurt. To ask how he liked it. But my legs also wobbled with the reality of his injuries, his mortality. Even without them, he had aged. His knees looked pointy through his jeans, and he was shorter than I remembered. But those baseball-mitt hands. I'd read once that human hair and nails continue to grow even after death. Would my father's hands ever stop growing?

"Cassie," he said. It was his Newly Sober Voice, gruff with shame. "It's great to see you. And you must be Duke."

Duke shook my father's hand. "Pleasure to meet you, sir."

Despite the circumstances, Duke seemed wired by a desire to impress my father. Before we'd left I'd walked into the bathroom to see him attempting to tame his curls with a slap of some dusty-lidded hair product. A tiny scab on his chin had dried where he'd shaved his usual stubble.

"Hi," I said stiffly, before turning to Andrew. "You ready, buddy? Need help with your bags?"

Andrew looked at my father, who said to me, "You've had a long drive. Stay the night, at least. It's Thanksgiving tomorrow!"

"We talked about this," I said to Andrew. "We'll have Thanksgiving back in Austin."

"I bought groceries," my father said. "We—"

I nearly dropped the car keys. "You drove? Was *Andrew* in the car?"

"I ordered stuff online," Andrew said, toeing the gravel with his black Converse. "It all got delivered. The turkey's already defrosting."

My pulse throbbed at my temples. Too much coffee, too little water. My eyes ached.

"Please." My father reached toward me, as if he might touch my shoulder, and then let his hand drop. "Just tonight. I've got Italian chicken pasta in the slow cooker," he added hopefully.

I wanted to remind him of our last phone call, the way he'd hissed: *Leaving at the first opportunity and then calling out of the blue with "you promised."* He'd sounded like he despised me. Now here he was, cooking my favorite meal. I'd never known which version of him was real.

"No, thanks," I said, right as Duke leaned into me, murmuring, "We were going to spend the night somewhere anyway."

I glared at him, furious that we couldn't be united on this one thing, but Andrew was already walking back toward the house. I couldn't read him. Did he want us to stay? Did *he* want to stay, despite everything?

My father clapped once, then winced, touching his ribs. "It's settled. Let me help with your bags."

"You're hurt," I snapped as I popped the trunk and yanked out my small duffel. "Hey, Andrew," I called, "wait up!"

I pulled up short inside.

"Do you like it?" my father asked behind me.

At first, I couldn't figure out how the configuration of my childhood home had changed so dramatically. Then I realized two walls had been knocked down, opening the dining room to the kitchen and the kitchen to the living room. The buttercream walls were repainted cappuccino-brown, the carpet replaced by white ceramic tile, shiny as veneers. The house felt masculine and country with the cherrywood TV armoire, the pine breakfast table with a star carved onto the back of each chair.

The brick fireplace mantel—the one from which my grandfather's urn had fallen—had been painted white, and the urn itself was missing. Instead there stood half a dozen framed photos: my parents slicing into a wedding cake; my parents and me on some lost Christmas morning; Andrew and our father, thrusting their saugeye at the camera, the fish's iridescent green scales catching the light. At this one, I felt an orphan's sorrow.

"The couch," I said suddenly, turning back to the living room. I avoided looking at his old leather chair, his preferred whiskey seat. "What happened to the couch?"

"What couch?" My father stared at the taupe microfiber set in its place. "Not that ratty old thing from when you were a kid?"

"Did you get rid of it?"

He frowned. "Well. Yes."

"You didn't even think to ask if I wanted it?" My voice was shrill. I was being unreasonable. But that couch was where my mother and I had watched *Dateline* together. Those were some of my happiest memories with her, watching bad things happen to other women. Maybe she'd been trying to tell me something. Trying to warn me: *Their bodies are our bodies. Their world is our world.* All the things she couldn't say out loud.

My father's bruised face concealed his emotions. "That couch was falling apart. But listen. I put some other things in the cellar in case you want to look later. Dinner should be ready soon."

"Smells delicious," Duke said. "If you need any help, I'm pretty handy in the kitchen."

I took my opening dully as my father led us down the short hallway to the bedrooms. "Duke owns his own restaurant."

"Well, it's a food truck now," Duke said, "but the plan is to be brick and mortar in a few years."

"A food truck, huh?" my father said. "Those are getting popular, I hear. What kind of food?"

I watched my father watching Duke, nodding along, agreeing that the perfect brisket came down to the bark, though I was sure he'd never heard the word *bark* applied to meat before. It was classic Sober John Bowman, earnestly interested in everyone. I had the wild impulse to interrupt, say, *Hey, Dad, remember that time you shoved Mom by the throat, and she was hoarse for a week? Good times.*

In the doorway of my room, my father said, "I made some space for you guys in the closet. Just in case." The rickety closet doors were open, showing an empty rod with a neat row of dry-cleaning hangers.

"No need," I said.

Duke thanked my father. "So," he added, with forced brightness, "this was your room, Cass!"

"I mean," I said, prickly and uncooperative, "not like when I was a kid, obviously."

But, in some ways, it was—the soft aqua walls, paint flecked to white in places where I'd once thumbtacked posters of Death Cab for Cutie and framed quotes like "Nothing bad happens to writers; it's all material." A quilted coverlet on the iron double bed my mother had bought for me when I was eight, such an exciting upgrade from a twin, a wooden trunk at its foot. There was the space beside my white desk where I'd tucked Andrew's bassinet, even though I always ended up bringing him into bed with me. *It's you and me, buddy,* I'd whispered. *I'll always take care of you.*

"Well," my father said, still in the doorway. "There's another blanket in the trunk in case it gets cold, and fresh towels in the bathroom. I'll just be in the kitchen." He smiled, more at Duke than at me, and retreated down the hallway.

"You couldn't have backed me up about not staying?" I snapped at Duke, kicking my duffel. "This isn't some happy family reunion, you know."

"How could I forget?" Duke shot back. Then he lowered his voice. "Andrew's the one who said they bought a turkey. It's got to be hard for him to say goodbye."

I sighed, rubbing my forehead. "I hate being here."

It felt like the most honest thing I'd said all day. *Ask,* I thought, surprised by this desire. *Why do you hate it so much, Cassie? What happened here? Ask!*

Duke tried to close one of the folding closet doors, and it stuck on the frame. He gave it a little rattle. "Should I help your dad with dinner while you check on Andrew or something?"

I sighed and glanced at my watch. Six o'clock. "I have to call Lore."

"*Now?*"

"It's my job, Duke." I let myself feel the pleasure of that statement, the jealously guarded dream brought to life. I wouldn't let it go. Not for anything.

LORE, 2017

The house was full: Mateo had come into town, and he and Gabriel and Brenda were sprawled like teenagers on the leather couches, wineglasses in hand, when I led Joseph and Michael to my bathroom. They only lived a minute away, but they liked taking Jacuzzi baths here. El chiquito, Joseph, tilted my wrist so that nearly half the bottle of fancy vanilla-scented bubble bath went in. Soon the bubbles were up to their slick, skinny shoulders, and they grabbed handfuls and blew them, shrieking with laughter. The bathroom floor shone with water and my blouse was soaked through, all three of us laughing so hard that Gabriel appeared in the doorway.

I waved him away. "Ay, mijo, we're just having a little fun."

When he left, I looked back at Michael and Joseph, their thick bowl cuts and flushed cheeks, and scooped the biggest handful of bubbles I could and blew them straight into their faces. One day, I hoped they'd remember that they could make a mess with their güela. That their güela liked making messes.

Afterward, I excused myself to walk Crusoe while I talked

to Cassie, who was in Enid after her father crashed his car like a pendejo. Pobrecita, having to become a mother to her brother almost overnight.

"So," Cassie said, "Sergio dropped Fabian off around eight. You went to a movie with the boys at seven and were home by nine, nine fifteen. When you were initially questioned on Monday, August fourth, you said Fabian was there when you got home, and that the four of you were home all night, which is obviously untrue. Why did you lie?"

I let out a rattling sigh. "When the police asked where I was that night, I told them." I had the receipts and ticket stubs ready, right there in my wallet, but they didn't ask to see them until later, once we were at the station. "I realized we were going to be suspects. I wanted them to leave so I could think. So I told them we'd all been together."

"Did you think Fabian was innocent at that point?"

"You got your one question," I said. "My turn: Are you going to confront your father?"

Cassie whispered, "What do you mean, *confront* him? I'm here to take Andrew away from him. It doesn't get more confrontational than that."

I stopped to let Crusoe sniff a mailbox. "Yes, but don't you ever want to make him take responsibility? For what he did to your mother? To you?"

The silence was icy. But after a moment, she asked, "Take responsibility how?"

My phone chimed with a text message from Mateo: *It's dark, are you almost back?* Sí, gracias, I knew it was dark. I had eyes. I wrote: *If I'm not home in 15 minutes send a search party. Make it big.*

"Just to hear him acknowledge it," I said. "I think it could be very healthy for you."

"I don't need him to acknowledge it." Her words were chiseled sharp. "I don't need anything from him."

"Bueno." I was four blocks from home. The evening air smelled like burning mesquite. The stars were magnificent, an endless echo. I thought of Cassie asking how long I thought I could keep up the double life once Fabian got home. I must have had an exit plan, she said. But I didn't. Not until I had no other choice. "Cuídate, mija."

CASSIE, 2017

My mother used to make Italian chicken pasta on deep winter nights, when the wind thrashed the thin branches of the old bald cypress out back. That smell made me feel like a kid again, belly cramped with nerves. What Lore had said about confronting my father—as if it would ever be that easy.

On my way to Andrew's bedroom, I passed my parents'—my father's—open door. He and Duke were still in the kitchen. Without thinking, I ducked inside.

The cream carpet, updated since I'd left, sank beneath my feet. My heart was pounding. I didn't even know what I was doing in here. The walls were painted a sage green my mother would have liked. He still had their mahogany four-poster bed, but there was now a gray duvet instead of their paisley comforter. The bed was made clumsily, the duvet pulled up to cover the pillows. The room smelled artificially clean, like the rest of the house, as if someone—Andrew, I somehow knew—had been liberal with the Febreze before we arrived. Underneath there was something sour and unwashed.

My fingers moved by muscle memory as I opened the first dresser drawer, shifting folded boxers and balled-up socks, skin catching on the unfinished wood lining. I took it drawer by drawer, fast. He'd kept mini bottles in here sometimes, tucked into undershirt collars and glasses cases. I'd never gotten rid of his booze again after the time I'd hidden his flask in the tree. But there was nothing worse than wondering if he was secretly drinking. I'd always needed to know how soon I could expect our world to fall apart.

On the fifth drawer, my hands stopped at something hard and cool—a small leather photo album. I glanced at the doorway, stepped through to the bathroom so no one would see me if they walked by. I was almost nauseated with the fear of being caught. I also felt reckless and wild, wanting to turn the whole house inside out to expose everything hidden in its folds.

The photos were of my mother. A teenager in a maroon Sooners T-shirt, standing on metal bleachers, mouth open in a cheer. In bed, taken in bad light with a cheap camera, blond hair half-askew in its scrunchie, arm beckoning the photographer closer. At a bowling alley, arms up in a V over her head, all the pins scattered. Reading something at a microphone during the school talent show, wearing a paper crown. In bed again, this time on her side, eyes closed, one swollen breast out of the white nightgown, eclipsing the tiny head that nuzzled up to it—me. The photo took my breath away. The intimacy. The transfer of milk and heat from her body to mine, my father moved enough to capture it.

"What are you doing?"

"Oh!" I dropped the photo album on the tile. "My God—Andrew. You scared me!"

He was standing in the bathroom doorway with an odd stern set to his lips. He gestured to the album. "What's that?"

"I— Nothing." I felt protective of it. "I was . . . I wanted to talk to Dad," I lied.

"He's in the kitchen."

"Yeah. I figured."

"Can I see?" Andrew held out a hand, and I gave him the photo album, watching as he flipped through. "I've never seen these before."

"Me neither."

The photos were so ordinary and anachronistic, yet somehow, they didn't feel random. It was as if my father had collected pieces of her that, together, hinted at her fullness.

Andrew looked up at me. His eyes flickered with something. Not pain, exactly. Longing. "What was she like?"

"Dad doesn't talk about her?"

"Yeah, but I want to hear it from you."

Had I never talked about her with Andrew before? Maybe I'd never wanted to remind him of what he'd lost—what he might think he'd taken, his life for hers. But he must feel the mother absence all the time, just like I did. How did withholding memories help? Maybe I didn't know how to talk about her without also talking about *it*— the drinking, the violence, the silence. Maybe I'd forgotten who my mother was apart from being a victim, an accomplice, a disappointment.

"She was funny," I said. "And really good at reading books out loud. She probably could have been a voice actor, she was that good. She took me to volunteer at the Salvation Army every few months because she believed everyone needs help sometimes, and if we could help, we should. She was"—I thought of us watching *Dateline*, assembling our cutout insects amid Charlotte's web—"a great teacher."

Andrew's lips were pressed hard together.

"Does he date?" I asked suddenly. "He still wears his ring. Has photos of Mom up. This album . . ."

Andrew nodded. "He's had a couple of girlfriends I've met. Nothing that serious, I guess."

I couldn't imagine my father with anyone except my mother, but it had been twelve years—he wasn't a monk. "What were they like?" I asked. "Was he ever—" How could I ask if he'd been violent?

Andrew frowned. "What?"

"Never mind. You know what?" I chanced a grin at him. "I think we should keep the album. Take it with us to Austin. What do you say?"

Andrew's fair eyebrows lifted in surprise. He grinned a little back, conspiratorial. Our first true moment of connection. "Okay."

I slung an arm across his shoulder and tucked the album under my shirt, holding it in place with my elbow as we walked out of the bathroom together. He glanced at the dresser; the fifth drawer still open.

"You know," he said, "it's kind of fucked up that you just got here and started snooping."

The swearing startled me, and I didn't know what to do about it. If I was going to be his guardian, should I tell him to watch his language?

"I wanted to see if he had any alcohol hidden," I said finally.

"Oh." Andrew shut the drawer for me, and we stepped into the hallway. "Did he?"

"Not in the dresser."

"Yeah. I think I got everything while he was in the hospital. He wasn't really hiding it, though." He squinted at me, something falling into place. "Did he used to hide it when you were here?"

My heart clamped.

"Guys!" my father called, his voice nearing. "Dinner! Oh—" He stopped short at the sight of us, our tucked heads and low voices. He glanced at his bedroom door.

"I was showing Cassie my room," Andrew said, clearing the hair from his eyes.

The leather album was warm against my skin. The bulge felt obvious. "I'm just going to use the bathroom. I'll be right there."

My father stared at me a beat too long. He pushed up his glasses, wincing when they caught the scab on his nose. "Sure. See you in a minute."

I squeezed Andrew's shoulder, unnerved by the smoothness of his lie. I used the bathroom—my bladder painfully full, I hadn't even realized—and then shoved the album in my duffel bag.

In the kitchen, Duke had made garlic bread, butter melted golden when he peeled back the foil. Andrew told Alexa to play some music, but it was all wrong, Ariana Grande instead of Stevie Nicks. My father struggled to drink from his glass of Dr Pepper with the neck brace. He noticed me noticing his hand tremble. I looked away.

"So, Andrew," Duke said, "play any sports?"

Andrew paused with a haphazard mountain of pasta halfway to his mouth. "I'm an orange belt in karate. I'm testing for first-degree green in two months."

Duke looked suitably impressed. "Wow. Can you show me some moves later?"

Andrew grinned. For the first time he looked like a kid. "Yeah, if you think you can keep up."

Duke laughed, and so did I. My father smiled, meeting my eyes with a silent, tentative question: *Isn't this nice? We're having a good time, right?* As if this were a normal family gathering, introducing my fiancé to my father for Thanksgiving.

God, this *feeling*. The strain of pretense, the forceful forgetting. The way it sometimes made me doubt what I'd seen the night before, the images rearranging into something milder, more palatable, the facts shifting beneath my feet. Sometimes I'd wished he would hit me, too, just so I'd have a physical mark to assure me it was real.

My old mattress squeaked with every movement. I used to hold so still as I read. If the rumble of my father's voice got too close, or I heard a distant clatter, I'd pull my headphones from the first drawer of my nightstand as if I were performing surgery, silent and precise. But I never actually used them. I didn't want to be caught off guard.

The house was drafty, and I'd taken a thick wool blanket from the trunk and laid it over the white coverlet. Duke's chest was warm against my back.

"So," he murmured, "your dad seems sober, doesn't he?"

"Nothing like a four-day hospital stay to force a detox."

I could feel Duke's irritation. "I'm just saying, it seems like he's trying."

I didn't respond, and the silence became hard to bear.

"What?" I said, turning around.

Duke reached forward, running a strand of my hair between his fingers. I couldn't see more than the shine of his eyes. "It's—it's such a big move, taking Andrew with us. Are we sure about this?"

I stiffened. "Yes. We're sure."

"But if your dad's getting better." Duke's thumb brushed my eyebrows, applying pressure the way I usually liked. "Maybe it should be more of a conversation between all of us tomorrow?"

I jerked my face away from his hand. "No. I'm not going to take that chance." Not again.

"I just think we should at least talk to Andrew," Duke insisted. "Make sure this is what he wants."

I sat up, the iron headboard pressing cold knuckles into my shoulders. "What *he* wants? Or what *you* want?"

Duke flicked on the bedside lamp. The LED glare was like the lights at a bar at 2 A.M., illuminating all the spilled beer and smeared makeup.

"It's not like I've had a whole lot of time to get used to the idea." His cheeks reddened. "I didn't even know your dad was an alcoholic before a few days ago."

"Well, you never worked very hard to get me to tell you about him! I mean, at a certain point, not asking becomes a *choice*, Duke."

Duke sat up in a furious rustle of covers. "You never wanted to talk about your family, so I never made you! I'm the bad guy for that?"

Duke was right. For our entire relationship, my natural disinclination to reveal met his natural disinclination to ask. A perfect match. But something had changed. I thought of Lore. The intimacy of her relationships, not only with both men, but with me. She might be holding something back about the night Andres was killed, she might even have had something to do with the murder, but she was honest about her feelings, her desires, and she forced me to be honest, too, or at least wish I could be.

"Duke, I have to tell you something." I focused on breathing through the blackness edging my vision. "About my dad. And me. When I was younger—" My phone buzzed. It was the number I'd programmed for Carlos Russo. "Shit."

Duke made a grab for my phone, to silence it, and I swiveled away, finger poised to answer.

"It's Andres's son," I said, already getting out of bed. "I'm sorry. It's important."

"And this isn't?" Duke's eyes were wide, the lines of his body tense.

"I just have to— Cassie Bowman speaking," I answered, before the call could ring out.

Duke scoffed. "Sure, but I don't fucking ask enough questions." He turned off the lamp and I blinked in the sudden darkness. My phone like a star, guiding me from the room.

"Carlos Russo," he said. "You been calling me. Leaving messages."

"Yes, I've been wanting to ask you some questions about—"

"That bitch, I know." Carlos's tongue sounded thick and unwieldy: *bish*. I thought about what Penelope had said about his hard times—he was drunk or high or both. Well. That could work to my advantage.

In the kitchen, I rummaged around in drawers until I found an old bill and a pen, leaned over the counter to take notes.

"She used us," he continued. "Used us and dumped us, like trash."

The phrasing was almost identical to Penelope's in the *Laredo Morning Times*. I imagined them as teenagers, trying to make sense of things. A line repeated to each other over the years.

"What do you think she used you for?" I tried to speak softly, not to wake my father or Andrew, but loudly enough to match his own volume.

"Who knows? Instant family, I guess. Maybe she hated her real family, maybe—"

"She didn't," I said, without thinking.

Carlos was quiet, breathing. "Then why?"

"If you ask me," I said slowly, "I think she wanted too many good things at the same time. She didn't know how to give any of them up. I don't think she meant to hurt you."

Carlos snorted, a wet, muddy sound. "She killed him."

I froze. "What?"

"She killed my father."

There was a crash, like he'd knocked a pot or pan to the ground.

"Carlos?" I said urgently. "Carlos? Are you there?"

"Shit. Hold on." More noise. "Okay. I'm here."

"Carlos, are you saying her *choices* killed him? Or . . ." I hesitated, hardly able to believe I was about to ask this. Carlos was obviously not in a good state. He'd self-medicated through his childhood trauma, and all that pain had probably twisted up into a story that depicted Lore as the monster she was in his mind. But there was also the gap in her alibi. And the gun she may have been carrying. "Or do you think Lore herself actually murdered your father?"

"That's what I said, isn't it?" His voice wobbled. I heard liquid being poured. A steadying swallow. "You know what I think? I think she's some kind of bruja. She makes people believe her. I bet she didn't tell you."

I was writing his words down verbatim, as quickly as I could. "Tell me what, Carlos?"

The seconds before he spoke again stretched like taffy, thinning, thinning. Then:

"She was pregnant."

LORE, 1986

On one of their weekends with Penelope and Carlitos, Carlitos asks, "How come your sister's never come to visit?"

It's May, and they're eating dinner in the new apartment, still only half-furnished, the walls bare. They could be anywhere. But at least they are somewhere, unlike so many thousands squatting in the husks of half-collapsed buildings, or city parks, or government camps. Fathers who had once left for work in the morning, mothers who had sent their children to school in clean clothes. And now those children, who had once traced painstaking cursive and practiced their times tables, cup their palms on Avenida Juárez, as if whatever you could drop in them would make a difference.

"My sister?" Lore gives a baffled laugh. She takes a bite of the calabaza con puerco Andres made.

"The one you were talking to after the earthquake," Carlitos says. "Remember?"

Lore swallows, the meat catching in her throat. She takes a gulp of water, coughing. "We're not close," she says, finally.

"But you said you loved her."

Andres and Penelope are watching her, identical looks of confusion on their faces.

"I thought you didn't talk to your siblings," Andres says, setting his fork down.

"I don't. But I figured they'd still care whether I was dead or alive." Her tone has taken on a clip of indignation, that first instinctive response to being suspected of something: make the other person feel bad. "I called her from Rosana's house."

Andres nods, thoughtful. "Why don't I go up with you some weekend? Surely if they care you're alive, they care you're married to someone they've never met?" He makes it sound like a joke, but Lore can hear the disturbance in his voice.

She smiles. "Unfortunately, I think the caring is limited to dead or alive."

"Why?" Penelope frowns. "I can't imagine not talking to Carlitos when we grow up."

Lore can't imagine not talking to her siblings, either. "I'll tell you some other time, okay?"

To her relief, they don't push it. She can sense it will come up again, though. As it is, Andres asks her twice in the next few months when she is thinking of moving to DF, and she says the same thing both times: when the economy improves. How can she leave her job right now? Especially with DF still in shambles? Andres never argues with this. No one can argue with a steady paycheck.

But he might, one day soon, insist on coming to visit her again. She can't blame him. They've been together nearly three years. If not for the temblor, she imagines it would have happened much sooner, because what is more unnatural—more dangerous—than a woman who claims to have no ties in the world?

CASSIE, 2017

Are you sure she was pregnant?" I asked Carlos Russo. "How do you know?"

"I'm the one—I'm—I found her test thing." The words came slower now, cottony. "In the bathroom. I didn't even know what it was. That's why I ashed—asked—my dad."

"When was that, Carlos?"

"The day before he left," Carlos said.

My breath caught. That fit with what Penelope said—something had happened to make Andres take the kids back to their mother's and buy a plane ticket to Laredo. Andres must have arrived in Laredo late Thursday, July 31, and either booked the hotel right away or after trying and failing to find Lore. Then he'd shown up at the bank Friday morning, thwarted from seeing Lore first by the board meeting and then by her doctor's appointment.

The doctor's appointment. Lore's "annual," her charmingly discreet code for a Pap smear. Carlos's words chimed through me: *I think she's some kind of bruja. She makes people believe her.* I thought of the plain little dinners we'd shared over FaceTime, laughing over our ham and cheese sandwiches. I felt a sick ache of betrayal, a pale echo of what everyone in her life must have felt at the time.

"Did you tell anyone about the pregnancy?" I asked. "Penelope? The police?"

But I knew, even as I asked. Carlos must have blamed himself—if only he'd never shown Andres the pregnancy test, his father might still be alive. So he'd done the only thing he could, all this time: try to forget. Until now. Until me.

"No," he said. Quiet and simple. "Mira, now you know. I gotta— I've got to go. Take care."

"Wait! Carlos!" I remembered my conversation with Penelope, months ago. "Hey—Penelope said to tell you her offer still stands."

He exhaled, a threadbare sheet on a line. "Yeah. You just tell her not everyone wants to get old."

Those words rang through me, desperately sad, as I sat at the kitchen table to write notes. So many lives irreparably damaged because of Lore, the implacable eye of the storm.

If she was pregnant and hadn't told Andres, that meant either she'd known—or decided—the father was Fabian, or she was still determining what to do about the pregnancy. Terminating would be the only way she could continue her double life. But the timeline was likely too tight for the doctor's appointment that day to be for an abortion.

Unless she'd decided to keep the baby. Maybe she'd weighed her options and decided to stay in Laredo, raise the baby with her original family, rather than lose Fabian, the twins, and her job to move to Mexico City. Maybe she'd already ended the relationship with Andres, or was planning to, and then Carlos found the pregnancy test. Even if Andres had never been aggressive before, I couldn't imagine more perfect circumstances for violence than the discovery of not only your wife's double life—but her secret pregnancy.

Then again, the same could be said for Fabian.

. . .

Duke was asleep, or pretending to be, when I returned to bed around three in the morning. His breathing remained deep and regular—a bit too regular, maybe—as I tossed and turned. "Duke?" I whispered at one point. Nothing. I thought I'd never fall asleep, but when I opened my eyes, it was morning and he was gone. *Went grocery shopping,* he'd texted me. *Let me know if you need anything.* Duke always harnessed his anger into executing complicated recipes. Not that Walmart was exactly Whole Foods. *Okay, thanks,* I responded. The read receipt appeared, then nothing. I swallowed, feeling as though I'd traded one form of guilt for another: Now that I was doing right by Andrew, I was letting cracks start to splinter my relationship with Duke. We would talk later, I promised myself. I would tell him everything. We would start fresh. It was time.

First, I had to call Lore.

The phone rang until it went to voicemail. After two more attempts, I reconsidered my approach. Maybe it was better to keep Carlos's revelation close for now. Until I figured out what it meant—and what to do with it.

In the kitchen, my father was wearing an apron with a small brown handprint decorated to look like a turkey, beneath which Andrew's name was written in careful, kindergarten-teacher print. The real turkey, bald and slick as a newborn, rested on the counter, and my father was squinting at his iPhone, as if reading instructions. His bruises were grotesquely shiny, as though coated with a layer of Vaseline. Must be nice not needing to hide them.

"Did you sleep okay?" he asked when I walked in. "Thought I heard you rustling around out here."

"I had a work call." Then, without knowing why, I blurted, "I'm writing a book."

"A book!" My father set down his phone, smiling. "You always did love to read. What's it about?"

Whatever had briefly opened in me closed. For fuck's sake. I wasn't trying to make my dad proud. "Never mind. Is there coffee?"

I was looking for the old coffeepot, the one he was always tipping into his thermos, with or without whiskey. I didn't see it anywhere. He gestured to a black Keurig beside the toaster.

"Coffee pods are in the drawer. Tell me about the book," he prompted again.

I slapped the Keurig's chrome lid shut. "My agent doesn't want me to talk about it," I lied.

"Oh. Right." He gave a self-deprecating chuckle. "I don't even know what an agent is."

Deborah. She'd told me to update her with any new developments— the phone call with Carlos fit the bill. Yet . . . the vibration in her voice when I'd shared my initial suspicions with her, the way she'd told me to keep records of my research, that we might be able to "use those artifacts later." I knew what she meant. Photos in the book, bonus content on the website. Clues inviting the reader to play detective with me. That wasn't the book I'd imagined, the book I'd promised.

Was it the book that would sell?

I willed the coffee to brew faster. God, my father looked ridiculous in that apron. Cheeks freshly shaven, the long lines of his dimples seared into his skin. Once, I'd stood beside him as he shaved, asked if I could do it, too. He'd squeezed a dollop of thick, pine-scented cream into my hands and showed me how to spread it evenly over my cheeks "like you're frosting a cake." Then he'd given me a disposable razor with the cap on, and I'd stripped the shaving cream off one stroke at a time. "You're a natural," he'd said, winking. "But it'll be another few years before your beard comes in." We'd both laughed.

"Cassie. When we last talked on the phone, I . . ." He looked pained. I was surprised he even remembered the conversation: *Who do you think you are?* "I'm sorry—"

"It's fine." I took my cup and hurried from the kitchen, stunned by my own cowardice. Breathless with anger—at him, at myself—I nearly barreled into Andrew in the hallway. He was clutching his crumpled pajamas under one arm, steam pouring from the open bathroom door.

"Whoa, sorry," I said, forcing a smile.

Andrew gave me a serious, searching look, and in a disorienting flash I saw my mother looking at me the same way, examining my body for injury after I'd lost control on my Rollerblades or fallen off my bike. He had so much of her, and he didn't even realize.

"You okay?" he asked. In one hand, his phone was open to a string of text messages. I suddenly wondered about his friends, what they knew, who he was going to miss.

I exhaled, ruffling his wet hair. "Yeah. Hey, I was thinking you could show me some of those karate moves."

"Really?" The lilac pockets beneath his eyes were faintly puffy, but he grinned, locking his phone screen. "Now?"

"Oh." I thought again about Deborah, the power she held over my career. I didn't want her to forget about me while I decided what to do with new information.

Andrew shrugged. "Whatever. We can do it later."

"No, no." Andrew was right here in front of me. I had to start getting used to putting him first. "Now's good."

Andrew's walls were bright green, the color of toxic chemicals in cartoons, vintage *Avengers* posters thumbtacked to the walls. Each figure was set against a monochromatic background, the angles of their faces sharp and geometric. The male figures had narrow, slit-like eyes cut into their masks, while Black Widow was entirely featureless, red hair swirling around a blank white face. Figured.

I set my coffee on his messy corner desk. "Where do we start?"

Andrew stood in front of me, bare feet firmly planted on the carpet. "I'll teach you some basic moves first."

For the next twenty minutes, Andrew taught me how to maneuver away from the imaginary grips of men much larger than I, men who might grab my wrist at a bar or push a forearm to my throat from behind in a parking lot. Andrew already had a wiry strength that surprised me. As we practiced, I wondered if my mother had ever thrust up a forearm like this to block a blow. I'd never seen her defend herself, but there was a lot I hadn't seen. Maybe she'd figured the easiest way through was to let it happen, knowing how quickly my father felt ashamed. If Lore had been threatened, she would have fought back. I knew it.

When Andrew determined I was ready to move on to crescent kicks and roundhouses, we went to the backyard. The house sat on half an acre, a thick tree line acting as a natural fence. The majestic bald cypress towered over the oaks and pecans. I used to wait all year for it to flame red in autumnal magic before dropping its lacy needles. Proof that things changed.

On the slightly rolling lawn, the lesson culminated in wild "flying kicks" that left us both laughing in the grass. We spread out as if making snow angels, cold dew dampening our jeans.

"See that?" I pointed to the low cloud hanging like a blindfold across the plaster-white sky. "That's called a nimbostratus cloud. It's going to rain later, but no thunder or lightning."

Andrew peered at the sky. A slant of sunlight cut through his fair lashes. "How do you know that?"

"Mom taught me."

I glanced at the old swing set. The metal chains gripped in my small hands, my father's palm between my shoulders, my mother's open arms in front of me, always prepared to catch me. They had tried to be good parents. For a while, they had been.

"Andrew," I said quietly, "how long have you known Dad's an alcoholic?"

He pulled a clump of grass from the lawn, staring at the exposed strip of earth. I thought of the crime scene photos—that line of skin between Andres's sock and the hem of his jeans.

"I don't know. A couple of years." He ripped a blade of grass in half slowly, deliberately. "He'd go from not drinking at all to drinking all the time, being kind of a mess, then back to nothing. Doesn't take a genius."

"Why didn't you tell me?"

Andrew shrugged. "Why would I?"

The sting of my irrelevancy spread in my chest. "But this time . . ."

"He wasn't stopping." He dropped the blade of grass, picked up a rock. "And the other stuff. Not cooking dinner, forgetting to pay bills. I think he was probably drinking at work, too, because he already seemed drunk when he'd get home. That time he forgot me at karate and we found him passed out—after that, my sensei said he could call someone for me. But, like, who? CPS? I thought they were going to take me away. So I told him I'd call you."

I had been a last resort. And even then, I hadn't come through for him. I braced myself. "Andrew, on the phone—you said he was getting mean. Mean how?"

Andrew clenched the rock, then hurled it toward the trees. "He called me an ungrateful little shit when I asked about the internet." His voice trembled. "I was just *asking*."

A wave of relief crested through me. "That's all?"

Andrew looked at me sharply. "What, that's not bad enough?"

"Oh, Andrew." I wrapped an arm around his shoulders. "That's not what I meant."

He shrugged me away. "He's better, though, right?" His eyes lifted to mine, and the anger had shifted to hope, guileless and open. I remembered how he used to look at me when I leaned over him in the bassinet—the grin when he recognized my face, the squirm of wanting to be lifted without knowing how to stretch his arms up for me. "He's sober now?"

I hesitated. "You've seen how it goes. He's better today. That doesn't mean he'll be better tomorrow. It's something he'll have to work at for the rest of his life."

Andrew pulled his knees to his chest, encircling them with his arms. In profile, his face was all sharp angles, like it had been chiseled by someone who didn't quite know when to stop. His baby softness almost gone.

LORE, 2017

After Thanksgiving lunch, everyone settled in to watch *Home Alone.* Gabriel and Mateo had been too old when the movie first came out, pero ahora con los niños we all laughed as Kevin set his traps for Marv and Harry. We promised we'd take Joseph and Michael to the striped Christmas tree tent on McPherson in the morning.

When the phone rang, I half expected it to be Cassie again. What had she wanted this morning, those three calls I'd missed? Normally we only spoke at six. Unsettled, I'd ignored them. Now my heart skipped; the caller ID said "Unknown." Finally.

The automated spiel came on, and there was a brief delay after I accepted the call.

"Lore?"

I smiled. "Hola, mi amor. I'm putting you on speaker. Gabriel, pause it. Fabian, we're all here. The boys, too."

"Happy Thanksgiving, everyone!" Fabian injected his voice with cheer, the way he was always so good at doing for the cuates when he was in Austin.

Gabriel gestured for the phone and held it close to Michael and

Joseph, who were lying on the floor beneath their *Blaze and the Monster Machines* blankets. "Say hi to Grandpa," Gabriel said. Joseph waved half-heartedly, his eyes on the paused image of Marv in a doorway, wild-haired and wild-eyed. "He can't see you, Joseph," Gabriel said, laughing. "The boys say hi, Dad. How are you?"

"Fine, mijo, fine. Same old. Michael, Joseph, ¿qué comieron?"

This question pulled them from their stupor, and they recounted all the dishes as I fought a wave of sorrow, imagining Fabian eating slices of dry turkey off a plastic tray. It wasn't fair. On the couch beside Gabriel, Brenda pulled out her own phone, scrolling and scrolling. I wanted to slap it out of her hands. Show some respect, I wanted to say. Feeling Mateo's gaze, I glanced at him, and he rolled his eyes toward Brenda. I smiled. I really did wish he would meet someone nice.

Michael was telling Fabian about our Christmas tree plans. "We're going to get a big one, one that's taller than Daddy, and I get to put the star on top!"

"No!" Joseph wailed, grabbing the phone. He searched the screen, still confused between FaceTime and speakerphone. "I want to put the star on top, Grandpa!"

It always amazed me, how, even with their perpetual whys, the boys just accepted that Fabian was in prison. As if prison were a city like Laredo, a place where people were born and sometimes stayed.

After a few minutes, I extended my hand. I wanted to talk to Fabian alone before our time ran out.

In my bedroom (now painted Cranberry Cocktail, beautiful with my gold damask comforter), I jumped straight to it: "Mi amor, has that reporter, Cassie, tried to schedule any more interviews with you?"

"Yes," Fabian said, "and I keep saying no. Why?"

"She keeps asking about that night."

Fabian was quiet. I pictured him standing at a phone bank. All our calls were recorded.

"Why?" he finally said. "¡Ya! What happened happened."

"I know, amor. I know. I'm sorry."

"We agreed," he said.

The line beeped. One minute left.

"I know." I sighed. "But she won't stop digging, y tengo miedo que if you don't talk to her . . ."

"It could all be for nothing."

"Exactly." I stared outside at the gnarled branches of the oaks. Sometimes branches separated only to come back together, the leaves on one indistinguishable from leaves on another.

"Fine," he said. "But, Lore."

"Yes?"

Another beep. Thirty seconds.

"Ten cuidado," he said.

Irritation poked like a splinter in my skin. I knew what I was doing.

And what I might have to do.

CASSIE, 2017

By six, the turkey was a golden sun in the oven. As expected, Duke had gone all out with the side dishes: twice-baked sweet potatoes with pureed chipotle peppers and maple syrup, a thirteen-layer potato gratin, roasted brussels sprouts with crispy pancetta. My father had dug three more aprons from a kitchen drawer, and at one point we all paused in our clumsy preparations to watch Duke—he was a marvel, an elegant flash of shiny blades. I'd stopped noticing his talent at home, but here, I saw it with fresh eyes. I was proud of him.

Still, there was a distance between us, the stilted aftermath of last night's unfinished conversation. We'd barely been alone today, but even when we had been, he hadn't brought up what I'd started to tell him about my father, and I hadn't apologized for taking Carlos Russo's call. Now he mostly addressed my father and Andrew—stories of his childhood on the farm, compliments on Andrew's peeling technique, questions for my father about aviation. Finally, my father pulled the turkey from the oven.

Duke whistled. "Now that, sir, is a Thanksgiving bird."

My father laughed. "As long as it's not still frozen in the middle, I'll call it a win."

Table set, I poured glasses of water for Duke and me, while my father filled his own glass and Andrew's with Dr Pepper.

"Before we eat," my father said, smiling with steamed glasses, "a toast. May this be the start of new traditions. New memories. Together."

Was he kidding? Had he forgotten why Duke and I had dropped everything to drive seven hours here? Seething, I clinked my glass against the others slightly too hard. It was the same every time he got sober, as if sobriety itself absolved him of everything that had come before. Repentance without acknowledgment or apology; forgiveness taken without being earned.

Throughout the meal, Andrew darted to the living room every ten minutes to update us on the football score. My cell phone and Duke's kept blowing up with his family group chat—pictures of Caroline's famous blackberry pie and coffee milk, videos of the new calf taking her first wobbly step. Light, cheerful messages, designed to uplift.

Separately, Caroline had texted me right before dinner: *How're you doing, honey?* I wrote back, *Been better. Can't wait to see you all for Christmas.* She'd responded, *And we can't wait to meet that brother of yours. Allie's already excited to get him on a horse!* Tears had sprung to my eyes. Andrew had a place in their family, just as I did. Her kindness, by extension, made me willing to overlook Duke's reluctance to bring Andrew home with us. When I laced my fingers through his between our places, he squeezed my hand.

My father smiled, noticing. "So," he said, "when's the wedding?"

Duke shot me an uncertain look. "We're thinking May on the farm. Right, Cass?"

I nodded and focused on cutting my turkey. The silence expanded, and I wondered if my father was imagining walking me down the aisle, giving me away, as if he owned any part of me.

"I'd like to contribute," he said instead. "I know how expensive weddings are and—"

"No," I said sharply, looking at him. His Eddie Bauer vest and tired, bruised eyes. If I didn't know about the potential for violence tucked somewhere in a locked drawer inside him, I'd never believe it. But that was all of us, wasn't it? Facades upon facades, only some were more damaging to believe than others. "I don't want—"

Duke put a hand on my thigh, cutting me off. "That's very generous, sir. But I'm sure we can manage."

I flushed warm with gratitude, wishing I weren't so surprised he was on my side.

"Well, the offer is open." My father smiled, but I could see the effort behind it, a conscious engaging of muscles. "So, Cassie," he said. "This book of yours—isn't there anything your agent will let you tell us?"

Duke looked at me quizzically. It was, of course, all I'd been talking about for months. Even here, with every nerve on edge, my mind was still clicking through scenarios in the background, shifting pieces around, trying to understand. Screw it. Quickly, I summarized the story for my father and Andrew: Lore's double life. Andres's sudden, mysterious visit to Laredo. The envelope that may have contained more than a note—the note with its dubiously cryptic message—the gap in Lore's alibi, the gun she may have been carrying. All culminating in Andres's murder and Fabian's conviction.

"That call last night was Andres's son, Carlos," I said to Duke. "It turns out . . . Lore was pregnant. That's why Andres went to Laredo. He'd just found out. Carlos thinks . . ." I hesitated, remembering Duke's reaction last time I'd shared my suspicions, and then I plowed ahead. "He thinks Lore killed Andres."

Duke dropped his fork, surprise clear on his face, swayed by someone else's belief in Lore's involvement. "That's . . . whoa. Does he have any proof? Do *you*?"

I sighed, crumpling the paper towel in my lap into a tight ball. "No. It's all circumstantial. Lore has all the motive and opportunity in the world, but Fabian is the one who left his print in the room and was seen around Andres's time of death. So he either went back on his own, out of jealousy or anger, or Lore convinced him to do it."

"But everyone knew everything by then, right?" Duke said. "So what would be the point?"

"Whose baby was it?" Andrew said suddenly.

I shook my head. "I have no idea. But I feel like the pregnancy is key." My leg was jumping. I tried to calm it. "What if she'd decided to stay with Fabian, but Andres, knowing or believing the child was his, threatened to take custody after its birth? Maybe Lore tells Fabian he's the father—true or not—to keep their family intact. That would give Fabian motive. And it would explain why she alibied him. Why they alibied each other."

Talking out the theories, feeling the pieces come together in a reasonable, plausible way, made my stomach churn. Because if Lore had—intentionally or not—manipulated Fabian into killing Andres, how would exposing it impact her life? Could she still be charged as an accessory? Could she go to prison? I imagined her garden replaced by a cell, talking to her grandsons through glass. Could I really take a sixty-seven-year-old woman away from her family for her remaining good years, when she'd been performing her own kind of penance ever since the crime?

But Andres deserved justice. His children—and Lore's, for that matter—deserved to know what really happened.

"Have you spoken to the ex-husband?" my father asked.

Ex-husband. *Ex-husband.*

"Oh, my God," I said.

"What?" Duke leaned toward me, more invested in the story than I'd ever seen him.

"I just— This is so stupid." I laughed, though it wasn't funny.

"I don't think I've confirmed through court records that Lore and Fabian are divorced. They must be. Lore hasn't said anything to the contrary . . ." I trailed off.

Then again, she'd also said she'd never been in another relationship. Could that be because she was still married to Fabian? Quickly, I pulled up the Webb County Clerk's website on my phone and searched for divorce records.

Nothing came up in either Lore's or Fabian's name.

My head spun. "I don't get it. How do you stay married to a woman who had a whole other life and family? And let's say I'm wrong about all this and Fabian did kill Andres without Lore's knowledge. How do you stay with a man who killed someone you loved?"

"Unless," Duke said, "like you said, they were in it together, and staying married protects them both."

"But how?" Needing to move, I carted an armful of plates to the sink. "He's already in prison."

I ran warm water over the dishes, then positioned a cup under the Keurig, slamming down the lid. Lore hadn't even told me this one fundamental thing about her and Fabian. But why? Because it raised questions of her complicity? God. What kind of crime writer was I that I hadn't confirmed this from the very beginning? What else had I missed because I enjoyed talking to her, because she felt like a safe space to share my own mistakes? Tears of frustration and shame lodged deep in my throat. She'd fooled me, just like she'd fooled everyone who loved her. And I'd let myself be fooled. Again.

"Maybe," my father said softly, "they forgave each other."

I turned. There was something on his face, an impression more than an expression, the final delicate ripple after a stone's throw in water. That was all it took. The anger that had been crackling in my chest since we'd arrived—no, since before then, since long before—blew open into a dark flame.

"Forgave each other?" I repeated, too loud, as the Keurig spat coffee. "What, like Mom forgave you?"

My father recoiled, a hand to his ribs, as if the words had pierced the tender flesh between each cracked bone, and God help me, it felt good.

"Cassie." He removed his glasses, then put them back on. Outside, the rain had started, a silent downpour. "I . . ."

"You what?" I remembered Lore asking me if I was going to confront him. It had meant something to me, that she thought I was brave enough to do that. I *was* brave enough, damn it.

My father cleared his throat. He glanced apologetically at Duke, of all people, as if sorry to mar his first impression. Then he turned to Andrew. "I'm an alcoholic."

"Obviously. And?" I was steely now. Indestructible. Vibrating with power. "What else?"

Lightning flashed, illuminating all the smudges on my father's glasses as he set them on the table. Maybe it helped to not see us clearly. Maybe none of us saw each other clearly.

"Cassie, I don't think this is the appropriate—" he started.

"*Appropriate?*" All the years of silence, of pretense and repression, coursed through me. All the times my mother had said it was an accident, all times she'd covered bruises with her Clinique foundation, all the times I'd read about murder because murder made me feel better about what was happening inside my own goddamn house. "You want to talk about what's *appropriate?*"

"Cass," Duke started, looking between us uncertainly. When conversations got too heated in his family, someone always shouted, "Table!" and that was it. The topic was tabled until emotions cooled. But I wasn't going to do that. Not anymore.

"Was it appropriate what you did to Mom?" I asked my father, low and cold.

Andrew's cheeks seemed to sink inward, his mouth pinched. "What's she talking about?" he asked my father.

My heart seized. "Tell them!"

My father's cheeks turned a mottled red below the bruises. Maybe he would show himself, shed the pretense like a translucent skin, and finally other people would see what I had for all those years. They'd know. We'd all know.

But he only pressed his palms together, so hard that his nails bloomed deep fuchsia in the center, capped with white crescents.

"Let's start with my ninth birthday." I clutched the counter to keep me upright. "Do you even remember?"

Unexpectedly, Andrew slammed a fist on the table. Dishes rattled. "Someone tell me!" he shouted.

My father lowered his face into cupped palms. Muffled, he said, "The day your sister turned nine, I was fired. It was during the holidays. Your grandfather died close to Christmas. He was a tough father—" He raised his head, looking at me with something like scorn, as if to say I had it good compared to him. "But his death hits me hard every year. With being fired on top of it—well. I went to a bar. I drank too much. Then I got home and—"

"I was helping Mom clean up after my party," I interrupted. This was my story. It filled my veins as much as my blood, and I was going to tell it. "You got home," I said to my father, "and Mom accidentally knocked the urn off the mantel."

At this, he stilled. Shook his head once, slightly.

"What do you mean *no*?" My chest was tight and sore, as if I'd been kicked.

"It wasn't her," he said softly. "You knocked it over."

"No. *She* knocked it over, and you hit her." The words came out small. I tried again. "You hit her. You smacked her right in the chest." I was crying now, a torrent of memory and hurt, a hand over my heart. The sorrow when she'd looked at me, as if seeing something irreparable break. My innocence. My trust.

Duke's spine stiffened. Andrew paled, looking between my father and me.

"You hit her," I said again. "You hit her. You hit her." The three words kept bubbling up, over and over, spilling out of me.

When I finally stopped, my father said, "She stepped in front of you."

"No."

He closed his swollen eyes. "I think you meant to wave at me. Something. And the urn fell, and I just—reacted. I didn't mean to. God, Cassie, I never meant to hurt anyone. Never. Not you and not her. I swore I'd get sober, that it would never happen again. She told me if I ever laid a hand on you, she wouldn't just leave me—" He opened his eyes, gave a painful almost-smile. "She'd kill me. I quit drinking, cold turkey. And God knows why, she stayed."

No. He was changing things. But I could almost feel the cool swish of my mother's sleeve as she darted before me. Her chest, right where my face would be. My bare feet dusted with my grandfather's ashes. But no. That wasn't how it happened. She had never protected me. I had protected myself.

I shook my head. "But you kept hitting her! Anytime you started drinking again. Right up until—" I looked at Andrew. "Right up until she got pregnant."

"Jesus," Duke said, a low hiss.

Sorry we're not your perfect family, I thought at him bitterly.

At some point, I had gone to the table. I was gripping the edge, my fingers searching for rough spots, seeking splinters. But the wood was varnished, too smooth. The leftover food was dull and congealed now, turkey like drying strips of human skin.

"I tried." My father looked at Andrew, whose chest moved fast with shallow breaths. Through clenched teeth, my father said, "You don't know how hard I have to try, every damn day, to be better than I am."

I exhaled hard through my nose. "We all have to try to be better than we are. Every one of us. That's no excuse."

My father looked me in the eyes. The only rage in the room was mine, and in a sickening whoosh, even that disappeared, leaving me shaky, hardly able to stand.

"I know," he said.

The room was pitched into the kind of silence that emphasizes every background noise: a Home Depot commercial in the living room, the fan humming over the stove, rain lashing the window. The room flashed white, and a clap of thunder jolted Andrew's skinny shoulders. He looked at me accusingly.

"You said there wouldn't be thunder."

LORE, 2017

After speaking to Fabian, I was feeling inquieta. I called Cassie.

"Lore. Hi," she said, strained. "Were we going to— Didn't we say we'd pick back up after Thanksgiving?"

"I'm returning your calls from this morning," I said, wondering now if they were what the cuates used to call "butt dials"—and what Michael adorably mistranslated as "booty calls."

"Right. Sorry, just—give me a second." The line went disconnection-quiet, as if she'd muted herself. "I just had a quick question: When did you and Fabian get divorced?"

The corners of my lips twitched in anticipation of Cassie's reaction. "We didn't."

"You didn't." Cassie sounded incredulous, though not as surprised as I expected. "You're still married."

"Yes." I moved toward the window and brought the drapes together. From the living room I could hear the music from *Home Alone*, the hijinks over, now the gentle, sad tinkle of a piano. Music for a forgotten boy, a scared boy, trying to be a man.

"Why didn't you tell me this before?" Her voice broke, like if she might burst into tears.

"You never asked. Mijita, are you okay? You sound—"

"I'm fine." Cassie paused, and I imagined her closing her eyes, breathing deeply. "Lore, just be honest. For once. Did Fabian really kill Andres?"

I froze. "Yes. Of course. Why would you even ask that?"

"Okay. Why did he do it? Why, really?"

"Why do you think?" Discúlpame, Fabian. "He needed to feel like a man again."

The answer, I sensed, was not what Cassie was expecting. But then, her questions hadn't been what I was expecting. *Be honest. For once.* That wasn't good.

"Did you know?" she asked. "When he left the house that night, did you know what he was about to do?"

I yanked decorative pillows to one side of the bed, piling them one on top of the other. I didn't want to think of his face. The anger. Dios mío, he was always so angry.

"No," I said. "Of course not."

"What about after? Did he tell you what he'd done?"

I sighed, folding down the comforter. I sat on the edge of the bed. Something about that music from the TV, the chill outside the window, and Fabian's voice in my ear—the memory was closer than it had been in years. I'd been so lonely. "He told me later that night. It was . . ." I tried to think of a word. "Horrible."

Cassie's voice, when she spoke, was softer, all the edges smoothed. "Can you tell me about it?"

I closed my eyes. I could see him so clearly, his dark eyes flitting around the kitchen. He was like a long-legged insect that had landed on the wall, that might launch in any direction the moment you stepped closer. His mouth opening: *I did something.*

And later, Fabian's bloodshot eyes, his shock, the sole survivor of some great massacre. He was the walking wounded, only it was I who had riddled him with holes. That was what I told Cassie, that though I knew Andres was dead, Fabian might still be saved. So I had lied to the police.

"You weren't angry?" Cassie asked.

"Of course I was angry! ¿Qué crees? A man I loved was dead, alone, lying there on some cheap carpet, and I couldn't bring him back. I couldn't make things right, couldn't—" I felt as if I'd swallowed a giant hook and it was scraping me inside. "I couldn't say goodbye."

Cassie was quiet, making room for my grief.

"But you didn't—" She hesitated. "You didn't hate Fabian?"

"No." I saw myself, stumbling toward him, both of us weeping. "How could I?"

"What happened next?"

My heartbeat was slowing. The past slinking away again, the present a warning glow. "Fabian threw the gun into the river."

"What about the wallet?"

My eyes opened. The wallet. The photo of Andres and me beneath the saguaro cactus, squinting into the sun. "Yes," I said. "That too."

"Did you plan it? Together?"

"We discussed it." I remembered how we'd waited for nightfall, how it had seemed to take so long, that terrible August day. The height of summer, when not even a storm can overpower the cruel sun for long. We had waited and waited, until porch lights flicked on and the remaining FOR SALE signs were silhouetted like gravestones.

"Is that why?" Cassie asked. "Why you stayed together? He killed Andres, you helped him hide it, you were . . . bound?"

"We are bound." I picked up the framed photo of us on my nightstand, our skin smooth and grins wide, cans of Schaefer Light on the wooden picnic table at the ranch. "But not how you're saying it. We're bound by love, by time, by our children. We're family. But the truth is"—I sighed—"at first there was no time to talk about hurt or betrayal. We could only talk about lawyers and police interviews and then bail and indictment and so on. He was gone before I knew it. And then everything became about the cuates—making sure they were okay, that they were surviving. Taking them for visits. And then, maybe six months into his sentence, he wrote me a letter. I wrote him back. And I guess that's how we healed. Eventually."

"Did he ask you questions? About Andres and your relationship? Did he want to know the truth?"

"He wanted to know *me*," I said, setting the photo back. "And I wanted to be known. I wanted to know myself. That's what it was all about."

"The affair? The second marriage?"

"All of it. I mean, there was love, of course." I thought of reading with Andres, riding with him, our fingers pointing to a mountain range, a waterfall, a lizard with its head thrown to the sun, its trembling bubble-gum throat. I remembered the way he kissed me and touched me, as slowly as he could for as long as he could, until we lost control. I remembered his hand pulling me from a building on the verge of collapse, and how we had stood in the ruins after, shocked at the completeness of loss. "But that wasn't why. Not really. I just wanted to know myself," I said again, frustrated at not being able to express how I felt, which was that I wanted to become new to myself again, to dig at myself—my mind, my heart—and witness the endless unveilings. I wanted to know all my possible selves, live every possible life.

"And I ended up alone," I said, with a hard laugh. "I told Andres I had no family, and then I lost them all." I remembered the hum of the refrigerator on endless nights. The only sound in the whole world. I shivered.

Then Cassie said, like an offering, "I confronted my dad."

I felt a furtive warm flicker, like maybe among all the wreckage I'd done something good. "And?"

"I don't know." She sniffled. "At least I know I'm not crazy. Andrew hates me, though. And Duke—"

There was a knock on my door. "Mom?" I stiffened at Gabriel's shape in my doorway. How he blocked the light. "Are you still talking to Dad? Because I—"

"I have to go," I said to Cassie.

"Right." Cassie went brusque with self-preservation. "Tomorrow at six?"

"I'll talk to you then. Oye, mija," I added. She waited. "I'm proud of you."

CASSIE, 2017

In the cellar, I couldn't feel the thunder.

I was three or four when I'd first sheltered down here with my parents. There were shelves bolted to the walls, emergency supplies. While the sky turned a dusky succulent green, my father had collected our musty sleeping bags from a hall closet and dragged the living room sofa cushions down the stairs. He arranged the cushions into a fort in the corner of the room, then slung the sleeping bags across to make a sloping ceiling. My mother brought down Tupperware dishes with sliced apples and strawberries and even a little cooler with chocolate ice cream. A low voice rumbled from the battery-operated NOAA weather radio, and this only added to the mystery, the magic. Back then, my parents were extensions of my own body, holding me before I even finished reaching for them. And that was how it felt, the three of us connected in our cellar fort as the invisible train tore up the world.

I toed aside several boxes, sweeping an old moving blanket off a chair. My mother's rocker, where she'd read to me until our two shapes had outgrown its contours, and then I'd outgrown her. I ran my hand across the carved back, the deep crack extending from one of the arm screws. Gingerly, I sat down, the cane seat creaking. I closed my eyes and rocked, remembering her arms around me, her fingers turning pages. Her nails short and coarsely trimmed, bitten, maybe. Her smooth skin and bony knuckles and blue-green veins. The animation in her voice, her cinnamon-and-cigarette breath on my cheek. Before I knew it, I was crying. Harsh, loud, ugly tears. Lore, saying she was proud of me. It had been so many years since I'd heard those words. Not since the day I'd gotten the thick envelope from UT. My mother had clutched me to her, hard and fast, knowing how quickly I'd push her away. Her lips to my ear. *I am so damn proud of you.*

Had she really taken a blow that was meant for me that day? Had she told my father that if he hurt me, she'd kill him? That didn't sound like the version of her I remembered, the story of her I'd told myself all these years. If she was willing to stand up to him for me, why not for herself?

"Cassie?" Duke's voice, at the stairs. A ribbon of light from the doorway.

I listened to his heavy approaching footsteps, stared at my own hands. My smooth skin and bony knuckles and blue-green veins. I tried to hold on to the image of my mother, the clarity of her voice, as if I'd stumbled onto the right radio frequency. But she was disappearing.

Duke stopped a few feet in front of me. I looked up, willing him to come closer. To say he understood. I wanted us to take Andrew and go home. I was ready for all of that. Finally.

He didn't move. "So."

I gave a thick laugh. "So."

He sighed, a hand through his hair. "Jesus, Cass. I can't believe you went through all that. Why didn't you tell someone?"

"My mom told me not to."

Duke frowned. "Yeah, but—a friend, a counselor, a teacher."

"She *was* a teacher."

"Okay, then someone else. Anyone." He shoved his hands in his pockets, as if he didn't know what else to do with them.

"I just couldn't." I tipped the chair back into a quick, anxious rhythm. "I couldn't betray her like that."

"*Betray?*" He shook his head, aghast. "Cass, you would have been helping her!"

"Yeah, well, you asked, and I'm telling you," I snapped. "Besides, you've met him—does he seem like a wife beater? I was afraid no one would believe me. Or that they would and then I'd be taken from my parents, or my dad would get arrested, or maybe nothing would change except both of them hating me."

Duke's face bloomed with pity. I looked away, wishing I hadn't seen it.

"But Andrew," he said finally.

I waited.

"You could have told someone any time, from miles away—"

I dug my nails into the wooden armrests. "Yes, Duke, I'm aware. You think I haven't been living with this guilt every day for twelve years?"

"But you didn't have to!" He took a step closer, almost pleading. "Why didn't you do something?"

I scrambled to my feet. It felt wrong, somehow, to have this conversation in my mother's rocker. I didn't want to taint my memories of it, not when so many other memories of her were already tainted.

"Why, Cass?" Duke asked again, softly.

My breath was coming fast, almost hyperventilating. "Because I could only save one of us, and I chose myself!"

Duke's solid frame seemed to cave slightly inward, as if I'd knocked the air out of him. "You could have told me," he said quietly. "We're supposed to trust each other. I thought we did."

A fist felt lodged in my throat. "You could have *asked*. You've had five years of me barely talking to my father, barely coming home, even for Andrew. It doesn't take a trauma expert to think, hey, maybe something bad happened there! Maybe she's staying away for a reason!"

"Yeah, but that was your business!" Duke slammed his fist on the work bench against the wall. A roll of paper towels fell over, and he righted it. "I'm sorry, but I'm not going to let you make me the bad guy because I don't pry into every single part of your past the way you do."

I took a step back, stung.

"And that's fine," he added, seeing the hurt on my face. "I've been happy to be an open book."

"Well, it's easy to be when the book is all good," I said.

"I guess that's my fault, too? I had a happy childhood, so I couldn't possibly understand?"

"Well, you're not being very understanding now, are you?" I crossed my arms hard against my chest. "You just found out my dad hit my mom for a decade—in front of me—and instead of blaming him or trying to understand what that was like, here you are asking me why, why, why, like I'm the monster." I laughed roughly. "Believe me, I've felt like a monster. I just hoped you wouldn't see me that way."

There was a beat where he could have denied it. It passed. And then it was too late.

At 2 A.M., I knocked softly on Andrew's door before stepping inside. He was in bed facing the wall, stiff and silent, spine curled like a snail. No one is so hard in sleep.

"Hey." I put a gentle hand on his shoulder. He jerked away. "I'm sorry, Andrew. That's not how I ever wanted you to find out."

He didn't move.

I sighed. "Okay. Well. We'll leave first thing in the morning. Are you packed?"

Andrew whirled around, glaring. "Are you kidding me? I'm not going anywhere with you."

"What? Of course you are."

"No." He sat up against the wall, beneath the poster of the Hulk. His small face was tight with rage, shadows beneath his eyes. "I'm not."

"Andrew, you were—you are—a kid. I was trying to protect you."

"Protect me?" His voice cracked. "How do you figure?"

"I thought things were good here." I heard the pleading in my own voice, and wasn't sure who I was trying to convince. "I didn't want you to think of them that way, Mom and Dad. Especially if Dad was doing right by you."

Andrew shook his head, resolute. His silky blond hair was rumpled. I wanted to press my nose to the crown of his head, the way I used to when he was a baby and smelled like nothing else on earth.

"I fucked up," I said. "So bad. But I promise I'll make it up to you."

Andrew set his mouth. "You can't make me go."

I dug my nails into my palms. He was right. I couldn't. Not unless I thought he was in imminent danger. Not unless I got lawyers and child protective services involved, which I couldn't afford, and the last thing I wanted was Andrew in the foster system in the meantime. He'd hate me if I put him through that.

"Andrew, please." I reached for him. His glare stopped me. "You think you know how bad it can get. But it can be so much worse. Trust me."

"Trust you?" Tears glinted in his eyes. "How can I trust you when you've been lying to me my whole life?"

LORE, 1986

It's the summer of the World Cup. What a commotion it's made, what political shrieking. From those who thought Mexico never should have been awarded the tournament—DF already hosted once, after all—to the Mexican artists and intellectuals outraged at the idea of the December draw being held at the Palacio de Bellas Artes, to Rafael del Castillo, the Mexican soccer federation president, saying there is no better way to show the world that Mexico is "on its feet." Which it isn't, obviously, and shouldn't the world see that? But Mexico, for better or worse, is made up of Mexicans, and Mexicans, for better or worse, are proud.

And so Andres surprises Lore with tickets to the quarterfinal, Argentina vs. England, at the Estadio Azteca. At first, Lore doesn't think she can be in a stadium without thinking of how the unidentified bodies were laid beside one another in stadiums around the city, three days of dry ice before the mass burials began. But she's swept away by the thrill of it: almost 115,000 people filling the stands. She'll never forget what will later be called Maradona's "Hand of God" goal, a streak of blue, a goal granted only because the referee hadn't seen the infringement, and then, right after, Maradona passing the English players one after another, none of his teammates available for a pass, a sixty-yard sprint all by himself, a feint and then his second goal in ten minutes. She and Andres are on their feet, screaming themselves hoarse, arms in the air and sweat streaming. They kiss as if something miraculous has happened, something redemptive.

Afterward, they go to some tiny nameless bar thick with smoke and riotous fans.

"Do you think Maradona should have accepted that first goal?" Andres asks. They're squeezed into a corner at a sticky highball table, drinking beer from lukewarm bottles. Lore is taking it slow.

Lore laughs. "What do you mean *accepted* it?"

Andres sweeps his sweaty hair back with his thumb and middle finger, a futile, habitual gesture that's become so familiar to her. "Remember Kant's categorical imperative?"

"We have a duty to act morally, and we can tell if an action is moral if we can universalize the moral principle." Lore grins, making a flourish with her beer. "The student becomes the teacher."

Andres doesn't smile. "So? What do you think?"

"Okay, well, first of all, I'm not a soccer expert, but I don't think Maradona himself has the power to accept or not accept a ref's call."

"But if he did?" Andres presses.

"I think you're suggesting that since the ref didn't see the infringement, and Maradona did, he shouldn't have taken the goal," Lore says. "Because it's not moral, since you can't say it's always for the universal good to . . ." She frowns. "What? It's not like he cheated."

"You don't consider benefiting from someone's oversight to be cheating?"

"I think he plays soccer," Lore says, more sharply. "I think it was the ref's job to score the match, and if he screwed it up, it's his fault."

"Even if Maradona knew better?" Andres's tone, too, from what she can hear in the loud bar, is changing, escalating. His body is stiff, shoulders hitched.

"I don't know! Are we really about to have a fight about the practical application of Kant's categorial imperative in the World Cup?"

After a moment, Andres sets his beer down, releasing it with a hand that has been clenched tight. "Sorry. You're right."

Lore kisses him. His lips are unyielding, and she pulls away. "Okay, what's wrong? It's not the goal."

Andres stares at the swordfish mounted on the faded brick wall behind the bar. Its skin looks shiny and hard, and Lore can't tell if it's plastic or if its gills once twitched in a midnight-blue underworld.

"What's really keeping you in Laredo?" Andres asks. "I know what you're going to say—your job. But will you ever move here, for good? With me and the kids?"

There's a replay of the Hand of God goal on the tiny TV at the bar. A cheer rises, deafening. Lore wants to say you can also determine a moral action by what gives the most happiness to the most people.

"Well," she says, when the noise fades, "when it makes sense, yes. But we have years of recovery ahead of us. You know that."

Andres's profile is statuesque, noble, like a soldier facing a losing battle. "What's keeping you there?" he asks again.

"Andres—"

"I know you're not close to your family. So is it friends? I still haven't met any of your friends."

"No. Andres, I've worked hard, you know. It's hard to imagine turning my back—"

Andres's mouth opens, incredulous. "Is that what you think I'm asking? For you to come here and be a housewife? Make me dinner every night?"

Lore fights the urge to leave the table. "Of course not."

"Well, then?"

"Well, then, what?"

They glare at each other in an unfamiliar angry stalemate. She knows what would make it better: if she told him about the test she took yesterday. The plastic tray and tubes and eyedropper, the illustrated step-by-step instructions she nearly dropped when Andres knocked on the door. She'd called out, "Just a minute! It's my stomach!" so she could finish waiting, the whole time praying, *Please, please, please,* as if God would know the rest. Then afterward, numb with shock, she stuffed everything back in the cardboard box and hid it under the counter, behind rolls of toilet paper and extra soap and shaving cream. She'll need to send Andres on an errand later so she can throw everything away properly before she goes back to Laredo.

But it would end the fight if she were to tell him, if she were to place his hand on her belly, though she's far from showing. She isn't even nauseous, the way she was with the cuates. It makes her wonder, with a terrible ache, whether it's a girl.

She wonders how Fabian would react if he knew. The first pregnancy wasn't ideal timing, either. But he spun her joyfully in his arms until she told him she was about to throw up all over him. Then he laid her in bed with almost comic tenderness. He covered her belly with his big warm hands and said, "Daddy's here, mijo."

"Or mija," Lore corrected.

"Or mija," he agreed, smiling. "Daddy loves you and can't wait to meet you."

She had burst into happy tears. She couldn't wait to tell her family, to tell Marta. She still thought, then, that Marta would be next. That this version of the future was inevitable, simply because they wanted it.

What would Fabian say this time? If she gave the cuates a few dollars and sent them off with their friends, where they always wanted to be anyway, and asked Fabian, "How do you feel about being a family of five?" Lore's heart warms at the image of a little girl in his arms, her eyes fluttering to sleep. Would Fabian see this image, too? Would joy jostle for room in his chest, expelling the bad energy?

More likely, it would push him over the edge. She can imagine him demanding how this happened and doesn't she remember how expensive babies are? And what about her job? They need her job. And wasn't she on the pill?

Yes, she was. But as of yesterday, she was five days late, which makes her about five weeks pregnant, putting the time of conception in late May or early June. She and Marta had a girls' night in right before the cuates' summer break started; they'll be juniors next year. She remembers moaning about it to Marta, how already they were in driver's ed, and soon they would be grown up and leaving her, and then they were reminiscing about their own high school years. They drank too much. Lore threw up, Marta holding back her hair, laughing that maybe they hadn't come so far since high school after all.

The next morning, Fabian surprised her by being amused by it all. He made coffee and chorizo con huevo and pressed a cold toallita to her head. And he kissed her. Gently, then not gently. The toallita fell to the side, the plate with its rust-red crumbs, and then he was lifting Lore's old T-shirt, taking a nipple in his mouth. She wriggled under him, and he pulled off her panties and slipped first one finger inside her, then another, her lips in the hollow above his clavicle. The house was Sunday-morning silent, the cuates sleeping in. Right before Fabian pushed inside her, he smiled, and she wanted to say, *There you are.*

She flew to DF the next night.

Telling Andres would buy her more time. But time for what? Decorating two nurseries? Two sets of doctors' appointments, of heartbeats and ultrasounds, when there could be only one delivery? One life after that?

Lore doesn't know whose child this is. All she knows is that it's the end.

She just doesn't know how soon.

CASSIE, 2017

Duke and I zipped up our toiletries and stripped the bed without speaking. By 9 A.M., I still hadn't seen Andrew. Duke was loading the car while I smoothed the bedspread over the bare mattress. A knock on the open door made me jolt in surprise.

My father looked as bad as I felt. His bruises had changed to a lurid green fanning out around the black, the swelling in his nose receding to reveal its new lumpy-clay shape. He cradled a long garment bag in his arms, as if it were a woman, passed out and flattened.

He cleared his throat. "I wanted to give you this. You might not want it, but—you might."

I remembered the fit I'd thrown about the couch. That was only two days ago. It felt like an eternity.

"What is it?" I moved closer. Curiosity, as always, edging out any other emotion.

"Your mother's wedding dress." He draped it over my arms carefully. The exchange felt strangely familiar, and then I realized why: Andrew, passed from my arms to his twelve years ago. "She'd have wanted you to have it."

I ran a hand up and down the bag, desperate to unzip it, to stroke and smell the white chiffon I'd only seen in photos, but I didn't want to share my reaction with him.

He sighed. "I'm not asking for your forgiveness. Or understanding. But you should know, we loved each other. I loved her more than anything."

I thought of Lore then. How she'd loved both Fabian and Andres, and all four children. We should be able to stop ourselves from destroying the people we love. Love itself should not be a destructive force. But I'd been reading true crime all my life: love was the *most* destructive force.

"Anyway." My father scratched under the neck brace. "I talked to Andrew. I'm sorry you drove all this way."

Such a stilted, formal way to acknowledge that my brother had chosen him over me. The remnants of last night's rage sparked in my chest.

"You could have killed him," I said, throat gravelly.

My father grimaced. "I know."

"You don't deserve him."

"I *know.*" My father's mouth twisted. I took a step backward as he clenched and unclenched his fists. "You, your mother, Andrew— you're all more than I've deserved. But Cassie, I swear to you, I want you and Andrew in my life more than anything, and I know how close I was to losing you both. I'm sorry. I'm so sorry for everything I put you and your mother through." His eyes were pinched in the corners, mouth trembling until he clamped his lips together. He breathed loudly, trying to control his emotions. "I'll never forgive myself."

I clutched the garment bag to my chest like a shield. How many times had he said these words to my mother and meant them? How many times had she chosen again to believe him?

"I'm going to call him every day," I said. "The second I hear you're drinking again, I'm coming to get him. I'll hire a lawyer if I have to."

Behind his glasses, my father's eyes flashed, a second of his other self, wrathful. Then it disappeared. "You won't have to," he said, and I wasn't sure if he meant because he would stay sober, or because he'd give up Andrew himself if he started drinking. It didn't matter. We knew where we stood.

Back in Austin, Duke and I moved around each other like considerate ghosts, careful that our ephemeral skins didn't brush. When our eyes met, he went back to cooking, or pulled on his North Face fleece to sit out back and scroll through Reddit. I let him go to bed first, relieved when he was snoring by the time I carefully slid in beside him.

In our five years together, Duke and I had rarely fought. Up until I'd started working on the book, our relationship had been all peaceful, easy accord. He was safe. He'd never let me down. But I'd also never given him the chance to. I hadn't trusted him to look at the broken parts of me and see anything other than ruin. Maybe it had been a self-fulfilling prophecy. Maybe everything would have been different if I'd told him about the abuse and leaving Andrew from the start.

Or maybe I knew all along how it would end up.

I couldn't help but think of Lore and Andres and Fabian. *There was love, of course,* she'd said. *But that wasn't why. Not really. I just wanted to know myself.* Even now, I had to admire this about her—the subversiveness of believing she was worthy of being known, by herself and others, whatever there was to find.

In the days after Enid, Andrew continued to ignore my calls and texts. I was forced to talk to my father each night. His sponsor was picking him up for daily meetings. Andrew was hardly speaking to him. My father understood. It would take time to make amends—with both of us. He would be patient. I could hear the work behind his optimism, all the cranking gears exposed.

My mother's wedding dress hung in our closet. A lace bodice, cap sleeves. An empire waist and gauzy chiffon skirt. I was taller than she was, but we were both slim, angular. The dress fit me, grazing the floor in my bare feet. The hem was slightly dirty, a hint of grass. It made me feel close to her, this evidence of wear. Sometimes, while Duke was at the food truck, I spent hours in it, sitting on the couch with my laptop, rubbing at the grass stains with my fingers.

Lore's pregnancy, which she still hadn't told me about, and which Andres had discovered the day before flying to Texas, meant I had to look at all the evidence differently. I read through the case file again from start to finish. I reviewed the evidence log and news articles and police tapes. I reexamined the crime scene photos, witness statements, and autopsy report.

Using index cards, I made a fresh timeline showing the Riveras' movements on the night Andres was murdered. I divided the cards into four columns on the coffee table, one for each family member. Lore at her doctor's appointment—I wrote *Pregnancy? Termination?*—from 3:00 to 4:30 P.M., returning to the bank at 4:45, shortly after Fabian opened the door to Andres. Oscar had said Lore was frazzled by Andres's unexpected visit, said he was "bothering her." After reading Andres's note, she had, according to Oscar, thrown "everything" in the trash. "Everything" could simply refer to the note and envelope. But Oscar had hung up right after I asked what he meant. If Andres had left something else for Lore, something small enough to fit in an envelope, what would it be?

A key.

What if he'd left her a key to his hotel room? She went and saw him, they had a confrontation. Maybe later, if she'd decided to keep the baby, she'd told Fabian it was his. Maybe she'd even told him, as she'd implied to Oscar, that Andres was threatening her in some way. Maybe Duke had been right, and Andres was a surrogate for Lore, the murder a kind of projected rage, a way to protect her while also punishing her. What had Lore said about the reason Fabian killed Andres? I searched through my dated interview transcripts—Thanksgiving, hard to forget. "He needed to feel like a man again."

It tracked. It was compelling. If Lore had a key to Andres's room, it explained how Fabian knew exactly where to find him. The question was: Was the murder premeditated? And how much did Lore know?

There was also the question of what had come of the pregnancy, the answer to which might explain everything or nothing.

Keep going, I thought. Make sure the theories fit the facts, not the other way around.

Cross-referencing witness statements, I added to the index cards. Gabriel and Mateo were alibied playing basketball at the park until 6 P.M., after which they walked home. Lore left the bank right after 5:15—maybe she'd intended to stay later, but the news about Andres had derailed her—and took the twins to Wendy's for Frosties, where their receipt was time-stamped at nearly 6:30. Then the movies from 7 to 9:15. Their night out still bothered me. But again, maybe she was worried Andres would ring her doorbell any minute. Maybe she was trying to keep her kids from finding out, a little longer.

That kind of desperation—that's what drives someone to murder.

Keep going.

Fabian getting picked up for the ranch between 5 and 5:30 and dropped off at home at 8. Lore's call with Marta around 10:30, close to when Fabian was spotted at the hotel. From 5:15 to almost 6:15, no one could alibi Lore. And from 8 to 9:15, no one could alibi Fabian, though he wasn't seen at the motel until 10:30.

That was the one incontrovertible fact, which seemed to prove that, despite what Carlos believed, Lore couldn't have directly killed Andres: it was Fabian, not Lore, at the hotel during time of death. It was the brick wall I kept hitting, though it had never moved.

Even as I struggled to fit the pieces together, Lore and I talked every night at six.

"Do you wish you hadn't done it?" she asked me, a week after Enid. "Things would be easier right now, right?"

I considered. If I hadn't blown up at my father, I wouldn't be stumbling my way through nightly phone calls with him. Andrew would be here. I wouldn't have seen the look on Duke's face in the cellar, as if I'd pulled off my mask and the face beneath was unrecognizable. Yet, I felt freer. By asking me to keep the abuse a secret, my mother had given me a seed to swallow, and it had grown into a poisonous vine. Now it was like I'd taken a knife to it, hacking and swiping, everything messy, but I could breathe.

"No," I said. "I don't regret it."

"Eso," Lore said, and I could hear her smiling.

"But . . . what should I do now?" I flushed. It felt ridiculous, asking for advice from a woman I couldn't trust, a woman I was actively investigating for her role in a murder. But Lore had gotten her sons to forgive her. She must have done something right. "About Andrew?"

She sighed. "Mija, you just keep laying yourself at his feet, no matter how many times he steps on you on his way to the door. You keep offering yourself and offering yourself. One day he'll turn around and you'll be there to help him. That's what being a mother is."

"A sister," I corrected.

Lore laughed. "Right."

LORE, 1986

The cramps start early in the morning of August 1.

All throughout the board meeting, Lore presses her hands to her belly, imagining the tadpole inside pressing back against her warmth and knowing she has a mother. The baby is a girl, she's sure of it, a girl she's planning to name Marta. Lore is only eleven or twelve weeks along, but a few days ago she could swear her daughter moved, a silky flutter deep within her body. She doesn't *want* to want this baby, but she does. Impossibly, the baby feels like she contains all three of them: Lore, Fabian, Andres.

The bleeding starts after lunch. Combined with the cramps, Lore knows immediately what it means.

Dr. Sosa, who delivered Gabriel and Mateo, is in his seventies, a slight curve in his spine, impatient though not unkind. He asks where Fabian is, and Lore says he's out looking for work. Dr. Sosa grunts, squirting cold jelly on Lore's stomach. He moves the ultrasound wand from side to side, pressing firmly. The small screen is black. There is a hollow echo where a heartbeat should be, a dark ocean of grief, and yet, like a flower pushing up through concrete, something like relief, because now she won't have to choose between Andres and Fabian. She won't have to decide which life to keep, at least not yet, and what kind of mother is she to feel this way about the baby she's just lost?

Then—a tinny, weak throb. A spot of light on the screen, like a star.

Lore gasps. "Is that—"

"There it is, all right." Dr. Sosa smiles, removing the wand and handing Lore a wad of tissues. "But your symptoms are concerning. Váyase a su casa. Put your feet up. Dígale a Fabian que you're not allowed to do any housework today. Doctor's orders."

Lore smiles weakly, dizzy with the faint gallop of her daughter's heartbeat. The panic returns, Lore's back to the wall while all she can hear around her is the gnashing of teeth.

She thanks Dr. Sosa, leaving with a pamphlet on "spontaneous abortion" that she throws into a trash can on her way to the car. Spontaneous abortion. As if the baby could tangle herself in the trip wire of her mother's mistakes and boom—gone.

The bank will be closing soon. She can sit behind the solid oak door of her office and let her blood pressure lower, her heart rate slow. Among the many things she knows herself to be, she is this baby's mother. She needs to breathe peace into her body so the tadpole will know it's safe to keep growing.

And then—then—well, Lore has no idea. All this time, all the work of splitting herself in two, of being wholly present in one life or the other to stave off the impossible future, and now the future is inside her, impossible to ignore.

CASSIE, 2017

In mid-December, my most recent request to interview Fabian was granted. My first thought, now that I knew he and Lore were still married, was that she'd told him to speak to me, that it must be to maintain the story they'd told for so long. Well, so be it. People reveal all sorts of things they don't intend to.

The interview was scheduled for Friday the twenty-second, a little over a week away, the same day Duke and I were due on the farm. Days passed, and I couldn't seem to bring it up. I didn't know how to make things better between us, but I knew this would make things worse.

On Tuesday, Duke came home from the food truck just after eleven. "I think we should talk about Enid," he said. No stalling, no preamble, as if he'd practiced the words in his mind a hundred times before saying them out loud.

I was on the love seat, rereading the witness statements. The neighbor blithely waving to Andres, thinking it was Lore parking in her usual spot in the driveway. Lore had described that house in such detail. All the projects she and Fabian had planned when times were still good—changing the wallpaper in the kitchen, renovating the bathroom, adding a pool. The only thing they'd managed to do before the peso devalued was add a carport because the driveway was too narrow for them to park side by side. Something about that was bothering me, but—

"Cassie?" Duke put himself in my direct line of sight. "Seriously. We need to talk."

I looked up at him and my chest ached, the reigniting of an old burn. I could still hear him in the cellar, asking me why, why, why. And the way I'd told him the absolute truth: I could only save one of us, and I chose myself.

"I know." I gestured to my laptop. "But I think I'm onto something important here. Can we do it tomorrow? Please?"

The swell of Duke's frustration was like a breaking wave. "Sure, why not? What's the rush?"

He stalked to the bedroom, slammed the door. We weren't normally door slammers, and I blinked away tears. Then I returned my attention to the witness statement.

The thought I'd been chasing, or the pulse before the thought, had disappeared.

The next morning, Duke pushed aside his breakfast plate.

"Cass," he said. "We can't keep going like this."

I stared at the remnants of his avocado toast. Sea salt like tiny shards of glass. "I know."

He ducked his head, trying to meet my eyes. "Can you look at me? I feel like you haven't looked at me since Thanksgiving."

I forced myself to meet his determined gaze.

"I'm sorry we fought." He shook his head, the emotion fresh. "It's just—there I was, shaking your dad's hand, helping him cook dinner, not knowing any of this stuff, and it made me feel stupid. And angry."

I grabbed our plates and took them to the kitchen, sweeping

leftovers into the trash. "But it wasn't *about* you. Or it shouldn't have been, at least not right then."

Duke followed me. "I can't help having a reaction, Cass. I'm human. In a relationship with you. And the Andrew thing—I never would have expected you to do something like that. It took me way off guard."

My throat closed, and I tried to edge past him, the narrow kitchen feeling too small with both of us crowding the sink. "Well, I thought nothing you could say would make me feel shittier than I already do. Guess I was wrong."

Duke exhaled, his hand sliding to mine. "This isn't coming out right. Look, I'm sorry we fought, okay? I love you."

The words were so close to what I wanted to hear, though still fundamentally off. They clattered through me like a pinball hitting every edge, leaving tiny dents. He might be sorry we'd fought, but he didn't see me, or my actions, any differently today than he had in Enid. And maybe he shouldn't. Maybe any decent person wouldn't. But his *I love you* sounded like he'd realized an item he'd bought was defective and decided, after lengthy consideration, to keep it after all.

"Okay . . ." I trailed off, deflated. "Well, I'm sorry I didn't tell you sooner. Or at all."

Duke smiled, relief etched all over his face. "It's okay."

A decision clicked into place. I stepped closer to him, so we were chest to chest. "I'm ready now, though. Anything you want to know, just ask me."

Duke roped his arms around my waist. "Cass, I told you. I don't need a list of everything that's ever happened to you in order to know you. To love you."

A small hollow opened deep in my sternum. Lore had said something similar, hadn't she? That Andres hadn't needed to know she was a mother, for example, to know her essential motherness. I thought she was wrong about that.

I felt exposed, soft and raw, unprotected and easily punctured. "Why do you love me?" I asked quietly.

Duke frowned. "Seriously?"

"Yes. Why do you love me?"

The question felt petulant, almost childish, and though my body pulsed with shame, I needed to hear his answer.

"Why do you think?" He leaned down, ready to draw me close for a kiss. I resisted the pull. "You're smart and beautiful. You've always supported my dreams. You get along so well with my family—I think they like you more than me now," he said with a small laugh.

The hollowness inside me expanded, cold. Maybe it was an impossible question, the reasons for love as unquantifiable as love itself. But still. Was that really what had held us together these five years? What he expected to hold us together for a lifetime?

The first weekend Duke had taken me to the farm, we'd bathed Ole Molasses, the horse that had tossed Duke when he was twelve, splitting his chin wide open on a rock. Duke had never given up on her. She was old now, and he'd murmured to her as we soaped her with huge half-moon yellow sponges. I was awed by the muscle of her chest and the heat of her breath, the shine in her onyx eyes, Duke's steadfastness to an animal that had hurt him.

"I hope this doesn't scare you," he'd said, as warm soapy water dripped down our arms. "But I'm in love with you, Cassie."

Ole Molasses had snuffled toward me, hot air from wide velvety nostrils. I leaned into her snout to hide the sheen of tears in my eyes. "It doesn't," I said, though of course it did. It terrified me.

I'd looked at Duke then, his tousled hair and flannel shirt, and what I'd felt were his mother's warm, strong hands on mine as she'd taught me how to milk a cow that morning, the udders warm and swollen and sweat-slick beneath my palms. I'd seen Duke's father in the maple of his eyes. I'd heard his sister Allie's whoop as she coached me into a trot on her own horse earlier that day and seen the easy way Stephie slumped her body against her father on the living room couch. I'd heard Kyle's surprisingly baritone voice singing Luke Bryan as he helped his mother mend a fence, and I'd seen Dylan kissing his wife, helping their kids collect eggs from the henhouse.

Duke said he'd fallen in love with me, and I thought I'd fallen in love with his family, and I was terrified of losing them.

The air between us crackled with a hurt I knew Duke didn't completely understand. I pressed my thumb into the prongs of my ring, wanting the skin to break.

"Cassie?" Duke covered my hands with his. "Are we okay?"

"Of course—" I started to say, but I stopped. I was ready to be honest. With him, with myself. "I don't know." Tears snaked up my throat. "No. I don't think so."

Duke stared at me.

"Duke, I can't come to the farm with you," I said.

"What? Why not?"

"I have an interview with Fabian."

Duke gave a short, relieved laugh. "Jesus. Okay. For a second I thought—never mind. When is it? Just come after."

I wanted to. I longed for Caroline's warm, lavender-scented embrace, for Allie to pull me aside and say, "Okay, why are you two being weird?" On Christmas Eve we'd all drink eggnog and exchange goofy but oddly useful Secret Santa gifts. We'd let the kids wake us on Christmas Day, though Caroline would have been up for hours, the house smelling like coffee and blackberry pie. Duke's family had made space for me within its fold. I ached to rejoin it.

But I was aware of a gulf opening inside me, a messy depth of wanting I didn't think Duke could fill, didn't think he *wanted* to fill, and fuck Lore's eighty-twenty rule, I didn't want to find myself trying to satisfy it somewhere else down the line.

"I'm sorry." I twisted the band around my finger. "I don't know why I said the interview thing. I can't come with you at all. Duke . . ." I felt dizzy, nauseous, almost worse than I had in my father's kitchen. "I don't think we should get married."

Duke went rigid. He dropped my hands. "Cass. You're kidding, right? Because of what happened in Enid? Because I didn't *react* right?"

"No."

Duke rubbed a hand over his face, then looked back at me as if

I were a mirage, flickering in and out of view. He reached for me, as if he could keep me solid. "Cass, this is crazy. We had a fight. It happens."

"It's not the fight," I said. "It's just—it's us."

Duke's mouth turned downward, a sorrowful expression better suited to an older man standing at the grave of someone he loved. I could hardly bear to know I'd put it there.

"You can't mean this," he said.

The room went wavy through my tears as I slipped the ring from my finger. "I do," I whispered.

LORE, 1986

The bank has that end-of-day rustle as Lore enters the lobby: customers making their final transactions, new-accounts reps tidying their desks, dust covers pulled over typewriters. Lore walks to her office and shuts the door, dropping her heavy purse onto the desk. She has just seen the envelope when Oscar knocks.

"Hey." He peers inside. "¿Tienes un minuto?"

Cramps grip her lower belly, twisting all the way to her back. "Actually, I'm not feeling well, so—"

Oscar steps inside, smelling like he just smoked a cigarette. He gestures to the envelope. "You had a visitor."

Lore looks down. Panic scissors up her throat. She would recognize Andres's handwriting anywhere—the deep slant of it, like a motorcycle leaning toward the road.

"He was here twice today looking for you," Oscar says coolly. "He said he was your husband."

Lore forces a laugh. "My husband? Well, he was obviously looking for someone else."

"That's what I told him." Oscar doesn't move.

"Okay." Lore's thumbs rest on the corners of the envelope, nearly trembling with restraint. "Oscar, I'm not feeling well, so—"

"But then he showed me a picture."

"A picture." Lore's brain is working too slowly. All she can do is repeat things, buy time while she scrambles for purchase. But she's falling.

"Of the two of you," Oscar says. "You were in a white dress. He said it was your wedding day. What the fuck, Lore?"

Lore's vision is collapsing toward a middle point, an avalanche of darkness sweeping in from her periphery. "Oscar, it's not—¿qué le dijiste? What exactly did you tell him?"

"Jesus Christ." Oscar pulls out a pack of cigarettes, lights one and takes a deep drag. He blows the smoke toward the window. The sun has disappeared behind thick sooty clouds, casting an eerie winter-like pall over the parking lot even though heat shimmers off the pavement. "So it's true?"

"Of course it's not true!" Lore half rises from her chair; pain pushes her back down. She groans. She needs Oscar to leave. Her daughter is in danger.

Oscar exhales another stream of smoke, and the smell nearly makes her heave. "Does Fabian know?"

Lore is sweating. "Oscar, look. You know Fabian was mostly in Austin for two years. Two *years*, Oscar, when it was just me and the cuates, in these times. I made a mistake. I slipped. I met him in DF. But Jesus, of course I'm not married to him! I actually—" Lore swallows, knowing there is no going back. "I actually broke it off with him months ago. He's been trying to contact me. I won't have anything to do with him."

Of all the lies she's told, this is the one that makes her hate herself. But she thinks of losing Fabian, losing the cuates. Almost losing her baby. Her eyes well with tears, and she turns that gaze up to Oscar, knowing its power.

"Please," she says. "No one else has to know. Right?"

Oscar smokes the rest of his cigarette in silence, staring at her.

"Fuck, Lore," he says, stabbing out his cigarette in her ashtray. "What is he doing here?"

"I don't know."

"Is he dangerous?"

Her thoughts are a frantic, spiderlike tangle. Nesting, hatching, ugly.

"I don't know," she whispers.

Oscar sinks into a chair across from Lore. His expression has become grudgingly protective. "Do we need to call the police?"

"No, no." Lore shakes her head. "But I need to know: What did you tell him?"

"Well, he introduced himself," Oscar says roughly. "As your husband. Said he'd heard a lot about me. I sort of laughed at first. I thought it was a joke, said Fabian must have hired a good plastic surgeon."

Lore closes her eyes, breathing deeply to stave off the nausea.

"The next thing I know he's pulling out this picture, and it's you, and he obviously saw that I recognized you, and he said, 'Are you telling me she's married? To someone else?' Then he starts demanding your address, which I obviously didn't give him. I was about to call security when he asked for some paper and an envelope." Oscar reaches across Lore's desk and taps the letter. "What does it say?"

She needs him on her side. Lore takes a letter opener and slits the envelope open, pulling out the note and a key. "Hotel Botanica. Room one fourteen."

Oscar scowls. "Doesn't look over to me."

She sweeps everything into the plastic trash can beneath her desk. "Well, it is."

Oscar stares at her for a long, inscrutable moment. Then he stands, reaches again for his pack of cigarettes. "You fucked up, Lore. Fabian's a good guy."

"I know." Her voice breaks. "Please, Oscar. Keep this between us?"

Oscar shrugs one shoulder. "It's none of my business."

Lore grabs her purse and rounds her desk. "Thank you," she says, rummaging through her purse for her keys to lock up. But her hands are shaking, and the purse slips from her shoulder to the floor, dumping dull blue tubes of lipstick, her powder compact, crumpled gum wrappers, business cards, and her wallet straining with too many receipts and not enough cash. Lore lets out a snarl of frustration, and Oscar watches, smoking, as she gathers everything back in, finally grasping her fistful of keys.

"I mean it, Oscar," she says, as they separate at the end of the hallway. He at the elevator, she at the door to the ladies' room. "Thank you."

Oscar grunts. "Just—be careful, okay? Se veía muy enojado."

She waits in a stall for her heart to calm. Oh, Andres, she thinks. Why did you come? Why now? Her back throbs with an ache that goes deeper than bone, radiating out from her most intimate places, and she thinks *Just a little longer* at the tadpole as she returns to her office and pulls the note and key from the trash can. *Just hang on a little longer.*

Andres knows Fabian's name now. He can look up their address in the motel phone book. She has to reach him first. Before she loses everything.

CASSIE, 2017

Duke packed his duffel for the farm right after our conversation. He hesitated at the door. "What are you going to do? For Christmas, I mean?"

I felt my aloneness so acutely then. I'd never had a huge group of friends. My college roommate, Em, was the only person I'd kept in touch with from those days. I thought I remembered she was going to see her husband's family in Chicago this year. My father had told me recently that I was always welcome home, but *this* was my home, this little bungalow on the East Side, with Duke, this home we could no longer share, and then what? For a frantic moment I almost took everything back. Then I remembered telling Duke to ask me anything, how there was nothing more he wanted to know.

"I'll be fine," I said to Duke, forcing a smile.

Duke's duffel fell to the crook of his elbow, and he hiked it back up. His eyes were bright with pain. "If you change your mind, you know where I'll be."

"Say hi to your family for me." *Your* family. No longer mine. Though they'd never been mine anyway.

I hurried into the bedroom before he could see me break down.

It was still a Wednesday, a workday. I poured myself a heavy glass of Cab and dragged the covers over my lap in bed. One of those once-or-twice-a-winter cold fronts had moved in overnight, and the sky outside my window was white as spilled milk—stratus clouds, horizontal layering with a uniform base, like the clouds are sewn together, my mother used to say, only you can't see any of the seams.

For the next two hours, I robotically scrolled through my Google alerts and recapped the most interesting murders I could find. I couldn't afford to get fired now.

The bottle of wine was half-empty, my nose raw from blowing into cheap toilet paper. The garment bag of my mother's wedding dress peeked out of our cramped closet. The clawed grip of yearning took my breath away. The family I had briefly imagined—Duke, Andrew, and me—was gone. I had nothing left.

Nothing but the book. Finding the whole of Lore's story, the truth of it.

It was nearly five o'clock. Oscar Martinez should still be at work.

He answered his extension with the same rough bark of his name.

"Oscar, hi, Cassie Bowman." Before he could say he didn't want to talk to me, I hurried through. "I just have a quick question. How did Lore's health seem to you that afternoon?"

He didn't have to ask which afternoon, and the question seemed to catch him just off guard enough to answer. "Pues, she'd come from the doctor, so I figured stomach virus or something."

"Why stomach virus?"

"Just. Seemed like it was hurting. Why don't you ask her? She'd know better than me."

Yes. *Yes!* I was getting somewhere. "One more question." I felt reckless with the wine. "Lore couldn't remember. Was the key Andres left metal or plastic?"

"Metal," he said.

I closed my eyes. I knew it. I fucking knew it.

"Thanks, Oscar," I said. "You've been a huge help."

I ate a bowl of leftover macaroni and made a strong French press coffee. I needed my head clear. I was too close to this. Too close to her. I needed to untangle the intimacies between us so I could see the situation clearly.

Now I knew for sure that Andres had told Lore where he was staying; he'd even left her a key. She'd seemed in pain after her OB appointment, which implied—what? That she'd had an abortion after all? On top of that, she could have been carrying a gun, and if what she'd told Oscar was true, Andres had been "bothering her."

By the time Lore saw Andres, he would have known about not only the pregnancy but also her double life. Maybe Lore had told him she'd gotten an abortion, and he'd lost his temper. Threatened her, attacked her. Maybe that's what she'd told Fabian later, and he'd gone back to take care of the problem. To "feel like a man again." Then he'd confessed to her and they'd planned how to dispose of the gun together. Her voice had rung so true when she said she couldn't hate Fabian. That they were family.

Something still felt off.

Have you spoken to the ex-husband? I remembered my father asking on Thanksgiving.

Well, I'd be talking to the current husband in two days, but that didn't seem soon enough.

Thinking of my father brought back painful flashes: the smell of coffee sputtering from the Keurig, the smudges on his glasses in the lightning-white kitchen. And the last words Andrew had spoken to me before fleeing to his room: *You said there wouldn't be thunder.*

Thunder. Rain.

I pulled up the original *Laredo Morning Times* story, the one that had started it all. Yes. That little writerly flourish I'd noticed on my first read: "Andres Russo was shot the evening before, on a day temperatures soared to a record-breaking 117 degrees before a much-needed rain cooled things off."

Someone else had mentioned rain, too. I opened my folder of interviews. Lore? Oscar? No—Sergio! He'd said Fabian had made a joke about it when they got home. I pulled up the transcript: "Pointed to his truck and said of course it had rained—he'd just washed it. That was exactly the kind of day he was having."

My heart pounded. Sergio said it had rained on their way to the ranch. That would have been just after five. Right in Lore's unalibied window. Thunder would cover the sound of a gunshot even better than music outside, splashing in the pool.

Okay. So Andres confronted Lore about the double life. The pregnancy. She told him she'd had an abortion. Or that the baby was Fabian's; that she was choosing him. Andres attacked her. She shot him. The sound of thunder covered the noise.

It was so simple. Except for one thing: Andres's time of death, during which Fabian was seen at the hotel. His fingerprint in the room. His *confession*, even if it was part of the plea deal.

Buzzing with caffeine, I returned to the crime scene photos. Fabian's fingerprint in that strange spot, on the base of the bed, and nowhere else. Even the glass of Scotch wiped clean, though only Andres's prints were on the bottles. Fabian could've picked up the glass at some point. Could've taken a drink for all I knew. Or maybe he wasn't thinking, frantically wiping down everything in front of him.

Like the interior *and* exterior door handles. If he'd knocked on the door and Andres had opened it, he wouldn't have needed to wipe his print off the exterior handle. If, though, he'd opened the door with a key, he would have.

I flipped through the photos, looking for something, but what? And then—I found it. The window unit, beaded with condensation. Hotel Botanica had central air and heat now—I remembered turning the thermostat down cold—but apparently not back then. On a 117-degree day, there was no way a window unit would have sufficiently cooled the space. Andres's time of death had been established as between 9 P.M. and midnight based on body temperature. But if the room was warm, delaying drop in body temp, couldn't that have given the impression he'd died later than he had?

Maybe Fabian had used Lore's key not to take Andres by surprise, but because he knew Andres couldn't open the door for him.

Because he was already dead.

Because Lore had killed him.

LORE, 2017

The week before Christmas, there was hardly a parking space left at the mall, even at Dillard's. The purses were all tiradas, shoes left in boxes on the carpet with tissue spilling out. White-knuckled hands clutched Starbucks cups, jaws set in determination. I could hardly imagine the mall thirty years ago, when Sears and Bealls had been the high-end department stores, when I'd taken the cuates to the sticky-floored movie theater beside the food court on that terrible night. I could never go back after that, not even when it became a dollar theater and would have been an easy way to pass my unanchored time. I was glad when they closed the doors and sutured it all up inside so it became something totally different. Sometimes that's what you need.

I finished my shopping and was home before six on Wednesday. I poured two fingers of Bucanas and waited for Cassie to FaceTime me, but it was a regular phone call.

"¡Hola!" I answered.

"Hi. How are you?" She sounded stiff and formal.

"What's wrong?" I asked, squeezing my glass. "Is it your brother?"

"No, no." She softened a little. "I'm just tired. Hey, I wanted to let you know . . . I'm scheduled to interview Fabian on Friday."

I hid a smile, though she couldn't see me. Qué linda, thinking she could surprise me. "Sí, me dijo. I was wondering when you'd mention it."

"I've had a lot going on." The distance was back in her voice. It set my teeth on edge. "I'd like to go down and see you first. Tomorrow. What do you think?"

I opened the back door, the rush of cold air like a splash of water on my face. It was supposed to be in the eighties again by Christmas, the way it had been so many other years. I could still see Papi at the rusty barbecue pit, white muscle shirt and burly brown arms, the silver glint of a beer can. Inside, Mami warming up the tamales. These days, it was as if past and present were unfurling at the same time, as if maybe it were still possible to change the ending.

"Sabes qué," I said, "that would be great. Mateo will already be here, and you still haven't met Gabriel. How's dinner? Six o'clock? We eat early because of the boys."

"Perfect."

We went quiet, like if we were both standing with an ear to opposite sides of the same door.

"Why don't we call it a night?" Cassie suggested. "I haven't been sleeping well. Let's touch base again tomorrow."

"Oh," I said. "Bueno. Take care, mija."

Something had changed. That's why I had invited her to dinner. It might be good for her to see us all together. To remember who we were, apart from the things that happened back then.

And if it turned out she knew more than she should—pues, I'd opened this door. Maybe I'd always known I would have to walk through it.

CASSIE, 2017

Before driving down to Laredo, I finally emailed my agent, Deborah, to set up a call. My phone rang as I passed the Border Patrol checkpoint on the other side of the highway.

"Cassie!" she said. "I've been waiting to hear from you. What's going on?"

"Well, I told you things seemed off about the day of Andres's murder. I spoke to Carlos Russo, Andres's son. It turns out Lore was pregnant, and Andres found out the day before flying in to see her—that was the reason for his surprise trip. Carlos thinks—" I hesitated. "He thinks Lore killed Andres."

Deborah sucked in a breath. "Okay. Any proof?"

My stomach tightened. "I spoke to an M.E. this morning. Andres's time of death was established solely by body temperature, which is apparently an outdated and incomplete measurement. Because of insufficient cooling in the room, TOD might have been earlier. Around the time Lore doesn't have an alibi. I told you she may have been carrying a gun. And it was apparently raining then, which could have covered the sound of the shot."

Deborah was silent, considering. "How do you explain the original husband's print and ID?"

"I think he went back to clean up after her, then took the blame." The first industrial parks were coming into view. The fast food billboards and trailers advertising nationalization services. In ten minutes, I'd be at Lore's house. No going back. "It turns out they're still married."

"You're *joking*!"

Suddenly, I wished I were. I felt like I had set something inexorable in motion, something ugly, though what could I possibly owe Lore if she'd been lying to me this whole time, if she'd murdered Andres and let Fabian go down for it, for *thirty-five years*?

"How sure are you that she killed him?" Deborah asked, clipped, excitement tempered by, probably, a laundry list of legalities. "Or at least conspired to kill him?"

I hesitated. "Seventy percent."

"That's a start. But not enough."

"I know. I'm getting into Laredo now to see Lore, and I'm interviewing Fabian tomorrow. I'm hoping to get a confession from one or both of them."

The line felt taut.

"The woman who lived a double life—and got away with murder," Deborah said, as if trying the words out loud. "This is highly marketable, Cassie."

Despite myself, a shiver of excitement ran through me. "Marketable . . . how?" I almost whispered.

Deborah laughed. "Don't get me wrong, your initial concept had everything: secrets, lies, love, death. It was hooky as hell. But this could have real-time, real-world impact. It's almost impossible to get a conviction overturned, but if your investigation exposes bad police work, gets the case reopened? There's a hunger for this right now. It could be big."

Big. Big meant money. If Duke and I were really over—the thought like a hammer to my chest—I'd be able to afford a place of my own. Somewhere with a room for Andrew, just in case. I could hire a lawyer if it came to that. With money, I'd be in a position not to fail him again. Because that's the thing about money—once you have it, you can afford to have a moral center.

Deborah's tone became more serious. "Right now, though, your only job is to find out the truth. Whatever it is, that's what you'll write."

Her words sobered me. "Absolutely," I said, as I took exit 4, stopping at a red light across from a Taco Palenque. The light turned green, and I crept left beneath the highway, sandwiched by eighteen-wheelers. Five minutes to Lore's house.

"Call me as soon as you know. And Cassie?"

"Yes?"

Deborah paused. "Be careful."

In Laredo, there was no evidence of the cold snap that had killed our three small potted succulents a few nights ago. The late-December evening felt like spring, a balmy breeze making inflatable Santas and Rudolphs sway drunkenly. The icicle lights dripping from Lore's roof felt absurd, like the only colleague who shows up in costume on Halloween. I smoothed my shirt, made sure my phone was recording, and knocked.

Lore opened the door holding a glass of red wine. Despite the warmth, she wore a red cable-knit sweater. I couldn't help noticing how similar it was to the one in the Christmas portrait with Andres's family.

"¡Pásale, pásale!" she said, giving me a hug and kiss on the cheek as she ushered me inside. So different from our first meeting, when she'd peeled off her gardening gloves with that exaggerated sense of inconvenience. "How was your drive? What would you like to drink? Everyone's in the kitchen." She glanced at me. Then she stopped. "Mija, ¿qué te pasa? Are you okay?"

I forced a smile. "Of course. Why?"

"You look . . ." She examined me the way a mother would: hand on my elbow, worried eyes taking in my dark circles, chapped lips. "Sad."

Oh, God. I ducked my head, pretending to search for something in my bag as I fought an unwieldy surge of emotion. Did Lore actually care about me, or was this an act? When she took my hand, I looked up. She was staring at my bare ring finger. Allie had been messaging me from the farm: *You broke up?!?!? Call me!* But I couldn't bear to hear her voice, to think of everything I was giving up by giving up Duke. *Soon,* I had texted her back.

Lore set her wineglass down on a side table and pulled me into a tight, rose-scented hug. "We'll eat dinner and then you'll tell me what happened," she said quietly in my ear. "¿Sí?"

I let my eyes close for a second. "Okay. I'll take that drink now."

She pulled away, squeezing my hand. That was when I noticed— the white walls and gold-framed watercolors were gone, replaced by rich color and bold abstract paintings. Lore smiled, following my gaze around the rooms that had never matched her vibrancy; the home she hadn't thought she deserved to create for herself.

"Do you like it?" Lore asked. "The furniture will be an ongoing project, pero ni modo."

"I love it," I said. "What made you do it?"

"You."

She smiled at me. Before I could ask her what she meant, we were in the kitchen. Mateo and Gabriel sat on leather barstools at the island, while Brenda, a petite dark-haired woman, arranged plastic dinosaur plates before two little boys at a miniature wooden table. Cartoons played from the living room TV, visible from the kids' seats.

"Everyone," Lore said, "this is Cassie."

I waved, embarrassed by the flush creeping up my neck. I focused on Mateo, the only familiar face. He looked more relaxed than I remembered in a blue checked button-down and jeans, a light stubble. His hair had grown slightly, waving up over the tips of his ears. His gaze lingered, curious and direct, as though he, too, saw something different in me. I'd emailed him several times since our strange late-night conversation, and while he'd responded each time, his answers were concise, nothing more than the bare minimum, as if he'd crawled back into himself. Maybe he'd been drinking that night. It would explain the late hour, the sudden willingness to talk. But a part of me hoped that wasn't it.

"Glad you could join us," Mateo finally said, and if it didn't sound wholly genuine, at least there was no hostility, unlike from Gabriel, who muttered, "Speak for yourself."

Gabriel was heavier than Mateo, with fleshy forearms resting on the island, though the resemblance was still uncanny—the same full, elegant brows, even the same way of sitting, elbows cocked out to the sides. But where Mateo was calm, Gabriel seemed on the verge of jumping from his seat even though no visible part of him was moving.

"Gabriel, honestly." Brenda pressed a button on the remote, lowering the volume on the TV. She came over and shook my hand firmly, her dark eyes sharp and assessing, though not unfriendly. "It's nice to meet you."

Soon we were sitting in the dining room, now painted a rich burgundy, the low light bouncing off a gilt mirror. My wineglass was full for the second time, my plate heaped with tamales, rice, and beans. A platter in the center of the table collected corn husks spackled with dough. Occasionally there was a clatter from the kids, who were eating at the small wooden picnic table in the pass-through kitchen—sippy cups dropping, an argument over the remote—and the younger one, freckled Joseph, eventually climbed onto Brenda's lap and pointed at me, asking in a theatrical whisper, "Who *that*, Mommy?" I wondered how Brenda would explain me. She answered smoothly, "That's Cassie. Say hi." Joseph tilted his head into Brenda's neck and kept his eyes on me, grinning crookedly as he lifted his hand. I smiled and lifted mine back.

Throughout dinner we talked about everything but the book—though, of course, everything *was* the book. The way Mateo and Gabriel seemed irritated by their own closeness, a subtle friction, rolling their eyes when they said the same thing at the same time, and how

Lore watched them with unabashed pleasure, content to let them dominate the conversation for long stretches of time though she was the clear matriarch, deferred to and respected. When our plates were clear and Michael and Joseph began chanting, "¡Nieve! ¡Nieve!" Lore brushed off Brenda's objections, winking at me as she went to the freezer and spooned them small bowls of chocolate Blue Bell. "¿Quién más?" she asked, grabbing more bowls from the cabinet. "Cassie?"

I wasn't hungry, but I didn't want to leave the table. I'd come here to learn the truth, and if the truth was what I suspected, it would upend their lives. Lore and I would never talk again over leftovers someone else had cooked. A different machine would crank to life, the arc of the moral universe bending at last toward justice. I would write the book, and Deborah would sell it, and this family would be splintered, and I would move on to the next story, whatever that might be.

"Ice cream sounds great," I said to Lore, forcing a smile. "Thanks."

Mateo scooted his chair back. "Here, I'll help."

A few times throughout dinner I'd caught Mateo looking at me. There was a warmth in his eyes that reminded me of Lore, but his mouth was firm, reserved. I couldn't read his expression, but even now—maybe especially now—I felt a pull toward him.

"Does Santa deliver presents in jail?" three-year-old Joseph suddenly asked from Brenda's lap, licking his spoon.

The adult Riveras looked from one to the other, a frantic silent exchange before Lore answered, "Sí, mijito. But he has to be quick-quick, because you know he needs to reach all the children in the world, most importantly."

Joseph nodded, returning to his ice cream, and everyone sighed with the universal relief of skirting a child's tough question. Michael was sitting on the floor watching something on Lore's phone, his tired, lulled face lit up by the screen.

Quietly, I asked Gabriel, "How often do y'all get to see your dad?"

All throughout dinner, Gabriel had tried to shut down any personal conversation quickly, as if he alone were aware of how closely I was watching and listening. Now he caught a drip of chocolate about to fall from Joseph's chin. He licked it off his finger, then tapped Joseph's nose, making him giggle. I softened toward him.

"Any chance we get." Gabriel lost every trace of warmth when he looked at me. "It's the least we can do."

I nodded, flooded with pity for Fabian, who'd been robbed of seeing his sons grow up, his grandsons being born. He'd missed out on so much. "I'm sure that means a lot to him."

Gabriel scoffed, a rough noise like coughing something up. "I'm so glad you approve."

"Gabriel," Lore warned. "No empieces."

On the surface, her face was impassive, but her copper eyes burned. What I didn't see at the mention of Fabian was guilt.

"No—if no one's going to talk about the elephant in the room, I will." Gabriel shifted his bulk forward, clearly meant to intimidate me. He lowered his voice for the kids' sake. "Mom's invited you here like you're part of the family, but you're just a leech, trying to cash in on us."

My skin prickled at the sudden attack. I looked at Lore as though she might defend me. She told Michael, "Go take the phone to the couch, mijito. Joseph, take your ice cream to the little table. You can put the TV on again."

I said, "I haven't made a penny off your family."

"But if this 'book'"—Gabriel made quotation marks around the word—"sells, you will, right? And does any part of that go to my mother?"

"I—" The truth was, I didn't know. The thought had never occurred to me.

"What I want to know is," Gabriel said, "why us? Of every fucked-up family in the world, why'd you choose ours?"

There was hurt beneath the anger, a glance I couldn't decipher between Gabriel and Lore. Mateo was rigid, a figure pinned in glass. I felt caught, stripped bare, the transactional nature of my relationship with Lore exposed, though perhaps it was only I who was sometimes in danger of forgetting. I had allowed her into my life nearly as much as she'd allowed me into hers, the boundaries in our relationship blurring with each confession shared.

"I thought your mother deserved a say in how her story was told," I said finally. "If she hadn't agreed, I would have moved on."

This, at least, I could cling to—Lore's permission. But I remembered my first night in the Hotel Botanica, the feverish, voyeuristic way I'd fallen into the case file, the crime scene photos, and the autopsy report the next day. How long would I have been able to resist the lure of a dead body? The story it had to tell?

Not very long, as it turned out.

"Moved on." Gabriel snorted. "Do you even hear yourself?"

I was sweating in earnest now, the house too warm for sweaters and accusations. Gabriel started to say something else. Brenda put a hand on his forearm, knuckles sharpening as she squeezed.

"Boys, bath time!" she announced. "Gabriel, help me, will you."

It wasn't a question, and she didn't wait for a response. She herded the boys out of the room, taking for granted that Gabriel would follow. His dark gaze didn't leave mine. He might be the only one here who saw me clearly for the threat I was to their family.

Finally, he scraped his chair back. "You don't fool me."

The intensity in his voice made me shiver.

Once he was gone, Lore and Mateo exchanged a weighted glance, a silent conversation I couldn't understand.

"Mateo, help us bring the dishes to the sink," Lore said. "Cassie, ven. You can help me wash."

At the kitchen sink, Lore carefully slid her rings over a small glass ring holder shaped like a swan. Her hands were shiny with soap. Her hair's natural curl was fighting her blowout, and a breeze from the cracked window kept blowing lightly frizzed ends into her mouth. She was barefoot, her toenails painted green and red, clumsily, as if Michael and Joseph had done it. I was suddenly overcome by the sweetness of the boys taking a bath here, when their own house was two minutes away. Did Lore have pajamas for them? No-tear shampoo and little hooded towels?

For a wild moment, I imagined abandoning the whole thing. I imagined telling Lore about the break—or breakup—with Duke and talking about where to go from here with Andrew and my father. I imagined being invited next Christmas, embraced by this family, becoming a part of it, the way I'd been a part of Duke's for the last five years.

But if I walked away, I'd be right back where I started, broke and blogging. Worse, I'd be without Duke, living in some shitty apartment with some shitty roommate, and worst of all, I'd lose the idea of myself that I'd clung to for years—that I was someone who would refuse to leave in the dark something that should be seen, should be *rectified*.

Who would I be then?

Brenda was putting the boys to bed. Gabriel and Mateo were talking in the living room over glasses of Scotch.

"Do they know?" I asked in a low voice. Whatever came next, I needed to know the truth. I needed to see it spread out before me, every pockmark and scar. I needed to understand what had happened and why. I deserved that, didn't I?

Lore handed me a plate, still dripping suds. Her smile was quizzical. "Does who know what?"

I tilted my head toward the living room. "That you were pregnant."

Slowly, Lore reached for the faucet. I dried the plate with a soggy dish towel embroidered with flowers.

"Let's go outside," Lore said.

LORE, 2017

I told the cuates we were going outside for some "girl talk" with our vinito, as if girl talk ever meant anything other than this: things that would shatter men's illusions. Gabriel had given me a hard, meaningful stare. *Keep your mouth shut.* I was never good at being told what to do.

I offered Cassie a throw blanket, and she shook her head before sitting on one of the wicker rocking chairs. I spread a rust-orange knit over my lap, its tasseled edges tickling Crusoe's cold snout. He circled, settled, sighed. Cassie's cell phone was on the table in front of us, recording. She was always recording. Vámonos.

"How did you find out?" I asked, gazing at the white lights wrapped halfway up the trunks of the oaks. String lights with large vintage bulbs hung like glittering vines off the branches. Mateo and Gabriel had held the boys up earlier to toss the wire around the branches as they screeched with delight, "More, more!" I always wanted more, too.

"I spoke to Carlos," Cassie said.

I looked at Cassie sharply. "When? How is he?"

Cassie shrugged. "He was drunk. I get the impression he's drunk a lot."

I ran my foot along Crusoe's side. His tail thumped. An ache opened in my chest. "Do you think it's my fault?"

Cassie stared into her wineglass. "I don't know, Lore. I can't imagine it helped, but then you have Penelope. People make choices."

"Yes," I murmured. "They do. Well, how did he know? Carlitos. Did Andres tell him?"

I watched Cassie realize. "Carlos was the one who found your pregnancy test," she said slowly. "He showed it to Andres, the day before Andres came here. How did you know Andres knew . . . if you didn't see him that day?"

Crusoe whined and stood, snaking his head between my knees. I scratched his knobby skull, rubbed his velveteen ears between my fingers. His black eyes shone.

"What happened, Lore?" Cassie asked.

We rocked beside each other like comadres, like viejitas, chairs squeaking. There was music coming from somewhere, faint notes of "Feliz Navidad." I pressed a hand to the side of Crusoe's snout, as if he were anchoring me here, keeping me from floating away to then.

"I've never talked about this," I told her. "Never."

Cassie nodded. Warm and lurid and fearful. "Take your time."

The sky had been low and ominous, the air smelling like a soldador taken to iron. At the Hotel Botanica, mothers were shoving towels back into bags, gritando a sus niños, "¡Cinco minutos más, eso es todo!" Wind whipped the straw roof of the palapa, plastic cups rolling toward the pool. Thunder growled in the distance.

I clutched the room key, but I couldn't make myself use it. It felt too intimate when the man inside could no longer be my husband. I dropped it into my purse and knocked instead, three short raps.

Andres opened the door with the glazed, wild look of a man realizing he was lost in the monte. He smelled like Bucanas. He stumbled back with hands raised, preventing me from touching him. The gesture sliced through me.

Inside, Andres grabbed a glass from the TV console. There were two empty mini bottles beside it.

"I'd ask if you want one," he said, "but it wouldn't be good for the baby." His furious, desecrating gaze landed on my belly. "Whose is it? Mine—or his?"

I placed a hand on my stomach. The way I'd felt earlier, como si the baby was a part of all of us, changed.

"It's *mine*," I said.

Andres slammed the highball back onto the TV console, making me jump. "This whole time? You've been married, this whole time?"

What could I do except nod? His repulsion shuddered through me. Where was the gentle man who'd understood when I declined his first proposal? Who made me caldo when I was sick, who smiled when my helmeted head butted against his on the moto? I never got to say goodbye to that man. Now this one stared at me como si I was a monster, a freak. I was wearing one of my skirt suits, and there was a dull, persistent pressure between my legs. I could feel my pelvic floor buckling, like a basket that might not be able to hold its weight for much longer.

"How could you?" he asked, bleak now, defenseless. "I trusted you."

"Andres, I—"

"No." He shook his head. "Not yet. God, I felt stupid. Can you even imagine how stupid? First, I find out my wife is pregnant and for some reason hasn't told me. Then I show up at her house and realize, oh, I don't have a key. She's not home, so I'll wait. Can you guess what happened next?"

I winced. The bank condo had been sold six months ago to some enterprising couple who'd be able to make twice their money on it in a few years.

"Yeah. Funny how you forgot to tell me you moved. Must have slipped your mind." His hair was disheveled, falling from behind his

ears into those shattered-bottle eyes. "And then, of course, I'm wondering why, if you've moved, you never gave me a new phone number. Why the old one has still worked. So I find a pay phone and
call—and call and call—but you don't answer. So there I am, in your
city, with no idea how to reach you or anyone who knows you." He
laughed. "Can you imagine? What phone number was that, Lore?"

"The bank pay phone," I whispered, staring at my feet. Qué
vergüenza.

Andres's laugh was strangled, like an injured animal. "How could
I be so blind?"

"You weren't!" My gaze shot up. I stepped closer, a hand outstretched. I wanted to comfort him somehow.

He shook his head, lips white with rage. "Oh, no? You're just that
good a liar? Have you done this before, Lore? Tell me the truth."

"No! Of course not."

"Of course not," he repeated. "I was the lucky first. Good for me.
You know what the worst part is?"

I waited. He obviously didn't want me to answer.

"This morning, when I went to the bank, I still thought there
must be some mistake. Some misunderstanding that would explain
everything." His laugh cracked down the middle. "I'm glad I finally
got to meet Oscar. He was very helpful. Your house," he added, with
a spark of vindictiveness I'd never seen from him, "your real house, I
mean—is very nice. I liked that picture of you two on the wall. The
ribbon cutting? You looked so proud."

I put a hand on the bed to keep from falling. "You went to my
house?"

"I have to tell you," Andres said. "I don't know who's the bigger
pendejo: the man who never knew where you lived, or the man who
never knew where you went."

"I'm—"

"Don't!" Andres's voice was the growl of earth splitting apart.
"You made a life with me, Lore, or at least half of one. With my kids!
How could you do this to them?"

"I love you, Andres! And I love Penelope and Car—"

"Don't say their names!" Andres roared. "Never say their names again."

I covered my face with my hands. Andres took my wrists and pulled them away, forcing me to look at him. Even then, I couldn't help wondering if this was the final time we'd touch. Even then, his grip tight on my bones, I wanted it to last.

"And don't think I didn't notice the other photos. You have kids of your own! All this time, I wondered how you were so good with mine, and it's because you're a mother. A fucking mother." He flung my wrists away, and my hands slapped against my legs. "What kind of mother does this to her children?"

"The kind of mother who's also a woman," I said, defiant, because, yes, I was a mother—in those painful seconds I was thinking of the cuates, wondering if they'd been home, too, wondering if they knew, and I was thinking of the tadpole, a hand to my belly, begging her to wait a little longer—but I was also more than a mother, and I always would be, even if I buried that self forever after this, because what was the alternative for someone like me, who felt most alive when waiting for the train to hit?

Andres scoffed, picking up his Bucanas.

"Did you tell him?" I whispered, hating myself. "About us?"

Andres stared at me. "All you care about is yourself. I don't know how I didn't see it."

The room was too hot, my fake-silk blouse sticking to my skin.

"Yes, I told him," Andres said. "I don't know what kind of man he is, and I don't care—he doesn't deserve this, either. No one does."

The cramps were getting worse. They felt familiar, too familiar, shifting from a warning, a deep ache, to something sharper, like a knife switched from back to blade. I didn't know how miscarriages worked—would I end up on the floor, legs spread, delivering a tiny corpse at Andres's feet? A wave of nausea overcame me, and I pushed past Andres to the sink, drooling into the drain.

When the nausea passed, I cupped water into my palms and drank it. Then I walked to him, palms out. "Andres, it was real," I tried to say. My last chance to try to make him understand. "I love you."

I closed the remaining distance between us, so close I could feel the heat from his body. He shoved me backward. I caught myself on the foot of the bed, stunned. I cradled my belly, imagining the tadpole inside, the grip of her translucent fingers loosening. My purse fell to my elbow.

We stared at each other, absolute strangers, capable of anything.

CASSIE, 2017

When he pushed me," Lore said quietly, "all I could think of was my baby. You have to understand—there's nothing a mother won't do to protect her children."

At Lore's words, I could almost feel the cold metal of my grandfather's urn against my knuckles as I knocked it off the mantel. I could hear my father's shout, see his wild swing, and feel the brush of my mother's sleeve against my cheek. The memory was dizzying, overpowering the one I'd replayed in my mind for all these years. My mother had stepped in front of me. She had blocked the blow.

She had threatened to kill my father if he ever hurt me.

"You had the gun," I said.

Lore nodded. She was rocking slowly, methodically. I could see how hard she was gripping the stem of her wineglass.

"The twenty-two?" I asked, for the recording.

"Yes," she said. "Fabian gave it to me for protection. I always carried it in my purse. I didn't plan it. It just happened."

I felt unsteady and disoriented, as if a film reel had been slowed down and then sped up. I set my glass on the table beside my phone, trying to control my breathing. Four months ago, I would have been buzzing with excitement, with triumph. Now I felt hollowed out, almost sick with adrenaline, with the truth. At the same time, a small, calculating part of me was thinking ahead to calling Deborah—*This could be big*—and then another part of me folded in on itself, receding, whispering with a mother's shattering gentleness, I'm disappointed in you.

"But, Lore—" I tried to make out her features. In the low light her face was all shadow. "How could you let Fabian take the fall for this?" My voice was reedy, accusatory. I tried to reframe the question. "How did Fabian get involved?"

Lore finished her wine. Her calmness was staggering, like a woman enjoying her last meal on death row, having long ago accepted her fate.

"I told him later that night. I realized . . ." Her fingers traveled to her collarbone. "I realized my locket had fallen off, probably when Andres pushed me. Fabian insisted on going back and getting it."

His fingerprint on the base of the bed. An unnoticed touch as he'd pulled a delicate chain from the carpet.

"I already told you the rest," Lore said. "About Fabian throwing the gun in the river, all that."

My head was spinning, flitting through my remaining questions. "That thing you told Oscar, about Andres bothering you."

For the first time, Lore flinched. "I shouldn't have said that."

"But then he did," I said. "Push you, I mean. You did feel threatened." I heard a kind of desperation in my voice, half like I was coercing a confession and half like a child, seeking the kind of confirmation I'd never received from my mother.

Lore stared into her glass, shoulders pulled forward. "Yes," she said quietly.

I nodded, engulfed by sadness.

"Bueno." Lore stood, folding the blanket neatly and draping it over her arm. "Now you know."

She didn't ask what I was going to do with the information.

Whatever she assumed—that I would go to the police, that I would break the story, that I would swallow her secret forever—she seemed not only resigned but at peace. Maybe she was relieved someone else finally knew, even if it would blow up her life, the way I felt after Thanksgiving. Maybe she was glad it was finally out of her hands. I didn't move from my chair.

"Cassie," Lore said, with exaggerated patience. "I'm tired now. We can pick this up tomorrow."

I almost laughed as I stood. Pick this up tomorrow. As if it were any other interview.

"Right," I said. "Okay. Well, I'll just be at the Hotel Botanica, if—"

Even in the dim, I saw Lore's eyes flash, stricken. Had I never mentioned I'd been staying there? Did she find it morbid, macabre? Maybe it was. Maybe I had lost sight of the line.

I followed Lore back into the living room, where Mateo was watching TV. He half stood to say goodbye. I told him not to get up. Gabriel and Brenda were nowhere to be seen.

On my way back to the hotel, the city felt quiet and festive. A wire Christmas tree sparkled on the roof of a bank. The air smelled like a freshly struck match.

And there was Fabian, inside a prison, experiencing none of it.

LORE, 2017

After Cassie left, I lit several candles and drew a bath. I looked at my body in the mirror as I undressed: my sloped shoulders and heavy breasts, my belly with the red lines where it folded over when I sat. Once, I'd imagined Fabian touching me again. His body a question mark around mine on a Sunday morning. Our hands giving seeds to the earth that it would return to us the following year.

When I was younger and still indulged in useless rumination, I used to ask myself whether I would do it all again, knowing how it would end. Como si one day, if I could say no and mean it, the years would flow backward and I'd find myself thirty-two years old again, a wedding invitation in hand. But I could never say no. How does one wish to have not known love? I was not that selfless.

That's one benefit of age, loss. I no longer lied to myself about who I was—or what I was willing to do for those I loved.

CASSIE, 2017

Perched on the edge of the bed at the Hotel Botanica, I imagined Lore, only a few years older than I, standing in a room just like this. A gun heavy in her purse as a man she loved loomed over her, transformed into a stranger by the pain of her betrayal. In her veins, something primal and instinctual surging—a woman who would do anything to protect her child.

Lore had never been blameless to me. That was the point. She was so hungry to know her own heart she was willing to destroy those she loved most, including—paradoxically—her children. She was supposed to be the one in control. She wasn't supposed to end up cornered by a man, driven to violence in self-defense. Such a sad, common thing.

Yet, Lore had survived. Women deserved to hear more stories of survival, fewer of the ones I posted on the blog—just yesterday it had been a mother suffocated by duct tape, discovered by her son; a serial killer targeting mothers and daughters across state lines; a woman mowed down by her ex-husband in a custody dispute. Men needed to know there were fucking limits. And if it had been self-defense, the law might be lenient on Lore, considering her age.

I remembered Lore winking at me while she ignored Brenda's objection to ice cream for the boys. I saw her wild roses, her newly color-drenched house. I saw the way she looked at Mateo and Gabriel, at Michael and Joseph, with a quiet ferocity that made me miss my mother so much I couldn't breathe. I saw Lore, in all her magnificent contradictions.

And she saw me.

Janet Malcolm wrote of the relationship between journalist and subject as a "deliberately induced delusion, followed by a shattering revelation." The interviews that feel more like conversations, like intimacies, are eventually over, translated to a black-and-white rendering in which the subject might not even recognize themselves. It's a gut punch, the subject left like all those women I'd read about at the start of this, who'd fallen for men shuffling wives like cards. The journalist like a con man, there for one reason: the story.

Had I, as the journalist, conned Lore into a delusion of intimacy so great that she believed I wouldn't reveal her as a murderer? Or had she, with her maternal caring, conned me into a sense of loyalty to her, instead of to the truth or the story or even to justice?

I reached into my laptop bag, pulled out the crime scene photos I'd seen so many times—the shape of Andres on that carpet felt as familiar as a lover's face in the morning light. Would he really have hurt Lore and, by extension, her unborn baby?

(What had happened to the baby? Lore must have miscarried after all.)

But questioning what Andres might have done if Lore hadn't killed him was a slippery slope. Not only could I never know, it meant I was trying to justify Lore's actions and, therefore, possibly keeping her secret. But there were more people than Lore to consider.

Penelope and Carlos deserved to know who had really killed their father. Maybe it would bring them more pain, though maybe it would also bring healing; maybe Carlos would take Penelope up on her offer, whatever it was, after all. Mateo and Gabriel and Gabriel's children deserved to know that Fabian was innocent; that he had made the ultimate sacrifice to keep his family intact. Fabian deserved to spend time with his sons and grandsons, to feel their weight in his arms. The justice system needed to be held accountable for the ways it had failed Fabian, failed Andres. This could be part of a much bigger conversation, a push for systemic change.

I could not hold myself responsible for what might happen to Lore as a result.

I threw on sweatpants and a tank top, trying to ignore how familiar this shirking of responsibility felt. I had passed Andrew to my father and hoped for the best. Now I was planning to pass Lore to the legal system and do the same.

But Andrew had been a baby. Lore was a killer.

No—she was someone who had killed under a set of specific circumstances. And couldn't that be true for most of us? If true crime had taught me anything, it's that if we never see that version of ourselves, it's only because we're lucky.

But still. A man was in prison for a crime he didn't commit. Would Lore's confession be enough to reopen Fabian's case, reexamine the evidence? DNA might have been science fiction then, but it wasn't anymore. Maybe she'd left some part of herself behind.

I searched through my bag for my phone, wanting to listen to the recording. A part of my brain, mercenary and untamed, imagined what Lore's words would sound like on a podcast or prestige docuseries on Netflix or HBO, what that might mean for the next book I wrote, what it might mean for my whole life.

This could be big.

"Fuck," I said out loud, disgusted.

I needed to think before I called Deborah. A question nagged at me: Once Fabian had been ID'd at the hotel, once his fingerprint had been found, why hadn't he turned on Lore? Yes, they were still married. But Lore herself had said the new, richer love between them had come later. Would Fabian really, in the immediate aftermath of Lore's betrayal, be willing to go down for thirty-five years for murdering her secret husband?

And where the hell was my phone?

LORE, 2017

I sank deeper into the bath, letting the water close over my face, my hair waving above me like seaweed. The horror of that night felt fresh, sticking in my throat. Andres's hand on my chest, shoving. The shock of it, the insult. The shock in Andres's face, too, as if he hadn't known before that moment he could touch me like that.

"I'm sorry." Andres had stumbled back, palms out. "I shouldn't have pushed you."

"It's okay," I said, so eager to give him my forgiveness. "I—"

"Just leave, Lore." Andres turned away, toward the windows. The first fat drops of rain were falling, smearing across the concrete walkway. "Go. I never want to see you again."

"Andres, please," I whispered. "Don't say that."

I stared at him, willing us to fall into one of those long unbroken gazes, pero he went into the bathroom and closed the door. I looked all around the room for paper and a pen, seeing a notepad beside the phone. He'd started to write me something: *Lore.* That's all. No *querida.* I didn't know what to write.

Finally, with Andres still shut in the bathroom, I left. Weeping, head lowered against the hot swirl of wind, clutching my stomach. The sky was as dark as the parking lot asphalt, and when I reached my car, I threw the notepad and pen onto the passenger seat and screamed.

I couldn't go home. Couldn't face Fabian. So I drove, the windshield wipers frantic and useless against the furious slant of rain. Water sloshed from the gutters back into the streets. I drove too fast. Wide, winding loops past the meat market where Papi picked up fajitas and sausage for Sunday lunches, and the cemetery where he would be buried only a few months later. Past the corn-in-the-cup stand where I used to take the cuates every Friday after school. Back downtown, past the bank and through the empty streets. The car sliding when I braked, fishtailing, and for a second I hoped that everything would end before I had to see Fabian's face.

CASSIE, 2017

I had just overturned my bag on the bed to find my phone when I remembered something Oscar had said—something about Lore being upset that afternoon. Something about her purse.

I slid my laptop from its sleeve, opening my notes from that call.

OSCAR: But look, after Lore told me how he was bothering her—I mean, we all make mistakes. I just wish—

CASSIE: Wish what, Oscar?

OSCAR: I don't know—that I would've done something to help. But Lore was very independent like that.

CASSIE: Let's go back. She said Andres was *bothering* her? Bothering her how? When did she tell you this?

OSCAR: When she came back to the bank that afternoon, after I gave her the note he left. She didn't go into detail. But again, that's Lore. You could tell she was rattled, though.

CASSIE: How so?

OSCAR: She was looking for her keys to lock up her office. Ended up dropping her whole purse on the floor. Everything spilled out.

Everything spilled out. But tonight, Lore had specifically said she always carried the .22 in her purse. If everything had spilled out, Oscar would have seen the gun. Whatever loyalty he felt toward Lore, surely he would have told the police if he'd seen her with the murder weapon.

Breathe, I told myself. Slow down. Maybe Oscar only *thought* the purse had emptied entirely. Because the alternative—that she wasn't carrying the gun—meant she'd given me a false confession. Why would she do that when Fabian was already in prison?

There's nothing a mother won't do to protect her children.

The calm, unwavering conviction in Lore's voice. A truth I could feel, despite whatever else she had lied about. Lore had a way of doing this, of making even the lies truthful. She had done it with Andres and Fabian, giving them something real even through her deceit. She'd done it with me, too. I thought about how Lore had claimed Fabian killed Andres to "feel like a man again." Maybe he'd tried to make up for his perceived failures not by killing Andres but by taking the blame for it.

Except—maybe he hadn't done it for Lore.

Gabriel and Mateo had been fifteen years old. Their friends Rudolfo Hinojosa and Eduardo Canales had confirmed they were all playing basketball at the park between four and six, which meant they couldn't have been home when Andres had pulled into the Riveras' driveway at four thirty. Even if they'd somehow known about the double marriage—and improbably kept it a secret—they'd have no way of knowing Andres was in town or where he was staying.

I returned to the neighbor's witness statement. He had waved at Andres, thinking it was Lore parking in her usual spot.

Her usual spot. The driveway that was too narrow for two cars to park side by side, so they'd built the carport. Lore parked in the driveway up front and Fabian in the carport out back . . .

Heart pounding, I entered the Riveras' old address into Google maps. The satellite image struggled to load with the hotel's weak Wi-Fi. Finally, the picture cleared. I zoomed in. Just as Lore had described, it was a gray brick ranch-style home. A corner lot. Around the side, an iron gate must lead to the carport. But the driveway, as she'd said, was built for two cars parked bumper to bumper.

Okay. So at four thirty, Andres had pulled into the driveway, where the neighbor had waved because he thought it was Lore. I opened the transcript for my call with Sergio, hardly able to breathe. When Sergio picked up Fabian for the ranch, "he was standing in the middle of the empty driveway, looking almost like he didn't know where he was."

The empty driveway meant Fabian's truck must have been parked in the carport all afternoon. Only, when Sergio dropped Fabian at home at eight, Fabian had, yes, "pointed to his truck and said of course it had rained—he'd just washed it."

"Shit," I said. "Shit, shit, shit."

Fabian's truck wasn't in the driveway when they left for the ranch. But it *was* there when he returned, at which point Lore was at the movies with the boys. Someone had moved it before six thirty, when she'd taken them for Frosties. It could have been Lore, but why? There was no reason to move the truck from carport to driveway if she wasn't going to *use* the carport.

Fifteen, though, was old enough to know how to drive. She'd told me Gabriel wanted to drive them home from San Antonio when she'd returned to the States after the earthquake. Yes, Gabriel and Mateo had been alibied at the park from four to six, but if there was one thing this story made clear, people lied.

Here was the other thing: it was storming from five to six, not exactly ideal basketball-playing weather. What if Gabriel or Mateo—or both—had gone home early and been there when Andres confronted Fabian? One or both boys could have taken Fabian's truck and killed Andres, maybe accidentally, maybe on purpose, returning home too flustered to remember to park in the carport.

Lore could have found out when she got home. Then taken the twins to Wendy's and to the movies not to make sure she was alibied— but to make sure *they* were. After all, times were tough. Tickets and snacks are a luxury when money is tight. And two fifteen-year-old boys out with their mom on a Friday night? Even the movie cashier had commented on it. Plus, Lore had just come from the confrontation with Andres (if it had happened the way she described). She'd been afraid she was miscarrying. Would she really pick that night for an outing? None of it added up, unless she'd done it for a very specific reason—to make sure the twins were seen as close to Andres's actual time of death as possible. It must have been a shock when the window was established as later that night, when Fabian was ID'd on the scene.

Jesus. *Maybe* Fabian would take the fall for Lore. But from everything Lore had told me about him, he'd *definitely* do it for one of his sons.

It finally made sense, why Lore had agreed to talk to me in the first place. I'd thought it was because she wanted to tell her story. But, I could see now, she wanted to control *me*, and she thought she could, a young nobody writer who would be all too eager to write exactly the story she told. And if I didn't—she always had this option, her own false confession, tucked away in a back pocket.

Once I'd told her I knew she was pregnant, she must have thought I was getting too close, that a confession would get me to stop digging. Like Fabian, she'd been willing to martyr herself for her son. And, if I was right, it had almost worked.

But which one was it? Who were Lore and Fabian protecting?

The answer came, silky and obvious. Gabriel's teenage volatility. His unbroken hostility toward me. The way he'd looked at me tonight, violence thrumming beneath his skin. And the way he'd answered when I asked how often they visited Fabian: *It's the least we can do.* The countless photos he posted of his sons with heartfelt captions for a man who couldn't read them: *There is no love like a father's love. Thanks for everything, Dad.*

I turned back to the bed to grab my phone—but it wasn't among the contents I'd shaken from my purse.

"Shit," I said again, a moment before the landline's strident ring fractured the silence. My heart hammered with the sudden noise.

"Ms. Bowman? You have a visitor."

The night was replaying by itself now, memories coming so clear and whole it was like if they'd been preserved behind glass all these years.

It had been just after six when I pulled up to the house. Fabian's truck had been in the driveway instead of the carport. I opened the back gate and sat in the car for a few minutes. I thought of telling Fabian what I'd told Oscar, that it had been an affair, a mistake. Even if Andres had shown Fabian the wedding photo, it wasn't obvious it was a wedding, with my short white shift dress and Andres in his guayabera. An affair. Fabian could forgive that, couldn't he?

The air was as soggy and hot as a dog's panted breath as I ran to the back door, but instead of Fabian, it was the cuates standing in the kitchen. Red-faced and dripping rain onto the linoleum. They were wearing basketball shorts and tennis shoes. I'd interrupted them yelling, but whatever they'd been saying was lost. They looked at me and then at each other. For a moment, they were two years old again, communicating in mysterious glances. Then Gabriel swallowed.

"Mom," he said, "I did something."

"Dame un minuto," I said, rushing to the bathroom. I couldn't hear about his latest fight or flunked test right now.

"I killed him," Gabriel said.

I turned.

The first twist came low in my belly. A sense of something pulling away, coming undone. I braced against the Formica counter.

"You did what?" I managed. "¿Qué estás—"

"I killed your other husband!" Gabriel yelled. "He's dead. I shot him."

And finally, finally, I saw the gun. The .22 Fabian had given me, which I rarely carried. It was usually in the gun safe. The cuates had known the combination for years, ever since they started hunting with Fabian. Now the gun was beside the stove, between the jarro and the spice rack.

"I don't—" I gripped the counter, moaning. "No entiendo. Gabriel, what are you talking about?"

"I was here, getting another basketball, when he came over." Gabriel glanced at Mateo. "I heard everything he said to Dad."

"Oh, God," I said, and the second twist came, a cataclysm of falling organs, and I ran to the bathroom, slammed the door, pulled off my pants and underwear, and collapsed on the toilet. A sob, a push, and something solid and slick slid out of me. Blood on the toilet paper, poinsettia-red. I clung to the pink countertop as I stood, shaking. I didn't want to look, but I had to bear witness, I had to give my baby that much, but she was gone; she had slid out of sight like a small animal going back to ground, and I was so relieved, so desperately relieved that I would never need to know how she looked when my failures unmade her.

I stumbled down the hall to my room, where I stuck a pad down to catch whatever was left. When I came back out, the cuates were sitting at the kitchen table, their heads in their hands.

"Mom," Mateo said, looking up. "Are you okay?"

"No!" I yelled. "No, I am not okay! Gabriel, start from the beginning," I ordered. "Dime qué pasó."

As he spoke, I felt myself withering, burning, turning to ashes. How could this be possible? Andres, poor Andres, who had done nothing wrong except trust me, dead, with a bullet hole in the chest I had kissed and touched, the chest that contained his beautiful heart. I wanted to race back to the hotel, to prove Gabriel wrong, to turn back time. But the stages of grief are a luxury of the innocent. I had to protect my son.

Gabriel, with his hair too long in the back. The barest hint of a mustache. Un niño nomás. Pero al mismo tiempo, no longer the child I recognized. He was someone new, reborn in blood, and I shuddered to think of what would become of him if he went to prison, surrounded by men who were already hard when he was still soft. A boy like Mateo, maybe he'd be able to keep himself whole. But Gabriel would shatter, then rebuild into something terrible. I couldn't let that happen.

"Give me what you're wearing," I said. "Los dos. Y traéme la ropa sucia from your bathroom tambíen."

Obediently, they stripped off their shirts and shorts, kicked off their shoes and handed me their socks, damp with rain and sweat. They changed and collected the rest of their dirty clothes, bringing everything wrapped in a towel, so neat and modest.

We're all going to need alibis, I thought as I started the wash. Gabriel said his friends, Rudy and Wayo—a brief flicker of recognition at those names, no time to dwell on it—would say he'd been with them at the park. I wondered how many other instances they'd covered for him, and what he'd done to need their protection. I wondered what he'd done for them in return.

I took the cuates to Wendy's for Frosties, made small talk with the cashier. Y luego straight to the mall, where I sat between them en el cine, my stomach doing a vuelta each time Gabriel's shoulder brushed mine.

For the first time in his life, I hated my son. But not more than I loved him.

I put a hand to my heart, as if I might still be able to feel the heat of Andres's palm. The last time he'd touched me. And that was when I realized: my necklace, the locket I always wore. It was gone.

CASSIE, 2017

With the white trellises beside him and the lights in the trees, Mateo was an oddly romantic sight in my doorway. He could be extending a hand with flowers, instead of the phone I'd left at Lore's.

"Thank you so much," I said, slipping it into my pocket. I was flustered, my heart still pounding after I'd come to my realization about Gabriel. And now, as Mateo's eyes crinkled slightly, more generous with smiles than his mouth, I was overly aware I wasn't wearing a bra, my nipples hard in the air-conditioning.

"No problem." Mateo slipped his foot against the door, holding it ajar as I crossed my arms. "Actually, I wanted to talk to you."

"Great. Why don't we go to the bar? Let me grab a sweater."

Mateo glanced behind him at the pool area as I zipped up my hoodie. "I think it's closed."

"Oh." I looked at the stool pulled up to the built-in desk. "Well, come in, then. Sorry, tight space."

Our shoulders brushed as I hurriedly closed my laptop. If he'd seen the street view image of his childhood home before sitting down, he didn't acknowledge it. He was frowning, taking in the faded floral wallpaper and venetian blinds, the fake fern and heavy, scarred wooden furniture.

"Why are you staying here?" His voice was neutral, stripped of inflection, which only made the judgment more obvious.

"Research," I said, embarrassed. I sat on the edge of the bed. Our knees were almost touching. "So. What did you want to talk to me about?"

"I wanted to apologize," Mateo said, "for Gabriel. He was out of line tonight."

My knee accidentally grazed his. I saw him notice the contact. He didn't pull away. He had that fresh-lit match smell, as if he'd driven over with the windows down. I liked that idea of him, enjoying a piece of the night by himself.

"You're not your brother's keeper," I said.

Then I wondered: How much did he know? That bribe when we first met—maybe it had been about more than protecting his family's privacy. Maybe it had been to protect his family's *secret*. And the late-night email exchange, the way he'd suddenly been willing to talk on the phone. Maybe he'd only wanted to get a sense of what I was learning. He could be here for the same reason. The idea saddened me, though what had I hoped? That maybe he wanted to talk to me not as the writer of his mother's story, but as myself?

"Okay, my own apology, then. You're obviously not someone who can be bought off," he added, as if reading my mind. "Plus, the shitty things I said about your abilities when we first met." He winced, sheepish. "I pulled out all the stops, didn't I?"

I laughed. "It's okay. I'd probably do the same in your position."

Mateo tilted his head, a curious, attentive gesture. I could see him doing this in exam rooms, stethoscope to his ear, listening to the gurgles and whooshes inside animals that couldn't speak for themselves.

"Does that mean—are you reconsidering the book?" he asked.

The question surprised me, made me want to clutch my laptop to my chest, protecting the months of interview transcripts and notes, the sample chapters and book proposal, the sense of purpose it had all given me, the sense of *promise*. No. I wasn't reconsidering the book. The book was everything to me.

"No," I said, gentle but immovable.

Mateo sighed, slumping forward with his elbows on his thighs. "Not that I expected you to say yes, but I'm disappointed to hear that." He looked up at me, something complicated in his brown eyes, and I realized—ridiculously, belatedly—how vulnerable I was, alone in this tiny hotel room with a man I hardly knew, a man who might be here to protect his family's secret. I pulled my phone from my pocket.

"Actually, that reminds me," I said. "I need to text my agent. She's expecting an update from me tonight."

I pressed the home button. Nothing happened.

"Sorry," Mateo said. "Your battery must have died."

His tone hadn't changed, but my breath hitched. An instinct, a learned fear—my dad retreating to his chair, hand on his drink—or one bred into us: a dark parking lot, keys between our fingers; dusk falling on a run, the sudden beat of footsteps close behind. I pulled my charger from my duffel and backed toward the nightstand, where I plugged in my phone without taking my eyes off Mateo.

Mom's invited you here like you're part of the family, Gabriel had said. *But you're just a leech.*

Maybe I was a leech. But I was a leech who was going to find out the truth, finally.

"Mateo," I said carefully, "your mother told me something tonight. She told me it wasn't your father who killed Andres."

Mateo stood, taking two slow paces toward the door, then back. "I know. That's why I'm here."

My hands trembled. "Go on."

Mateo placed a palm on the TV console. "The kitchen window was open. I heard her confess. Cassie, you can't write that."

I startled at the sound of my name in his mouth. Familiar, almost intimate.

"Why not?" I glanced at my phone, waiting for it to light up with charge.

"Because it's not what happened!" He began pacing again, four large strides from the door to the bathroom, tense and fast. The room tightened around the space he was claiming, back and forth, back and forth.

"It wasn't your mother, either, was it?" I stabbed the home button on my phone. Nothing.

Mateo didn't answer.

"When did you find out?" I asked, almost dizzy.

Suddenly, too suddenly, Mateo stopped moving. He reminded me of an animal you'd encounter in the wild, something elegant and strong, eyes fixed to yours, muscles twitching. Antlers that could take you apart if it was cornered.

"About what?" he asked, low.

About Gabriel, I meant to say. But something in the way he was staring at me. It clicked, a final understanding. *Can you even imagine what it was like,* he'd said in our first conversation, *opening the door to someone who tells you that everything you believe about someone you love is a lie?* His voice tight with outrage. As if he'd been there. As if he'd heard it.

"Oh, God," I said. "You were there, when Andres came to the house."

Mateo's whole body seemed to deflate, like a man reaching the end of a very long journey.

He sighed, looking down. "They've changed the carpet," he said. "But otherwise, this room looks exactly the same."

LORE, 2017

Someone pounded on the bathroom door. "Mom, come out, get dressed—hurry!"

"¿Qué pasó? ¿Los niños?" I kicked the drain with my heel, and it sucked back its first slurp of water.

"No, they're fine," Gabriel said. "It's Mateo."

Five minutes later, we were going fifty, then sixty, down Del Mar, past Starbucks and H-E-B and the Maverick (now called something else) where I used to call Andres, and the Wendy's where I'd taken the cuates the night he died, though back then the tile was ugly brown rectangles, and cigarette smoke cut through the scent of hot oil. We passed St. Patrick Church—both instinctively making the sign of the cross—and Rangel Field, where the cuates had briefly played Little League before discovering basketball and thank goodness for that because it hurt to watch them strike out, their little shoulders slumped as they looked up at the bleachers, as if we would ever do anything but cheer for them.

We swooped left under I-35 a full second after the red, and I gripped the handle above the passenger door. "Gabriel, what is going on?"

His panza strained against the seat belt, and I remembered a carnival where the cuates had driven bumper cars and Fabian and I had laughed at how they leaned over the wheels like viejitos straining to see the road.

"We have to get there. What room is she in? Do you know?"

"Cassie? I have no idea. Gabriel, dime ahorita qué está pasando!"

Gabriel glanced at me. When the cuates were younger, they always knew it was serious when we switched to full Spanish.

"He said he heard you two talking." We were on the highway now, going seventy, seventy-five, even though the exit was half a mile away. "He said he had to stop it. Brenda called me to help her with Joseph, and when I came back out, he was gone. What did you tell her? Did you tell her—about me?"

"Ay, Gabriel." My fingers reached, out of some ancient habit, to my chest, but the locket was long gone. I grabbed the collar of my cardigan instead, rubbing it between my fingers. "You think I could do that to you?"

Gabriel swerved onto the exit. As usual, the cars on the access road didn't yield, and Gabriel punched the horn, then finally swung into the right lane and into the motel parking lot. He exhaled, pointing. "His truck. I fucking knew it."

We ran from the car to the lobby, where a skinny kid who barely looked out of high school was staring at his phone behind the front desk.

"Cassie— What's her last name again?" Gabriel asked me.

"Bowman," I said to the kid. "Cassie Bowman. What room is she in?" I didn't understand Gabriel's distress, but it filled me like a strange vapor, making me light-headed and unsteady.

The kid looked at his computer. "Hold on. I need to call her first."

The phone rang and rang. Gabriel loomed over the counter, a heaving mass.

The kid glanced at us. He had an angry sprinkling of acne on his chin. "That's weird, she was just—"

"What's her fucking room number?" Gabriel growled.

"Please," I said to the kid. "I'm her—" I hesitated. "Mother."

The kid shrugged. "Fine, whatever."

He gave us the room number, and we ran down the cement walkway. Gabriel pulled ahead of me, so I felt like I was chasing him, chanclas slapping the ground, breath ragged. The pool area was empty, the water lit from within. Bugs clustered on the lights. I was panting, choking on my own heartbeat.

And then we were at the door, Gabriel jiggling the handle. He pounded the aluminum with a fist: banging, banging, banging. Was this Andres's old room? I thought I would remember, but they all looked the same. All I knew was that no one was answering and something was horribly wrong.

"Mateo!" I yelled. "Cassie! ¡Abre la puerta!"

Finally, after what seemed like hours, the door opened.

Mateo looked ten years older than he had at dinner tonight. "Well," he said wearily, stepping back. "This has always been a family affair."

CASSIE, 2017

Lore and Gabriel pushed into the room, and while Gabriel shoved Mateo into the corner, Lore pulled me so tightly against her I couldn't breathe. I felt like a child whose mother had picked her up hours late from school—fury cutting through the relief—and I almost pushed her away. We were here because of her, because of all the lies she'd told, everything she'd needed to have, but then it seemed we were here because of me, because of everything I'd needed to have, and her grip on me was strong and solid, so I dropped my head to her shoulder, succumbing, as always, to the care that still felt so real. But I didn't take my eyes off the brothers, who were conferring angrily, too low for me to hear.

"Are you okay?" Lore pulled away, searching my face and body. She glared at Mateo. "¿Qué hiciste?"

"I'm fine." Those moments of terror seemed surreal now, a tide lurching back toward the horizon, leaving only damp sand as evidence of its presence.

"It was you," I had whispered to Mateo, losing feeling in my hands and feet, as if the center of my body were disconnected from the earth, as if nothing could keep me from floating away and disappearing, just another vanished woman. A laugh had been trapped in my chest. A lifetime of true crime had brought me to this moment, though it sure as hell hadn't taught me how to get out alive. Maybe I could shove past him to the bathroom or the door, I'd thought, though he'd probably grab me before I managed to turn the lock. Maybe I could keep him talking until my phone charged, then try to get the SOS call slider to appear. Andrew's self-defense lesson rushed into my mind—if Mateo grabbed me from behind, I'd throw my head back into his chin or nose, and if I had an arm free, I'd stab my elbow into his solar plexus, I'd hook my foot around his so he couldn't yank me backward, I'd fight, at least, I'd fight like hell, and I'd scream, and I'd make sure that even if he killed me, my body would tell the story.

But Mateo hadn't taken even one step closer. He'd stood near the door, motionless. His hands loose at his sides. His stare was earnest and sad, waiting for something. For me, to give him permission to carve open his skin and bone, exposing everything glistening within.

He watched as I neared, my heart hammering. When we were close enough to touch, he said, "I'm really fucking tired of keeping secrets."

Trembling, I took his hand. He looked startled at the sight of our palms pressed together. I was startled, too. Then he laced his fingers through mine. I whispered, "Tell me."

Now Lore's voice hardened. "Good. ¡Ahora alguien dígame que está pasando!"

Mateo's shoulders sagged. While no one was looking at me, I unlocked my phone, finally charged just enough. I opened Voice Memo, hit record. When Mateo met my gaze, I said, "She needs to know."

He nodded, jaw clenched. To Lore, he said simply: "It was me."

Lore looked warily between the three of us, as if trying to anticipate a cruel punch line. "What are you talking about?"

"It was me," Mateo repeated, more firmly. "I—"

"No, güey." Gabriel clapped a hand around his brother's shoulder. He said something I didn't understand. Not English or Spanish or any other recognizable language, but a rough, nonsensical series of consonants and vowels, meaningless sounds.

Lore clapped her hands once, loud. "Stop it! ¡Ya con tu secret language!"

Mateo took a step forward and Lore shrank back—not afraid of him, I understood, but of what he was about to reveal.

"I killed him," Mateo said. "It wasn't Gabriel. It was never Gabriel."

"Mateo!" Gabriel dug his fingers into his brother's arm. "¡Ya cállate, cabrón! What are you doing?"

Mateo shrugged him away. "Well, what's the alternative? Let Mom do it now? Let everyone in this family go down for it but me? She confessed tonight, Gabriel. That's why I came. To make things right—finally."

"No." Lore looked at me with a flame of accusation in her eyes. I had come into their lives and shaken every tree it had taken them thirty years to grow, shaken so hard that now the roots were pulled from the earth, tangled and searching. "It was me," she told me. "I did it."

"No," I said, more gently than I felt. Lore had, after all, been lying to me. Lore was always lying. "You didn't."

"I was home," Mateo said, "when he came to the door."

Lore shook her head. "You were at the park."

"I left the park." Mateo glanced at Gabriel. Something passed between them. "Dad was out back working on the stupid gate, so he didn't hear me come in. I went straight to my room. I heard the doorbell ring and was coming out to answer. Dad got there first. I was in the hallway. I heard everything."

For the first time, anger flashed across his face, rusted-old and fragmented. I knew that kind of anger. I'd seen it in my father. I'd felt it in myself.

"He asked for you," Mateo said. "He sounded confused. So did Dad. Then the guy must have seen the picture on the wall, the one of you and Dad at the store. He started saying, 'That's Lore! That's my wife!' They were both yelling, and I just wanted him to go away. And then he did, but he told Dad where he was staying, said they needed to talk." He gave a hard laugh. "I don't know what he thought they were going to talk about."

Lore was motionless, combustible. "Mateo, stop," she said, but the command emerged as a plea.

"I went back to my room. I didn't know what to do. Everything already felt so . . ." Mateo searched for a word. "Precarious."

Lore's voice cracked. "It did?"

"Of course it did," he snapped. "You were never home. Dad was in his own world. Everyone was broke. We had friends—right?" he said, an aside to Gabriel, "—who'd lost their houses, who were selling drugs. It felt like we were next."

"That's not—" Lore blinked quickly. "That's not how I remember it."

"I'm not surprised," Mateo said, though it was matter-of-fact, not bitter. "Anyway. Tío Sergio came to pick up Dad, and then I was by myself. I was afraid we were going to lose you to this complete stranger. I felt like—I needed to be the man. So I took the gun and Dad's truck. I just wanted him to leave. I still hoped maybe he was crazy. Just saying stuff. But then I saw you, leaving his room."

Lore's whole body was shaking violently. I wanted to guide her to sit down but knew she'd erupt if I touched her.

"You looked upset." Mateo's eyes pleaded. "You were crying, your shirt was twisted. I knew then that it was true. But I also thought he'd hurt you. Did he?"

Lore put a palm to her chest. I thought of the shove, wondered if it had really happened. "No," she said. "Never."

Mateo sighed, looking at me. "Maybe it was what I needed to think."

"Mateo, stop talking!" Gabriel boomed. Mateo was undeterred. The story poured from him now, unstoppable. His eyes were half-glazed with memory.

"I knocked, and he answered right away. He obviously thought it would be you again," he said to Lore. "I told him who I was, asked if I could come in. And then it started storming. You couldn't hear anything except thunder and water. He was telling me how sorry he was. How he hadn't known. How he"—Mateo gritted his teeth—"loved you. How he had two kids of his own. A son my age. He stepped toward me like he was going to, I don't know, *hug* me, and I thought of how you looked, coming out of his room, and . . . I don't know. I took out the gun. And I shot him."

The room was achingly silent. I felt a lurch of nausea, a terrible sweeping sadness.

"I didn't mean to." Mateo took a step closer to Lore, stopped. "I think back, and I don't even recognize myself. I was just so . . . angry."

Lore was weeping quietly into her cupped palms. She stared at the carpet, as if she could see Andres. As if she might fall to her knees and feel the heat of his life escaping.

"Did he say anything?" she whispered. "Did he suffer?"

Mateo shook his head. "It was instant," he said, but his glance flicked in my direction. Andres had drowned in his own blood. There was nothing instant about it. For once, I didn't want to replace a lie with the truth.

"I don't understand." Lore looked at Gabriel. "Why did you say it was you?"

Another silent communication passed between the brothers. A question, a decision.

Gabriel sighed, rubbing his goatee. "I guess it doesn't matter now. But I had started dealing. I'd been doing it for a few months. It was such easy money. Mateo didn't want anything to do with it."

A tired realization dawned on Lore's face. "Rudy and Wayo." She almost laughed, a sorrowful sound. "The chucos. You tried to tell me," she said to Mateo, who stood stoic, a silent confirmation. Back to Gabriel: "That's why you two were fighting. Spending less time together."

Gabriel nodded. "That's why Mateo left the park that day."

"And why they said you were both there," Lore said.

"We all had skin in the game," Gabriel said. "God, it was stupid. But I felt like—it was my fault Mateo was home. He never would have done this if I hadn't made such stupid fucking choices."

"You two." Lore shook her head, the motion seeming to take more energy than she possessed. "Always protecting each other."

"Besides." Gabriel's voice broke, and he gave a rough little shrug. "I knew it would be easier for you if you believed it was me."

The air in the room thickened, threatening to drown us all.

"I'm so sorry." Lore stepped toward her sons. She snaked her arms around their waists, her cheek pressed into Gabriel's chest. "I'm so, so sorry."

They encircled her, shielded her from my gaze, trapped her inside their pain.

LORE, 2017

In the silent darkness of my bedroom that night, I remembered being pregnant with the cuates—bowing beneath heaving waves of nausea, catching the ripples and thrusts beneath my skin, staggering with their growing weight upon my bones. Toward the end, I was so desperate to get them out, to be alone again in my body. I didn't understand that I would never again have one body. That from then on, the cuates would be my organs, my tripas and corazón, pulsing and exposed, constantly under threat.

Andres had told me once how he used to wake to his mother watching him sleep. His mother who had miscarried so many times, whose need and love were too heavy for him to bear. He said he'd never understood it until he had children of his own—the sweet relief of watching them sleep, knowing that in those moments, at least, they were safe.

I had nearly told him the truth then.

The terror of being a mother never disappears. You only learn to absorb it into your body, to whisper it to sleep with the lull of everyday routine. But every so often it roars awake again, the knowledge that your children could be taken from you at any time, and that without them, your one, intact body may as well burn to ash.

All night I thought of the grip of Gabriel's hands on the steering wheel. The way we'd run down the motel corridor as if expecting— what? Was Gabriel trying to stop Mateo from revealing the truth? Or had he thought Mateo could hurt Cassie? The thought made me stumble toward the bathroom, retching. Nothing came out of me but tears.

I called Cassie in the morning, once I heard the front door slam: Mateo, out for a run. Good. I didn't want to see him yet. Gabriel— what he'd said about it being easier for me if I believed it was him. Even at fifteen, he'd known his brother was my favorite. My heart felt like tenderized meat, beaten soft and pulpy.

Cassie agreed to meet me at Mami and Papi's house, and she was waiting in her car when I arrived. I said a silent prayer to the God of earthquakes and Abraham that my sacrifice might be enough.

"¿Cómo estás?" I asked, giving her a kiss on the cheek.

"Not great." Her skin was nearly translucent, with lavender ojeras she didn't bother covering with makeup. The sun shone off her light hair, pulled into a somber low ponytail. "How about you?"

"Same."

Cassie nodded, waiting while I opened the padlock at the chain-link gate and led the way up the short, cracked cement walk to my parents' front door. The house looked so small now. A battered antique dollhouse, overloved and forgotten.

"What are we doing here?" Cassie asked, following me inside.

"I want to show you something."

The house was hot and musty, despite our weekly cleanings. Most of the furniture remained. I could still see the front room as it had been on so many Sundays: the long gleaming wood dining table sheathed in plastic, every chair taken, voices loud, arms reaching over each other to slap food into the children's bowls. Papi had died so long ago, but I swore I could still smell the charcoal smoke and

Old Spice. And there was Mami in the kitchen, covering the last of the tortillas with a secador, griping at me for complaining about her Carlo Rossi. I was breathless with longing for everything I'd lost.

"In here." I led Cassie into the living room. Before we went any farther, I asked the question that had kept me up all night: "Cassie, did you think Mateo was going to hurt you?"

She looked down at the shag carpeting, toeing it with her boot. "For a second, yes."

"Did he . . ." I put a hand against the wall. "Threaten you?"

"No." Redness traveled up her neck in faint splotches. I studied her more closely. "I don't think he meant to scare me. I think it was just me, thinking the worst of people, like always."

I wanted to be reassured. But I kept remembering Mateo's voice when he talked about shooting Andres. A kind of dreamy awe behind the regret, as if, even now, he was impressed with the shape his anger had taken, the shape he let it take: the crescent-moon curve of the trigger.

Cassie met my eyes. "I think Mateo made a mistake. But still—"

"Wait." I hurried to the corner of the room. "Before you say anything else, just wait."

I knelt, grabbed the carpeting, and pulled. As always, the floorboard beneath it lifted, too. I reached inside and pulled out a thick collection of letters, held together with deteriorating rubber bands.

Cassie crouched beside me, blue eyes wide. "Are these . . . ?"

"All the letters Andres wrote to me. And a few other things." I lifted a Ziploc bag with one photo inside: Andres and me beneath the saguaro tree. Me in my cheap white shift dress, Andres in his white guayabera. Rings on our fingers.

"Oh my God." Cassie reached for the bag. "The photo from the wallet."

I handed it to her. "Gabriel told me he'd taken the wallet to make it look like a robbery. He gave it to me to get rid of."

"Along with the gun?" Cassie asked.

I nodded. My chest hurt, remembering how the wallet had sat beside the gun on the kitchen counter. Gabriel hadn't actually removed either one of them from his pockets. Mateo must have set them there before I arrived.

"And Fabian?" Cassie asked. "How did he find out about everything?"

"He was home when we got back from the movies," I said.

He'd been slumped at the kitchen table. "Gabriel, Mateo, go to your rooms," he'd said.

The three of us had looked at each other, realizing Fabian was inhabiting an entirely different reality from ours.

"No, Fabian," I said. "We need to talk, all of us."

Fabian's dark eyes flashed with tears. "Cuates, I said go to your rooms!"

But they followed me to the kitchen table. I explained, repeating every word Gabriel had parroted to me while Mateo—what had he been doing? It was so hard to remember now. That must be because he was acting normal, or whatever could pass for normal in those circumstances. It was Gabriel who alternated between screaming at me and wiping furious tears, all of us sweating because it was so damn hot outside and too expensive to keep the AC lower than eighty. Fabian's eyes had sharpened, his pupils dilating. He made Gabriel repeat the story four or five times. He asked what Gabriel had touched, and Gabriel said the door handles and the nightstand, where the wallet had been sitting, and the stupid glass of Scotch, which he said he'd drained after shooting Andres. Then I issued the final blow.

"My necklace." I reached for the empty space at my chest. "I think it fell off in the room."

Fabian's mouth opened and closed. "You went there?"

My pad was heavy. My body ached with the remnants of what it had so recently held. "To end it."

Fabian closed his eyes. "What did you touch?"

I told him about washing my mouth in the sink, the door handle on the way out, the nightstand where I'd taken the notepad. He looked at the clock on the microwave. Though it was after nine, the storm had passed, and the sky had cleared to a sleepy, twilit blue.

He stood up, standing straighter than I'd seen him in months. "I'm going to take care of it," he said. "I'm going to take care of everything."

CASSIE, 2017

Lore again buried her arm beneath the floorboards. She pulled out a tiny Ziploc bag and handed it to me. I held the bag between two fingers. Inside, the gold locket still shone. But its delicate chain was tangled, darkened with time and—I looked closer—something else.

"Fabian brought it back to me," Lore said, sitting back on her heels. "I couldn't bear to wash it. I know how that must sound, but I couldn't rinse him away like that. So."

In my pocket, I could almost feel my phone getting warmer, as if the recording could sense the importance of this moment.

"This is Andres's blood?" I asked, hushed, reverent.

Lore nodded. She gestured to the letters, the photo, the necklace. "You have everything now. Even—" She bent forward, pulling out yet another bag with a Hotel Botanica notepad and pen. Andres's abandoned letter: *Lore*. "Only his fingerprints and mine will be on this. They can match his handwriting to the other letters. And, of course, you have my confession." She paused, as her meaning fell into place. "You can get your big book deal with this, right?"

I jolted to my feet. "Jesus, Lore, after everything? You didn't kill Andres!"

Lore's knees cracked as she stood. "But I'm willing to say I did."

I fixed my eyes over Lore's shoulder, at the painting of the Virgin Mary cradling her infant son. Would she have taken his place if she could? I crossed my arms, still clutching the baggie with Lore's necklace. I unclenched that fist—I didn't want to risk damaging the evidence.

"What kind of journalist do you think I am?" I asked quietly. "What kind of person?"

Lore smiled. "The kind who reads about people's tragedies and wonders how she can use them for herself. But, mija, I understand. Really. And I want you to get your book deal. You deserve it."

I gritted my teeth. "Please don't try to manipulate me, Lore."

"I'm not," she objected, but a smile played at the corners of her eyes, reminding me of Mateo.

At the thought of him, my stomach clutched. Last night, as they'd all trailed out of my room, Mateo had leaned down to whisper, "Do what you've got to do." His lips had grazed the curve of my ear, making me shiver.

"Lore," I said. "You told me Andres shoved you—that you were scared for the life of your baby. You used everything you knew about my family history to create a situation you knew I'd be sympathetic toward—didn't you?"

For once, she had the decency to look guilty. "It's your instinct to see women as victims," she said. "I don't blame you, with your mom, with the work you do. Besides, it could have happened that way if he were a different kind of man. And I can say that," she added, fervently. "I can say, looking back, I don't think he would have hurt me. I'll say I panicked after he pushed me. That part did happen. Please, Cassie. Let me do this. Don't you think I deserve to pay for everything?"

A few months ago, I might have said yes. But she'd lost two men she'd loved. Her sons had moved away from her. Her father had died.

Her mother had disowned her, dying before they could reconcile. Lore had spent the last thirty years in the ashes of what she'd destroyed. More importantly—*she hadn't killed Andres*. There was nothing to consider here.

"I have an obligation to the truth, Lore," I said. "I can't ignore Mateo's confession. I can't let Fabian stay in prison. How can you? How can all of you allow a man you claim to love rot behind bars for a crime he didn't commit?"

"Rot?" Lore laughed. "Do you know how many men he's helped get their GEDs? How many he's taught English? He'll be done soon. You would expose everything and make his sacrifice worthless? For what? Who wins, besides you?"

I flinched.

"Go talk to Fabian," Lore said. "Then call me."

I drove north into a cold front, the temperature plummeting from eighty to fifty in two hours. The sky was moon gray, scudded with altostratus clouds. My mother had described this kind of sky as layered like a cake, so that if you took an imaginary knife to it, it would spill either rain or snow, depending on the temperature.

I'd had so little time to idolize my mother, to see her as a keeper of knowledge and wonder, before I flattened her into one pathetic thing, no longer worthy of my love or curiosity. She was a mother, yes, and as a mother she had failed me in profound ways, but only now could I imagine starting to allow in other memories, other parts of her. I might never understand why she'd stayed with a man who hit her—except that last night, at 3 A.M., I'd called my father and he'd answered and he'd listened, the way Penelope said Andres had listened to her, and I could imagine maybe, if he kept going to meetings, if he stayed sober, maybe one day I could see him as more than his failures, too, the way my mother must have seen him, the way Lore and Fabian and Gabriel and Mateo were able to see each other.

Whoever writes the history has the power, my mother said.

What I wrote about these crimes—these people—would define two families. It would claim sovereignty over their memories. It was the only time in my life I'd felt powerful.

After a tedious sign-in process, I was led to the prison visitation area, a long, narrow room lined with plastic chairs facing a glass partition. The room smelled like body odor and burning, like the heater had kicked on too strong. As I sat down, I had to try not to overhear the one-sided updates about lawyers and Christmas plans.

Fabian was already waiting. At first glance, in his white prison uniform and wire-rimmed glasses, he looked like an old man in pajamas. The dark hair I'd seen in newspaper photos had faded to steel gray, shaved close to his head. His face was raked with deep lines, like freshly tilled soil. But his forearms twitched with a younger man's ropy muscle, and his dark stare, the potency of his dislike, reminded me of Gabriel.

"Thanks for agreeing to see me," I said into the phone.

He raised his eyebrows, a silent *Get on with it*.

"Okay then." I took a breath. "Fabian, I know what happened that night. To Andres."

"Congratulations." His voice was uncannily similar to the twins'. "So does everyone else."

"Have you spoken to Lore today?" I asked.

He hesitated. "No."

Before I could change my mind, I lowered the zipper of my sweater. Fabian's eyes widened.

"Is that . . . ?" he asked.

"Yes."

There was a clatter beside me as an elderly woman struggled to set the phone back on its base. She pulled a crumpled tissue from her pocket, wiped her eyes. Blew a kiss at the window.

"Do you understand?" I asked.

Fabian's eyes searched mine. "No."

"You should probably call her."

For a moment, he didn't say anything. Then he shook his head. "Pinche Lore."

"She is a force," I said wryly, and he laughed, his shoulders finally relaxing a little.

"That night," he said, quiet, like a gift, "I was standing at the river. It was dark. I could see every star. And you know how I felt?"

I leaned forward. I hadn't expected anything new from him. "How?"

"Proud." Fabian tapped his chest with a fist. "I'd done nothing but fail my family for years, but that night—that night I saved them. Do *you* understand?"

I heard Lore's voice in my mind: *You would expose everything and make his sacrifice worthless?*

Lore had given me the number of Fabian's former parole attorney. After twenty years of model behavior, Fabian had allegedly been in a fight the day before his second hearing. He'd apparently been surly and uncooperative during the hearing itself, and after parole was denied, he'd never requested it again. "You'd be surprised how often that happens," the lawyer said. "They figure they'll just be denied, don't want to go through the heartache. Some people even think their outcome will be better in prison than out. Who knows? Maybe Mr. Rivera found some kind of purpose in there."

I wondered how Fabian would feel when he found out it was Mateo, not Gabriel, whose mistake had placed him here; whether it would even matter. But it wouldn't be me who told him.

Fabian pressed his hand to the glass, and I touched the swirl of his fingerprints, leaving my own behind.

"The print you left in the room," I said. "Was it really an accident?"

It had been bothering me, how meticulous Fabian had been about cleaning everything else, everything but this. Almost as if he'd wanted to get caught, or at least give the police a solid reason to turn away from anyone else in his family.

Fabian's dark eyes crinkled in the corners. "Of course it was."

I shook my head. "You're a good man, Fabian. A good father. But you should apply for parole again." I thought about what to say next, what it would mean for all of us. "You're not doing them any good in here anymore."

Fabian's throat moved as he swallowed, and he nodded, just once. "Thank you."

"Take care," I said. "Maybe I'll see you again sometime."

My phone rang as I merged back onto I-35: Deborah. Her third call today. She'd emailed me with the subject line: *Confession???*

Your only job, she'd told me, *is to find out the truth. Whatever it is, that's what you'll write.*

But her subject line said it all. I knew the truth she was hoping for—the "highly marketable" version. I understood. A part of me, diminished if still alive, scrabbling, clung to the same idea. I could see that version of my future, the one I always wanted, so clearly.

I pressed my thumb into the tip of Lore's locket.

Maybe there was an alternative.

The Austin skyline came into view as dusk was settling. My father had texted me earlier: *If you don't have other plans, you can always come home for Christmas. I think Andrew is ready.*

I glanced at the clock. If I drove straight through, I'd be there by midnight.

Epilogue

LORE, NOW

Sticks and stones may break your bones, I used to tell the cuates, but words will never hurt you. That's not true, though, is it? Words leave scars. They change history.

That day at Mami and Papi's house, I told Cassie to talk to Fabian. To see if exposing Mateo would feel like justice. And if not, I told her she could still write the book with my blessing, including the parts most people didn't know. She could write about what Andres's note had really said, and the last time I'd seen him, in the motel room. She could even write about the pregnancy. It would not be the explosive reveal of Mateo's confession, but it was still a confession of a kind. She could even tell the story of how she'd found out "the truth." I'd been reading more true crime, and writers seemed to like doing that—putting themselves into the book. I saw the gleam in her eyes. The sort of excitement that comes from knowing secrets, telling secrets. Being right at the center of everything. We were more alike than she realized.

She surprised me, though. She took her time. Did her research. Después de su breakup, I invited her to stay with me for a few weeks.

We could work on the book. She could save her money. She ended up staying with me for three months. We found a good deal on airfare and went to DF together. In the end, she wrote the book from as close to my perspective as she could get. She ended it just as I arrived home after leaving Andres at the hotel. My hand on the back door-knob, still unaware—in the book, as in life—how everything would end; how it had already ended for Andres. Because this was all true, she could avoid outright lying about Fabian pulling the trigger. The reader, she said, could infer the rest based on the known "facts" of the case. Then she had included the first letter Fabian wrote me from prison; the first letter I sent him in return. A new beginning.

The reviewers called it an "extraordinary feat of journalism," how close Cassie managed to get to my psyche, my voice. How she "laid bare" a "beautifully flawed" woman (like if she had spread me naked for everyone to see) while "resisting the temptation to glorify the murder." This was, they said, the truest kind of crime book.

That made me laugh a little. Because, of course, there were slight bends in the truth that even Cassie didn't know about. I'd told her that Andres and I went to Chapultepec Park on the night we met—when actually that came later, our midnight walk in "the lungs of the city," the way we'd murmured beneath the shivering canopies of ahuehuete trees.

In reality, the night we met, at the wedding, we danced until three in the morning, invisible among the press of bodies on the floor. It was like if we were standing at the edge of a cliff while the world collapsed around us and all we had was this moment, an eternal present, everything permissible, everything forgivable. I'd laughed into his chest, smelling his damp-cotton sweat and the inexplicable tang of oranges on his fingertips, my red dress stuck to my skin, and as the edges of the night bled into morning, I took his hand and we stumbled into that caged elevator together.

Afterward, Andres had stood naked at the window, looking down at the Zócalo. Shadows pooled at his shoulder blades, the small of his back. I'd stared at him in fascination. This man who was not my husband. As my skin cooled, shame coated my throat. I went into the bathroom and cried while I ran the water, thinking it felt like a hundred years since I'd sunk into that tub, my fingers tracing the gold rope holding back the drapery. I had been another woman then.

No—I just hadn't yet admitted the woman I was.

I didn't like thinking about this first time, not then and not now, so many years later. The carelessness of it, the cliché: *Okay, well, I have an early flight tomorrow, it was nice—ha, ha—it was nice to meet you.* I'd gone home and tried to block it from my mind. But he'd called me at the bank—his sandpaper voice, *Yes, I'm looking for Ms. Crusoe.* And I realized what I thought had ended had only just begun.

It was the second time I met him that we went to Chapultepec. And it felt . . . pure. Real in a way the wedding night had never felt, the details lost to wine and tequila, so much tequila. When I returned home from the second trip, I remembered everything: his hand clasping mine to his chest on the bike; the way he'd asked me if I wanted children; and how we'd kissed, with abandon and desperation.

Mexico City, the constantly sinking land. Even now, we're sinking. Do you feel it?

I feel it.

And so Chapultepec, over time, had obliterated the original memory. It had *become* the original, fused together with the wedding. This felt, to me, like the truth. Truth is a malleable thing.

Cassie would never have understood this folding and refolding of memory into a new shape, a true shape. Not then, anyway. Not at the beginning.

But now—with the book out, the accolades, the story we maintained and the one we've held between the five of us—now, Cassie might understand.

ACKNOWLEDGMENTS

I have been writing stories since my third-grade teacher gave us small white hardback books with empty pages and asked us to write and illustrate what we wanted to be when we grew up. I wrote about being a singer (I couldn't sing; still can't) and accidentally fell in love with writing. My whole life after that has been an effort to get to this book you hold in your hands. What a miracle, that you've chosen to spend time with this story. Thank you.

I am profoundly grateful for parents who have supported this dream since I was a child. My mom gave me her love of reading, transferred to me as a toddler in her lap, and my dad gave me his stubbornness, his willingness to take big leaps, to not let fear of failure—or failure itself—mean the end. Mom and Dad, your love and belief in me are why this book exists. Thank you.

Bock and Lob, you may have preferred being soul skaters to coming to my reading parties, but you've read everything I've ever written—including about twenty drafts of this book, in Amanda's case. Thanks for being my number one fan, manita! I'm so grateful to have siblings who are also friends, and whom I can count on for brainstorming, endless text exchanges, and the perfect mimosa recipe.

Thank you to my extended family: Caro, Matthew, Charlie, Tessa, and the whole Collins crew in Australia—Jude, Jode, Justin, Katie, Sammy, and Elle. I hope that by the time you're reading this we've all been able to be in the same place together again, with champagne in hand.

I'm not sure I would have found my voice as a writer without the MFA program at Texas State University. There, for the first time, I began setting stories in South Texas, a place I used to think didn't belong in literature because I never saw it there. I gave my characters familiar names, let them speak Spanglish when it suited them. I grew convinced that not only do Mexican Americans belong in literature, we make it better. I'm grateful to those who came before me and showed me the joy of seeing parts of my world reflected back.

Thank you to Amanda Eyre Ward for the support and encouragement, and for letting me know, on my previous novel, that the story began on page 200! Thank you to the Best Art Friends, May Cobb, Julia Fine, and Sarah Morrison. You are my writing and motherhood soul mates, and I wouldn't want to be on this journey without you. Thank you, too, to the incredible authors who blurbed this book. I will be grateful for the rest of my life that you put your names on my work.

My publishing dream was just that until my shooting star of an agent, Hillary Jacobson, made it a reality. Writers don't like to talk about the novels in drawers, but when my first one didn't sell, Hillary told me she'd stick with me for the next hundred if that's what it took. Thankfully, it took only one more—but Hillary edited countless drafts with me over eighteen months, until we'd given it the best chance for an editor to fall in love. Hillary, I will never be able to thank you enough. I get to do what I love every day because of you.

Thank you also to my UK agent, Sue Armstrong, for finding the best home for this book at Michael Joseph, and to Sophie Baker and Jodi Fabbri at Curtis Brown for the dream of seeing this book translated into multiple languages. Thank you to my film/TV agent, Josie Freedman at ICM, for a career (life?) highlight I hope to be able to talk about one day.

ACKNOWLEDGMENTS

And my editors—I can't imagine working with more brilliant, generous people than Jessica Williams and Joel Richardson. You two saw the book not only for what it was, but for what it could be. I'll never forget reading your first twenty-page edit letter, balking at the work ahead (still!), and then, on a second read, realizing how damn lucky I was to have you on my team. Thank you for loving this story and devoting your considerable talents to helping me tell it as best I could. At Michael Joseph, thanks also to Clio Cornish and Grace Long for stepping in so reassuringly during Joel's paternity leave. My book has always been in such amazing hands.

Thank you to Julia Elliott for the cheerful and always helpful production coordination on the U.S. side, and to copy editors extraordinaire Cecilia Molinari and Laura Cherkas, who ensured, among other things, this did not accidentally become a time travel novel. Thank you to Ploy Siripant for designing my stunning U.S. cover—you brought my book to life in a way I never dreamed—and to art director Lee Motley and picture researcher Alice Chandler at Michael Joseph for the months of research, consideration, and conversation that went into designing my gorgeous U.K. cover. I'm so grateful. Thank you also to Eliza Rosenberry and the publicity, sales and marketing teams I haven't met yet, but who will champion this book in ways I likely can't even imagine. It has been a joy working with you all.

And finally, my whole heart of love and gratitude to my husband, Adrian. Not every man would sit next to a twenty-year-old girl on a flight who calls herself a writer and ask to read some of her work then and there. Even fewer would move across the world ten years later and ask that girl to marry them. Thank you for the years of brainstorming with me about murders and double marriages, and for every single time you took the kids so I could write. Thank you for believing in me. This book wouldn't exist without you. I wouldn't want to exist without you.

And to Jo and Jack: I love you more than you'll ever know.

ABOUT THE AUTHOR

Katie Gutierrez has an MFA from Texas State University, and her writing has appeared in *Harper's Bazaar*, the *Washington Post*, Longreads, *Texas Monthly*, and more. She was born and raised in Laredo, Texas, and now lives in San Antonio, with her husband and their two children. This is her first novel.